Overflow

Kiara Mills

AOS Publishing, 2024
Copyright © 2024

Kiara Mills

ISBN:978-1-990496-46-2

Cover Design: Jessica James

Visit AOS Publishing's website:
www.aospublishing.com

*For everyone who made me into the person I am today,
and my family especially (you know who you are)*

A Note from the Author

This book was written on the unceded traditional territory of the Lheidli T'enneh First Nations, part of the Dakelh peoples' territory. The fictional town of Belle also sits on the traditional territory of the Lheidli T'enneh, nestled between the Fraser River and the Yellowhead Highway, right across from the Chun T'oh Whudujut, or the Ancient Forest Provincial Park. Chun T'oh Whudujut is a small sliver of the only inland temperate rainforest in the world, and it was not protected against logging until 2012. In *Overflow*, this protection is largely thanks to Katherine Selene, but in the real world it is because of the Lheidli T'enneh First Nations, the University of Northern British Columbia (UNBC), and the Government of BC. *Overflow* is an ode to what the land we come from can mean to us, and how the relationships we build there become who we are. It is a reminder to protect the land and to protect each other.

From the bottom of my heart, thank you to the Lheidli T'enneh peoples for upholding the health and wellbeing of the land I live on. I hope to continue to expand my knowledge of it, and its people.

1

RIVER WATER / WARMTH

Isaac hears the yell from the river as soon as he sets foot out of the car. "Did you hear -" he starts, looking over the roof to his friend, Iris, who nods. Her jaw is set with focus, and he wishes for just a moment to know what she's thinking.

The world around them goes quiet, the trees holding their breath, waiting, creeping closer to the precipice of something, something wrong, something capital W wrong. If Isaac focuses, he can feel the pull of the river, *come to me*, it's whispering, *come to me, come to me, come to me*. He shakes his head to drown it out, but the pull only gets stronger.

"Do you really think that we're supposed to be here?" He asks Iris, the remaining light fading as the sun slides behind the trees on the horizon. It takes what's left of the heat with it and goosebumps raise on Isaac's arms. He already knows the answer to his question. Everything that Isaac is experiencing, she must be experiencing tenfold, the same energy in her blood.

"Yes," Iris says, gathering her hair into a messy bun at the top of her head, ready to face what it is that's coming. "It's for us to find. Don't you feel it?"

Isaac presses his lips together and nods, solemnly. He does feel it. It's a buzzing in the tips of his fingers and the roots of his teeth, an uncanny knowledge that this is exactly where they're supposed to be right now. That doesn't mean he has to like it. He very much does not like it. "I don't want to go in blind," he complains.

"We don't have time for anything else," Iris counters, pushing up her sleeves. As if on cue, there's a large splash and another, louder yell, something that could be help, but sounds more like panic without words.

Iris is down the trail towards the river in a split second and Isaac watches her nearly disappear before he steps out to follow her. She's always been the one who acts first, who tells him his thinking is overthinking, and she's usually right. She's right to be running toward the river, too, but that doesn't mean he's any happier about the situation, or the fact that it's nearly dark.

1

They know what is happening is all according to Prophecy - *the secret to the secrets themselves will be skimmed from the River's edge -* but that doesn't mean they have details. A book of Prophecies is a good idea until the Prophecies come into fruition and all they have to work with is the puzzle of words and double meanings they've been given. It never makes sense until they're in the moment, and sometimes not even then. Who would have guessed that the *secret to the secrets themselves* was a person? Not Isaac. Not any of them.

The shadows make it hard to see and even though he's travelled this path hundreds of times before he doesn't trust his muscle memory, extending his hands out in front of his body, out in front of his body, the chill of the evening uncomfortably itchy under his skin. There's that buzzing again in his bones, in his veins and his nervous system, electrifying him, pulling him forward towards the river. It builds, intensifying with every step he takes. He's bound to this river, just as he's bound to Iris and this godforsaken town. He's bound to whatever it is that they're walking into.

Water splashes and they're close enough now for Isaac to hear a desperate gasp for air. The hair on the back of his neck stands up. *Someone's going to die,* he realizes, *someone's going to die here.*

Isaac's hands brush up against Iris's back, her skin just as cold as his and together they stand at the mouth of the trail, surveying the scene in front of them. The river flows as it always does, tumultuous and tempting, and at its edge stands a giant man, the silhouette of him bleeding into the evening as if he is more *night* than human. His hair is pulled into a low ponytail, and he's holding someone under the shallow water, his face filled with anger, filled with disgust. The person is struggling against his hold, but Isaac can sense that they're losing energy and they're losing it quickly.

Iris starts to shift forward away from him and into the clearing before he has the chance to say anything, and he almost starts after her before changing his mind. He will be no better for her in the open than he will be here, in the shadow. If it goes south, there's still a chance he could get away unnoticed.

As she steps into the last of the remaining light her hair catches fire in it, a soft halo in the wisps falling around her face. *"Stop,"* she says, and her voice rings out clear and loud, amplified by the silence of the trees around them.

The man looks up, his grip still firm around the person under the water. His face is written with crude arrogance, and it makes him appear both eternal and fleeting, young and old. His edges sharpen and blur, night and then man and then night again. Isaac is certain he's never seen him before. "Why should I?" he sneers, and his voice is a low growl that makes Isaac's skin crawl. He realizes he was right to question the man's humanity.

He closes his eyes, letting the river whisper to him, letting it sing its song for a moment – *come to me, come to me me me* – bringing with it a fear so pungent it makes tears well up. It makes his heart and stomach and lungs twist and his knees buckle. The fear is so strong it makes him want to puke in the bushes and run back to the car where he won't have to be anywhere near it. He doesn't, he can't, he won't. This is where he's meant to be.

"The river doesn't want them to die here tonight," Iris says, raising her arms from her sides, palms open to the sky. This snaps Isaac out of his reverie, and he follows her movements, palms up at his sides. He is a vessel, and his energy is hers to use if she needs it.

"And you think you speak for the river?" The man laughs, loosening his grip on the person in the water. "You think you know anything of its wants? Its needs?"

The reflected fear inside Isaac intensifies as he watches the person try desperately to lift their head out of the water and fail. If he focuses, he can feel the burn in their lungs, the fatigue in their body. "Iris," he warns, and tries not to notice the man turn his gaze from Iris.

"Is this your pet, witch?" he laughs, mocking, the wicked look in his eyes peeling Isaac down to his core. "An empath? Is this all you bring with you?"

"He's all I need," Iris hisses back, and then the air tightens around them as she starts to call in energy.

The well inside Isaac opens, with it comes the familiar pull at his core, not uncomfortable physically but uncomfortable knowing that something is being taken from him in a way he can't fully quantify. His eyelids droop with fatigue, and goosebumps rise on his skin, side effects of the energy loss. Somewhere in the animal part of his brain, alarm bells are ringing, but he pays no mind to them. *It's just Iris,* he tells himself, *it's just Iris, I am a vessel, and she needs me, nothing bad will happen to me, it's just Iris.*

Light begins to pour from Iris's hands, and she directs it towards the man, whose head snaps up, sneer still clear on his face.

"You – think –" he says, his body glowing bright orange, "you – know – what –" his hands let go of the person in the river and immediately begin to burn, "you're doing – and you – don't. I – will – win," and then he laughs, high-pitched and ear-grating. The laugh turns into a scream, his mouth opening wide as he falls back into the current, one step, two steps, three steps before he loses his footing and is carried downstream, there in one moment and gone in the next, underwater, or dissolved into it. Magic is a strange creature, and Isaac is certain the man was made of it. Isaac is also certain that whatever he is, he isn't dead – scattered, maybe. Disoriented. He doesn't resurface.

"Get him out," Iris whispers, her attention on the body in the water that's still visible.

"Right," Isaac manages to say and then he's moving again, worry bubbling up in his chest. He reaches out to feel something from him, but all he gets is an overwhelming void where warmth should be.

The man has managed to drag himself mostly out of the river and he's coughing wretchedly, a pile of bare skin and white t-shirt on the shore. He looks pitiful and small and nothing like the secret to anything.

Isaac doesn't know what to do, so he looks to Iris, who only holds up her still glowing hands to him. She can't help. For her to touch him while she's super-charged like this is for worse things to happen to him than drowning.

The man has finished coughing up river water and he's pushing himself up, looking at Isaac with something dangerous behind his eyes, a wild animal who's been cornered. "Don't touch me," he hisses, and Isaac stops, a foot away.

"We have to leave," Isaac tells him, aware that Iris is hovering a safer distance behind him. There's still magic in the air and it's not hers. She doesn't have to tell him that they need to leave as soon as possible.

The man shivers violently and tries to get to his feet. He stands for an unsteady second, and then pitches forward, only staying upright because of Isaac's hands on his shoulders. "Don't," he says again, and Isaac releases him.

"We have to go," Isaac repeats.

The man narrows his eyes at Isaac, and then another shiver wracks his body. He doesn't move an inch towards Isaac or towards the trail to leave. "How?" he asks, and it's an impossible question to answer. Isaac doesn't know how or where or when to start. *How?*

Iris pipes up from behind him. "Magic," she says, "we'll explain everything when we can, but we need to go. *Now.*"

Something in her tone moves the man. He nods, and takes a step forward, stumbling.

"Here," Isaac whispers, offering his arm, and this time the man doesn't protest, instead leaning his soaking body against Isaac's, tense and cold and *scared.* "What's your name?" Isaac asks, as the man shudders against him.

"Parker," he says, through chattering teeth. His show of bravado at the shore is dissolving into a need for survival, for warmth. He stumbles again as they step onto the trail and Isaac tightens the hold he has on his arm.

"I'm Isaac," he whispers, not sure if there's anything else to say. Not sure if he should keep Parker talking.

"Hi," Parker slurs, and Isaac's heart dips into his stomach.

"Hi," he replies, his concern building.

"Where are we?" Parker asks as they spill out into the open where Iris is rooting around in the trunk of Isaac's car.

"We're at the cabin," Isaac says. He shoots a meaningful look at Iris.

"Oh," Parker says. "Who are you?"

"Isaac," Isaac says again, and Iris holds up the emergency blanket he keeps in case his shoddy car breaks down.

"I'm cold," Parker whispers. His teeth have stopped chattering.

"I know," Isaac says, "here. This is Iris. She has a blanket for you. Oh – and a sweater."

Iris nods. "You're going to have to take off your wet clothes," she says, solemnly, giving the awkwardness of the situation some weight.

"Right," Parker whispers, and he slides away from Isaac. The tips of his fingers are a sickly blue in the little light left from the sun, and they don't close around the edge of his t-shirt tight enough to pull it over his head. He sways dangerously, reaching out to Isaac to steady himself. "Can't." His voice is so quiet. His eyelids are drooping.

"Isaac, come on," Iris says as he looks to her once again for help. *It's to help him. It's not weird,* her expression says. "I still can't –"

"Here," Isaac turns his attention back to Parker. He wrestles the t-shirt off him, and then the sweater Iris offers onto him. "Turn the car on," he tells Iris, tossing her his keys. In the back of his mind, he prays that the heating won't shit the bed like it does sometimes when he needs it the most.

Parker sways again, and Isaac drapes the blanket around his shoulders. "Come sit," he tells him, guiding him to the backseat of the car. Parker sits.

Isaac painstakingly unties his shoes and pulls them off his feet.

Iris is there again, offering up Isaac's emergency socks from the glovebox.

"I don't –" Isaac starts again, but Park's already fumbling with the button to his jeans. He manages to undo them, and then Isaac is uncomfortably peeling them off his legs and shoving the warm socks on. He's not thinking about the fact that he can feel the chill of Parker's body six inches from his skin, and he's *not thinking* about what it means that Parker has stopped shivering entirely. "Get in all the way," he tells Parker, and he listens. Isaac adjusts the blanket, so it covers all of him, and then shuts the door.

"Do you want me to drive?" Iris asks, but Isaac shakes his head. Driving is a welcome piece of control that he can keep to himself.

He steps into the car, assaulted by his miraculously working heating system, and then his foot is on the gas pedal and they're moving and the adrenaline pumping into his system can *stop*. Everything is going to be okay. He's here and Iris is here, and the half-drowned man who must be so very important is here, too. Finally, finally, finally, things are happening. *The secret to the secrets themselves.*

He glances in the rear-view mirror to see that Parker's eyes are closed, hardly holding onto consciousness. His eyes wander to the road and then to Iris, who's already looking at him, expression heavy with post-magic fatigue. With just this glance he knows that she's thinking ahead to the next prophecy, too.

Two to twine in divine time: the Understanding and the Understood, the Protector and the Protected, together at last.

"Do you think – ?" He starts, and she nods, once.

"He has to be, Isaac." She says, and her voice is soft.

Isaac guides the car into his driveway and takes one last look at Parker in the mirror. *Is it you?* He wonders, and then the adrenaline is back in his veins, what little control he had in the car, gone. They're moving again and Parker is being bundled inside and buried in blankets and Isaac's only thought is a plea for him to stay alive.

****

Parker is asleep in the guest bedroom upstairs and neither Isaac nor Iris have even tried to close their eyes. Isaac's nerves are alive and singing in his body, and while Iris looks dead tired, she's determined to stay awake.

Isaac managed to slip Parker's phone out of his pocket, and they used his face to unlock it once they realized that he has a sibling or a friend and the lack of contact from him was beginning to worry them.

C: *Park, where tf are you?*

C: *PARK!!!!*

C: *jfc, if you're out fucking in the woods and you don't have the time to tell me that you're fine i'm going to be PISSED!!*

The absolute last thing that they need is to get someone else involved, especially if that someone else is the RCMP. So Isaac texted them back, trying his best to imitate Parker's frantic typo-ridden communication.

Park: everything good. sorru will explaib tomorrow. spending hte night

He even sent the address, just in case they remained dubious, and they read it, but didn't respond.

"What if they're onto us?" He asks Iris, tapping the screen so it doesn't go black. He feels a little bit disgusted by himself for sending the message, for deceiving C, for pretending to be Parker.

"It's not like he's in danger," Iris says, putting her hands around the mug of coffee that's sitting in front of her. "He'll go home tomorrow and maybe he'll tell them that it wasn't him texting and maybe he won't, and it'll be no harm no foul."

Isaac grimaces, and finally lets the phone lock. If Parker really is who he thinks he is, it's just going to make it that much harder for him to trust them once he realizes that they've invaded his privacy. It's going to be that much harder for him to trust *Isaac* once he realizes that he invaded his privacy.

Two to twine in divine time: the Understanding and the Understood, the Protector and the Protected, together at last.

The words have been running around in his head all night, and he's trying to tell himself that it's impossible to know if the other half of the Prophecy is Parker, but that feeling that he had when he stepped out of the car at the river is still nestled in his mind. It's a feeling of rightness, of alignment. He wants to ask Iris if she feels it, too, but he's already asked three times and her answer has always been *yes.*

"What are we going to tell him when he wakes up?" He asks instead, and Iris closes her eyes.

They've been throwing around possibilities all night. They could tell him everything, immediately. They could explain that they figured the thing that was drowning him in the river is an ancient, magical force they've nicknamed the Ghost, and that he's mentioned several times in their book of Prophecies. They could explain that Iris is a witch and Isaac is an empath and they're part of a larger group of well-meaning witches and intuitives called the Hell Club.

Isaac was the one who mentioned this, and Iris had shut him down. He goes ahead and mentions it again. He thinks that, if anything, Parker at least deserves the truth. He deserves to make his own decision.

"We don't want to scare him away."

"So, what? We lie to him? He was *there* at the river last night! If he didn't see exactly what happened, he knows the consequences of it."

"If he goes to the cops or if he tells anyone else, we're screwed."

"What's your suggestion then?" Isaac asks, scared of her answer.

"We put a spell on him. He tells us how he ended up by the river, and we make him agree to be quiet about it."

Isaac presses his lips together. "That's not fair."

"None of this is fair, Isaac," she sighs, and he knows that he's already lost the battle. "He has to be eased into it, or else he'll run. Like a frog in boiling water."

"At least let him make the choice to keep it a secret," he says, a compromise.

She nods. "Deal."

They spend most of the night in silence, Isaac lost in daydreams and Iris flipping through the books she has stored at Isaac's house for the workings of a spell to get Parker to spill his guts. Isaac refuses to help.

Suddenly she groans, and Isaac looks over at her, raising his eyebrows. "No luck?" He asks.

"No – I just – you're right. It feels wrong to put a spell on him. If my parents ever found out –"

"Oh, good," he interrupts, "I'm glad you're listening to the expert." He's trying to make it a joke, but he is glad that she's reconsidered – to break Parker's trust like that, right out of the gate, seems cruel. It seems like, if anything, it will push him away when they need to be bringing him closer.

She rolls her eyes, and Isaac grins at her. "I'm just going to find something that might help him focus and he can choose whether to take it or leave it."

"Sounds good to me." Sounds *much better.*

"Does that mean you'll help me?"

Isaac shrugs, and gestures for one of her books, figuring that it might be helpful to distract his mind. The Prophecy is still dancing around in the back of his head, and he's trying not to let it get out of hand, but he's always been a daydreamer. A romantic. An overthinker. He keeps imagining Parker smiling at him, inviting him closer. He keeps imagining Parker in the passenger seat of his car, laughing, reaching over to turn the volume of Isaac's music down, so he can hear what he's saying properly.

Even reading through the book of herbs doesn't do a great job of distracting him, and he sits back after a few minutes, glancing at Iris.

"Do you think – ?" He starts, one more time.

"Yes."

2
TRUST ISSUES

It feels as though cotton has been shoved through Parker's eye sockets and removed through his mouth. His whole head feels gauzy and unfocused, his body brittle as if it's been formed by hardened sugar and not bones and muscles and skin. He tries to look at himself in the mirror of the bathroom, but something feels not-quite-right, off in a way that he can't put a finger on.

He presses the heels of his palms to his eyes and counts to ten three times. He presses the tips of his fingers into his temples and counts backwards from five six times. He splashes cold water over his face and looks again at the distorted image of himself before he wipes it off on the towel sitting beside the sink.

This is not him. This is not his life. The face staring back at him is still an imposter, someone else whose body he's stepped into.

He counts his fingers, to make sure there are still five on each hand. There are. He touches his nose, his eyebrows, the top four of his incisors, all four of his canines. They still feel like his, but they can't be. He doesn't remember much of what happened last night, but he remembers the cold, the struggle, the water in his lungs. He remembers clinging to someone's arm, Isaac, his warmth. He remembers another with glowing hands, though he doesn't remember her name. It was a dream, like something that happened to someone else and he's trying to see it through their eyes. Could he be dead? Is this what death would feel like? Dissociation?

He steps back into the bedroom he'd woken up in, looking at the sheets thrown to the bottom of the bed where he'd gotten up and out in a crazed haze. The room is dark blue, the sheets red and orange and black, in stark contrast. There's a nightstand beside the bed, and it looks expensive, made of solid wood, an elegant lamp, and a pile of clothes – his clothes, dry and folded – on top of it. The curtains on the window are open to a neat backyard, framed perfectly with trees that touch the sky, and he moves towards it, looking out and taking a deep breath.

Parker concludes that this is an old house, in the richer part of this strange town, and that he has not died and gone to heaven. *If this were heaven,* he thinks, looking down at the sweater he's wearing, *then I'd be wearing something with a band that I know.*

Movement catches his eye through the window, and he looks down to see the man from last night, Isaac, leaning against the railing of a porch, facing the house, flicking a lighter against a cigarette. Once it's lit, Isaac looks up, directly into the window, and for a second Parker holds eye contact, his heart in his throat. Isaac is beautiful with his honey-blond hair tucked back into the hood over his head, his long fingers pinching the cigarette, his lips pulled downward, into a frown. He seems familiar to Parker, in a vague way. He's probably seen Isaac come through the coffee shop where he works, or maybe in passing at the grocery store, on the sidewalk, anywhere else in Belle. It's a small town.

Isaac looks away first and says something that Parker can't hear toward the door into the house.

Parker remembers, once again, the night before, hands on his shoulders, head underwater, new hands under his arms, a woman whose hands *glow,* and he steps away from the window. It was Isaac and Iris? – *Iris* – the two whose house he seems to be in, that killed the man who was drowning him, and that makes them dangerous. That makes them unknowable, unpredictable. Isaac may be beautiful, but he is also powerful, and Parker is going to have to tread carefully.

Of course, if they wanted him dead, they could have just let him drown in the river.

He grabs the pile of clothes and holds them to his chest, taking a deep breath, and one final glance around the room before he steps, barefoot, into the hall. This time, not in a rush for the bathroom, he takes his time to survey the photos on the wall which consist of a collage of portraits documenting the growth of a boy with white-blond hair (Isaac), and a three-piece painting of the woods he'd so wrongly entered the night before. He takes a minute to examine the paintings, two of them of the river at different angles and the middle one a cabin. The way they're set up makes it seem as if the river is feeding into the cabin, fueling it, leading to it. Parker takes a step closer and leans forward, his breath fogging the glass of the frame, and in the cabin windows, through the partially cracked door, he sees a soft, red glow. It's in the water, too, faintly, but mixed into the undertones of the paint.

He straightens his back and blinks several times, fighting away the dizziness, the uncertainty of what he's seeing. The hair on his arms is standing up. Whatever it is that he's gotten himself into, it's not normal. It's not safe. He should have never moved here. He should have told his sister she could fend for herself.

The noise of a kettle whistle shrieks into the air from downstairs, and it makes him jump. He holds his bundle of clothes tighter to his chest, and takes a deep breath, trying to calm his racing heart. *Just get it over with,* he tells himself, *just leave, just get out of here.*

He follows the soft whispers that have started, careful on the stairs because the soft sweatpants he's wearing are several inches too long for him and he doesn't want to trip and make an even bigger fool of himself. An even bigger target.

The stairs open into a dining room, and through it he can see two people, Isaac, sitting on the counter, watching him intensely, a mug of something warm in his hands, and Iris, pouring water from the kettle into two more mugs. In the dim kitchen light, they look more human than they had last night, more human than Isaac had on the porch outside. In the dim kitchen light, they are real and concrete, not something from a dream, not something his overactive imagination has cooked up for him.

He steps off the last stair and approaches them with caution, digging his fingers into the fabric of the jeans he nearly drowned in. He wants to avoid Isaac's piercing gaze, but he finds he can't, and he comes to a stop a few feet away, words dying in his mouth.

"Morning," Iris says, finally, turning to look at him expectantly, her hair pulled back into a messy bun, loose strands falling free around her face. "Would you like some tea?"

Parker opens his mouth and looks to Isaac who hasn't moved. "I –" He starts, and realizes how sore his throat is, how raw and dry the water he'd swallowed last night has left it. Behind Iris's shoulder, Isaac takes a sip from his mug, finally breaking eye contact with Parker.

"It's peppermint," Iris says, and her voice is soft, comforting, a white flag. "With honey. It'll help your throat." She holds out one of the mugs she'd just been pouring water into, and he finds himself taking it, holding his clothes with one hand.

It's warm, and he feels comforted. "I," he starts again, trying to speak around the scratchiness, "I don't even know you." He wants to get across that he shouldn't be accepting the tea from her, a stranger, but she only raises her eyebrows at him like he's spoken a fact with no connotation attached. He opens his mouth to elaborate, but Isaac leans forward then, putting his elbows on his knees and holding his mug with both of his hands.

"You will," he says, and there's not an ounce of doubt in his voice.

"You sound so sure," Parker replies, and Isaac nods.

"It's all part of the plan," he says, smugly, and Iris shoots him a glare over her shoulder.

"Um," she says, "yeah, sure." She pulls another mug from the cupboard and holds up a vial of something green. "Do you remember anything from last night?"

Parker blinks at her, his fingers that aren't around his mug digging into his clothes. *Of course I remember,* he wants to tell her, *I almost drowned,* but he doesn't. "Bits and pieces," he says, instead, wary. She seems like she's going to offer him whatever it is in the vial and he's not sure he wants it.

"Would you tell us what you remember?" She asks, dumping the vial into the mug, and then filling it barely a quarter of the way full with hot water. She doesn't look at him while she's doing it, so he turns his gaze to Isaac, who *is* looking at him.

"Why?" He asks, and Isaac blinks, thinking about something very hard.

Parker likes that Isaac is easy to read – he has an honest face, an amiable face, a handsome face, and Parker can see the gears turning in his head. Iris, on the other hand, doesn't seem as open. She still hasn't turned to face him, but he can see that her lips are pushed together in a frown.

To his dismay, it's her that answers him. "The thing that tried to drown you last night wasn't a man," she starts.

"No shit!"

"No, I mean –" She sighs, "I mean that we know what it was. We call it the Ghost."

"Why did it try to kill *me*?" Parker puts his mug down on the counter.

"Because you have a secret that it doesn't want us to know."

"What?"

Isaac also puts his mug on the counter, and then he slides off it neatly, his fingers wrapping around its edge. "Belle is full of magic," he says, and his voice is soft, comforting, "its entire future is laid out in Prophecies –"

"Isaac," Iris warns, but Isaac only shakes his head at her, focusing back on Parker.

"There was a Prophecy for last night. It talks about secrets being drawn from the edge of the river – you were drawn out of the river. Therefore, you have a secret that we need."

Parker blinks at him, flabbergasted. He doesn't have any secrets. He's a shit secret-keeper, a shit liar. If he had a secret everyone around him would know it by now. "I –" He starts, but Iris cuts him off.

"It doesn't have to be a known secret," she says, "maybe it's an ability that you don't know of yet. Either way, you're very important to us."

He looks back and forth between them, trying to patch what they're saying together. They're magic, yes, Iris had said that last night. It makes sense, too, with what he knows of this place and now what he's seen. Only magic could explain the burning man and Iris's burning hands. Him being important to them, though – that's what doesn't make sense. He only just moved to Belle at the beginning of the summer, and, sure, he's endured tarot readings from friends at house parties, and maybe he's even bought a couple of crystals in the hopes they'd bring him romance or focus or wisdom, but he's not *involved* with anything that could come close to magic. He doesn't *know* anything about the thing that tried to kill him – the *Ghost* or whatever Iris called it.

"You still haven't told me why I should tell you what I remember from last night," he reminds them, trying to buy himself time to process.

"Ah," Iris says, "yeah. Did the Ghost say anything to you? Mention anything? Maybe it let you in on something – an answer to what you'll bring to Hell Club."

"Hell Club?" Parker feels the horror drip from his tone. Who in their right mind calls something Hell Club?

"That's uh –" Isaac starts, grinning, "We call ourselves that. Iris and I and our friends."

"That's a stupid name."

"Names aside," Iris cuts in, "did the Ghost tell you anything?" She's turned to face him, the mug with her green substance held tightly in her hand.

Parker sighs, and closes his eyes, trying to remember, trying to think. He remembers showing up at the river for the promise of a hookup with some guy named Eric, and then he was waiting for twenty minutes longer than he should have, the burn of rejection creeping up his spine. He remembers feeling stupid and used, and he was just about to call his sister, C, and leave when the man materialized from the shadows, snapping a twig as if it were an afterthought, as if to appear more human. Parker remembers the hair on the back of his neck standing up, asking if the man's name is Eric even though he knew the answer. He remembers the moment he decided to run, and the way that the man, the Ghost, sighed and side stepped so easily, hardly moving his legs to fall into place beside Parker. He remembers the Ghost's hands grabbing his shoulders, wrenching him backwards, and then his arms wrapped around Parker's shoulders, dragging him down to the water. He remembers the noise that he made, the animal cry that he hoped someone, *anyone* would hear. He remembers the sinking feeling in his gut when he realized that he was about to die here, in the river, and there was no one to save him, there was no one to help him. He remembers the shock of the freezing water as the Ghost threw him in, the way it electrified him and drove him to attempt escape, he remembers the way the Ghost's hands clamped down on his wrists, pulling and bending until he gave in and then he was plunged under. He remembers water in his mouth and in his eyes and desperately trying to suck air in when he fought his way to the surface for an instant. He remembers trying to scream.

He swallows and shakes his head. When he opens his eyes, Isaac is looking at him with such a kindness, an openness, an understanding, that Parker is certain he's read his mind. *Can you hear my thoughts?* He asks in his head, but Isaac doesn't seem to hear anything – if he does, he doesn't show it. "The Ghost didn't say anything," Parker says, and then, smaller, "I don't really want to think about it."

Iris deflates in front of him. "Are you sure?" She asks, "I have – I picked up something that my dad said would help you remember."

"I don't want to remember anything more than I already do." Parker says, ready to take a step back as she rolls forward on the balls of her feet.

"But we need –"

"Iris," Isaac says, reaching out to put a hand on her shoulder, "we have time." They share a look, Iris annoyed, and Isaac firm, and then Iris nods.

She puts the mug down.

"Alright," she says, disappointed, "if you do want to remember, or if something else comes up, just let me know."

Parker nods. He adjusts the clothes he's holding, pulling them even closer to his chest. He feels small, tired, helpless. The enormity of what happened last night and the gnawing feeling that this is just the beginning have caught up to him and he wants to go home, to lay in his bed and curl up in his blankets and process what it is that Iris and Isaac have told him.

"We rescued your phone," Isaac says softly, and he pulls the device from his back pocket. "Um, C kept texting you so we let them know that you were safe." He grins sheepishly, and Parker unlocks his phone to check. "I hope that's okay."

Parker opens the conversation with his sister and sees that he's right. "You didn't do anything else, did you?" He asks, once again suspicious. He thinks that if it were Iris telling him this, he would feel violated, but Isaac's shaggy hair and his easy smile and the way he dips his shoulders down when he answers smooths out any worry that Parker has.

"That's all," he says.

"Okay."

The silence is palpable, Iris looking at Parker and Parker looking at Isaac and Isaac looping his thumbs into the tops of his pockets.

"You should take our numbers," Iris says suddenly, and gestures for Parker's phone.

"Why?" Quite frankly, Parker never wants to see them again. Parker never wants to see *one* of them again.

"The Ghost didn't kill you last night," she starts, taking his phone when he hands it to her, and typing her info in, "but that doesn't mean it isn't going to try again."

Oh. Right. Parker's heart sinks deep into his chest cavity, and in his mind, he's swallowing water, and he's so cold and the arms holding him down are so strong. "I don't want to die," he whispers, and Isaac gives him a grim little smile.

"Then stay in contact," Iris says, her voice cool. "We'll protect you to the best of our ability. We have to if we're going to figure out what your secret is."

What my secret is. Parker nods, tight-lipped. He takes his phone back from Isaac, who's programmed his contact in with two heart-eye emojis. When he looks up, Isaac has a real smile, just for him.

"We should get you home to C," he says, "they must be worried."

Parker nods, and follows him out of the kitchen, into a foyer where his shoes are sitting, dry, by the door. "They probably are," he whispers back. He doesn't say goodbye to Iris, and she doesn't say goodbye to him.

"Who is C?" Isaac ventures, pulling a coat on over his sweater, and slipping his socked feet into slides. "If you don't mind me asking."

"My sister."

"Oh."

"I'm uh – I'm still wearing your clothes –"

Isaac shrugs, and opens the door, gesturing Parker outside. "You can keep them," he says, unbothered, "at least for now. I don't think this is the last time we'll see each other."

Parker doesn't reply as he gets into the passenger seat of Isaac's red car, sinking as far into the sweater as he can, trying not to show that he's cold, that the morning air has got to him, that he wishes he had brought a goddamn coat to his hookup last night, and maybe some mace.

Isaac turns up the heat and hits his palm on the radio, which spits out only static. "Piece of shit," he mutters under his breath, towards the car. "Sorry," he says, now to Parker, "I don't know how this car is still living. We call it the Shitbox." He gives the radio one more half-hearted slap, and the voice of a man fills the silence.

" – the world is overrun with spirits," says the voice, "and one day they won't be able to be stopped."

Isaac twists the dial until music starts. "Sorry," he says, again, "there's this old man – John, we call him Old John – anyways, he broadcasts all sorts of shit. I don't know how he hasn't gotten in trouble yet."

"C goes for runs by his house," Parker offers, amused by the car troubles, "she's obsessed with trying to figure out what the things on his fence mean." Old Man John with the paranoid words on his fence. Parker has seen some of it, when he bothers to join C for her runs, but he isn't as interested as she is. To him, they're just ramblings of a sad old man with nothing better to do. To C, they're a mystery.

"He was a part of Hell Club," Isaac says, backing out of his driveway, "at one point. A long time ago. We think he helped write the Prophecies."

Parker sighs. He doesn't reply. He doesn't want to think about what it is that he's gotten himself into. He doesn't want to think about magic and *Ghosts* and drowning. He doesn't want to think about anything at all.

"You're going to have to tell me where your house is," Isaac says, softly, like he knows Parker doesn't want to talk. "I'm an empath, not a mind reader."

Parker sits up a little bit straighter. "Turn left - does that mean you're going to manipulate my emotions?"

Isaac lets out a startled laugh. "No," he says. He turns left. "I usually keep my guard up. It gets too exhausting, and I can't do that, anyway. I can only tune in."

Parker doesn't reply, instead looking out the window and watching the houses pass by. He's certain he knows where his house is from Isaac's, but there's a chance he could be wrong and he doesn't want to miss the next turn. "Right," he says, recognizing the house on the corner. He's surprised they live so close together - if he grew up here, they'd probably have taken the same bus to school.

Isaac turns right. "I would never, even if I could. You should know that."

His tone is earnest enough that Parker believes him. "It's the third house on the left," he says.

Isaac pulls into his driveway. "Iris was right," he says, "you should stay in contact."

Parker reaches for the door handle. "I will."

"I'm serious."

"So am I."

He makes the mistake of looking over at Isaac, who's staring at his hand. He watches as Isaac's gaze moves up his arm, to meet his own, his eyes dark with something like want. He gets the feeling that Isaac isn't telling him something.

Isaac swallows, Adam's apple bobbing in his throat. The air in the car feels charged for a moment, and when Isaac opens his mouth Parker thinks he's going to say something important, something solidifying, but all he says is, "See you later then."

Parker's disappointment melts on his tongue, and he nods. "See you later." He gets out of the car.

He walks towards his house. He grabs the spare key under the flowerpot on the porch, not looking back at Isaac, who's still waiting in the driveway. He puts the key in the lock, turns it, opens the door, and reaches down to replace the key in its hidden spot.

He hears the window of Isaac's car roll down, but he still doesn't look back.

"Parker," Isaac says, and, *finally*, Parker turns.

"Yeah?" He closes the door.

"Why were you even at the river last night?"

Isaac read C's texts. Isaac *must* know why Parker was at the river. Isaac seems like a lot of things but thick isn't one of them. Parker heads back down the porch stairs, back to Isaac's car, so that he doesn't have to shout it across the neighbourhood. "I was supposed to meet a guy."

Isaac nods. "What guy?"

"His name was Eric."

"How old was he?"

"Like 23, I think?"

"Did you get his last name?"

"No?" He says, his brows furrowing. "Do you usually get the last names of your hookups?"

Isaac shrugs. "It's a small town," he says, "I usually already know them." He's grinning.

"Do you know an Eric that's 23 years old, then?" Parker asks, trying not to let his tone get sharp.

"Yeah," Isaac says, his grin getting bigger, "it's too bad he didn't show up. He's hot."

Parker feels the burn in his cheeks immediately, and he looks down at his feet. "Guess I missed out, then," he mutters.

"Guess *he* missed out," Isaac corrects, and Parker's heart flutters.

"I should go," he says, and then he flees.

"Bye!" Isaac calls after him, and he waves.

Parker tries to focus on his feet, so he doesn't trip. He tries to focus on his heart, so it doesn't pound right out of his chest. He tries to hear anything past the roaring in his ears.

He makes it inside, and closes the door behind him, waiting until he hears Isaac driving away before he attempts to breathe again. *What the fuck is happening?* He asks himself, half-hot with embarrassment and half-hot with something akin to curiosity. He's glad that it's late enough in the day that no one else is home to witness, as he kicks off his shoes, taking his bundle of clothes downstairs to his bedroom where he crashes. He doesn't mean to, but he falls asleep, his mind spinning.

3
ALL THE SOLDIERS GO MARCHING

The autumn breeze is cool on Isaac's face as he settles down into the damp grass beside Iris. All day they've been tracing things, whispers, trying to discover where the Ghost is hiding, what it is that it's plotting. All day there's been nothing – maybe a hum in the trees here, or the hair standing up on Iris's arms there – and Isaac is the kind of tired that he always is, maybe more so. He's bone tired, death tired, dreading the next morning tired.

"I don't want to think anymore," he whispers, closing his eyes against the darkening sky and Iris murmurs in agreement. All day, they've been thinking, debating Prophecy and placement and their upcoming plans. They've been talking to their friends, to Iris's parents, to Isaac's aunt, about the energy that's shifting in their town, the something that's coming for them, sitting just on the horizon, looming.

They've been walking, too, and they found themselves back at the part of the river where Parker had been half-drowned. Isaac waded into the water until it was at his knees, and he felt the anger in it, the thirst for blood. He's sure that rivers aren't supposed to be bloodthirsty yet here it was, swirling and swirling and crashing into the shore, crashing into the rocks, crashing against Isaac's legs, stinging his skin with its intent. It was then that Isaac had started to feel the pit of dread open in his stomach, and it's been growing larger as the day goes by, deepening and darkening, eating all sense of hope he thought that he had.

"Has he texted you?" Iris asks, turning her head to look at him, her eyes dark in the fading light. He can feel the heat emanating from her body, only a few inches away and a thread of nostalgia winds its way around his heart. This is where they always end up – together, on the ground, below a sky full of stars.

"No," he groans, embarrassment gripping him with its heavy fists. He can't believe what he'd said when he was dropping Parker off, how *blatantly* he'd been hitting on him. "He's probably never going to text me, Iris." This is another factor for the gnawing pit inside him. Here is a beautiful man that has been hand-delivered to him and here he is, already messing it up. He's never going to hear from Parker again because of his hubris.

"He will," Iris says, smirking, "you know he will."

Isaac rolls his eyes at her, and they lay in silence for a while. The breeze ripples through the leaves on the trees above them, and the birds that stay for winter chirp their songs to each other. Somewhere in the distance, someone hammers something loudly and somewhere closer there's the noise of a family outside, enjoying one of the evenings before the weather becomes cold and icy. The smell of early dying things wafts into Isaac's nose and then all he can think about is Parker and water and Parker under water and how he had also been dying like the leaves and the trees and the grass.

"What do you think it feels like to drown?" He asks Iris softly, and she takes a minute to process the question.

Finally, she says, "I think it would feel hopeless," in her wistful voice and this makes Isaac's heart hurt in an achy kind of way, deep down at the bottom. He also thinks it would be hopeless and lonely and terrifying. "Didn't you get any of what he was feeling?"

He had. He'd felt the fear coursing through him as if it were his own, the twist in his chest and heart and stomach. He'd felt it so badly that his knees had buckled, but this, as everything he feels is, was only an echo. What Parker felt would have been much worse – more like the earth was shattering around him, more like every ounce of hope had been drained from his muscles. He doesn't want to admit that he was in Parker's head, so he lies. Iris doesn't need to know this, either. "No," he doesn't explain.

"That's probably a good thing." Iris sighs and pushes herself off the ground, offering him a hand which he takes graciously. When they were younger, he used to feel bad when he told her lies like this, but Iris has a different way of processing. It takes more for her to feel something, it takes connection and time, and she has to logic her way into it. She can logic her way out of it. Fear is different to her – she can shoo it away with a stick. She could walk into the water Parker was in last night, stick her own head under and scream until it moved away from her. She's *powerful,* and she isn't afraid of herself. She isn't afraid of anything, and Isaac loves her for it, but doesn't feel bad when he's lying to her about these things, because he's realized that they aren't the same.

"I don't want to go to the Clubhouse tonight," he admits, as he wipes the dead grass off the seat of his pants and looks at her, trying to sway her, trying to get her to agree to cancel their weekly meeting. He knows it's useless.

"We have to," she says, "we have to tell them what's happened."

"We *have* told them what's happened."

"We have to come up with a plan."

He frowns. "I still don't want to."

"Neither do I." But here they are, going anyways, because the weekly meetings are tradition. They're fun. They're a good excuse to catch up with their other friends, even if nothing magical is happening.

Together the two of them head back into Isaac's house, the sunlight nearly leached from the sky behind them, the chill turning from nibble into bite. As Isaac turns to close the door behind him, he catches a glimpse of motion between the trees, close to the ground. He waits for a moment for it to move again, and then it comes into full view - a fox, small and brown. Her big ears are alert and pointed towards the house as she sits in a clear spot between two pine and watches the house patiently, just close enough that Isaac can see her big amber eyes staring directly into his own.

He tilts his head, and the fox mimics the movement, unmoving otherwise. He straightens his neck, and she does the same, not breaking eye contact.

"Hi," he calls out the door and into the evening air. "Are you a friend?"

The fox stands, stretches, shakes out her fur, and then sits again, indignant.

Isaac takes a step forward, his mind swimming. He's heard of these things before - messages and messengers and omens of good and bad. He's not sure what it means, but he knows that it must be important, he knows that the fox is here for a reason. Iris steps out beside him, and he can feel the excitement radiating off her.

"Do you have something I should know?" he asks her, the fox, and she tilts her head again, eyes sparkling with something like mischief. "Do you mean well?"

The fox's chin dips down, and then back up, and she stands again.

"Thank her," Iris whispers, her voice tiny, full of awe.

He straightens. "Thank you for coming to me," he says, "it's an honour."

The fox snuffs and watches him for another moment before she trots back into the shelter of trees, disappearing almost immediately. As soon as she's gone, Isaac ushers Iris back inside and closes the door, locking the knob and the deadbolt.

He knows that the experience was incredible and that he really should be glad, but something doesn't sit right with him. Something feels off. Something is making the pit in his stomach grow and churn and he can't name it.

"Jesus," Iris whispers, "that was incredible."

Isaac nods, silently, her awe soaking into him, urging him to share it with her, but he can't. "We're going to have to look up what foxes mean," he says, instead, and her grin disappears.

"Is something wrong?" she asks, immediately on guard.

"I don't know," he replies, "it just felt weird." It felt like the fox was keeping a secret from him, something important, and she wasn't about to give it up easily. It felt like the possibility of something bigger, something so big that everyone knows about it except them. It felt otherworldly, foreign, indescribable.

Iris nods, reaching out to squeeze his arm. "We've been waiting for this for a long time," she says, "but it's all going to work out. It has to."

Isaac puts his hand over hers and gives her a smile, something reassuring. "I know," he whispers back, and he knows that she's right. Everything's going to be okay. They just have to figure out what it is Parker has for them, and then they need to use it to stop the Ghost from doing what they think it's going to do. Simple, really. Probably. Maybe.

***

Isaac and Iris bundle Isaac's cousin Chip safely into his booster seat which isn't a two-person job, but they make it so, Isaac doing most of the bundling and Iris watching with approval, engaged in polite conversation with Chip.

"You mean to tell me that your classmate believes his dog speaks to him?" She asks, her eyebrows raised, and he nods enthusiastically.

"He said she tells him when she's sad and when she's happy and when she's scared. I asked Polly to tell me when she's sad or happy or scared, but she didn't say anything." He pouts and Isaac sits back, his buckling and pulling and pinching finally finished.

He gives Chip a skeptical look and Chip grins back, his curls falling into his face from all around. "Let me know if she does," he says, and then his face breaks into a smile because Chip just happens to be full of light. "I want to hear what she has to say." Isaac can only imagine the chocolate lab being happy. Happy all the time – happy to see her people, happy to play with them, happy to pee on their shoes. So happy everyone else also must be happy.

Iris chimes in that she'll need to be included and Chip promises wholeheartedly that he will *call* them both right away when it happens. He even giggles and both Isaac and Iris feel their hearts swell with his gentle innocence. Despite everything the kid still believes in miracles.

More than anything, Isaac wishes that Chip doesn't lose this. Just the thought of his cousin being broken down by the world is hard for his mind to comprehend, to hold on to. He would do anything to avoid it, anything to prevent it. He knows that Iris would do the same.

He climbs out of the backseat and makes sure that all of Chip's extremities are still inside before he closes the door. Iris grins at him and mouths the word *kids* and he shrugs his shoulders. To be honest neither of them would be truly surprised if it turned out that animals could talk. To be honest it wouldn't surprise them if Chip could coax every animal in the world to speak to him, he has the right kind of patience. The right kind of belief. The right kind of light inside of him.

He reminds them both of Isaac when he was younger but neither of them will ever say it. Chip isn't allowed to grow up to be Isaac. Isaac won't allow it. There are better people to aspire to be, people who are going to go somewhere, be something. People who aren't going to be stuck in this good-for-nothing town in the ass crack of nowhere.

Isaac starts his car and is just about to back out when the front door opens and Chip's mom emerges, a cardigan that's not large enough to cover her pregnant belly draped tightly around her shoulders. She waves and then holds up a toque and a plastic container full of sliced carrots. Isaac raises his eyebrows at his cousin in the rear-view mirror. "Forgetting something?" he asks, and Chip says "I don't want to wear it," and Iris says, "It ruins his hair!"

Which is an exchange that happens every time they take Chip out with them during the colder months of the year.

Isaac rolls his eyes at Iris, who's grinning, and slides out of the car and up the porch steps to meet his aunt. "You'd think we'd remember by now," he says, and she chuckles, the warm light from inside making her honey-coloured hair glow.

"This kid is going to be the death of me," she says, passing the snack and hat to Isaac, her hands going down to her belly afterwards. "You guys be safe, okay? Make sure he wears it." She leans forwards, a look of exhaustion and worry and motherly affection written over her lips. "Don't let him stay up too late."

Isaac nods. She doesn't have to tell him that she's worried for him to know – his questions about the energy in town have tipped her off to something, although she doesn't know the specifics of what Hell Club does – and he's grateful that she doesn't ask him any questions. She trusts him.

Mel raised Isaac, his own parents – her sister and her sister's husband – left him with his grandparents and her when he was just a baby. The sisters haven't gotten along since. He and his mother don't get along. He's worlds closer to his aunt and he would be okay if he never saw his mother again.

Mel had Chip when Isaac was fourteen, and he likes to help as much as he can, despite her worries that he would end up the same as she had: young and responsible for a child. She doesn't want the same feelings she has for her sister to fester between them, but Isaac loves her with his whole heart. "I know, Mel," he says, giving her a small smile.

She nods, and then sinks deeper into herself, looking tired. "I just have to say it," she whispers, and Isaac understands – it's Mel's job to look after them, and it's hard to turn it off.

There's a moment where neither of them seems to have anything to say, and then Isaac holds up the toque and the carrots, and says, "Thank you. We'll see you later – back by eight! I know!" And then he's heading down the stairs of the porch hurriedly because he knows if he stays, he's going to start saying things that he shouldn't be saying. He knows that one inquiry from his aunt, and he'll tell her everything. He'll tell her about Parker and the river, and he'll tell her about the Ghost and its reappearance. He'll tell her that the world is moving forward, and life is happening and happening and happening and he's only starting to come to the realization that he can't stop it. He'll tell her that he's smoking again, and he can't shake the feeling that there's something coming, something bigger than him and he can't wrap his mind around it, he can't fathom the speed at which it's approaching. If he stays for even a second longer, he'll tell her every thought he's had in the past twenty-four hours.

"Bye!" She calls, before he hears the front door shut, and his heart darkens with guilt.

Maybe he *should* tell her. Maybe she'll have advice for him – she usually does. If Isaac has experience with the magic around Belle, Mel has the same experience tenfold with magic everywhere. She ran the family business for a while – performing Rituals, words, and actions that make the magic of the earth available to those who can't feel it, who can't call to it and selling Artifacts, items touched by magic and changed by it – so he's sure that she could give him something. He's sure that she would be happy to investigate things, to help, but asking her to help means getting her involved and being involved in the Hell Club is dangerous. It's not a death sentence, but it's a pair of shackles keeping them here in Belle. It's a feeling of unbelonging when Isaac leaves his town, and he doesn't want his aunt to be tied here, too.

He opens the door of his running car to Iris and Chip discussing the importance of hats in the prevention of heat loss from the body, and he tosses the hat in question to Chip, who only looks up at him with mild disgust.

"My hair," he protests, holding it away from him like it's a dog with fleas.

"Just wear it until we're out of sight of your house," Isaac retorts, putting the car in reverse and waving to his aunt, who's appeared in the window, a head peaking through the curtains.

Iris waves, too, and turns in her seat to take the toque from Chip and wrestle it onto his head. "There," she says, "now you'll be warmer."

The smile that had appeared on his face immediately disappears. "But my *hair*," he protests again, squirming in his seat.

"We're going into the woods anyways, Chip, no one's going to care what your hair looks like." Isaac has been hit with a wave of fatigue. This whole fight with his cousin seems pointless – wear the hat, don't wear the hat, what's the point of arguing with a seven-year-old who clearly has his priorities straight, however vain they may be.

As soon as they turn off of Chip's road, his hat is off, flung to the other side of the car with disgust. "*I* care what my hair looks like," he retorts in an airy voice and Iris and Isaac share a look.

"Good luck to Mel when he's a teenager," Iris whispers under her breath and Isaac snorts.

"Good luck to us all," he says, softer, and Chip starts to tell them about the ins and outs of being seven years old. Who said what and who did what and what offensive things his mother has said to him (nothing out of the ordinary) and what his father hasn't allowed him to do even though he really wanted to (operate the heavy machinery of his woodshop and eat leftover Thanksgiving pie for breakfast).

Isaac tries his best to listen to everything that Chip is saying and be active in the conversation, as he usually is, but he's so tired. Chips words seem to slide off him like rain on an umbrella, and he feels bad. He's usually a much better cousin, and a much better listener. The trees in front of him start blurring together and he blinks them back into focus. The sinking feeling is back in his stomach, and it's reminding him that he has no idea what he's doing, that there's so much of the Prophecies and what's to come that is unknown, and unknowable. He's walking into this blind.

He pulls the car up beside an old truck and shifts into park. Chip says something that sounds like excited gibberish from the back seat and Iris is already out and helping him unbuckle himself from the monster that is his booster seat.

It takes a moment for Isaac to will his legs to move, and he hoists himself out of the car, into the cool night air. Out here it smells like tree and dirt and the river is moving not that far away – the same piece of river that tried to drown Parker, the same piece of river that Isaac waded into earlier today and felt its anger.

"Are the others here yet?" Chip asks Isaac, pulling on the sleeve of his jacket like he can't contain his excitement.

Isaac gestures at the truck. "You tell me." He quips, but Chip doesn't get the sarcasm. He takes off at a run to the cabin door and throws it open, disappearing inside and leaving the other two behind. "No loyalty," Isaac mutters, joking, fond of his cousin all the same.

"He just loves everyone," Iris says back. She knocks her elbow against his as she passes him, giving him a smirk over her shoulder, barely visible in the dim light shining through the cabin windows. "Reminds me of someone," she adds, betraying the unspoken rule between them that they're not to compare Chip to Isaac.

Neither of them comments on it further. Isaac grimaces and moves to follow her inside, where they can hear the voices of the others now that they've become accustomed to the silence of the trees. Someone laughs, high-pitched and on the verge of a giggle - probably Eve - and Isaac's heart trips in his chest. He's not sure he can face them and tell them that he doesn't know what's coming, that he's trying to piece together the Prophecies and their places in all of them. He knows that they've been working on it just as hard as he has, that they're no farther along than he is, but somehow, he's more disappointed in himself. He's had the longest to sit with this information, the longest to digest it, and explore it.

He found the book at the Clubhouse when he was only seventeen, and it took him a month to build up the courage to show Iris. That month was full of reading and re-reading, memorizing, trying to make sense of the new world he'd been plunged into. Finally, when he'd done as much research as he could on his own, he gave Iris the book and let her help him. She started pulling tarot cards, meditating, reading through her mother's journals to get a better idea of the Ghost and what it is that it wants.

The rest had come in their own time. Eve and Derek, the lovers, catching a glimpse of the Prophecy book tucked into Isaac's backpack in their final year of high school, asking what it is. Chip insisting that he be taken to see the cabin and then getting so swept up in the talk of magic that he couldn't sleep for days after, riding the wave of his excitement. Dahlia, the most recent, sitting on the porch of the cabin one night, waiting. She, like Iris, can feel the energy in Belle, and she claimed that it brought her to them, whispering until she couldn't stand it anymore.

Isaac loves them all with everything that he has, and he doesn't want to disappoint them. He feels like he's disappointing them, because he doesn't have the answers that they need, that they want.

Iris stands at the door for a second, before she turns back. "Ready?" she asks, adjusting the messy bun she's wrapped her hair into, looking like she's ready for war.

"Just give me a second." He's not ready. He needs to - he needs to think for another minute.

Iris nods, and the door opens, light spilling out and illuminating her in the most beautiful way - her eyes, her skin, the way her hand braces against the wood - and then she's swallowed by the cabin, met with noise from the others already inside. Isaac tries to pick out their greetings to her, but it sounds like static. He thinks that he hears his name, but the door closes over it, and he sighs.

He wishes, for a moment, that he'd brought his cigarettes so he could give his hands something to do to stop their shaking. It would calm his nerves, it would give his brain something to think about other than spiraling and spiraling and doing that thing that it does where the edges of his vision go black and his heart drops to the bottom of his pelvis, between the ilia, beating like a kickdrum.

His fingers find the edge of his phone in his pocket and dig it out, just to see if maybe the electronic *thing* which he hates can replace the drag of smoke in his lungs. His finger hits the power button, and it pops up that he's gotten a message from an unknown number:

hi, it's parker,

and then his heart really does do the thing where it drops to his pelvis and he turns off his phone, shoving it deep back into his pocket. He swings the door to the cabin open without thinking – without realizing what he's done, because Parker, the man from last night, the half-drowned man, the incredibly beautiful man, has texted him and he's texted him so much sooner than either he or Iris had expected.

Isaac hasn't the slightest idea what to say to him.

He blinks into the sudden light to find several pairs of eyes looking at him expectantly from all corners of the one-room cabin. "Hey guys," he says, grinning at them, trying to feign normalcy even when he's still half-shocked at the text message and the speed at which he'd moved to get away from answering it. Shouldn't he be *excited?*

The room is cramped as always, and he walks through the limbs splayed on the floor to lean at the desk by the woodstove, right beside Iris, their elbows touching. The rest of his friends nod at him, smile at him, wave at him, and then go back to their conversations. Dahlia, wrapped in a blanket scarf, is listening with intense interest to Chip's talking dog story, one of her hands splayed on the table they're sitting on, her nails painted black. Eve is sitting in the only real chair in the cabin, ever-present sunglasses perched on her head despite the dying light of the evening. She looks amused at whatever Derek is telling her, his hands moving through the air crudely to demonstrate, his body angled almost painfully towards her from where he's seated on the arm of her chair.

Iris raises her eyebrows at him. "All good?" she asks, and he shakes his head.

"He texted," he whispers to her, digging his phone back out of his pocket.

"What?" she exclaims, reaching for it as he lights up the screen. "He texted you twice!"

Isaac leans over to see, but she holds it up and away, her eyes flicking back and forth as she reads, a smile beginning at the corners of her mouth. "He's cute," she says, after a moment, already typing something.

"Asshole," Isaac mutters as he tries to look again, and she moves the phone away. "At least let me see what he said." The fire of embarrassment at his behaviour earlier in the day is burning deep in his stomach, and he desperately needs confirmation that he hadn't overstepped his place.

Iris wiggles her eyebrows at him, and then places it back in his palm. "He answered right away," she says.

Isaac only glares at her, opening his phone.

Parker: *hi, it's parker*

Parker: *i hope it's not too early but i'd like to see you again if that's okay. i'm still really confused abt what's happening but i've been putting together some questions that i'd like answered. can we meet soon?*

Isaac: *yes. come to the cabin right now. we're having a meeting – we can answer some of your questions.*

Parker: *the cabin by the river?*

Isaac's heart is in his throat. He confirms the place with Parker, and then shoves his phone back into his pocket. "Why did you do that?" he asks, even though it's a useless question.

To get Parker acquainted with those that can help protect him. To get Parker some kinds of answers. To test him, to see if he's really interested, if he's curious enough to keep coming, if he has the hunger for the unknown that they so need him to have.

Iris shrugs. "He seemed eager enough."

Isaac: *that's the one.*

Parker: *be there in like ten minutes*

"He's coming," Isaac whispers, and Iris grins.

"That's a good thing, Isaac," she says, knocking her arm against his, her excitement radiating from her in waves, making the nervous pit in his stomach jolt, the fire burning hotter.

He swallows, and nods. "I know," he says, "it's just that –" he can't finish. It's just that Parker is the person from the Prophecy, *two to twine in divine time*, and Isaac has promised him answers that he doesn't have. That none of them have. It's just that Parker is the sort of beautiful that makes Isaac's knees weak with want, and his hands are the sort of hands that Isaac can't stop seeing intertwined with his own, on his body, fingers hooked in his mouth. It's just that this is the kind of desire that makes him do stupid stuff, that makes him lose his mind just a little bit, that makes him lose his confidence. It's just that the enormity of it astounds him. It's just that the unknowns of it all scare him.

Iris leans a little closer to him and reaches out, touching his hand. "It's all gonna work out," she says, "don't worry about it."

"Yeah," he says, and he feels her resolve flicker for a moment. "I know." He flips his hands, and captures hers, squeezing her fingers before letting go.

"Ready?" She asks, and he's not but he says yes anyways.

Iris stands, and the others in the cabin look at her. The already dim light of the cabin becomes dimmer, and the shadow that she casts along the wall becomes larger, distorted, less human-shaped. Isaac used to fear her power, when he didn't understand it, but now it's comforting. Now it's easy to see her magic and believe that between them all, there's enough power to be able to do something. Now it's easy to see her magic and believe that if Iris is on his side, nothing is impossible.

She sits back down, beside him, and Isaac's skin prickles with her heat, with the heat of the Protections she's called down onto the cabin, the Protections that her and Dahlia worked so hard on, that keep anybody they want out *out* and anybody they want in *in.*

Eve leans forward in her chair, looking eager. "What happened at the river?" she asks, her eyes glued to Iris. "Who is it?"

As if on cue, there's a knock at the door of the cabin, and Isaac is up on his feet in half a second flat. He hears Iris say behind him, smug,

"Just wait," but his heart is beating so fast that he can't hear any of the responses.

He opens the door maybe a little bit too fast, and then Parker is there, the light from the cabin casting shadows across his face, so close that Isaac can smell the warmth of his soap on his skin, can make out the pockmarks of acne scars along his cheeks. "Hey," he breathes, and Parker looks up at him.

"Hey," he says. "I – uh – hi." His eyes turn to the ground, and Isaac pushes the cabin door open further to reveal the others, to invite Parker inside.

"Come in," he says, gesturing, and Parker follows, glancing around before he stuffs his hands into his pockets. To his friends, Isaac says, "This is Parker," and Parker says, "Park," and then the room explodes with introductions.

4
ANSWERS?

Parker stops at the door of his sister's bedroom, running the text message he received from Isaac through his head over and over. He wants to go to the cabin, and he's already told Isaac he'll be there. The only problem is the physical journey.

The cabin, which he's discovered is open for community use (something about its historic significance), is only a fifteen-minute walk from his house, but he's rather averse to travelling it alone in the dark, especially after last night. This leaves one option, which is to ask his sister to drive him, and she has made it clear that she's still annoyed with him for making her worry.

He's also thought about *not going,* but there's a loneliness that's been fermenting inside of him unchecked for too long and the promised presence of Isaac and answers to the questions he's been brainstorming all day is too much. He needs to know more about what it is that tried to kill him, the Ghost, and about the secret that makes him so special. He needs to go to the cabin because he needs to see Isaac again, now that he's recovered. He needs to know that he didn't dream either of his rescuers up and that what happened at the river really happened.

He's been thinking about it, turning over the events in his mind. The man, the not-man, the Ghost, holding him under the current, Iris glowing, Isaac's hands gentle and warm. The specifics of it are slipping out of his memory, becoming fuzzy, more feeling and colour than real happenings. He was cold and wet and drowning and then he wasn't, and he needs to know more about it all.

He takes a deep breath, about to knock on the door in front of him, when it opens.

"Jesus, *Parker,*" she hisses, staggering back, her hand pressed to her chest. "You scared me. What are you doing lurking out here?"

"Sorry," he mutters, stepping over the threshold and into her room. "Sorry, I was just about to knock. Also, I am not *lurking.*" He was most definitely lurking.

"What do you want?" He was hoping that her annoyance might have faded throughout the day, but the way her eyes are narrowed tells him that he has not been forgiven and will definitely be in more trouble after he asks her to drive him and doesn't promise any answers.

"Can you do me a huge favour?"

She sighs. "I won't pick you up when you're done," she says.

"I didn't even tell you what I wanted?" He questions, taken aback. He was expecting her to tell him off, to remind him that he can get his own license and car so he can drive himself places after dark.

"You want a ride," she deadpans, "what else would you be asking for?"

He throws up his hands. There are a million things he could be asking for.

She only raises an eyebrow.

"Yeah, yeah," he says. "I need a ride. I can tell you more tomorrow."

"Why can't you tell me tonight?"

"Because I don't know if he's worth telling you about yet," he admits. He wishes he could tell her about what happened the night before, but he gets the feeling that it's probably not a great idea. Isaac and Iris didn't specifically say not to tell anyone, but he got the idea that Hell Club works on a need-to-know basis and C doesn't need to know. Besides, if he told her that he'd nearly drowned then she wouldn't drive him, and he'd have to walk.

"Fine," she mutters, pushing past him, through the door and into the hall. "Coming?" She calls out over her shoulder, and he nods.

On the drive, C remains quiet, and Parker's heart is a jackhammer. The loneliness is back like an uninvited guest, lingering on the fringes of his thoughts so he pushes it out and deep down into the recesses of his chest. He's not doing this solely because he's lonely and Isaac has a pretty face. He's doing this for answers.

"Why am I taking you into the woods?" C asks, turning into the short driveway that leads to the cabin. "Why are there two cars here?"

"It's - uh - well - um," Parker stutters, struggling to find an answer that's going to quell the thoughts that C is having, and C puts her hand up to stop him.

"Never mind," she says, "I actually don't want to know the answer to that."

"It's not what you think," Parker says, sheepishly, as she comes to a full stop.

"I don't want to think anything," she says, pushing her hair back behind her ears, eyes flashing in the light from the dashboard of her SUV. "I just want to know that you're going to be safe."

Parker swallows. He's sure that Isaac and Iris and the rest of their friends are going to keep him safe – it's what they told him they were trying to do. He remembers last night again: cold and wet and drowning, and then none of those things. "I'll be safe," he tells her, nodding.

"Alright," she says, "but I want to know about everything tomorrow."

"Yeah, of course. See you later." He pulls himself out of the car, listening to her pull away as he walks to the cabin.

It's darker here than it had been at his house, and the fear of seeing the Ghost again drives him to lift his knuckles to the door before he has the chance to check his text messages again. He knocks, once, twice, three times, and then pushes his hands deep into his pockets.

In the dark, chilled under his sweater, he feels the energy from the freezing earth and the trees and the river, and Parker kind of likes it. It's coming from the cabin too, and if he looks close enough, un-focusing his eyes just a touch, there's a red glow surrounding it like the paintings in Isaac's house.

It feels right that he's here, like something in him is aligning that he hadn't been aware of before. His entire body is buzzing like it's been filled with bees. Excited, nervous bees.

The door opens and in front of him is Isaac, his blond hair tucked into a toque, his face in shadow, his hand wrapped neatly along the side of the door. The inside of the cabin smells like smoke, and Isaac leans forward, closer to Park. "Hey," he says.

"Hey," Park replies. "I – um," he starts, but his voice cracks and betrays him. "Hi." Heat rises in him, and he looks down at his feet, awkward.

He feels the shift in Isaac, then, the warmth and the welcoming emanating from him. "Come in," Isaac says, and he pulls himself out of the doorway, gesturing for Park to step inside, and Park notices all the other pairs of eyes on him.

He stuffs his hands into his pockets, and looks again at the floor, swallowing. He figured that there would be several people here – Hell Club, Isaac and Iris's friends – but somehow this is more than he thought. He feels self conscious. He feels stupid. They probably all know that he was nearly drowned last night, and it makes him feel dirty, as if it's *his* fault. As if there's a running joke being played on him, and he doesn't know what the punchline is.

The door shuts behind him, and Isaac's warmth seeps into him from his shoulder.

"This is Parker," Isaac says, and Park flinches.

"Park," he corrects because he forgot that he told Isaac his name is Parker. His name is only Parker to his parents, and only when they're angry.

Isaac nods, "Park, then," he says, and he points at the child sitting on a desk. "This is Chip," Chip beams.

The woman beside Chip, who is tall and looks annoyed, nods at him. "Dahlia," she says, and her nails dig into the wood of the desk a little bit tighter.

Another woman, with mousey brown hair and sunglasses perched on her head stands, and offers her hand to Park, grinning. Her grip is firm, and her hands are warm and soft in his, the tips of her acrylics brushing against his palm. "Eve," she says, "it's so nice to meet you."

He nods, getting the impression that she means exactly what she says. "You too," he says, feeling the awkwardness slip its icy fingers onto the back of his neck.

"This is my boyfriend, Derek," she says, and then Derek is standing beside her, incredibly tall and wide and full of tattoos.

"Hey," he says, and he holds out his hand, too, which Park takes, only a little scared, until Derek smiles at him, and then places his hand on Eve's waist, ushering her back to their chair, where he perches on the arm, his back pressed against her shoulder.

"And you've met Iris," Isaac breathes, still beside him. He gestures to a stool between Eve's chair and where Iris is standing, watching him, and Park sits, self-conscious.

Everyone here seems so *interesting* – Derek with his tattoos, Eve with her kindness and her winged eyeliner, Dahlia with her sullen silence, and Chip with his childish excitement – they seem like they belong. He feels out of place in his ratty sweater with holes around the sleeve cuffs. His face is stubbly, his hair is just-rolled-out-of-bed messy, and he feels unkempt, unfit for so many eyes.

He pulls his ratty sweater sleeves around his hands, and searches for somewhere to look that isn't a stranger, that isn't going to make him feel even more out of place. He finds Isaac's gaze, as Isaac pushes himself onto the table beside Iris, and Isaac gives him a small smile, a small nod. *You're okay,* he seems to be saying. *Don't worry about it.*

"Have you told him about the Prophecies?" Eve asks, leaning forward, her elbows on her knees, directing her question to Isaac.

"A bit," Isaac says, "the basic premise. The one about his secrets."

Eve nods, and then something passes through her expression that looks almost like a tease, and Isaac shuffles his hands uncomfortably from his sides to the table underneath him.

"So you know that you're important to us," Eve says, focusing on Park, that half-smile still on her face, like he's missing out on the joke.

"I guess?" Park questions. "But I don't really understand how. Or why."

Eve gives Isaac and Iris another look that seems like an eye roll. *Are you serious?*

"We didn't want to scare him off too early," Iris says, shrugging, and Park catches her gaze, which is warmer than it was at Isaac's house, but still intense. She's looking at him like she knows him, knows all his secrets already, knows every single sin that he's ever committed. She's looking at him like she is not of-this-earth as he is of-this-earth, that she exists on some other kind of ethereal plane that he will never know about.

Whatever part of himself that he thought was brave shrivels up and dies in the fire that has become his nervous system.

Iris blinks and looks away, as Park balls the material of his sweater tightly in his hands, his teeth pressed together at the back of his skull so hard he can feel the headache already. Everyone else here seems friendly enough – except maybe Dahlia – and he doesn't know what he's done to warrant Iris's soul-searching judgement.

"I'm not going to get scared off," he says, his voice coming out whiny and petulant like a child's. He wants to hunch his shoulders with embarrassment, to hide himself in the dark corner of the cabin, but he doesn't. "If the Ghost is going to try to kill me again, I want to be around people who know how to protect me. I'm not stupid." He looks back to Iris at the last part and sees something lift in her eyes.

"No one said you were," Eve says, and her voice is soft, "but it *is* confusing. It *is* scary. It was for all of us when we were first learning. Right, Derek?"

Derek nods, enthusiastically. "It's a lot all at once."

Park swallows, pressing the balled-up fabric of his sweater harder into his palms. He swings his gaze back to Isaac, who's watching him too. Everyone seems to be watching him, and the pressure of it is building up, threatening to crack his foundations, threatening to spill over the sides. He doesn't know what he's supposed to be for them, or why it's him that's involved. He doesn't know anything about magic, or Belle, or the Ghost. He doesn't have any secrets.

Isaac must sense it in him, because he says, "We'll go at your pace. What questions do you have right now? What do you want to know?"

"Isaac," warns Dahlia, "what if he goes to the RCMP or something?"

Park looks at her, in disbelief. "I'm not going to the police."

She narrows her dark eyes at him for a moment, judging, and then she nods, finding him to be telling the truth. "Fine."

"What do you want to know?" This time it's Eve that asks, and Park sighs.

"What's the Ghost?" he asks.

Eve bites her lip and looks to Iris. Iris looks to Dahlia, who shrugs, and then Iris lets out a breath. Chip, who's been quiet this whole time says:

"The trees."

Just as Isaac says, "Everything."

"Oh, come on," Iris says, annoyed. "You guys are so cryptic," she points her attention at Park. "The Ghost is the protector of something called the Sorrow. The Sorrow is an amalgamation of the energy of the earth, the trees, the plants, the water, you name it. It absorbs everything that happens on the land - logging, violence, pollution. In every encounter we have recorded of it, it's screaming. Or crying. That's why it's called the Sorrow."

Park blinks, absorbing. "So, the Ghost is a guard dog? And the Sorrow is literally the earth's sadness?"

Iris nods. "Basically. The Ghost only comes around when the Sorrow gets to a certain point of despair - the point of no return, I guess. It uses the same energy of the earth that I do to work its magic, but it's different than a witch. It exists on a plane of space or time that we can't really comprehend, just like the Sorrow. That's why we can't hear it."

"But it can switch into our plane? And that's what tried to drown me?"

"It takes different forms," Iris continues, "but yes. That was a part of it, the part that it uses to communicate to us. In most cases, it's more of a shadow or a darkness, hence, the Ghost."

"Sometimes it's dust," Eve quips, but doesn't expand.

"I don't understand - why is it here, then? Why does it care about me?" Park is baffled. Park is desperately trying to scrape together his wits, so he doesn't seem baffled. He's trying to take it in stride, as if otherworldly guard dogs and screaming powers in alternate planes of existence are a normal Thursday occurrence for him. He can tell he's not doing a great job.

"There are the Prophecies," Isaac cuts in, "a book of them. They speak of the 'End of Times,' where the Ghost reaches its full power and pulls all of humanity into its homeland so the earth can recover. They speak of one person who can stop it, or extend it and we - well, we think that may be you. You're the one with the secrets, which means you could be the one who knows how to -"

"I don't know anything," Park cuts him off, the pressure once again boiling in his chest, threatening to crack him open. He pulls the collar of his sweater away from his neck, and swallows, looking at Isaac, hoping that Isaac understands. "I didn't even know that magic existed before - before last night. I -"

"That's why we're here," Dahlia says, "we're here to teach you and to make sure that the Ghost doesn't kill you or draw you into it." She seems warmer now, more accepting of his presence, his confusion.

"What happens to the people it draws into it?" He probably should have asked this already, but something tells him that he already knows.

"They die," Eve confirms, "or they come back different."

"Different how?"

"Ready to do anything to give the Ghost what it wants."

"How many people have come back?"

"Just one."

"Who?"

"My mother," Iris says, "she came back long enough to protect the forest from old-growth logging and then she disappeared again. We never found a body."

"Oh, god," Park breathes, "I'm so sorry." He suddenly feels like he's in over his head. These people – they know things. They've seen things. They've lost loved ones and he clearly has no idea how to help them. He doesn't even know where to start. He has no idea what he's supposed to do, or why he's the one who's involved.

He stands, abruptly, ignoring Isaac who says his name, and then Chip who says it more urgently.

"I just – I just need some air," he says, and he beelines for the door, ashamed that he's giving them the idea that they were right about him, that he is a coward, that he is being scared off. "I'll be back – I just – " he opens the door, and the cool air feels nice on his face.

He steps out into the night, and above him are a billion stars, bright against the black night. Even though he feared the dark before, it feels better than being in the cabin. He stumbles down the steps onto the hard ground and takes a deep breath and then another, filling his lungs with fresh air, feeling as the oxygen absorbs into his body, tearing through his throat.

"Park, wait!" says Chip again, but then the door slams shut between them.

There's a moment where he hears the clatter of feet hitting the floor inside the cabin, and then there's the loudest noise he's ever heard and it's inside of his skull, ricocheting from ear to ear and then he's falling and his vision is black and his body is on the ground and it's so cold and there's nothing he can do. He's helpless, his limbs unmoving, his tongue and his teeth numb. He can't tell if his eyes are open or closed, but everything is black, dark, not even a shadow in his sight. He tries desperately to move his fingers, to move *something,* but nothing happens. The noise echoes, rattling his bones, and he – he wants nothing more than for it to be over. He feels like he's floating, like nothing is real. He holds onto the feeling, drifting further and further away from the noise. Drifting further and further from himself. He's a passenger in his mind, stranded from his body.

He remembers telling C that he'd be safe here. If this is how he dies, she'll never forgive herself for leaving him. He reaches out again, trying to wiggle his fingers, but the connection between his mind and body is severed. There is only the terrible noise and endless darkness his subconsciousness is floating inside.

Suddenly there's a hand on his shoulder, and he's brought back into his body all at once. It *hurts.*

"Fuck me," someone says, far away, and then Isaac is whispering to him. "You're okay. You're okay. Don't move, yet, okay? Shit - he's bleeding. You're okay, Park."

Park still can't see, and the panic rises in him, but he can't say anything, either. He's aware of his body, of the feeling of it, of his shoulder, which houses the warmth of Isaac's hand, but he can't *move.*

There's another pair of footsteps on the gravel, and another pair of hands probe at his forehead. He hears Eve say, "It's just a skin bleed, he'll be okay."

Isaac's hand moves from his shoulder to his face, his thumbs pressing gently on Park's eyes, and then Park blinks them open, Isaac and Eve coming into focus in his vision. He tries to open his mouth, but nothing happens, and Isaac's thumbs move, matching his thoughts. They press against his lips, and then Park gasps, breath and words tumbling out of him.

Isaac's fingers slide from his skin, for a moment, and then reappear on his chest, right over his heart, and feeling and control come back to Park's body all at once. He jerks, sliding away from Isaac and from Eve, feeling the burn of tears starting at the back of his throat and desperately swallowing them. He doesn't want either of them to know that he is terrified. That he can still hear the ringing in his head. That he'd been so far away from himself.

He takes a deep, ragged breath, and then another. Neither Eve nor Isaac says anything. Neither of them touch him.

Finally, he gathers himself together enough to ask, "What *was* that?"

"A Protection spell," Eve clarifies. "You left before we could deactivate it."

Park finds himself nodding, as if this is a perfectly normal explanation. As if nothing he's just learned, as if the all-consuming fear he's just felt aren't anything extraordinary at all. As if it all makes sense.

"Nothing in and nothing out without permission from the witches," Isaac continues the explanation. "The same would happen to any of us if we tried to leave without Iris or Dahlia taking them down."

Park pulls his knees to his chest and presses his forehead against them. *Of course.* Of course, they wouldn't let him leave - he's special to them. Of course, he had to run out like a fool and embarrass himself. Of course, Isaac had to be the first out the door after him, of course it had to be him that pulled him back into his body.

"I'm sorry," Isaac offers, and his voice is velvet soft. "I know it's a lot. I'm sorry we didn't tell you about the spell."

"I just – I guess I don't understand, but why me? Why did the Ghost choose me?"

Eve and Isaac shrug in unison.

"Your guess is as good as ours," Eve says, "but it did choose you, and that means that you're one of us now."

"Great," he says, through gritted teeth. He doesn't see the perk.

The door to the cabin opens behind them and Iris pokes her head out. "Everything okay?" She asks, and Park realizes that the rest of them are waiting politely inside for his fit to be over, for his pain to be finished.

"Yeah," Isaac says, "but I think I'm going to offer Park a ride home. Are you coming?"

Iris nods. "Let me get Chip."

"Do you want a ride?"

Park nods, as Isaac stands, offering his hand to Park who takes it. He stumbles while he pushes himself off the ground, and Isaac steadies him, hand in hand and hand on opposite elbow, his fingers strong. He doesn't let go until he's sure that Park's not going to fall right back down, and then he leads Park to his car, turning on the engine and cranking the heat up.

Park bundles himself into the passenger seat, and then Isaac whispers that he'll be back in a minute. Park watches him go back to the cabin and exchange a few words with Eve and Derek who have emerged from the cabin. None of them look at him, but he's almost certain that he's the main point in their conversation. He sees Isaac's lips make his name more than once.

He turns his gaze to his lap with shame, staring at his hands, at the stupid ratty sleeves of his sweater. All the rightness that he'd felt standing at the door to the cabin has disappeared and it's left a taste of acid in his throat. All he can wonder is what he's gotten himself into. All he can wonder is whether he'll be okay. All he can wonder is what his secret is, and what's so important about it.

The backseat door opens and Iris slides in, and then the other side opens and Chip is hoisted into his car-seat and Isaac buckles him into it deftly.

Despite himself and his misery, he finds himself pulled into the warmth that the three have with each other. Chip and Isaac and Iris are arguing about Chip's hair and his hat and how his hat ruins his hair, and the argument seems well-rehearsed, well-oiled, as if they've had it a million times before.

Park likes the routine of it. He likes that Chip still puts the hat on when they turn the corner to his parents' house and acts like he's been wearing it the whole time. He likes how Isaac and Iris make unbuckling and delivering Chip to the front door a two-person job. He likes how the light from the front door of the house glows around them and makes them look like they did the night at the river.

He likes how Iris seems relaxed, how she laughs when Isaac makes a stupid comment. He likes how Isaac smiles at him when he catches him looking, how it doesn't seem awkward. He likes how Isaac pulls into his driveway and says, "Stay in touch, okay? Please?" and then stays in his driveway until the front door closes behind him.

He likes Isaac. He even likes Iris more than he had the first time they met. He likes Chip, and he likes Eve. He likes the people. He doesn't like the secrecy or the magic or the not-knowing things. He doesn't like how he embarrassed himself in his panic. He doesn't like that he knows the power that Iris has now – the floating uselessness of his body is something that he knows is going to haunt him.

More than anything, he knows that he needs to stick close to them. More than anything, he can imagine that he doesn't want to stray out of their protection. More than anything, he knows he wants Isaac's hands back on his face, back on his chest, the careful concern in them, the warmth of his palms. More than anything he knows this.

5
A MESS TO BE MADE

"*What did you think* of Parker?" Eve asks as she rubs lotion onto her face, more of a shadow than a person in the dim light of the room.

Derek looks up at her and leans back on the palms of his hands. He had thought that Parker was frightened. He had thought that Parker was confused. He had thought that Parker shouldn't have any reason to come to them for protection after how they'd treated him - but Eve has the sparkle in her eye that means he's not supposed to answer with *those*. "He didn't really have *anything* to him," he says, instead, remembering his aura, his energy, the lack thereof. "I don't know what I was expecting but it wasn't him."

From the Prophecy, he'd been expecting someone with grandeur, someone who already knew about Belle and the magic which swirled in the air around it, the history, and the Ghost. He'd been expecting someone who took up more space - someone who had the confidence of someone like Isaac, of someone like Iris or Dahlia. Someone intimidating - someone taller? He doesn't think he's ever seen anyone so grey.

Eve squirts more lotion onto her hands and motions for him to sit up. He does so and she straddles him, bare skin against bare skin, and dabs the lotion over his face, rubbing it in in concentric circles. "I feel bad for Dahlia," she admits as Derek closes his eyes, leaning into her touch. "For Isaac to end up with someone like him instead of someone like her."

Derek opens one eye. "Dahlia didn't have a chance. Not when he's known about the Prophecy for so long."

She sighs. "No, I know that, but like energy wise, you know? Like someone so bland. That has to hurt her feelings a little." She stops rubbing circles and cups his cheeks in her hands, planting a kiss off-centre on his lips.

"She didn't have to be so rude to him, though," Derek says, wrapping his arms around her and pulling her closer, so their chests touch. "He was already confused, and she just seemed so *angry*."

"I mean, isn't that just Dahlia? And I'm confused, too, I guess." She pushes her cheek into his shoulder, he feels her breath against his neck, warm and steady. "Like I know we're supposed to keep him alive but what does that look like?"

Derek falls backwards onto the bed, bringing her with him and eliciting a noise of surprise as she readjusts. "I don't know, babe," he sighs. He thinks he would be more content if he'd never been a part of the Hell Club, if he didn't know about any of this and he and Eve were free to live their lives separate from the magic in Belle. He wraps his arms tighter around her and squeezes his eyes together tightly.

"Imagine if it had been us that found him at the river instead of them," Eve says, her breath still on his neck, her weight on him calming, "we wouldn't have been able to do anything."

"I know."

The world around them goes silent for a few moments, and Derek cherishes their closeness. He doesn't want to have anything to do with Parker. He doesn't want to have anything to do with the Prophecy – he just wants to hold Eve and breathe with her and watch her grow old. He wants to see the good she would do as a doctor, and he wants to watch her walk down the aisle towards him in a beautiful dress and he wants to buy a house together and talk about their days. He wants more of chasing each other around the house with NERF guns, he wants more of making her breakfast and more of shared lazy Sunday mornings. He wants to walk down all the streets of their town with her, and he wants to make her laugh at the stupidest of things, he wants her to be happy. He wants to be happy with her. That's all he wants.

"What are you thinking right now?" She asks, putting her weight on her elbows so she can look him in the face. "Like right now?"

"You," he says, opening his eyes so he can see her, her hair braided behind her head, the crooked way her lips are angled like she already knew he was thinking of her. "I'm always thinking about you."

She smiles, so big it lights up the room. So big she can't possibly know what's going to happen. So big he must smile too. "Liar," she says, but they both know she's only making fun of him. She lays back down on him, this time her head on his chest, and she says, "I was thinking about you, too," and he angles his head so he can kiss the top of hers.

"Night baby," he says, and she says it back, her voice muffled, already falling asleep, even as he stares at the ceiling, unable to.

"I love you," he whispers, after she's flopped off him and has snuggled herself into blankets, pushing her back into his ribs, safe and warm and perfect.

"Lumf you too," she says, half asleep, everything he's ever wanted. The rest of his worries fall away – Hell Club ceases to exist, the Prophecy ceases to exist, Parker and the Ghost cease to exist.

"It'll all be alright," Isaac had told him earlier that night, worry written through his face, and Derek hadn't believed him then. He still doesn't completely believe him now, but things seem better. 'Alright' seems more believable than perfect. Anything seems believable when Eve is beside him.

He falls into an uneasy sleep in which he's being chased, chased through a never-ending forest by a thing without a name and when he wakes up, he's drenched in sweat and Eve is poking him with urgency.

"What?" he asks, groggily, and she wrinkles her nose.

"You're gross," she says. "Sweaty and gross."

He huffs. "So, you woke me up?"

"Yeah," she replies, "but you woke me up first."

He turns his back to her and wraps an arm around his pillow. "Go back to sleep," he groans, and she scoots away from him.

"Okay, sweat monster," she replies haughtily, and Derek slips back into the dream where he's running, and Eve slips back into a dream where she's losing him everywhere.

6

WHERE TO EXIST ALONE

Isaac shakes the bowl of food at the tomcat he's been trying to befriend for the past month. "I swear I'm not going to hurt you," he tells him, pinching the edge with his fingers and pushing it as far from his body as his arms allow. "See? No harm."

The cat sits, just beyond the bowl, and stares at him with his big gold eyes, unmoved by Isaac's muttering.

"Fine," he sighs, setting the bowl down on the porch railing and moving away from it to lean back into the corner, digging in his pockets for the box of cigarettes he'd stashed in them on his way out. The cat seems pleased with this development and stands, moving to dig into the food in the bowl.

Isaac lights a cigarette and watches him, fascinated by the violent way in which he's eating, his mouth wide open, piling as much kibble as he can into his mouth and swallowing it whole. "It's like I don't feed you at all," he muses to the cat, taking a drag and crossing his arms in front of himself. The morning is cold and so is he, absorbing the chill of the air, feeling the uncomfortable prick of goosebumps raising along his skin. This is what he gets for not wearing a sweater, this is what he gets for waking up at five-thirty in the morning to feed a stray cat that hardly cares what time the food comes as long as the bowl is full.

It's the first night in a long time that he's spent in his house alone and the quiet of his morning has been deafening. He woke up without the snores of Iris coming from the spare mattress in his room, and he went through the motions of making coffee without having to measure portions for two. He didn't get to tease her about the ungodly amount of cream she pours into her mug, and he didn't get to participate in their morning dream debrief. It's already been a devastating morning and it's only six o'clock.

Not to mention the cat's distrust of him, despite feeding him for months now. Not to mention the doom looming on the horizon. Not to mention the dwindling day light and the frost on the lawn, the smell of cold on the air. Not to mention the panic in his body when he watched Park fall from the wards, the pleading look he'd given Iris to pull them down faster. Not to mention the nightmare he suffered through, where he hadn't gotten there in time, where he'd watched Park float further and further from his body, unable to help.

He takes another drag of his cigarette, and the cat jumps down from the railing, trotting off back into the yard.

"Goodbye to you too," he says, letting sarcasm bleed into his words.

The cat continues trotting towards the woods, unbothered by neither Isaac's snark nor the frozen dew on the grass. Isaac watches him until he disappears and then lets out a sigh, wondering what the next step is, what their plan is. How he's going to talk to Park again.

He presses the cherry of his cigarette into the ashtray and leans his elbows into the wet wood of the porch railing, immediately feeling colder. He knows the Prophecies, of course he does, he could recite them by memory alone, but it's still unclear to him the degree to which the Ghost wants Park dead, and what keeping him alive will truly look like. It's unclear to him when and why and how they're meant to be together – should he be waiting for something? Pursuing Park? Giving him space? Or should he be focusing only on how the next Prophecy fits into the picture? The next Prophecy is the one that he's worried about, the one that he knows the rest of Hell Club is worried about.

One will be taken; too late too late, down the Ghost hole they fall.

He and Derek have theories. Derek thinks that it's going to be him, *the One that falls*, and Isaac thinks that it might be, too. Derek is the only one who doesn't have any kind of insight, any kind of magic and that could make him the martyr. It could make him a target.

Isaac shifts his feet back and pushes against the railing, stretching out his back, feeling the muscles in his shoulders pull and lengthen, his biceps tense and relax, his hands taking on the pressure. The cold is getting to him, but he doesn't want to go back inside and face his empty house. The idea of being alone is a night terror that leaves him screaming every time.

He knows that Iris will be over, eventually, and the text messages will trickle in from his other friends, from the Hell Club group chat, from Mel. He knows that he's never truly alone, it's just the mornings that are hard when there aren't any other bodies around. It's just the waking up and the doing things – the menial activities of every day that keep him alive and functional.

Feeding himself and bathing himself and clothing himself all seem pointless when he's *by* himself. He doesn't care about these things, not really. Hence why he's smoking again, after a year without. Hence why he's still outside in the cold, freezing and doing all he can to avoid going back into his house.

Sometimes he thinks his stability is all an elaborate rouse, so that his friends don't worry about him and when he's alone like this, the rouse slips and his cracks show. Sometimes he thinks that his loneliness is a wild animal in his chest, and he's trying so hard to keep it inside, to keep his desperation for company to himself that it's turning against him, its claws and its fear digging deep into his heart, taking over.

He clenches his molars together and stands as the cold finally reaches his bones. He affords one last glance to the trees, searching for either his tomcat or his fox and finding neither. He still hasn't investigated what the appearance of the fox meant, but he's certain that she was in his dreams the night before as well, watching with soulful eyes as Isaac tried and failed to help Park. He almost doesn't want to know, doesn't want to see another bad omen, or accept its existence.

His mind conjures up the Prophecies and the words spin around like a kaleidoscope. *Two to twine* and *the secret to the secrets themselves* and *down the Ghost hole they fall.* His mind conjures up Park, on the ground, bleeding from his forehead, and he closes the door behind him, taking a deep breath. He watches Park's terror and pain fade into apprehension, into something small and hurt and desperate to understand what Isaac and Eve are telling him.

He pulls his phone out of his pocket and stares at the conversation that had drawn Park out to the cabin, the promise for answers.

He falls into the leather armchair in his parents' study and taps at the screen when it starts to darken. Really, he should probably let Park reach out when he's ready. He should be focusing on the One who falls, and who it is and what it means for them.

His fingers start typing.

can we meet again today? i want to give you something.

Isaac wants to give him more information and more reason to trust them. He wants to try to right the accident that was last night, that was the Protection spells rendering Park half dead in the gravel outside the cabin.

He doesn't expect the immediate typing bubble, but it pops up so quickly that Park must have been in the chat, too.

i get off work at 2:30. can you meet me here after?

yeah.

It takes a moment for Isaac to realize that he's stupid – he doesn't know where Park works.

where's here?

right. pippa's.

i'll be there

will you keep your protection spells at home?

Isaac lets out a breath of amused air, despite himself.

yes.

He doesn't bother telling Park that he can't weave Protection spells, or that he's so incredibly sorry he couldn't have gotten there sooner or told Park about them immediately.

promise?

cross my heart.

okay:)

He turns off his phone and flips it facedown on the desk once again, not before looking at the time to see that it is only 6:27 and he has a *long* time to sit and think about what he's going to say to Park.

He wants Park to read the Prophecies, and he wants to explain more about the magic that winds its way around Belle, but he doesn't want Park to realize that they're bound together by a Prophecy. He wants Park to think that his interest in him is genuine and not fated, because it is. Isaac is sure that if he met Park under any other circumstance, he would be pursuing the man just the same and he doesn't want there to be any doubt in Park's mind.

He also is scared that he's going to scare Park away, just as Iris is. He's aware that it all seems like a fantasy, that because Park hadn't grown up in Belle and he doesn't know their folklore, their history, that it must sound exactly like the kinds of things that drive people away from small towns. Premonition and magic and prophecy and ancient spirits hell-bent on vengeance. If Park hadn't already felt the effects of it, he would probably be writing Isaac and Hell Club off as weird, stir-crazy, cabin fevered. He might still think that.

He flips his phone back over and texts Iris:

park agreed to meet with me again today

im so nervous

what if he thinks i'm weird????

Iris replies two hours later, at a decent time of the morning.

Isaac, you are weird tf

But you're also hot

And nice

And you smell good

It'll be fine

Apocalypse or not, you KNOW how to seduce a man so just do what u do ;)

He's glad that she's telling him it'll be fine. He knows it will be (probably) but hearing it from someone else makes it real and the claws around his heart give just a little bit.

your faith in me is greater than my faith in myself

Oh COME ON!!!!!

Like I know half of this is because of the Prophecy but like you've never not made someone fall in love w you so why do you think now is going to b any different

GO GET YOUR MAN (but don't scare him away pls we still need him)

low stakes hey?

Don't you know it ;)

As much as her enthusiasm is over the top, he loves it. She knows how to make him feel better. She knows how to encourage him, to ease his worry. If Iris believes that it'll be okay, it'll be okay.

7

THE WHOLE DAMN THING IS BACKWARDS

There's been something scratching at the back of Iris's brain, and she needs to talk to someone about it. She's not sure that Isaac will understand, so she's at Dahlia's instead, showing up on her doorstep in the small hours of the morning and being ushered in for tea.

Dahlia is the only person that she knows that will be feeling what she's feeling – the two of them are cut from the same cloth, the same magic, the same power. Dahlia is less acquainted with the specific energy in Belle, but she's learning fast, and Iris is impressed. She can only imagine the amount of power that Dahlia can wield in her own home.

"Tea?" Dahlia asks, opening the cupboard she's dedicated solely to warm drinks. "I have Earl Grey."

"Oh, yes, please," Iris says, leaning over the counter and settling her hips further into her stool. "I've been trying to cut down on coffee."

Dahlia looks over her shoulder, her eyes sly. "How's that going for you?" She asks, and Iris shakes her head.

She's been a notorious coffee drinker since she was fifteen, and the sudden decrease in her desire has left her family flabbergasted. "No one believes me." Isaac hasn't stopped making her coffee in the morning, but she's never shared with him her plans for stopping. Besides, she still *likes* coffee, she just doesn't like making it, and her days with Isaac make that easier for her. All the coffee and none of the hassle.

Dahlia laughs and pours hot water into Iris's favourite mug at her house, handing it to her. "What made you want to stop?" She asks, her arms disappearing into another cupboard for a second and coming back into view with sugar.

"I don't like making it anymore," she says, pulling her tea towards her and scooping a teaspoon of sugar in. She's about to ask for milk when Dahlia opens the fridge door and pushes it across the counter towards her, always a step ahead. "I'm so busy these days – I just –" She trails off, tired. She knows that Dahlia will understand.

To be connected to the energies in Belle right now is to be exhausted. Iris can sit down or lay in bed all day, and she'll still be bone-tired by the end of it. She can go outside and stand in the trees, something that usually gives her energy, she can spend the day with Isaac, she can drive for hours, or she can guzzle eight cans of energy drink, and yet, she always ends up just as drained as she was in the beginning.

"I get it," Dahlia says, leaning against the counter opposite of Iris, her mug cupped between both of her hands. "I've been sleeping for like twelve hours a night and I'm still so tired."

Iris nods. There's something happening, something that she's aware of, but can't put her finger on yet. "It's like a storm brewing."

"Oh *God,* I know. Like the moment right before the torrential downpour starts."

"And you've forgotten your umbrella." Iris smirks. Talking with Dahlia is easy. She smiles easily and she laughs easily, and she understands in a way that no one else really can.

Iris is jealous of Dahlia, too. Dahlia has her own place - an apartment with an open concept, and natural lighting that floods in when her curtains are open. She has the time and the ability to make herself breakfast and dinner every day. She has a whole set of matching dishes, matching pots and pans and placemats on her dining room table. She has seasonal dish towels.

Dahlia came to Belle for a job - a well-paying job. She had already gone to university when she was called into the Club. She already had direction and purpose, and Iris sometimes must turn away when Dahlia is talking so that she doesn't see Iris's hunger for the same. Her envy.

Iris has alwaysmeant to go to school. She was supposed to start her university degree as soon as she graduated, which would mean that she should be in her third year already. She's not sure what she would be doing, but she suspects that it would be something where she can help people, where she can educate them, where she could share her compassion and her empathy, and she could make an impact on the world around her.

Instead, she's here in Belle, still living with her parents and helping them run their metaphysical shop. Instead, she's still fighting with her sister - Kat - over who gets to use the bathroom first in the morning and texting her stepmom that she shouldn't wait up when she's spending the night at Isaacs. She's still shopping at the same grocery store that she always has, walking the same streets and buying her coffee at the only café in town. She's stuck in the place she grew up in, always spinning around the place with the same memories.

At least Dahlia had the chance to choose.

"What do you think the Ghost is going to try next?" Dahlia asks, snapping Iris out of her self-pity.

Iris doesn't know. She's been thinking about this too, trying to anticipate what's coming next, where the next strike will be, where the rain will finally start falling. She has a bad feeling about the bridge across town, but she's not sure if it's because something is brewing there or because that's the spot she last saw her mother and it's just residual energy. She has a bad feeling about Pippa's café, but according to Isaac, that's where Park works so it makes sense that she has a bad feeling about it. She doubts that the Ghost will try anything to him there, though – it's too public. There would be too many witnesses.

In her mother's accounts, the Ghost likes privacy. The Ghost likes trees and water and mud. The Ghost likes to crush and drown and bury and disappear, taking people with no trace.

"I don't know," she says honestly. "I don't feel anything super localized. I didn't even feel anything that night at the river until we were basically in it." Usually, she can feel when something as strong as the Ghost is using the same source that she does for magic. Usually, it's a prickling at the top of her skin, a buzzing in her ears that gets louder the more that it is used. Neither had happened the night that Parker almost drowned and that terrifies her – she and Isaac had walked in almost completely blind, something that she knows Isaac is used to, but she *isn't*.

Dahlia has her eyes closed. "I think –" She starts, and then she stops again, focusing on something, her eyebrows furrowing together, mouth set in a straight line.

Iris leans forward, her mug scraping across the counter as she does so. She reaches her right hand out to Dahlia, and touches her, her skin hot. There's a spark, a pulse, a rhythm, and then Dahlia opens her eyes.

"Do you know the abandoned bridge just North of Old John's property? On that hiking trail?"

Iris nods. It's the bridge she's been thinking about. When she focuses on it, her bad feeling grows into something bigger – something that fills her abdomen and her chest cavity, something that feels like a dark, curling smoke of dread and terror, something that ebbs and flows but never really goes away. Something that looks familiar but is *wrong*, somehow. Wrong in a way that is gut-wrenching, terrifying, indescribable.

Iris sighs. The Ghost might take other people, but their main priority is Parker. The Ghost absolutely cannot take Parker. "We keep the kid away from the bridge until something happens."

Dahlia's frustration is apparent in the set of her shoulders. "What about everyone else?"

Iris doesn't know what else they can do besides causing irreversible damage to the bridge and closing the trail – even then people might still come across the Ghost in the area. Just because they've localized it to the bridge doesn't mean that the Ghost will take someone *on* the bridge. It might go a little bit upstream to the RV campsite, or it might go downstream to Old John's house.

"I don't know," she says, honestly. "I don't think we can do anything."

"Story of my fucking life," Dahlia says, and Iris agrees.

"It's not like anyone would listen to us, anyways," Iris states, sadly, and it's true. It's in the records of the Hell Club.

No one ever listens to the people who speak for the land, who speak for the trees and the energy that lives there. No one listens to those who preach peace and tolerance, who speak of the connectedness of the beings in the world; they only listen to those who speak of money, or corruption or violence. In its own way, the Ghost is only trying to protect what it loves, something that Iris *very much* understands.

It's the kind of understanding that makes her wonder why she's fighting against it – it's not like it's evil. It's not like it's something that can ever be truly stopped.

"Is Isaac meeting with Park again today?" Dahlia asks, and Iris nods.

"Yeah, he texted me this morning."

"I hope it goes well."

"Me too."

They both know it will. They both know that there's never been a person who Isaac couldn't get to fall in love with him.

8
WONDERFUCK

Park is alarmed by the text message that Isaac sends him in the morning before he leaves for his shift. *I have something to give you.*

He continues to be alarmed by the thought of Isaac meeting him after his shift, so much so that the customers notice he's not his usual cheery self. One regular, an old man who always (*always*) orders a large americano and drinks it straight, even goes as far as to ask Park if he's gone through a breakup or something similar and Park hastily states that he's nervous for a date this afternoon. A *date*, which is exactly not what he and Isaac are about to go on. The regular laughs at him and moves on, but his coworkers – his coworkers are *relentless*.

Sky, his manager, who is only a few years older than him and shows up high ninety percent of the time, overhears this conversation, and tells Riley, Park's favourite co-worker. Riley, in turn, tells Cadence, who is the only one that has the guts to bring it up to Park and ask him for details.

"We heard you have a date this afternoon," she says, cornering him when the café is slow, closer to the end of Park's shift. "And you've been avoiding us all day."

"Yes," he says, "that's on purpose." He doesn't want to have to explain that it's not a date, or that he doesn't know what it entails. He knows that Isaac is interested – he made that *very* clear the first morning when he dropped Park off – but he isn't sure if this is the kind of meeting that he should be taking as romantic. He's sure that if those were Isaac's intentions, he would state them. Isaac doesn't seem the type to beat around the bush or keep hidden agendas.

Cadence raises her eyebrows at him, and he sighs.

Riley yells from the break room, "Wait! I'm coming!" and Park rolls his eyes, maybe not so discreetly. There isn't a way for him to get out of this interrogation.

Riley appears, tying their apron back up behind their back and grinning broadly. "Who is he?" They ask.

Park debates giving them a fake name, but they're both locals and in Belle everyone knows everyone. If he makes up a name, they'll know, and the likelihood of them knowing Isaac Paige is exactly one hundred percent. "Isaac," he says, and Riley nods.

Cadence takes a step back. "Isaac Paige?" She asks.

Park nods. "And it's not a date. We met by the river, and I left something there. He wants to give it back." His lie isn't wrong. It's just not well thought out, and he realizes this when Riley furrows their eyebrows.

"How'd he get your number?" They ask.

"He found me on Facebook, actually."

"But he knew your name?"

"We talked for a while at the river." Park is sweating.

"But he asked to come at the end of your shift?"

"Yeah."

"And you're nervous to see him?"

Cadence is grinning at this point, and Riley is acting as if they're just pointing out the obvious. Park wishes he could explain to them what really happened, why Isaac is really coming. Having to rely solely on the people from Hell Club for his information about Hell Club is frustrating, but he can't talk to his friends about it. If he does, he'll probably be locked up, or worse - he'll lose whatever kind of protection that he gains by befriending the club. If it hadn't been for them, he would have been dead, and according to them his life will continue to be threatened. He doubts that Cadence and Riley could do what Isaac and Iris did that night at the riverbank. He doubts that they have any kind of idea about the energy around Belle or else he would have heard about it by now. The two of them are terrible gossips.

"Yeah."

"Did you know Isaac Paige was a slut in high school?" Cadence chimes in and Riley gasps.

"No slut shaming!" They yell, but they're laughing and so is Cadence.

"I'm not!" She yells back, and then to Park she says, "I'm not slut shaming. I'm just saying that he slept around *a lot*. He wasn't quiet about it, either, and he was always very open about not being straight."

Park blinks at her. He tries to comprehend the version of Isaac that he's been introduced to - quiet, softspoken, kind, also intimidating - to their high school Casanova version of him. He can kind of see it. Isaac seems to make people feel safe, and he is, of course, *gorgeous*. Park supposes that these two things could be a deadly combination. Obviously, it's a deadly combination – he's already developing an embarrassingly large crush on the other man.

"Did either of you ever sleep with him?" He asks, trying to turn the conversation away from himself, but he feels guilty immediately. It isn't his business who Isaac's slept with – not at all, especially when they haven't had any conversation about romance yet.

Neither Riley nor Cadence seems to mind, though, and Riley shakes their head. Cadence's grin gets even bigger.

"I did," she says. "And not in high school, either."

"You've *never* told me this," Riley accuses. "How have you never told me this?"

"You never asked."

"Was it good?"

Park watches the exchange, wide-eyed. Intrigued and ashamed and glad that he is no longer the one being interrogated.

"Of course, it was good, it's Isaac Paige," Cadence says, and it's Riley's turn to roll their eyes.

"He's always been on such a pedestal, hasn't he?"

"Has he?" Park inserts himself, yet again. Desperate to learn more. "What kind of pedestal?"

"The good-at-everything one," Riley clarifies, "he was always good at school and good at people, and he was always so kind, but not like performatively. He just was Isaac, and everyone loved him for it."

Park nods. This sounds like the Isaac he's met.

"But anyways – you say it's not a date, do you?"

"It's not a date!"

"But you want it to be, don't you?"

"Fuck off," Park says, feeling heat coming to his cheeks. He so incredibly, stupidly, wants this to be a date. He so incredibly, stupidly, wants Isaac to take him somewhere where they can talk alone, and he wants Isaac to tell him more about Hell Club and then maybe tell him more about himself, and then maybe Isaac tells him more about the ulterior motives he's had this entire time.

Their conversation is interrupted by the door jangling open, and a wave of customers coming in. Riley gives Park a look that says *this isn't over,* but the people keep coming in and they don't stop coming in until it's 2:25 and Park is staring out of the windows, waiting for Isaac and the Shitbox to show up and Cadence is smirking at him.

"He's going to be late." She says at 2:29, when Park is excusing himself to go put his coat on.

At 2:31 when he comes out from the staffroom, Isaac is there, leaning on the table by the window, smiling at him and showcasing the wrinkles around his eyes, his mouth. The afternoon light floods in behind him, illuminating his hair and the white parts of the shirt he's wearing.

"Hey you," Isaac says, warmly, and something deep in Park's stomach squirms with delight. Hey *you.*

"Hey," he says. He knows that Cadence and Riley are watching, so he flips them off behind his back, hoping Isaac doesn't see it. "What's the plan?" He questions, desperately wanting to leave the café so that he doesn't have to deal with Cadence and Riley's prying eyes.

"I was hoping you'd be okay with coming over to mine? I brought it with me just in case you –"

"Alright," Park cuts him off, and Isaac's mouth turns up into a grin.

He turns to head out the door, holding it open for Park.

"Will there be anyone else there?" Park asks, suddenly, realizing that this is a possibility. He desperately doesn't want Iris or any of Isaac's other friends to be there. He wants Isaac all to himself so he can ask him questions and he can watch the way his fingers press into each other when he's thinking and so he can admire the shadows that his eyelashes cast on his cheeks.

"No," Isaac reassures, "it's just me." He opens the passenger seat door of his car, and Park thanks him, climbing in, immediately hit by the warmth and the *Isaac* smell of the car. The door closes behind him as soon as he's all the way in, and Park closes his eyes for a moment, to ground himself. There's a familiar feeling of anxiety in his stomach, and he desperately wants it to fade.

He opens his eyes and realizes that Isaac has parked in a spot which is visible to Cadence and Riley who are most definitely still watching from their place behind the coffee counter. He's going to have to explain why if it's *not a date* Isaac is bringing him away somewhere and opening doors for him. He doubts that playing it off as Isaac being chivalrous will stop Riley's pestering during their shift tomorrow.

The driver side door opens and Isaac slides in. "How are you feeling today?" He asks, gesturing at Park's forehead, which bears the mark of the Protection spells from last night.

Park's bones melt a little bit at his concern, but he shakes it off. "I'm okay," he says, and his voice is smaller than he wants it to be. Being alone with Isaac once again makes him feel vulnerable, even if he's not saying anything particularly big or full of emotion. He's more aware of the other man than he ever has been before – their elbows are almost touching and Isaac's eyes in the sunshine turn to liquid honey. His breathing is even and slow and loud.

"Good," Isaac beams, "I was worried that maybe the magic would leave something residual. I'm glad it didn't." He turns the keys in the ignition and the engine splutters to action.

Instead of Old John's station, this time there is music. Park doesn't know it, but it's soft with a steady bassline and it makes him feel like he's in a movie. It's comforting. He wonders if it's the band on the hoodie of Isaac's that he still has. "Residual?" he questions, and then, "I forgot to bring your clothes back for you."

He really had planned on bringing them today, but in his haste to leave in the morning, he forgot the hoodie hanging on the back of one of the kitchen chairs and the pants on the table, just in sight enough for one of his parents or his sister to ask about them. Just one more thing for him to be worrying about all day.

"Oh, that's fine. I'm sure this isn't the last time we'll see each other."

Park's heart jumps with hope – he doesn't want this to be the last time he sees Isaac. He tries to hide his excitement by gripping onto the fabric of his jeans and clearing his throat. "Oh – uh, okay."

"And I was hoping there was nothing residual, because sometimes that can be written into the spells. Sometimes there's an extra awful thing that happens a few hours later if whoever is affected gets through the first wave. It's complicated magic and I didn't really think that Iris and Dahlia would go through the trouble, but it still – it still worried me a little bit." When Park looks over at him, his mouth is pressed into a tight line, and he's looking straight at the road, avoiding eye contact.

Park realizes that this is a kind of confession, and he wants desperately to reach out to touch Isaac. He wants to press his fingers into his forearm or run the back of his hand against Isaac's cheek. *I've been thinking about you, too*, he wants to say, but he doesn't. It's too soon. It's too much. Instead, he says only, "Oh."

"They're good at what they do," Isaac continues, "but they're not about to make more work for themselves that they don't need to."

"That makes sense."

Isaac pulls the car into his driveway, and then sighs as he cuts the engine. "I'm sorry," he says, "I really wanted this to be a time where you could ask anything you need to know about and I'm just rambling. I'll – um – I'll stop now."

Park nods, still watching him as he turns, meeting Park's gaze, finally. Park wants to move, wants to say something, but he finds that he can't. There's too much that he's seeing in Isaac's expression, and it's entrancing. The back of his throat goes dry.

"Do you have any questions?" Isaac asks, and his voice is hardly loud enough to be heard.

Park thinks for a second that whatever it is he's feeling, Isaac must be feeling, and he straightens in his seat, swallowing. He breaks eye contact. "Yeah," he mutters, "I do."

Out of the corner of his eye he sees Isaac make a *well then go ahead* gesture, and he sighs. All his questions are to do with Isaac and not with Hell Club, or the Ghost. All his questions are secret ploys to have Isaac's hands back on his face like they were last night. Finally, he settles on one that doesn't seem too personal, one that he's sure will tie back to Hell Club.

"Why are you still here?"

"What do you mean?"

"Why are you still in Belle? I mean – I'm sorry – I asked my co-workers about you, and they said you were good at school, that you earned scholarship money and everything." Park is curious why he would choose Belle over that – over an education and a bigger city that he doesn't know everyone's name in.

"Oh," Isaac sighs, his hands returning to the steering wheel, tightening around it. "Yeah, that's a good question."

Park watches Isaac's jaw work as he tries to navigate the right way to answer the question. "I –"

"Do you want me to tell you the real reason?" Isaac asks, and his voice has become incredibly serious. His eyes are unwavering, open, honest. The brilliance of them is almost shocking, and Park isn't sure if he would rather look away. He doesn't.

"Yes." He doesn't have to think about his answer.

"Okay."

"Okay?"

"Once you're a part of Hell Club, you don't get to leave Belle." Isaac's whole body turns to face Park, to gauge his reaction.

"What?" *Don't get to leave Belle.* Something sounds like a warning in his words, but Park isn't sure what.

"I mean – like – I guess you can, but you always come back. You'll always be rooted here. At most you might get a few years before you get called back."

Park blinks at him. "So you *can't* leave."

"I could, but I'm always going to end up back here, so what's the point? Besides, everything with the Prophecies is happening now, so I can't." There's a frustration in his voice now, and Park realizes that he's hit a sore spot. Isaac *wants* to leave.

"What would you do?" He asks, wanting Isaac to keep talking about himself so that Park can learn. He mirrors the other man, turning his body towards him, intrigued. He supposes that if he grew up here, if he was stuck here, he would want to leave, too. He would want to leave more than anything. Belle isn't a town for people who don't want it; it isn't a town to raise a family or to start a career. It's a dead end.

Isaac shrugs. "There isn't any use talking about it, is there?" He asks, but Park is sure that he would love to talk about it. Park is sure that Isaac is bursting at the seams wanting to talk about it. Park is sure that Isaac is bursting at the seams to talk about anything that Park brings up, and Park wants to hear it all.

There's something about Isaac that seems restless, where before he had been quiet, softspoken, calculated. Park thinks it might be nerves – is Isaac *nervous*? About *him*?

"Want to head inside now?" Isaac asks, and Park nods.

A sense of eagerness is bubbling up inside of him, and he's giddied with it. Isaac is nervous about being around him and Isaac is going to give him answers and he's going to get to watch the way that Isaac talks with his hands and he's going to get to watch the shadows from Isaac's eyelashes dance across his cheeks just as he wanted to. It feels like things are finally starting to fall into place for Park. It feels like the beginning of something that he can hold onto. It feels like the beginning of something beautiful.

9
LOOKING LIKE A HEART ATTACK

There is nothing that Isaac wants more than he wants Park to finish reading. Every single nerve in his body is on fire, waiting as Park flips page after page, reading with his eyebrows furrowed. He hasn't said a word, and the silence is crushing Isaac, making him itch and yearn for something – *anything.* Any kind of noise or acknowledgement to keep him from overthinking.

He would even take more questions like the one Park asked him out of left field in his car. He's been thinking about it ever since, mulling it around in his head.

What *would* he be doing if he wasn't trapped here? Probably nursing – although Isaac isn't a fan of conventional jobs. Careers. He's been spoiled by the idea that he can dip into his family's business any time he wants – he would make more there than in any nursing job – and he wouldn't even have to go to school. It's not what he really wants, though. Selling things not meant to be sold has never really appealed to him. He wants to help people, he wants to make a difference to someone, to something. He doesn't want to tear them down.

"What does this mean?" Park asks, suddenly, startling Isaac from his thoughts.

He motions for the book and Park turns it towards him, pointing at the exact line that Isaac did not want Park to notice. The line about them, together. The one that Isaac has been replaying in his head for the past three years, since he first read through the book of Prophecies. It hadn't made sense to him until he made sense of the rest of them; until he knew what was supposed to happen and Iris and Eve and Derek confirmed his suspicions.

Two to twine in divine time: the Understanding and the Understood, the Protector and the Protected, together at last.

He's not sure if he should tell Park. He hesitates for a second, before he jokes weakly, "Cosmic romance?" And the hesitation is what gives it away to Park.

"What does it really mean?" He asks, gesturing for the book back, and Isaac reluctantly pushes it across the table.

"Can I tell you when you finish reading?" He doesn't want Park to leave before he's gotten to the end. It's important that he knows where this is going. It's important that he grasps the gravity of their situation and what's really at stake.

It's not like there's a ton of Prophecies left, either. Only two, really, and then some theories chicken-scratched onto the last page.

Park's eyebrows raise, but he nods, returning to the words, his fingers tracing each sentence, like he's worried that they're going to fall off the paper if he doesn't hold them there.

Isaac looks away, scared that he'll do something stupid – touch Park's hands or reach out a foot to hook around Park's ankle – or he'll say something stupid – *it's us in the Prophecy, by the way, you and me* – and he can't risk it.

Park finally flips to the last page, and then gives Isaac a dark and contemplative look, his fingers resting on the final Prophecy. *When the Ghost calls, one will doom all.* "Does every single one of these come true?"

Isaac nods. "In some way or another. So far."

"So why are you guys fighting it? It seems clear that we're doomed."

"It's what we have to do," Isaac whispers, swallowing. "We might be able to delay it – to push it back. This dance with the Ghost has been done before and –"

"And you don't have any other choice, do you?" Park closes the book.

He's putting it together so fast, Isaac thinks, he's working through what it took Isaac ages to figure out. "It's like a curse," he whispers, "some sadistic game that the Ghost likes to play. Like a cat toying with its food."

"And now I'm a part of it?"

"Yeah."

"What if I don't want to be a part of it?"

Isaac shrugs. "I tried to avoid it, too, in the beginning. I started having nightmares, and then I woke up in the middle of the night and I couldn't breathe. I started coughing up black dust and wandering off like I was sleepwalking when I was wide awake. I tried to hide the Prophecies, but I always dug them up when I went wandering, and I always ended up at the cabin."

"I don't get a choice."

Isaac shakes his head. "I'm sorry." And he is. He wouldn't wish this on his worst enemy. The weight of the world is resting on his shoulders, on all their shoulders, and it's not an easy thing to bear. Especially when it's so likely they'll fail.

Park is quiet for a minute, staring at the tips of his fingers, thinking. "What about the cosmic romance?" he finally asks, and Isaac's heart thrums in his chest a thousand times faster.

"That's about - um - oh, shit - um -" He can't seem to push the word past his lips. *Us.* That's all he has to say. It doesn't matter anymore now that Park has read the Prophecies. Nothing matters. He knows the stakes.

"Us." He finally says, looking away, looking at anything except Park. He feels the heat in his face, and he pulls his hands back to his body, so that every part of him is safe from Park's rejection, from his scorn.

Park is very quiet, and Isaac waits in suspended agony for him to say something, for him to do something. He can't make himself focus on Park, and he can't make himself move away. Instead, he waits, for what feels like forever, like a child about to be scolded.

"Us?" Park asks, a million moments later, and his voice sounds so incredulous that Isaac sneaks a glance at him, at the hopeful tilt of his head and the lean of his shoulders across the table, closer to Isaac.

"Yes."

"So, your interest in me is because - because of some *Prophecy?*"

"No - no, well I mean, yes, that's what brought us together, but it's not all that. The Prophecies don't make things happen; they just tell us what's coming. We probably would have met anyways and you - well - you're - I mean, um, you're *really* hot." Isaac's whole body is on fire. He's so embarrassed. He's so worried that he's pushed Park too far. This is so much more awkward than he thought it would be.

"Oh," is all Park says, and there are several more moments of heated silence, until he says, very small, "I think you're really hot, too."

Oh, thank God, Isaac thinks, and then there's a grin plastering itself to his face, so big that he can feel the ache in his cheeks already. "Do you now?" he asks, allowing himself to fall into his normal confidence, his normal flirting.

"Yes." Park is looking once again at his fingertips.

"I guess we'll have to do something about that then, won't we?"

A smile starts to creep over Park's lips, and when he meets Isaac's gaze once again, he looks slyly pleased, like he's just won a prize he knew he could all along. "I guess we will."

"Are you free tomorrow?"

"Tomorrow?"

"Don't sound so enthusiastic," Isaac deadpans.

"Yeah – no – I mean, I am enthusiastic. I just – that's like four days in a row?"

Isaac shrugs. "Is there a problem with that?"

"No. Not at all. I get off work at 2:30 again."

"I'll be there."

"Alright." A beat of silence, in which Isaac can hear the blood pumping through his arteries like waves hitting the shore, and then, "I think I should be going, though. Dinner with my parents and all."

Isaac nods. It's getting late. "I'll drive you home."

"Can I take this with me?" Park picks up the Prophecy book, "I want to read more. I'll probably have more questions when I'm not – when I'm not distracted." He smiles sheepishly.

"Yes. Take it. Ask as many questions as you want."

Park nods, and trails Isaac to the door. "Thank you," he says, as they're poised in the doorway, about to step outside.

"For what?"

"For telling me all this."

"Oh – it's no problem. I think that the more you know, the better."

Park only nods, holding the book tight to his chest as if it can guard him from the chill of the evening.

They drive to Park's house in near silence, and then say their goodbyes, finalizing their plans for tomorrow. Park walks towards his house, and Isaac watches as the hope drains from him, his shoulders hunching. He turns around once, at the door, to give Isaac a curt wave, which he returns, and then Park disappears into his home.

Isaac backs out of his driveway, and when he gets back to his house there's already a text message from Park.

first question: does tomorrow count as a date?

He can't help the butterflies that start tumbling over each other in his stomach.

yes.

10

HALLELUJAH IS RIGHT

Cecelia, C, sees the hoodie thrown over the kitchen chair and the folded sweatpants on the table before either of her parents are awake, and she moves them to Parker's room, so neither of them have the chance to ask him about it. This doesn't mean that *she* won't be asking about it.

Who is this man that her brother seems smitten with? She wants *answers.*

She thinks about texting him right away that she moved the clothes, but she would rather him sweat it out a little – punishment for not giving her the details yet. Punishment for going out to see him *three days in a row* without telling her anything. He hasn't told her he's seeing him today, but she figures the appearance of the clothes means he's going back. What a dick.

She slips on her running shoes, and zips up her windbreaker, stepping into the cold morning air. It's starting to turn to winter, and she's not a fan of running in the cold but she's even less of a fan of treadmills, so she has vowed to herself to weather the winter for as long as she can. It hasn't been easy, and it's only October.

This whole move hasn't been easy. She misses her friends. She misses her job. She misses Starbucks and McDonalds and the fucking *movie theater.* Only stupid little towns don't have movie theatres and somehow, she's ended up in the *stupidest,* smallest town.

She can run the whole perimeter of this place in an hour. One. Hour. She does it every day and it gets more boring each time, like putting together a hundred-piece puzzle that she's already solved.

It starts with their next-door neighbour's house, the one to the right, the Melbourne's: white with red trim and it looks like it came right out of the seventies, and it continues with the Wallace's, also straight from the seventies. Down the street a little further is the Webb's and *their* house looks like it's from the *sixties,* which is *crazy.*

C hates this place. She hates it with every fiber of her body, mind, and soul. The second she turns eighteen she's leaving, going back to the big city. The silence here is *deafening,* and it's not even total; the neighbours know everything about everybody. There is no such thing as a secret here.

She's surprised that her parents agreed to move to this place. There are some secrets that they would like to keep - some secrets they're running from, or at least trying to keep very, *very* hidden, especially from the churchgoers. Especially from the small-town people whose small-mindedness leads to them thinking that a queer son and a queerer *daughter* are shameful. Jokes on her parents, though, the only church in town has a pride flag waving out front, and it's even the progressive one.

Not that it's any kind of redemption - it's just nice that they're acknowledging the existence of the gays. It's just nice that C knows her and her brother will be marginally safer if they decide to walk down the road with their lovers. Not that she has a lover.

She's outside of Pippa's now, and the open sign is just being turned on, but not by her brother. By the manager, the one that's always high and can't be bothered to care. Park says he likes her, but C has met her and she's not too sure. At least Park has people that he works with that are supportive. Not like the people he knew before, who were so passive aggressive about his queerness, about his upbringing. At least he has people who aren't judging him.

C, however, is having a much harder time. It's high school and she has the appearance of any other church girl, though she's not much one for church and her thoughts around girlhood ar ambivalent. Her feelings on gender aside, she's not even allowed to wear shorts out of the house, and a tank top would probably send her mother into cardiac arrest. Gym class is the only place she's been able to sneak something revealing in and that's because she hides her workout gear in the hideous scoop neck shirt and sweats her parents bought her. She likes the looks she gets when she's wearing revealing clothes - she likes the attention. She doesn't like the way other people's eyes feel on her body, but that's the price of being wanted, sometimes.

As it is, she likes attention but not from anyone. She doesn't like the church kids because she's an atheist, and she doesn't get along with the alt kids because they think she's a church kid. She wants to join the LGBTQ+ club, to meet other kids like her, but she doesn't know a thing about dungeons and dragons and she's too scared to ask. She wants to join the volleyball team - her serves have their attention - but the volleyball team consists of almost all church kids. Her only solace so far has been the quiet kid, who she usually ends up sitting beside: Kat.

Kat is okay. Kat doesn't seem interested in hanging out outside of school – she works and devotes a lot of her time to her hobbies, Kat's words not C's – but their classes are almost all the same, so they end up sitting together and walking together and eating lunch together. At first, C did most of the talking, with Kat just watching from behind glasses too big for her face, but she thinks she's drawing Kat out of her shell. They talk more now, and C doesn't feel as bad for her big mouth.

She knows she talks a lot, but it's easier for her to process her thoughts out loud. It's easier for her to ask her questions than it is to keep them inside, and she's aware that it makes her weird and loud and awkward. Park has told her more than once, in his concerned older-brother tone that she hates, and it always sparks a fight between them. She knows that he doesn't mean it in a hurtful way – he really is just worried about her – but sometimes it gets under her skin. She's already different enough, he doesn't have to point it out.

Despite this, she still spends most of her time with Park. She knows that he only moved to Belle with their parents because he's worried about her. She knows that he has enough money tucked into a savings account and a decent enough resume to have stayed working in the city, renting his own place. She almost resents him for coming with them – for having the choice to stay and choosing this godforsaken place anyways, for having the ability to get them a place away from their parents and not doing it.

She knows that it's not like that – their parents would *never* let her live with her brother alone, not while she's under eighteen. God forbid the things he would start whispering in her ears, the things he would force upon her.

She's at the road that follows the river now, and she can hear the water hitting the shore just a few hundred feet away. Some part of her wants to go and step into it, feel it kiss her ankles and pull her further down. Some part of her wants to walk straight into the middle and let it take her, let her body go with the current.

She does none of these things. She stays on the road, keeping the same pace she has this whole run. She's a half hour in, now, and her favourite part is still ahead.

There's a creepy old shack at the corner of Main and the Highway, right by the river. The townspeople call the man that lives there Old John, and Kat told her he's the scariest looking man alive, straight from a horror movie. C hasn't run into him, but every morning when she passes the house, she hopes he's outside, sitting on the deck or warming up his truck or painting over the last weeks nonsensical fence quote.

C has asked Kat about the quotes, too, and Kat told her that she can't be bothered to pay attention to them anymore. He's been doing it for years and the fence quotes usually mirror the nonsense he's spewing on his radio channel, not that anyone bothers to listen to that, either. C listens. C listens all the time, the mans claims of ghosts and energies and magic magic magic, all seeping into her ears and letting her dream that maybe there's more to Belle - maybe this place *is* special.

She wants to know. She wants to see the scary old man and ask him about it herself, but she can never bring herself to go up the driveway, to knock on the door.

As she gets closer it becomes more apparent that today will not be the day that she runs into him accidentally - no lights are on in the house and his truck isn't in the driveway. The fence bears the same quote as it did last week (*isn't it that we all die? I think that's it, what it is*) and it makes just as much sense as it did when C ran by yesterday. She hasn't had the chance to tune into his broadcast. She's started writing all the quotes down in her notes app so she can keep track of them.

She asked Kat if Kat writes them down, but Kat shook her head, saying that it's not important. None of it is important - it's just an old man rambling, but C is convinced that it's more. Besides, Kat's parents run a metaphysical shop, so she must have knowledge about what Old John is talking about, not that she'll give C any information, much to C's annoyance.

She's nearing the end of her run, now, and it's all uphill. She hates this part. One time she took Park on her run with her, and all he did was complain. He told her that she should start the other way, so that this would be downhill but she's the one who is going to end up with fantastic legs by the time they move, so he can suck it. To Park's credit, he has run with her several times since, when he's not working the early shift and he hasn't complained again.

Her pace slows and her breaths get deeper as she starts to slog her way up, her shins and her arches starting to feel the ache of the pavement beneath them. The cold air is starting to get to her face and the tops of her ears, but she's so close now she can't stop, she can't stop, she can't stop.

She slows to a walk as she gets to the Baldwin's house, a few to the left of her own. It's been modernized and it looks like it could be from the early two-thousands, although C knows it was probably built in the seventies. *Her* house was built in the seventies, and it most definitely hasn't been updated.

There is not an ounce of her being that wants to step inside the door to her house. There is not a single part of her that wants to say good morning to her dad who will be awake and eating breakfast in the kitchen, and there is even less of her that wants to talk to her mom who will want a detailed schedule of her day ahead. She knows that in their own way, they care about her, and Park and they care a lot, but there's just so much that they won't acknowledge.

When Park came out, both C and Park thought their mom would be okay with it. They thought their dad would take some time, but they were sure he would come around eventually.

When Park came out, their mother cried about the grandchildren she would never have, and their father just happened to find a cross that he thought Park would like the day after at a thrift store, the King of Passive Aggression. They haven't really talked about it since, but sometimes C will catch their mother listening to Park talk about his love life to C and then feign disinterest after. She thinks that maybe their mom is finally warming up to Park's homosexuality, but she can't be certain. Park thinks she's giving Georgia too much credit.

C slips back in through the door and takes off her runners, unzips her windbreaker. She wipes the cold sweat off her forehead with her sweater sleeve and enters the kitchen where her dad is eating his cereal at the table.

"Morning, Dad," she says, nodding in his direction.

"Morning, Kiddo," he responds, and she closes her eyes as she pours herself a glass of water, gulping it down.

He wouldn't be calling her kiddo if he knew that she's gay. He used to call Park buddy and now he only calls Park Parker. Park hasn't explicitly told her that it hurts, but she's noticed.

"It's cold out this morning," she muses, taking two slices of bread and stuffing them in the toaster, trying to be as efficient as possible. She grabs a travel mug and siphons sugar into the bottom, then coffee, then cream.

"Winter's just around the corner! How long do you plan on running outside for?"

She grimaces. Always with the pestering. If her dad had his way, she would have never been allowed to start running outside. She would have always been cooped up at the gym in town, on the godforsaken treadmill. "I'm going to run outside until it's absolutely too cold."

"Okay, well, just be careful, kiddo." He stands up, and places his dishes in the sink, giving her a hug goodbye and a kiss on the top of her head on the way out. "Have a great day! See you this evening."

She returns the niceties and sips her coffee, pulling out her phone and typing a message to Park. *Moved your clothes, don't worry the Terribles didn't see*, but she deletes it. She thinks she deserves to be mad that she still hasn't gotten the details about this stupid hook up. She debates texting Kat that she's sick and she won't be in school today, but she doesn't.

She wonders what Kat would say, if she'd be concerned or not. Maybe she'd hardly care. Maybe she'd be worried. They have been spending more time together in the past couple of weeks, and C is glad to be growing on her. She has high hopes for their friendship.

Her toast pops and her mom enters the kitchen all in the same minute.

"Morning, C," her mom hums.

Cecelia responds, her back turned to her mom, digging through the fridge for the jam.

"Any big plans for today?" The most annoying question in the entire world.

"No, not really." She does the same four classes every day, and then she comes home to do homework alone in her bedroom. It's thrilling.

"Alright, honey. We'll see you tonight, then, yeah?" She nods, hugs her mom, and continues to spread her jam.

She feels the tears burning at the back of her throat and she pushes them back down. This isn't the time or the place to cry. She'll wait until she gets home tonight and maybe she'll have a hot bath with one of the bath bombs that she's been saving since Park bought them for her last Christmas. She can cry then, when no one will see her, or hear her.

It's not worth it to cry now, when there might be more to cry about this evening.

75

11
SWEATER MATERIAL

The only thing in Park's mind is the image of Isaac's face when he realized which Prophecy Park was questioning. The immediate shock, the way that Isaac stopped for a moment, worry passing through his eyebrows, his shoulders tightening, the debate that so clearly was happening in his head. When he said *cosmic romance?* Park knew that he was trying to brush off something important, and he's glad that he pushed. As awkward as the explanation had been, at least he got one and Isaac – Isaac really had handled it with as much grace as possible.

Park hasn't doubted for a second that Isaac is interested in him beyond the Prophecy. The Prophecy does add something – pressure, reassurance – but Isaac is right. They would have met each other anyways.

He closes his eyes for a second, feeling the warmth that Isaac sparks in him, the butterflies, the embarrassment of the entire conversation. It feels so far away, and it's only been a few hours. He and Isaac have been texting, back and forth and back and forth in an endless conversation, getting to know each other. He's astounded by how easy it is, how rapidly his trust in Isaac is growing.

He's not sure about the others from Hell Club – Iris and Dahlia scare him, but Eve seems nice and so do Derek and Chip – but he's sure that he can rely on Isaac. He's sure that he can trust Isaac. Isaac hadn't held back on him when he was talking about the Prophecies, he'd explained as much as he could in the amount of time that they had, and Park is certain if he texts Isaac another question about them, he'll answer earnestly.

The Prophecy book itself is laying untouched in the far corner of his closet, where C won't find it. He knows that she's interested in Old John and his ramblings, he knows about her obsession with his fence paintings, and her dedication to figuring out if there's a deeper meaning behind it all. He knows she's invested in the magic within Belle without even knowing it's real, but he can't fathom bringing her into Hell Club consciously. Isaac's words are echoing around in his brain, the chains that connect them both here now, and he can't subject C to it. He knows how much she hates this place, how much she wants to go back to their home in the city, how out of place she feels. He couldn't live with himself if he ruined that for her - if she could never leave Belle again.

There's a knock at his bedroom door, and he lifts his head. "Yeah?" He hopes it's C; he can't deal with his parents bullshit this evening.

"Can I come in?" C. Relief washes over him in waves.

"Yeah." The door opens, revealing his little sister. "Is that my fucking sweater?" He asks, and a grin splits her face open.

"Don't ask for it back." She sits on the edge of his bed, and then flops down so she's laying perpendicular to him.

"Wouldn't dream of it." Despite everything, he's not stupid. "Thanks for moving those clothes this morning, by the way."

"Don't mention it." It's C's way of gloating. "Do you want to go on a walk with me?" This is C's way of asking him to have a conversation away from where their parents can hear.

He sighs. He's so tired he can barely keep his eyes open - it's been a long, exciting day, and he just wants to sleep. He wants to be able to continually check his phone for messages from Isaac undisturbed.

"Please?"

He sighs, and checks his phone, an image of Isaac popping up in his head, the easy smile, the slanted line of his neck leading to his Adam's apple, the flipped collar of the flannel he's wearing resting against it. His first two fingers pressed into the book, tracing over the Prophecy, the way he wouldn't meet Park's gaze while he was hesitating to tell Park what the Prophecy was about.

"Yeah, fine," he breathes, knowing that he's going to drive himself insane if he doesn't talk to someone about Isaac, and he hasn't mentioned anything to C for a while now - not since the river, at least. She's probably itching to hear all the information he has about his *hook up*. There's also the fact that he did say he would talk to her in exchange for her chauffeur services. He's itching to hear about school, and her budding friendship with Kat.

"Sick." She's out of his room and up the stairs before he can muster the energy to get out of bed.

He's worried about C because she's lonely and she's having a hard time adjusting and she hasn't mentioned anything, but he's sure there's an internal battle happening inside her about God and about gender and about coming out to their parents. The least he can do is listen to her tonight.

He heaves himself up and out of bed, up the stairs and to the front door. The TV is blaring from the living room, and he doesn't bother checking in with his parents – they don't seem to care much about his comings and goings anymore, and while he's grateful, sometimes he just wants them to *act* like they care. Even if it's not real. Even if it's all a lie.

C is already waiting for him on the porch and she makes a hand motion for him to hurry up so he makes a show of slowing down the process of putting on his boots and his coat. She flips him off.

Finally, he opens the door and steps out to meet her in the crisp evening air. "It's cold," he complains, and she rolls her eyes.

They walk in silence for a minute and then,

"Who's the lucky man?" C asks him as soon as they're out of sight of the house and therefore safe to talk about their queerness. Safe to talk about whatever they want.

He rolls his eyes. "He's just this guy that I went out to meet. He's my age, and he's kind of weird but in a really good way – like he's super nice, and he's also really pretty and –" He cuts himself off, feeling the heat rise in his cheeks. He stuffs his hands in his pockets and looks at the ground so he doesn't have to suffer through C's amused stare. "He's nice," he finishes lamely.

"What's his name?" C's phone is in her hands. She's good at digging, and she'll have found all of Isaac's social media by the time the evening is over. She'll have a history of everything that he has ever done by tomorrow morning. Her friend, Kat, has an older sister and between the two of them they seem to know everything about everyone and C loves to hear it all. It will only take a day before C knows more about Isaac than Park does, and it makes Park nervous to answer her.

"Isaac," he says, finally, still not looking up from the ground.

"Do you have any photos?"

"No." Park hasn't even looked up Isaac on social media yet.

"Didn't you meet him on a dating app?"

"*Oh* – yeah, you're not allowed to see those."

He can feel the distaste reverberate through the air, and when he braves looking at her, her nose is scrunched but she's typing on her screen, pulling up Instagram. "What's his last name?"

"C," he says, but she's already found him. Apparently, Isaacs from Belle are rare.

"Parker, this is a beautiful man."

"Give me that," he says, reaching over, but C pulls her phone out of his reach and continues to scroll down his feed.

"Parker, how did you pull him? Holy shit *look*." She brandishes the screen at him, and he squints at a badly taken photo of Isaac with one hand on Iris's shoulder, smiling a smile that takes up his entire face to the camera.

It's a terrible, dark and grainy photo, but he has to admit that Isaac looks incredible. Isaac looks terrifyingly beautiful with his smile and his dimples and the intimacy with which he's looking into the camera. There's nothing more attractive than someone looking at something or someone they love, and he so obviously loves the person taking the photo. He so obviously loves Iris – the ease with which they're standing speaks for itself.

"You're drooling," C smirks, pulling the phone away to keep stalking.

Park stuffs his hands further into his jacket pockets and lifts his shoulders to his ears. The same embarrassment courses through his body, and he pushes down the realization that all he wants is the same ease around Isaac as Iris has. All he wants is Isaac to look at him like he was looking at the camera. His heart is beating dangerously hard in his chest.

"He smokes." C shows him a photo that Isaac is tagged in, where there's a cigarette held between his fingers.

"I know," Park says. The first morning after his drowning, Isaac was smoking on the porch, and then earlier he had smelled like smoke. It wasn't strong – Isaac must have tried to cover it – but it was there.

"That doesn't bother you?" C is still scrolling.

"There are worse things to worry about." He doesn't want to admit to his sister that he's always kind of liked the smell of cigarette smoke. He doesn't want to admit to her that he's smoked before, on the back steps of the first guy he slept with, so many years ago. He certainly doesn't want to admit that he liked it then.

There are a lot of things that Park doesn't want to admit to C, and smoking isn't even in the top five. She's not religious, but sometimes he thinks that the rules and the judgement they grew up with have stuck with her more than him. She swears she's okay with stuff like weed and sex and alcohol, but sometimes he'll mention it and he can see her trying not to recoil. She still goes to church on Sundays with their parents.

The rational part of Park knows that this is because she wants to keep up her appearances. But the small, selfish part of him thinks that maybe the things she tells him about her beliefs and her queerness are an act to keep him close, too.

It's not fair. He knows that. She's just afraid of their parent's rejection - and he's not angry about that. He's been through it.

She's just young, and there are a lot of things that she's been sheltered from. It all looks so intimidating looking at things from the outside - he knows what it's like. Mostly. There are things about her that he'll never understand as much as he tries, and that's fine. He just - he wants to trust her more. He wants to stop doubting her. He wants to support her and help her, but every time he tries, she brushes him off.

"I'll ask Kat if she knows more about him," C says, finally shutting her phone off, seeming satisfied with what she's found. "I'm sure she will."

"Of course, she will," Park rolls his eyes. "Kat knows something about everyone."

"You're acting like you don't like her."

"I've literally never even met her! Besides, everyone has something to say about *everyone* in Belle. It's not just Kat."

C shrugs. "She's my only friend here," she whispers, and Park feels the mist of loneliness that falls around her. "And sometimes I think that she only hangs out with me because I'm convenient and she doesn't have to talk as much."

Park and C have this in common - the self-doubt - and it makes Park incredibly angry whenever it flares up in C. Himself, not so much. "What do you mean?" As far as Park has heard, C and Kat are glued together at the hip when they're at school, and they would be outside of school, too, if Kat didn't work at her parents' shop.

"I just feel like I annoy her. I text her too much or I talk too much and sometimes I think that maybe I'm just too much, you know? Like she's only putting up with me because she thinks she has to, or because she pities me?" It's C's turn to not make eye contact as Park thinks about how to comfort her.

Back in the city C has friends. C has so many friends – not a day went by when she wasn't at someone's house for study club or whatever it was that they did, whatever made C happy. C used to *smile*, and now she just worries.

"C you are incredibly likeable," he starts, "and if she just felt obligated, I think you would probably be able to tell. Most people can't hide that easily."

"Maybe." She doesn't sound convinced.

"Maybe you should talk to her about this? Get her side, especially if it's bothering you so much?"

She sighs. "I don't know how to bring it up."

"Just tell her you want to clear something up with her that's been bugging you. If she's really your friend, and I think she is, it'll be no big deal to have a conversation about it."

"Maybe." Still not convinced.

Park decides not to push her, and they keep walking in silence, both deep in thought. Park wants to say something more, to make her feel better, but this might be something that she needs to figure out how to do on her own. All he wants to do is push her to express her doubts and her feelings because God forbid she ends up in friendships and relationships like he did when he was her age. With people stepping all over him because he didn't know how to say no, because he didn't know how to stand up for himself.

He wishes he could tell her about Hell Club. She would love it – she would love the magic, and she could meet Isaac and Iris and Dahlia, – who Park is sure she would adore. She would want to know everything; she would be so eager to learn.

He wishes he could tell her that he was almost drowned in the river, by an ancient eldritch power, and it will probably rise to try to kill him again. He wishes that he could tell her about the thrum in his veins now, the way the crisp air smells so sweet and how he can sense the energy radiating out around him, like he's connected to something bigger than his body, a living and breathing part of a larger living and breathing thing.

Instead, he settles on, "I'm going on another date with Isaac tomorrow."

"That's like four days in a row."

"I know."

"You usually never go on a second."

Except that one time, and then the time that he didn't tell C. "Yeah, I know."

"He's different?"

"He's better than anyone I've ever met." Which is so incredibly true the moment Park says it out loud. He's certain that Isaac has good intentions. He's certain that Isaac will only get better the more he gets to know him.

"Good." She seems satisfied with this.

"You approve?"

"Let me talk to Kat." *Please talk to Kat about how you're feeling, too,* he thinks, and he hopes she hears his silent plea.

"Cadence told me he's slept around a lot."

"And you think that would change my mind?"

Park shrugs. A couple of years ago, it would have.

They've made it back to their driveway and it's clear that neither of them wants to go back inside. Back inside is tension and a type of quiet that never ceases to be unsettling. Back inside is something that calls itself a safe place but is anything but.

"It doesn't."

"But smoking does?"

"Smoking can kill you."

She has a point. "We all die anyways."

"Edge lord."

"Shut up."

They finally broach the porch, and C sighs once again. "I fucking hate this place."

"Yeah, I know," Park's voice is small. If he ever thought about going back on his promise to not drag C into Hell Club, this cements his will to keep it from her.

"I can't wait to leave."

"I know," he whispers.

C must notice that he's not agreeing with her, but she doesn't say anything. She just goes back into their house, her lips pressed together tightly. "Goodnight," she says, and she heads through the kitchen, to her bedroom upstairs, and Park goes back into the basement.

He resumes his position, laying in bed and checks his phone for a text from Isaac, finding several. He scrolls through them, and then takes a deep breath, settling himself, bracing himself to reply, trying to push the growing worry for his sister out of his mind.

He types out a reply to Isaac, and then he makes the mistake of closing his eyes after it's sent, falling asleep almost instantly.

12
INTERLUDE I

Derek's morning follows the same routine every day. He gets up, he kisses Eve on her forehead, he gets dressed, he brushes his teeth, and he makes a pot of coffee. He pours his into a travel mug and he makes a bagel for breakfast.

Sometimes Eve wakes up and meets him in the kitchen, where she kisses him, and he complains about her morning breath, and she laughs at him. She'll take her mug of coffee and sit at the dining room table, still half asleep, and he'll bring his breakfast over. Eve will muster the energy to look alive, and Derek will eat his bagel at the speed of light. He'll get up, put his shoes on and give her another kiss before he leaves for work. They'll say *goodbye* and *I love you.*

Sometimes Eve won't wake up and meet him in the kitchen, and on these days, Derek eats his bagel over the sink because he doesn't want to dirty a dish and he leaves her a note on the coffee maker. It differs every time, but it always ends in *have a good day, I love you.*

Either situation ends in Derek getting into his truck and driving to work for another long day of answering calls and pressing buttons and talking to people about their money. It's not glamourous, but it pays well, and Derek isn't one to complain.

He might not love his job, but he loves Eve, and he loves the life they have together. He loves that he can call her on her lunch break, and she'll answer and they'll get to talk about their morning together, the ups and the downs. Eve works at the only beauty salon in Belle and as such she gets to hear about all the town gossip. Derek doesn't get the town gossip, but he hears about all the events that are planned, about all the get-togethers and fundraisers. They like to trade information.

When Derek's shift ends, he gets back into his truck and drives home. Sometimes he stops to pick up groceries first, and sometimes he stops at the local chocolatier to get something sweet for Eve. Sometimes he stops to pick up flowers. Sometimes, he stops in the parking lot of the pet store, and he *thinks* about going in and seeing the kittens that are up for adoption, he thinks about the face that Eve would make when he walks through the door, the way that she would *adore* the newest addition to their family.

He's never gotten the courage to go in, but he likes to tell himself that he's working up to it. One day he'll get home and he'll give Eve a cat and she'll have another creature to pour her love into. She'll have another being to be there for her when he –

"What are you thinking about?" she asks, putting her phone facedown on her chest and turning her full attention to him.

"You." He's *always* thinking about her. He will *always* answer her question in this way and sometimes he thinks she asks just to hear it.

"Romantic ass," she snickers, but she's smiling. "What are you thinking about for dinner tonight?" Neither of them felt like cooking when they got home, and now they're in the should-we-order-out-or-make-something-easy limbo.

Derek groans. Even mac and cheese sounds like too much of a chore. "We should order," he says, already pulling up the menu of the only restaurant in town that does delivery. "Whatcha want, baby?"

"Wait – hold on, did Parker and his sister just walk by?"

"I mean, they live down the street, don't they?" Derek doesn't see why this is any of their business, but Eve is up and at the curtains, watching them. "You're being a creep."

"Shouldn't we follow them to make sure they're okay?"

Derek scrunches his nose and puts his phone down. "I'm sure they're fine?"

"But Iris said that we should always be keeping an eye on them, didn't she?" Eve is craning her neck to see them, now, as they leave the view of the window.

"I don't see how an evening walk would warrant us following them."

Eve lets the curtain fall back over the window, and she turns to face him, a pensive expression on her face. "But what if the Ghost attacks while they're out? What do we tell Iris then?"

"We say, 'we didn't feel like being totally creepy and following Park and his sister on their evening walk.' I think that's perfectly reasonable."

Eve shrugs. "I suppose."

"Now, come here and tell me what you want," he whines, "I'm so hungry."

She smiles, and Derek's insides melt. "Me too. Whatcha getting?"

***

"When is Zac coming over again?" Chip asks, his hands around his favourite superhero toy. "I miss him."

Mel sighs. She hasn't spoken with Isaac for a few days. "I don't know, honey," she says. "I'll ask him, okay? Maybe he can come watch you tomorrow after school."

"Why not you?" He looks up at her and her heart melts, like it does every time.

"Mommy has some running around to do tomorrow afternoon," she says. She has a doctor appointment in the city, and she knows she should have texted Isaac already. She should have texted their sitter, too, but she's been so preoccupied.

Her sister, Shannon, Isaac's mom, called earlier in the day and from what she described Mel is convinced she's about to drive their entire business into the ground. Not that she was doing particularly well with it to begin with, but it seems despite her successful career and her head for business she doesn't have a head for magic, or the possible consequences of it. Mel almost believes that she's trying to ruin the business just because she can – how will she pay her penance to their father and to Mel if there isn't a business left? But the money she generates from it must be too great. She's worried that Shannon and her husband Carter are starting to take too many risks, and that this is going to get them in trouble, with the law or with magic she's not sure. Neither would be good.

When she voiced her concerns to Walt, he only smiled and rubbed her back comfortingly.

"They'll work it out. You know they always do," he said, helpfully, but Mel has seen what happens when they *don't* work it out and she doesn't want to have to run in and pick up the pieces of her older sister's failure, yet again. Sometimes she thinks that's all she's good for.

She has lunch planned with Shannon, and she hopes that her sister will be able to put herself back together by then. If not, she might not be willing to help this time. If not, she might just turn a blind eye.

It's an empty threat and she knows it, but it still feels good to think about.

***

Old John paints frantically over his fence: *isn't it that we all die? i think that's it, what it is,* doesn't seem right anymore. He needs to change it and he needs to change it before whatever terrible thing that's been brewing in the air around his house finally boils over. Before the Ghost tires of his nonsense and decides that time is finally up for the old man.

He's been seeing it in his dreams, the black dust, the amber light, the giant ominous presence that he's felt before. The one that moved his hand across the pages and hid the books of Prophecy in the clubhouse. The one that he and Katherine Selene worked with, so long ago. The one that's turned venomous with its anger, with its grief.

He wishes that he could turn back time. He wishes that humanity hadn't hurt its master so. He wishes that the screaming in the back of his head would stop so he could get some *goddamn* sleep. He wishes that it would just be over already.

He shakes his spray paint can and the whispering of the river rises in volume around him, becoming deafening, becoming impossible to ignore. He feels the dread in the pit of his stomach start, and he knows that if he turns around the Ghost will be forming behind him, all dark fragments of memory and feeling and magic. He is sure that it will be wearing his face – his younger face – and he is sure that it will be here to swallow him whole.

evil doers beware, he paints, and then the whispering river becomes the screaming river and the air around his house is dark with dust, alive with energy. All at once he feels young again, alive alive alive.

"John," says a voice from behind him, and he does not turn to look. He keeps spraying paint.

evil doers beware, the time is

"I think that's quite enough, John," the voice says, and it is not unkind. It is familiar, and it is warm, and it sounds like everything he's ever lost coming back to him all at once. A hand touches his shoulder, and he finally stops.

He stands, and turns to face the Ghost, its face his face but warped. His face, but young and pointy and uncanny. "You told me you would come when the time is right," he says, the spray bottle loose in his hand.

"The time is right," the Ghost says. It is not angry. It is not chiding or hateful. "A new Prophet has found their voice."

"I'm scared," Old John whispers, and his knees are shaking. Suddenly his life does not feel so long. Suddenly he wishes he had more air to breathe and moments to enjoy. Suddenly he wishes he could have done it differently – maybe he could have saved them all if he had just burned the book. Maybe he could have saved Katherine if he had just – if he had just done something, anything different. The idea of being replaced doesn't sit well with him. He wishes he could tell them what he knows and pass along his wisdom. He didn't get enough time. He was never going to have enough time.

"I know," the Ghost says, and John gets the sense that it wishes things were different, too. He gets the sense that the Ghost loves its people as much as it loves its master, and he knows then that none of this could have been different. To think so is to think that one can change fate, that one can rewrite the world.

"I'm sorry," John says, and he feels the hotness of tears on his face. "Will she be there?"

The Ghost shakes its head. "No," it says, so softly that John isn't sure it said anything at all. It opens its arms to him, and he steps forward. "It's time to go now."

Old John takes a deep breath, and then he steps into the embrace, allowing its arms to wrap around him, pushing his face into its shoulder. When he disappears, it feels a lot like going home. It feels a lot like love.

Behind him, in the physical world he leaves behind, the spray paint can hits the ground with a clang, and rolls into the ditch, the only evidence of an old man, no more.

13

GUILT AND OTHER NIGHTMARES

"You told him?!" *Iris* says loudly, both incredulous and proud. "How'd he take it? How'd it go? What'd he say?" She pushes her tarot deck into her chest, grinning at him.

Isaac shrugs. He thinks it went as well as it could have. "I'm seeing him again today."

"Really?" Her eyes get even wider than they were. "He must have taken it well then!"

"I think he had a crush on me already, and we got most of the heavy lifting done at the cabin." Isaac lowers himself to the floor. This feels like a conversation that he wants to hold from the safety of the rug Iris uses to meditate on in her little reading room. "And I think that maybe some of the Prophecy stuff hasn't really sunk in for him yet. He didn't really have any questions for me, and I feel like he should. Maybe he'll have more today."

"I think that's fair. It's a lot to process all at once. I took weeks to really understand what everything meant." Iris did take weeks. She didn't talk to Isaac for days after he showed her, at first because she was angry he kept it from her for so long and then for showing her and damming her to be stuck in Belle with him. She was always more interested in leaving than he was.

"You also already knew a lot about magic," Isaac whispers, "and you and I could ask Mel or your dad about it."

"Park has us, though."

"I think he's scared of you."

She frowns and presses her tarot cards further into her chest. "Scared or intimidated?"

"Both, probably. I think you should talk to him about stuff – maybe you could explain your role better to him. Maybe you could help unlock whatever it is he's supposed to give to us." Isaac has been thinking about it, and he's sure this is the right way. Iris has the most knowledge of the greatest number of things – divination, meditation, witchcraft – and therefore the most to impart on Park. All Isaac can do is give him his interpretations of the Prophecies and hold his hand through it all. (Isaac *really* wants to hold his hand.)

"Yeah," she mutters, "yeah, okay. I'll see if he'll want to get together sometime."

Isaac closes his eyes, so many things running through his head. There's Park, and then there's the *One who falls*, quickly moving towards them. There's Derek and his insistence that it's going to be him that disappears, and there's Eve and the strange, wild way she's been looking at him, like she knows something he doesn't. There's Park and Isaac and the way that Isaac's insecurities are creeping up his spine, making him doubt himself and his ability to give Park any kind of relationship, any kind of commitment, anything but confusion and lust.

That's why he's here, with Iris, requesting a tarot reading. He wants to know how he should be moving forwards with Park, what he should tell him and let him in on and what he shouldn't. The tarot cards might make the dance he's complicated inside his head easy again.

"I was thinking I could bring him for a walk out by Old John's - you know the bridge?"

"No," Iris's hair moves over her polyester shirt as she shakes her head, "not there."

He pushes up on his elbow so he can raise an eyebrow at her, and she takes this as her cue to start shuffling her deck, bending the cards and then allowing them to fall together again with a decisive *snap*. "Why?"

The moon flashes at the bottom of her deck and she shuffles again. *Snap.* "Dahlia saw the Ghost by the bridge." *Snap.* "Sorry, felt not saw."

Isaac groans and flops back onto the floor. "What else are we supposed to do?"

"You could go out to the Lookout." *Snap.*

"No! He's going to think I just want sex."

Snap. "Does he know the Lookout is a hookup spot?"

Isaac sighs. Park probably doesn't - if he had, he doubts that he would have agreed to meet anyone at the Clubhouse. This doesn't mean that he won't figure out what the Lookout is as soon as he sets eyes on it, though, and he doesn't want Park to think he's only after one thing. "No, but I don't want to run the risk of him putting it together."

"Do you think he would care?" *Snap.* Then the tap-tap-tap of Iris's knuckles knocking on the deck. "Cards are ready."

"I don't know," he says, and he doesn't, and he doesn't want to think about it. He waves his hand at her, listening as she starts to shuffle for jumper cards. "Do your worst, magic lady."

Iris has been reading tarot for him for years, and she is *scary good* at it, which makes him more nervous for what her cards are going to tell him. He's never been good at romance, even though he's always been charming. He's been interested in people before – certain entanglings that were more than sex – but those were before he knew about the Prophecy.

Sometimes when he thinks about it too much, he regrets how he acted in high school, and for a short time after. He regrets sleeping with so many people – not because it wasn't fun, or because he feels any sort of shame from it, but because he was doing it for attention. When he was younger and more insecure, he loved it when he caught the eye of someone new and they were excited he was talking to them. He liked the glances in the hallways, and the whispers between them and their friends. He liked feeling wanted, feeling worthy.

He'd done a lot of things to stay on that high. He'd lead people on. He'd hurt them. He would sleep with them, but never commit, and he let some of them believe they could change him, that they were special enough he would settle down.

He's better at setting boundaries now. He's better at keeping expectations exactly where they should be, and he's not so invested in the attention. He used to think it was the only thing worth anything, but now he knows better.

"Oh, *Isaac*," Iris laughs, and Isaac closes his eyes. He hates it when she does this.

"It's bad, isn't it?"

"I mean, it's not good."

Isaac pushes himself back up on his elbows to see her cards lined up, none of them the ones that he associates with good things or happy times except maybe the nine of cups. "That one's good, isn't it?"

Iris rolls her eyes. "I'm getting that you're going to have what you want, but at what cost? Like, look," she gestures at the knight of pentacles, "you're stubborn, you're working hard for what you want.

You've got the long run in mind, but that doesn't change the fact that you're stuck." The eight of swords.

Isaac snorts. This is exactly what he and Park were talking about. Fuck these cards.

"So, you're like okay, what am I supposed to do? Choose between something that you really want, or give it up entirely and break your own heart by walking away?" Justice. Three of swords. Nine of cups.

Isaac points at the last one, the one in the deck that he hates the most but pulls quite often. "Let me guess, I'm having nightmares about it." He is.

"Well, yeah. Let me pull a couple more to see how you can move forward."

"Apparently I break my own heart, or I get everything I've ever wanted," he says, gesturing at the cards on the table in front of her. "Obviously."

Four more jumpers fall from Iris' hands, and she signs. "Stop overthinking it. If you keep going the way you have been, and you stop thinking about it, it'll all work out. The big picture is out of your control, but you already know that."

The Prophecy, of course. He doesn't really have a choice, does he? If he doesn't continue to pursue Parker, if he turns his back on the Prophecy they'll be pushed together anyways; the illusion of choice.

If he pursues Parker, they'll get more time together than if he turns his back. If he pursues Parker, they have more time to figure out what his secret is, more time to find happiness before the world ends. So, until then, he just needs to keep doing what he's doing, and not thinking about the rest of the Prophecies Not thinking about how this isn't even what he wants to be doing. And thinking about how angry he is that he's stuck here, fighting a battle that can't be won.

"Can they tell me something that we don't already know?" He asks, annoyed.

"Sure. But, you know, sometimes you have to be reminded of this stuff."

Isaac doesn't bother replying. He knows she's right. He did need to be reminded that this is the only choice. This is the only viable path forward.

"God, I can't even. These cards know you so well. Look." She holds up the three of cups and the high priestess. "Just be his friend, right? You already knew that."

Isaac presses the heels of his palms into his eyes. "I hate your cards," he mutters. He can hear the smirk on Iris' face as she collects them and puts them back in her desk drawer.

"I don't know, man. Honestly, we know it's going to work out anyways, don't we? Just be yourself."

"But I'm so awkward. You should have seen our conversation yesterday, Iris. Literally all of me was so *red*." He's almost red just thinking about it.

"I'm very aware of how red you get," she says, leaning on her forearms and looking over to him, still on the floor. "You're like a little tomato."

"Shut up." But he's grinning at her, and she's grinning back.

"But in all seriousness, you have to think that he's probably feeling the same way. I mean, at least you *knew* you were destined to fall in love with someone like that. And he's been texting you non-stop since, so it can't have been as bad as you're thinking it was."

He sighs. He realizes that it must have been a lot for Park to process, but Park didn't seem as surprised as Isaac thought he should be. Park didn't seem to have as hard of a time accepting the Prophecy as Isaac had.

Isaac was angry when he first realized that the Prophecy was about him. He was seeing a boy at the time, a nice boy with kind eyes and hands that lingered on Isaac's body like he was afraid of losing him. Isaac had loved him, and the thought that they weren't meant to be together had cut him down to the bone. When they broke up, Isaac was inconsolable, tired and sad and angry. Angry that it had ended and angry at himself for being unable to make it work; angry that he didn't get to choose for himself.

Obviously, he hadn't known Park then, and he's not angry anymore. Park has been nothing but great; he expects Park will only get better as they get to know each other. Most people do.

"I know," he sighs. "I just worry."

Iris nods. "Are you nervous for today?"

"Yeah, I am." It feels like there is a spider walking across his nerves, nothing big enough to be a bother, but enough that he's aware of them. He closes his eyes again, and in his pocket his phone starts vibrating, indicating a call, but he ignores it.

"It'll be okay," Iris says, and he knows she's right.

It's all going to be okay. It's all going to work out – until it doesn't, but he doesn't have to think about that right now. He just has to follow the path that he knows is right for him, and that's all there is.

14
THE SOFTEST TOUCH

Park is a bundle of anxiety, and he only gets more tightly wound as the hours of his shift go by.

It's Cadence and him working for most of the day and he hasn't dared to tell her what's happening after he gets off. She grilled him on what happened yesterday as soon as he walked through the door, and he tried very hard to give her as little detail as possible. He told her that he's going to see Isaac again, he just didn't say when.

She implied that he was lucky to be getting a second date, and he's starting to think that maybe Cadence is a little bit jealous. From what he gathers, Isaac wasn't super interested in her after they slept together, and she wanted him to be.

When 2:30 hits and Isaac is once again leaning against the window table, he feels Cadence's stare and he flips her off behind his back for the second day in a row. He already hears what she's going to say to Riley when they get on in the back of his mind. *Park is* special *enough to keep seeing Isaac.*

"Hey, you," Isaac says, just as warmly, and Park feels the heat rise in his chest just the same.

"Hey," he replies, weakly, the affection he's growing towards Isaac curling like smoke around his heart. He follows Isaac out the doors, into the cool autumn air, and it feels nice on his warm cheeks, his warm hands. "So, what's the plan?"

"I was thinking we could go for a walk over by Old John's place – they have a little informational trail that's kind of cool - but Iris says that it's a bad idea." Isaac opens his car door for Park, and Park brushes by him close enough to smell his aftershave which is sharp and inviting.

"Why is it a bad idea?" He questions, hoping that Isaac can't feel the sudden spark of *want* that's started a fire of impure thoughts in his head. He wants to press his chest into Isaac's so that he can get closer to his skin, so he can inhale that smell again, so he can run his fingers through Isaac's messy hair. They haven't touched each other since the Protection spell backfired, and all Park has wanted all this time is Isaac to reach out and broach the gap between them.

Isaac's lips have skewed slightly to the side in amusement, and the fingers that curl around the edge of the car door have tightened around it, his knuckles paling with the effort. Park is certain he knows what Park is thinking. "Her and Dahlia sensed the Ghost in that area."

"Sensed?"

"They can tell when magic from the source they take from is being pulled out. They're connected to it." Park watches Isaac swallow, still leaning into the car from the street. At the base of his throat, his pulse is jackrabbiting, and Park gets caught on it, imagines his teeth against it.

"Oh," he says, and straightens in his seat, pushing down his thoughts. "So, what's plan B?"

Isaac leans forward. "Get food? Are you hungry?" He steps back for a moment, looking over the roof of his car, and Park turns his head to see what's grabbed his attention.

There's nothing there, so he focuses back on Isaac. "Sure," he says, even though he already ate. It doesn't really matter what they're doing – he just wants to get to know Isaac. He just wants to talk to him.

"We can get takeout, if you want? Go back to my house?" He glances back over the car and Park gets the feeling that he's suggesting this for a reason. He seems uneasy, worried.

"Sounds good to me," Park replies.

Isaac's smile breaks out across his face once again, but there's still something that Park is sure he doesn't want him to know about. He closes the door and hurries to the driver's side. "Sorry," he says, slumping into his seat, "I just – I thought I saw something out near the highway, a shadow. It's gone now."

"What do you think it could have been?"

Isaac shrugs, and suddenly he seems tired. Park can only imagine how stressful it's been for him to be balancing the End of the World and the coming Prophecies and explaining things to Park. "Could have just been my imagination, honestly. I didn't get much sleep last night."

"Nervous for something?" Park asks, grinning, hoping that his off-hand comment doesn't offend Isaac, hoping that he chuckles or that he smiles, just a little bit.

He grins, "Yeah, actually. There's this really cute guy that I'm going out with – definitely nervous for that."

"Oh, well," Park starts, not sure where he's going, "I'm sure the really cute guy is just as nervous as you."

"Are you?" Isaac asks, his eyes darkening as he leans forward, out of the sun.

"Yeah," the word is a breath on Park's lips, and he feels like Isaac is going to reach out, going to touch him, going to do *something* but he's interrupted.

His phone, in the middle console, starts vibrating, and the moment is broken. Isaac checks the caller ID, the screen lighting up his face, harsh in the shadows of the car. "Sorry," he says, "it's my aunt. She wouldn't be calling if it wasn't important."

Park nods as Isaac answers, looking apologetic. He chews on the inside of his lip as Isaac listens, wondering what it was that Isaac was going to do. His mind is wild with possibilities, and he tries not to think about any of them too hard. If he does, he's not sure he'll be able to control himself, and he'll give too much of his emotion away to Isaac, who will read it and know more than Park wants him to.

"I'm sorry," Isaac says again, snapping Park out of his reverie. "Chip is still at his school. He was supposed to be picked up by his sitter, but something happened, and my aunt can't reach them." He drops his phone back in the console and pushes his fingers into his temples, barely containing his disappointment, his annoyance.

"Okay," Park blinks, unsure if Isaac is going to cancel their date, if he's going to want to drop Park back off back at home. He doesn't want Isaac to.

"I can drop you off," he says, "if you want." The disappointment is more obvious in his voice, and Park shakes his head.

"You don't have to. I like Chip," Park says, and Isaac lets out a deep breath.

"I'm sorry it's not at all what we planned but –"

"That's okay," Park reassures, "really. It's all good. Shit happens."

"Okay," Isaac nods, relieved. When his eyes meet Park's, he seems almost hopeful. "Okay, well –" He checks over his shoulder into the backseat and pulls a sweater off of the car seat, "Here we go, I guess." He straightens, and starts the car, pulling out onto the road and letting the soft music from his speakers fill the silence.

It's mostly quiet between them as they approach the school, and Park can't help but wonder if he's made a mistake. He stays in the car as Isaac goes into the office, coming out a few minutes later with a disgruntled looking Chip, whose hat is pulled down over his curls. Isaac is holding his backpack, and some sort of form, and he looks out to the car, meeting Park's gaze and keeping it for a second as he shepherds the boy closer. Park smiles, and Isaac's face warms, though just a little.

He wonders if maybe he should have got Isaac to drop him off back at his house, if maybe the strain of looking after his cousin and trying to maintain conversation with Park will be too much. Isaac already seems so tired.

The back door opens, and the backpack is the first thing through, followed by Chip, who climbs clumsily into his car seat, his small hands pulling the buckles around himself, but not clipping them. "Hi, Park," Chip says brightly, and Park pulls himself around the passenger seat to smile back.

"Hi," he says, trying to be just as bright. "I see you're wearing your hat today."

Isaac turns so he can roll his eyes at Park, theatrically, so Park knows it's in good nature, directed more at Chip's insistence of avoiding hats than at Park.

"Miss Webb made me put it on," Chip glowers, and Isaac lets out a small *aha* before closing the backseat door. "I told her I hate it."

"Don't you get cold without it?" Park asks, and Isaac shakes his head as he once again steps into the drivers' seat and starts the car.

"It's a fight you absolutely won't win," he tells Park, putting his hand at the back of Park's headrest to look behind him as he backs out of the parking lot and onto the road.

Park's breath catches in his throat with the proximity of Isaac's arm, but he can't show it because Chip is telling him off for telling him he'll be cold, and he's worried that Isaac will catch onto the stutter of his heart. "Alright," Park says, and Isaac gives him a side glance that says *I told you so.* "I guess I'm wrong."

"You are," Chip huffs.

"Sorry to interrupt," Isaac says, "but, Chip, do you want to stay at my house tonight, or yours?"

"We can stay at your place?" Chip asks excitedly, bouncing in his car seat, and Park can't help but smile because he's smiling. He really hadn't been lying when he told Isaac that he likes Chip; the kid is *infectiously* happy and outgoing.

"If that's what you want." Isaac shoots another glance at Park and there's something like yearning in it. Something that makes Park's teeth ache.

"Yes!" The answer is immediate.

"Okay, we just have to stop at your house to get your overnight stuff."

Chip hums with excitement in the back, and Isaac sighs.

"He'll ask you to stay the night, too," he says, softly, pulling into his aunt's driveway. "You can say no."

Park is certain he can't say no to the kid, but he thinks that this is less about Chip and more about Isaac. He seems otherworldly exhausted, like he could use someone to lean on while he's babysitting. "What if it's you that asks me to stay instead?" He asks, raising an eyebrow.

Isaac swallows, his hand on the door. "You can still say no," he says, voice even softer, vulnerable, "but you are welcome to. I mean – to stay."

Park nods. "I'll think about it," he says, but there isn't much thinking to do.

***

Park volunteers to cook the three of them dinner, which consists of several boxes of macaroni and cheese, by Chip's request.

Chip and Isaac are sitting at the island stools, Isaac watching Park intently and Chip tracing his way through a book that is just slightly above his reading comprehension.

Park is trying very hard to not notice that Isaac is watching him, but he's doing a piss poor job. Every few minutes he looks over his shoulder to see the other man's eyes on him, and his stomach drops a little bit with nerves.

He isn't sure how the previously planned date would have gone, but he assumes that this afternoon with Chip is *worlds* better. At first it was awkward, but Chip is a great icebreaker, and they'd played card games for a while before Chip asked to go outside, and then they'd played chase in the yard until Chip was tired and it was time for dinner.

He can't help but think that it's incredibly attractive to see how good Isaac is with his cousin, how attentive and present he is, and Chip makes Isaac smile more than Park has ever seen him smile before. Isaac might have been worried about taking care of Chip, but he's handling it swimmingly.

He really is beautiful, and Park is drinking everything about him in. If Park hadn't already mostly made up his mind about spending the night, he has now.

"Mac's ready," he announces, "I'd get bowls, but I don't know where they are."

Isaac chuckles and slides off the stool, walking towards Park and brushing by him as he reaches for the cupboard right beside him. The contact is startling, and when Isaac brushes by him a second time it leaves Park wanting more. To top it off, Isaac looks over his shoulder as he sets the bowls down, a smirk present on his face, telling Park that he knows *exactly* what he's doing.

Park swallows, grabbing the pot of mac and cheese, and the hot plate hanging by the stove. He places both on the counter beside Isaac, and Isaac starts scooping into the first bowl.

"Tell me when," he tells Chip, and Chip doesn't say when until the bowl is heaping. "You better eat all of it, rascal," he says, and Chip nods enthusiastically.

He passes Park the spoon, fingers lingering just a second more than what could be considered normal, and Park's heart stutters yet again when they touch. Park wants so badly to kiss Isaac, to press their chests together, to hold him close, and from the way that Isaac has been watching him he's made it clear that's what he wants too. But they'll have to wait. They'll have to wait until after Chip is in bed and sound asleep.

"Can we watch a movie after?" Chip asks, through a mouthful of macaroni.

Isaac looks to Park. "Are you staying tonight?" Even though they both know the answer.

"Yeah," Park breathes, and it feels good to say.

A pleased expression passes through Isaac's face, and he says to Chip, "Yeah, and I'll even let you pick."

Chip grins with excitement. Park isn't certain there has been a point where Chip hasn't been grinning with excitement.

Park is excited, too. A movie means that he'll have an excuse to touch Isaac, it means couches and blankets and closeness. It means that he'll at the very least be able to rest his head on Isaac's shoulder or press their arms together.

The anticipation for the movie seems to drive everyone to eat faster, and Chip finishes his entire bowl, which surprises no one.

Isaac wordlessly collects dirty dishes and deposits them in the sink, to deal with later. "Pajamas before the movie," he tells Chip, and Chip takes off to the guest room upstairs which he told Park is his room. "He's going to fall asleep halfway through," he says to Park, "he does it every time."

Park smiles, "I fall asleep during movies, too," he admits, and Isaac rolls his eyes.

"Great, so I'm going to be the only one crying at the end." But he's smiling too.

"Yeah, sorry about that."

"Thanks for staying," Isaac says, more serious, "Chip really likes you."

"I'm incredibly likeable," Park jokes, "and I thought you said it would be Chip asking me to stay." Isaac stops for a second, thinking about what to say next. Park watches him look to the stairs that Chip disappeared up, and then back to Park, mischief glinting in his eyes.

"You are incredibly likeable," he starts, "and I have my own agenda."

"What's on it?" Park feels like they're getting dangerously close to something, like they're standing on the precipice. Isaac takes a step forward, and his body is inches away. The sharp scent is overwhelming, and it's making Park's mouth water.

"Can I kiss you?"

"Yes," Park breathes, falling off the edge. He's glad Isaac asked because he's certain he wouldn't be able to get the words out.

Isaac closes the distance between them, leaning down so their mouths meet, his hands landing on Park's sides - Park's around his waist. The warmth of Isaac hits him first, and then his breath, and then his lips, soft and forgiving against his own.

Park thinks his heart might explode, and there's not a single thought in his head except *Isaac. Isaac Isaac Isaac.* Isaac, leaning in to deepen the kiss, pulling Park in with his hands, an easy give and take between them. Every nerve in Park's body is alive and on fire, every piece of him that's in contact with Isaac is hot and electric and Park doesn't want to step away, ever. He doesn't want the kiss to stop.

Isaac's hands move slowly to Park's back, and he pushes Park further into him, slipping his tongue into Park's mouth and making him let out a sharp exhale of surprise. Park can feel the ghost of a smile against his lips and he pushes harder into Isaac, chest to chest, leg between leg, his hands wrapped tightly in Isaac's hoodie, and then –

"Isaac!" Chip's voice from the top of the stairs, "I'm ready for the movie."

Isaac pulls away from Park, but leaves one hand on his waist, to steady them both. "Alright," he calls back, but he's still looking at Park, his eyes dark with *want*, "we'll meet you in the living room. Can you get the TV going?"

"Yeah," Chip mutters, and Park watches him round the corner into the living room without so much as glancing at them.

"You're good at kissing," Isaac says, his lips swollen, red. He hasn't taken his hand off Park, and Park has to fight the urge to take it, to pull Isaac back to him, to finish what was so rudely interrupted.

"You too," Park says, not wanting to admit that this is the best kiss he's ever had.

"We should –"

Right on cue, Chip's curly head pokes around the corner. "I can't find the remote," he says, and Isaac chuckles.

"Coming," he says, and he starts towards the kid, Park following reluctantly. "Can I kiss you again?" Isaac asks, softly, just before they get to the living room, and Park makes a small noise of affirmation.

Isaac turns and he places a kiss so soft on Park's lips that Park wonders if it happened outside of his imagination.

His head is reeling as he sits down on the couch and Isaac hands him a blanket, which he wraps around himself gratefully. He doesn't know how Isaac is functioning as he digs through the armchair cushions for the remote, and finds it, turning on the TV and turning off the lights before joining Park on the couch. Park feels like his bones have been pulled out of his body, like he's one big blob of Jell-o, warm and red and hazy. There's nothing in his head but *Isaac*, and the way that *Isaac* felt against him, the way that *Isaac's* mouth felt against his, his hands.

Chip takes a seat on Isaac's other side, and Isaac wraps an arm around them both.

"*How to Train Your Dragon*," Chip says, as soon as Isaac clicks the Netflix icon, and Isaac chuckles.

"How did I know?" He asks.

"You can read minds," Chip replies.

"Hey, I told you not to tell anyone about that," feigned anger.

"Too bad." Flippant. No shame. Isaac ruffles his hair, and he groans, turning so that his feet rest against Isaac instead. "You're the worst," he huffs, and Isaac raises his eyebrows at him.

"Am I?" He asks, unwrapping his arm from around Park to tickle Chips feet, until the boy is laughing so hard he's almost crying. Park watches with great amusement, blanket pulled around his shoulders, still in a haze but smiling.

"Take it back and I stop," Isaac says, and Chip finally gives, still laughing.

"You're not the worst," he breathes, and Isaac pulls his hands back.

"I knew it," he says, and Chip recovers, his giggles fading but not his excitement. He pushes a pillow against Isaac and leans on that, grabbing his own blanket.

Isaac lifts his arm up, inviting Park to come back in, everything about him soft, warm, open, vulnerable. Park leans against him, breathing in the smell of vanilla and deodorant, the smell of man and of Isaac. He squeezes Park's arm, and starts the movie, before reaching over to tug on the blanket and pull it over himself so that Isaac and Park are snuggled under it, together. His hand finds Park's, and Park's heart soars out of his chest with happiness.

It doesn't take long for Park to give into the unwavering desire to let his eyes close, and he drifts into a dreamless sleep, full of something that feels like safety.

***

Park wakes up to Isaac pulling away from him gently.

"Oh hi," he whispers when he sees that Park's eyes are open. "The movie's over. I'm going to get Chip to bed."

Park sits up groggily, and nods, rubbing at his eyes. "Sorry I fell asleep, I really did –"

Isaac smiles, "Don't be," he says, and then, "meet me in my room?"

Park raises his eyebrows; he doesn't know where it is.

"Right," Isaac carefully lifts a sleeping Chip, "last door on the right up the stairs."

"Okay." Park stretches, not wanting to move from the little nest he's wrapped in on the couch. He watches as Isaac disappears out the door.

There's a small part of him that can't believe he agreed to stay the night, but the rest is screaming at him to get off his ass and up the stairs so he can be in Isaac's room when he's done tucking Chip in. o he can kiss the man again, this time uninterrupted, this time with more tongue and more hands and maybe less clothes. He's not sure if it's too early for sex – he wouldn't mind – and he knows what he's heard about Isaac, but this seems different. It seems like Isaac is taking his time with Park, and Park is okay with it. He would, however, like there to be less clothes involved, whatever they decide.

He finally peels himself from the couch and treads upstairs, through the last door on the right and into Isaac's room.

It's clean, the surfaces covered with neatly arranged items – there's a desk that has a laptop and a sketch book, paintbrushes tucked neatly into a metal stand, and various pens and pencils in another beside it. A bookshelf stands with its first few shelves filled full of books, arranged in no order that's obvious to Park, and the last shelf full of what he assumes are used sketchbooks. There's a nightstand with a lamp and a bowl that houses cigarettes and an array of lighters, a charging cord laid haphazardly across it, and a bottle of melatonin. In the corner is a dirty laundry hamper, and a dresser with an open drawer, the pile of clothes in it disturbed like Isaac took from the bottom in a rush and didn't bother to put it back in order. The walls are an off-white, and there are string lights on every available surface, draped over the desk and bookshelf and hung from the ceiling, wrapped around the headboard of the bed, and stapled into the wall around the door. There are posters, too, arranged tastefully, some for bands and some that remind Park how he met Isaac, botanical drawings of herbs, and different depictions of tarot cards. He steps to read a flashcard that's handwritten and finds the recipe for weed brownies, right next to instructions for a hex.

Park smiles, and steps back, taking it all in.

There's a small noise by the door and he looks over to see Isaac leaning on the doorframe, where he hadn't been just a few seconds ago, watching Park from under his eyelashes, vulnerability clear as day on his face.

"Weed brownies?" Park asks, pointing to the flash card, and Isaac laughs.

"Those are an Eve special," he explains, stepping into the room and closing the door behind him. "You should ask her for some one day – you won't be disappointed."

"I will," Park says, and he sits on Isaac's bed, finding it much softer than he would have thought.

There's quiet for a moment, as Isaac bites his lip, and Park continues to drink in the room around him, and then Isaac asks,

"Do you want some clothes to sleep in?"

and Park nods, maybe too eagerly.

"T-shirt? T-shirt and pajama bottoms?"

"Just a t-shirt." Park isn't picky. He'd sleep in his jeans if he had to.

Isaac digs through his dresser for a minute, and then passes Park theshirt, before going back to get his own pajamas. Something about this feels more intimate than the kiss they'd shared earlier, and there's an awkward tension in the air that's making Park nervous.

"If you want to change in the bathroom, that's fine," Isaac says, softly, "it's just next door if you don't remember."

Park nods, and stands, taking Isaac's shirt with him. It seems safer to change in the bathroom, besides, splashing some cold water on his face might help bring him back into this world. He closes Isaac's bedroom door softly behind him and finds the bathroom, wincing when he turns on the light.

Everything that's happened today feels surreal, he realizes as he leans over the sink, splashing his face once and then twice with cold water. It seems like it's been a week since Isaac picked him up from Pippa's, but it's only been seven hours; it feels like an eternity since Isaac kissed him, but it's only been two and he was asleep for a good portion of it.

He looks at his reflection in the mirror and he realizes he's a mess. His hair is everywhere, smushed against his head on the side he was leaning against Isaac, and his eyes are puffy from his nap. He sighs, and closes his eyes against himself, taking a minute to gather his thoughts.

He's at Isaac Paige's house, who is both the man that he has a crush on and the man that he's destined to fall in love with according to a Prophecy. Isaac Paige is beautiful.

He's spent the whole afternoon with Isaac and his cousin, Chip, and he's been amazed by them the whole time. He cooked dinner for them, and Isaac, the beautiful man, kissed him in the kitchen and put him in a whole-body trance because Park has never been kissed like that. He's never been kissed so *gently*, so *sweetly*.

He's never been welcomed so wholeheartedly into someone's home, into someone's life, and the ease with which it seems to come to Isaac is incredible. This house feels safe, Isaac feels safe. He can't believe that just a few days ago he was debating whether Isaac is trustworthy – there's no doubt in his mind, anymore. Isaac is nothing but genuine.

Park takes off his sweater and shirt, and replaces them with Isaac's, which is just a little bit too big on him, but it's soft and it smells like Isaac. His jeans come off and he feels so naked with both his arms and his legs bare. He can't look in the mirror.

He leaves the bathroom and knocks on the bedroom door, waiting for Isaac's confirmation before going back in. The fairy lights are all on, and Isaac is sitting cross-legged on the bed, looking at his phone. He's wearing only a t-shirt and boxers, and Park thinks this is the first time he's ever seen Isaac's arms bare. Somehow, he expected tattoos, but there aren't any, at least that he can see.

Isaac turns off his phone, and leans to plug it in, letting it drop on the nightstand. "Hey, you," he says, and Park's heart kickstarts in his chest. Isaac stands to meet him, and takes the bundle of clothes he's holding, neatly stacking it on the desk chair, and turning his full attention back to Park.

He grabs Park's wrists and pulls them so Park steps forward and they're in contact again, this time with less fabric between them. Park's hands settle around Isaac's waist, and Isaac whispers so softly that Park barely hears him, "Can I kiss you?" And then they're kissing again and Park's eyes are closed and behind them all he can see are bursting colours, all he can feel is heat as their limbs tangle and Isaac pushes into him harder than before.

He toys with the edge of Isaac's shirt, running it through his fingers, and when Isaac bites down on his lip, he tests the water and brings his hands under it, "Okay?" He asks, between kisses, just like Isaac's been doing, and Isaac breathes a *yes*, and then Park pushes his hands up, between Isaac's shoulder blades, feeling the muscle there, the bone, digging his fingertips in for a moment before traveling down, to his hips which are softer, and his abdomen, which is softest. He keeps his hands here for one beat, then two, relishing in the warmth, and then he slides them to Isaac's chest, where he splays them, pushing Isaac back so he can remove the shirt entirely, but Isaac understands what he wants and stops kissing him just long enough to get it over his head.

"Your turn?" He asks, tugging on the bottom of Park's shirt and Park shucks it, letting it drop. They make eye contact for a moment, and Isaac opens his mouth to say something, but closes it again. His hands at his side are open and he seems to be looking for words.

"Is something wrong?" Park asks, immediately feeling vulnerable. Did he do something? Did he fuck it up already?

"No," Isaac shakes his head quickly, "no, nothing's wrong. I just – I want to set boundaries and stuff before we get – um – too carried away, I guess."

"Oh," Park breathes a sigh of relief. "Yeah, boundaries." He doesn't know what to say – no one's asked him about his boundaries, no one's ever asked him if what they're doing is okay like Isaac has been. It's nice, he thinks, and then he remembers that this is probably standard. Isaac is acting like it's standard.

"Is there anything that you explicitly don't want to do tonight?" Isaac asks, sitting on the edge of the bed, and patting the space beside him. "I don't really want penetration, but I'm okay with other stuff."

Park nods, "Me too," he says, and takes a seat so that he's pressed against Isaac. He doesn't know what else there is that he doesn't want, he doesn't know what else Isaac means.

"Hickies?"

Oh. "Below the collarbone."

"Me too. What else do you like?"

Park pauses, trying to think, trying to come up with something so he doesn't seem like a complete idiot. Most of the time he just takes whatever it is he's getting. Most of the time it's quick, and there isn't really a say in what happens.

Isaac breaks his hesitation, and smiles, leaning forward to press a kiss to Park's shoulder. "We can try things," he says, "but if you don't like something, let me know, okay?"

Park nods, unable to look at Isaac, feeling the dread of realization building in him. He knows that his past interactions weren't great, but sitting here now, with someone who's trying to talk to him, who's making it about their joined pleasure instead of just taking what he wants from Park - it's horrifying.

"I like biting," Isaac says, "and scratches."

"Okay," Park whispers, blinking furiously.

"Do you want to set a safe word?"

"I -" he starts, and then his throat betrays him and the words stick.

"What's wrong?" Isaac is immediately more attentive, his hand on Park's thigh.

"No one's asked me stuff like this before?" Park admits, taking a deep, shaky breath. "I - I've never used a safe word. I thought that was just for, like, kinky stuff -"

Isaac shakes his head. "No, not always. They're for any kind of intimacy, so that you're comfortable." He squeezes Park's thigh, and the gesture makes the emotions well up inside of him once again.

Park closes his eyes. He knows that this is all basic stuff, but it's new to him. He's never been asked what he wants, what he likes, what they should use as a safe word. For him, sex has always been an act of need rather than want, of take rather than give, and now that he's thinking about it, some of the situations he's put himself in before were not ideal.

He's embarrassed that Isaac's acts of the bare minimum have stirred such emotion in him, but then Isaac is pulling him in closer, wrapping his arms around him, running his fingers through his hair, and it all seems okay. Isaac isn't judging him.

"I'm sorry for killing the mood," Park says, after a minute.

"No," Isaac replies, "no, no. Don't be. Don't ever be. You didn't kill the mood. This is a conversation we needed." There's a soft kiss planted in his hair, and Park's heart melts. They're quiet for a few minutes, but it's not awkward. It's a million things unspoken that Park is sure Isaac is piecing together, understanding.

"Do you want to keep going or do you want to go to bed?" Isaac asks, finally, rubbing his hand up and down Park's arm, and Park blinks.

"We can kiss a little bit more," he says, and then adds, "if you want."

Isaac laughs, "I do want," he says, and then they're kissing again, soft, and slow and sweet. Isaac's hands are warm, and his mouth is sure in making its mark, turning Park's world into a kaleidoscope of reds and purples and yellows, turning him back into warm jelly, full of limbs and lips and desire.

They don't stop kissing for a long time, and when they do, Parker is exhausted in the best kind of way. Together, they crawl under the covers, and Isaac wraps his arms around Park, pulling him close, as close as he can be, chest to back, hands wrapped around wrists, skin against skin. Park melts into him, breathless and full of elation, full of something that feels like safety.

"Goodnight," Isaac whispers, sleepily, using a hand to smooth down Park's hair so it's not in his face and then returning it to where it was wrapped gently around Park's wrist, thumb to pulse.

"Goodnight," Park says back, and he falls asleep wrapped up in Isaac.

15
SOMETHING GOES WRONG

Mel should not have left the business. She was aware that her sister would send it into a nosedive, yet she left anyways. *Live and learn*, she thought, but she had lived. She had learned, and yet, here she is once again, cleaning up after her *useless* sister. She loved her sister once, but that love is very far away.

"Of course, Mr. Allan," she says in her best professional voice. It's a little out of practice, and it makes her feel like she's twenty years old again, playing at knowing what she's doing. It seems to charm him all the same. "I understand that you are frustrated. I'm working on trying to fix the situation at hand, and it should be under control shortly. Your Artifact will be back with you this evening."

The man narrows his eyes at her, his pupils beady under his bushy eyebrows. He reminds her of a muskrat, slimy and wet and scheming. "I should hope so," he says, "or else I may have to look into other means of obtaining my Artifacts."

It's a weighty threat and they both know it. Mr. Allan is and always has been one of their main buyers. He collects Artifacts like they're hobbies – learning their ways, their curses, and then tossing them aside, into his fancy warehouse of horrors – and he and Mel's father used to be friends. Without his support, the business will start crumbling at the foundation, and as much as Mel promised she wouldn't come back full time, she would rather walk into hell backwards than let it collapse. Her father would, too.

She nods at Mr. Allan, and gestures for him to step out of the dusty office in her sister's house, where she's supposedly conducting all her deals. "My father or I will be in touch soon," she says, as she shuts the door behind him.

As soon as she hears the front door open and close, she lets out a long sigh and leans against the wall. Her feet hurt and her head hurts and her back hurts and her belly is so heavy. *Why now?* She thinks to herself, as she stands upright and collapses in the office chair behind the old, empty desk.

She has done everything in her power to teach Shannon about the ins and outs of Ritual Magic, and the dos and do-nots of Artifacts. She genuinely has no idea how her sister has the capability to fuck up to this capacity – if she weren't so appalled at the incompetence, she might be impressed. It's a wonder, really, that the woman is lawyer. It's a wonder, really, that she can keep her own goddamn head above water.

Mel pulls her phone out of her purse, and pauses before she presses her father's contact. He is the heart and the soul of the business, and he usually doesn't like to be disturbed unless it's a true emergency – he's trying to retire, but is finding it impossible, especially after the death of his wife – but Mel is certain that she can't finish the clean up on this one by herself.

Her thumb touches the button, and the answer is instant.

"Hi, Mel," says the voice on the other side, and it fills her with relief.

"Dad," she breathes out, "I need your help."

Mel has done everything in her power to shield Isaac from their family business but she's sure that Isaac would be great at it. He has the temperament for magical things, and he knows what's worth taking on and what's not. He's good with people, too, balancing emotions and words and he usually gets exactly what it is he wants without ever having to try too hard. If she worked with him, she's sure that he would fare much better at it than his mother, but he's busy with the Ghost in the woods, and she's not sure she wants to subject him to the infinity that is the business. There will always be buyers and sellers, and there will always be Artifacts and Rituals, and none of the four of them are reliable or trustworthy.

She, herself, has tried to retire many times, and it never seems to stick. There's always something that drags her back in – her sister screwing up, a deal that's just too good to let pass by, or the desperate need for money to support her family. She loves her husband with all her heart, and she supports him in whatever it is that he wants to do, but sometimes the woodshop doesn't bring in enough revenue and, well, they have a second child already well on the way. Sometimes she must fall back on the business, and he understands. He may not be fully in support – Ritual magic stinks to high heavens, and many of the Artifacts are life-threateningly dangerous – but he understands.

"Dad," she says, as he steps up on the porch. She gives him a kiss on the cheek, and he returns it. "Thank you for coming."

"No problem, Mel," he says, adjusting the sleeves of his suit. "Where is she?"

"She's inside. She's been crying almost the entire time I've been here." The *she* in question is her older sister, and the tears are endless because of the same figurine that caused her last screw up. Mel isn't sure why Carter let his wife near it again, but here they all are.

The two of them enter Shannon's home and Carter stands like a ghost in the corner, dark bags under his eyes, the skin around his mouth tight and fraught with worry. He looks like Isaac if Isaac were balding and hadn't slept for three days. Mel has always disliked him.

"Thank you for coming," he says, gratefully, wringing his hands out in front of him, "I tried to perform the Ritual you did last time but it didn't work. I forgot something." Mel's upper lip curls, and he notices, but says nothing.

His father-in-law, more forgiving than Mel, nods softly. "It takes time to get it right. You stay here, we'll only be a couple of minutes."

Carter nods, and Mel looks away from him, following her dad deeper into the house, to where the wailing is now audible. If she could, she thinks, she would just walk away and let the figurine consume Shannon. They might all be better off for it.

"She's going to need to take some time off," Mel says, letting her annoyance peak through, "she did last time, too. I can't keep up with things right now - I'm -"

Her dad gestures to her belly, "I understand," he says, "you need time with your children. I'll take over for a little while, give her time to recover."

"Thank you," she says, "the clients will be grateful as well. Mr. Allan seemed - tense - when I told him what was happening." The clients will be grateful, and not only Mr. Allan. There's no one better than Victor Wright in the industry. He lives and breathes Rituals and Artifacts, and he's been performing them and selling them for the past forty years.

"It's too bad you're not interested in taking over for her," he says, his hand on the doorknob to the room from which the wailing is coming, "you've always had a better head for this stuff."

Mel sighs. She's been thinking about it, but it would mean leaving her home and moving back to the city, or at least a very long drive a couple of times a week. It would mean uprooting Chip and Walt or having to rely more heavily on their sitter and Isaac for childcare. If they move, they will have to leave Isaac behind completely, and Mel doesn't want to abandon him. She knows the circumstances are different, and he would understand, but the less parallels she can draw between Shannon and herself the better. "Give me another few years," she says, tiredl.

Her dad nods, "You know the business isn't going anywhere."

He opens the door, and there on the ground, weeping, is Shannon, clutching an ugly silver figurine to her chest like a child.

Mel isn't sure why this stupid figurine has such a hold over her sister – it's supposed to affect those that have lost children, and Shannon has only ever had Isaac. As far as Mel knows, Isaac is still looking after Chip, and they're doing great; she called them earlier to double check.

"Do you have the salt?" Her dad asks, his eyes on his weeping daughter.

Mel digs in her purse and produces a very large box of table salt. She watches as he draws a circle around Shannon, who seems so caught up in her grief she doesn't notice that she's no longer alone in the room. For a moment, Mel almost feels bad for her, and then she shakes it off like a dog shaking water off its coat.

Shannon has done nothing to deserve her pity.

"The branches?"

Mel points wordlessly to where there are branches of prickly rose laid out across the bed.

Her dad nods, and strides over, picking them up and producing a knife from the inside pocket of his jacket. Without flinching, he cuts a line in his palm, and lets the blood that stems from it drip over the branches before he places them, one on each side of the circle. North and then East. South and then West.

It's an eerily familiar scene, something that her and father have been doing together for decades, and she knows that if she were to look at his palm, the ragged scar tissue there would mirror her own. It's been so long since she's performed Ritual magic, and the adrenaline of it is sitting at the base of her cervical spine, ready to spill. She likes doing it – she always has – she just hates the consequence. The smell. The healing hand. The fact that the Rituals she's paid to do are generally filled with shame and hate and blood.

Carter probably forgot the blood, she thinks suddenly, and it fills her with a mild disgust. The man has been dealing with this for how many years, and he's still too squeamish for blood? Laughable. Where does he think real power comes from? Certainly, he must be aware that all Ritual requires sacrifice, however small. Certainly, he must know that this particular Ritual requires mother's blood, and Shannon most definitely has some of her own kept around here somewhere, just in case it's needed. (It doesn't have to be fresh.)

Her dad holds out his unbloodied hand, and she takes it, stepping carefully to meet him at the North end of the circle. She produces her own small knife, and punctures a finger, letting a single drop fall to the salt.

Around them, the air feels electric with energy, and it courses through Mel's body, as if the blood she gave were still in her veins, and with it, the magic required for the Ritual. Her and her father become conduits, livewires, for just a sweet second and then it courses into her sister.

Shannon opens her mouth to let out a wail, and instead, a spirit falls out, full of tears. She is inky in her half-formed self, with long dark hair and eyes that are glassy with pain. The spirit looks out, towards Mel, towards the one with the blood that has tied her once again to her prison, and Mel's heart lurches.

"It's okay," Mel tells her, "your loss is unimaginable, but you must grieve for yourself."

Anger stirs in the spirit's eyes, and Mel is grateful for the salt and the roses that bind her in the circle. She would kill Mel if she could. She would kill them all.

Victor takes a deep breath. "Go now," he says, "you are no longer wanted here. Go back to your haunt."

The spirit's gaze turns once again into sorrow, and her mouth opens in a scream. Mel cannot imagine the pain she must be in, the pain she's forced to endure every day. She wishes they could fully banish her, so that she could have some peace but the Artifact that she's tied to, the challenge she presents buyers, is worth a high price. There's something about the pain of her loss that the buyers enjoy, and there's always one willing to take her, there's always one who thinks they can handle the darkness she brings. Often, they can't. Often, they suffer the same fate as Shannon would have if Mel and Victor didn't show up.

They watch as she sways, pulled back into the figurine, still pantomiming a scream.

As soon as they're sure she's safely contained once again, Victor breaks the salt circle, and snatches the figurine from his eldest daughter, who seems empty, slowly coming back to her body.

Mel opens the door, planning on yelling at Carter to come comfort his wife, and comes face to face with the gaunt little man.

"Thank you," he says, hurrying towards his wife, whispering all sorts of sweet things in her ears as if she didn't almost ruin everything for everyone in the room.

Mel looks on distastefully for a moment, thinking again about the time she used to love her sister, the ancient time when they used to get along. It was the time before Shannon had Isaac and subsequently abandoned him to her and their parents for the dream of law school. It was the time before they were both adults.

Victor stands to leave, the figurine balanced in his uninjured hand, and Mel leaves with him, not giving another glance to the two on the floor.

"I'll take care of it from here, Mel," her dad says, when they're free of the house, and she leans to give him a hug.

"Thanks, Dad," she says, softly. "When do you think you'll be around to visit your grandkids?"

He shrugs, "Soon," he says, and she knows the memories of Belle are bittersweet for him. He raised his family there, he lost his wife there, and the mountains remind him of her more than anything. He usually only comes home for holidays.

She chews on her lip for a second, before she nods, and they say goodbye at the gate. She climbs into her car, and rests her forehead against the steering wheel, ready to make the drive back to her hotel room, ready to sleep until morning when she'll be back at it again, driving back home. She's grateful her dad can help. She's grateful that he's dealing with Mr. Allan. She's grateful that she doesn't have to worry, and she hates her sister – for herself and for Isaac.

Her phone dings with a text, and she looks at it, wearily. It's Isaac, providing his mandatory goodnight report, telling her that everything is a-okay on the home front, making her feel a million times better.

Most of all, she hates Shannon for Isaac. She hates her for everything she's missed in his life, for the sweet kid he was, always willing to forgive her absence, always inviting her to his birthday parties and his school events. She hates Shannon for every letter he ever wrote her that's sitting unopened in the desk drawer in her upstairs office. She hates Shannon for every hope she ever gave him that one day she would be his mother. She hates Shannon for feeling like she lost something when she never even tried to have it in the first place.

Finally, she starts her car and heads back to her hotel room where Walt will wrinkle his nose at the smell of magic but let her sleep in the same bed anyways. Tomorrow, they'll be back home, and the business will be taken care of and her and Walt and the new baby and Chip will be under the same roof once again.

16
A LATTE LUST

Isaac has been in a daze for the last few days. He's relived the night Park stayed over so many times he can hardly remember what is real from what he's embellished. Park's hands, warm and strong, on his abdomen, on his chest, between his shoulder blades. Park's nose against his, the curve of it, the way they fit so well together.

He's trying to be practical about everything, trying to stay present so he can get his chores done, so he can get his grocery shopping done, so he doesn't accidentally drive off the road, but every time he lets his mind wander, Park is there. Park is there, nestled against him, sleeping on the couch, sleeping in his bed. Park is there, laughing with Chip, indulging his cousin's probing questions. Park is there, watching Isaac watch him, the hint of a smile tugging at the corners of his lips.

He's down bad. He's down *so* bad.

Two days have passed since he dropped Park off, back at his house, and the smell of him lingers on his pillows, on his blankets, in his car, and it's driving Isaac crazy. His thoughts are full of yearning and lust, and he's embarrassed for himself, for the magnitude of his feelings and the way everything plays back when he closes his eyes. *I'm young and I'm stupid and I should try to get my thoughts under control,* he tells himself, and then – and then he remembers brushing an arm across Park's back, the electricity of the unexpected touch.

He sighs in frustration and picks up his phone, checking for messages from Iris or Park or Eve or anyone to distract himself. There's a meeting tonight and Park is going to be there. Isaac is picking him up from work once again, and Iris is coming over after her shift so the three of them can talk some things through.

He makes the mistake of closing his eyes and Isaac's mind replays the moment that Park is looking at him as if he's just asked a question in another language, and his eyes are glassy, and Isaac's stomach is turning itself into knots because he's putting the pieces together and coming to the conclusion that nobody's taken the time to go slow for Park, that no one's given him the voice to set his boundaries.

This instance repeats in Isaac's mind more than anything else. The turn of Park's head away from him, his hands tight on his own knees, the far away look in his eyes, as if he's reliving something. He wants to ask Park about it, to dig further, but he's sure that it's something that Park will have to mention on his own, and Isaac will continue to ask for boundaries, to communicate to the best of his abilities. More than anything, he wants to be able to create a place where the two of them are comfortable with each other - with each other's bodies and with each other's expectations.

He wants - *oh god, how he wants* - Park's mouth back on his and he wants Park to do that thing with his tongue that made him squirm.

He checks his phone again and there's still nothing. Park told him this morning that he's working the early shift again, and Iris is also at work - appointments for tarot readings until five - and then she's closing the store. This leaves him alone with his thoughts until at least two-thirty.

He sits in his grandpa's old leather chair and plays with the corner of his phone case. He's been wondering about Mel too - she doesn't usually spend the night in the city when she goes for her doctor's appointments, and she most certainly doesn't come back stinking like Ritual magic. She's always tried to shelter him from the family business, but there's no amount of sheltering that can hide the rankness that follows someone around for days after a Ritual. There's no amount of sheltering from the anger that shadowed her face when he dropped Chip off.

Mel is only ever angry about one thing, and that is Isaac's mother. He'd been too scared to bring her up, but he's sure that's why she stayed in the city; to clean up another mess Shannon made. Shannon, his mother, absent for most of his life. If she's fucked up in the same way she had before, that means she'll be coming back to Belle, back to their family home, while she recovers, and Isaac desperately does not want either her or his father in his space.

The house he's in is the house he grew up in, for the most part. It's his grandparents, and he acts as its keeper - since his grandmother died, he's mostly alone in it, his grandfather hardly ever coming home - but when his parents come back to Belle, they stay in it with him, overwhelming him with their noise, their presence. The last time they came back Isaac needed to escape to the room that Mel keeps for him in her house - he used to spend more time there, when he was a teenager, when his grandma was dying, and his grandpa was becoming more distant – but this time he can't. Who will refill the bird feeders? Who will leave food out for his cat? Not his parents, that's for certain.

Neither of them is good at caring for anything other than themselves and each other, and they've made it clear to him time and time again. They handed him to Mel, to his grandparents, when he was just a baby, and they haven't looked back. His mother's career and her work in the family business, however terrible she may be at it, always come first and despite all the hope that Isaac used to have for them, it's never changed.

Even now, something deep in his chest is telling him that this time it will be different, that this time it will be better, but it won't be. He's been down this narrative before, too many times to count.

The only thing his parents are good for is money, and they seem to throw it at him just to make him go away. They don't care if he comes or if he goes. They don't care about anything that's happening in his life. They've made it crystal clear, and this time nothing will be different.

He checks his phone again. It's only been ten minutes.

He groans and lets his head fall back into the cushy leather. He should be thinking about the meeting tonight – about what their plan is, how they're going to move forward now that it's been a while and the Ghost hasn't continued its pursuit of Park, now that the *One who Falls* is looming over them like an uninvited dinner guest – but he can't because all he can think of is Park and Park's hands and Park's hands on him –

He is *insufferable.* He needs a hobby.

He has a hobby, it's just that art isn't feasible right now. He's tried, but all that comes out of his paintbrushes are blobs. Blobs that are intangible from other blobs, not even worth the title of abstract – his inspiration is dead in the water, and it has been for a long time. He hasn't painted anything in many, many years. Not like he used to. He used to be good at it, creating art like he was breathing. Everyday he'd have a new idea, a list in his note's app, of paintings he'd start and then half-finish and then paint over and start something else, something more fun. Sometimes he'd rapid-fire finish paintings, and they'd hang on his walls until he got sick of them. Sometimes he wouldn't pick up a brush for a week and there would be an ache in his stomach, a craving, a build-up of emotion that was begging to be released. If he thinks about it too much he can feel it, even now, even after so long. An ache that begs him to do something, to make something, but he – can't – he might never pick up a brush again, and that's okay. It's okay for now. If he makes something now, he's sure it will be an ode to Park's leg pressed against his, Park's amused half-smile, and he's not ready for that. That's too much, even for him.

He wonders if Park is thinking about him, too. Maybe he's distracted at work. Maybe he's seeing Isaac's face every time he closes his eyes. No, *no*, he's not going to imagine that. It's a line of thought that is just going to make him insecure. It's a line of thought that will make him second guess himself and he can't do that. He shouldn't do that. Park clearly likes Isaac, and that's what he's been showing Isaac with his emotions and his actions and his words and that's all Isaac needs to worry about.

He swallows and wonders if it would be a terrible idea to camp out in Pippa's, just so he can see Park again. He could bring a notebook and sit in the corner seat that he and Iris used to study at a million years ago when they had something to study for. He could write out his thoughts on the One who Falls, and he could do it all while being within Park's proximity.

He would only be there for an hour and a half. He could tell Park that it's all part of the plan, that Iris felt the Ghost somewhere near by and they wanted someone around just in case, but he's certain that's a lie Park would see right through. Maybe Park would think he's crazy, maybe Park would reconsider, would wonder what it is he's getting himself into.

He doesn't want to come across as overbearing. He doesn't want to come across as desperate. He's just excited, and he can't wait until 2:30.

He lets out another deep groan and presses his hands into his temples.

He'll just go outside. He'll drive around town for a bit, clear his head. He'll get to play music and think while he's moving instead of while he's sitting still and maybe that'll make everything better.

***

Pippa's is empty when Isaac steps through the door half an hour early because driving did not clear his head as much as he hoped it would and the thought of going back to his house for the measly amount of time he'd have before he would have to pick up Park is nauseating. Still, he feels a shiver of anxiety run down his back, worried that maybe Park will think he's being clingy. Being weird.

Park is leaning against the counter with his back turned to the entrance, talking with Riley. The two of them turn their attention to the door, and Isaac sees Park straighten when he realizes it's him. For a moment, Isaac waits for his daydreams to come crashing down, waits for Park's face to become cloudy, waits for proof that he's embellished a little too much into his memories, but Park smiles instead.

"Hey!" He says, brightly, and Isaac notices Riley smirking behind him.

"Hi," Isaac replies, relieved and excited all in one. "I – um –" He had a plan. He came up with a plan while he was driving but it slipped completely from his mind the second Park looked at him.

"You're early," Park says, but he's smiling slyly, like he's pleased Isaac is here.

"I was so bored at home," Isaac complains, "I went for a drive, but it ended early and now there's no point in going back until you're off."

Park's hands come together in front of him, and he looks away quickly, and then over his shoulder at Riley, who only raises their eyebrows. "Oh," Park says, focusing back on Isaac, and Isaac realizes that he must feel put on the spot. "We haven't been super busy today; I might be able to slip out ten minutes early."

Isaac nods. "Okay," he says. "I can - I can come back -" He half turns his body to leave, but Park is shaking his head.

"No, no," he says, "that's not – no, we're not busy. Stay. *Please* stay. Please order a coffee so we have something to do. Riley's cleaned everything twice already."

"Three times," Riley pipes up, wringing a tea towel in their hands, "I'm on three now." They pointedly avoid eye contact with Isaac, and he swallows. He hasn't talked to Riley in years – they used to be in the school council together. They'd always been pleasant with one another, but not close. Rilley was better friends with Eve.

Park's face breaks out into a reassuring grin. "See?" He says, and then, "Whatcha want? On the house."

He shrugs, tasting stomach acid at the back of his throat. He's never been this nervous around anyone in his entire life. How much does Riley know? What can Isaac say in front of them that won't embarrass him, won't embarrass Park? Is he allowed to flirt? Can they flirt publicly? "Whatever you like to make," he says, and Park rolls his eyes.

"No, really," he says, "what's your order?" He's leaning forward, over the counter, his thumbs hooked under the edge, leveraging himself. Isaac can see the veins in his hands, and he has to tear his eyes away.

"Vanilla latte with double espresso," Isaac says, and Park's stupid grin tells Isaac that Park noticed Isaac's looking. "With oat milk."

Park's grin gets even wider, taking up the entirety of his face. "Gay," he says, and Isaac lets out a chuckle. Park looks up at him from under his eyelashes, like this is exactly what he wanted out of Isaac, like he could tell Isaac is tense, and he wanted him to let loose. Just a little. "Coming right up."

Riley clears their throat from behind Park, and Isaac's eyes find them, but their glance flicks away, uncomfortable. "I - uh, the bathrooms. I'm going to clean the bathrooms," they say, throwing their tea towel on the counter and swinging their arms back and forth.

Park watches them go, amusedly. "You make them awkward," he says, pressing the espresso. "I've never seen them shut up like that."

"I don't know why," Isaac admits. He's never done anything that he can think of that should make Riley awkward around him. They've always been friendly.

"I'll ask them later." Park seems to be adding art to Isaac's latte, and Isaac resists the urge to lean over to see it better.

"Fancy," he breathes, and Park's grin comes back.

"I'm learning," he says, and he hands the drink to Isaac, their hands brushing for the briefest moment, making Isaac's heart much louder in his chest. "Try it."

Isaac raises his eyebrows, *impatient much?* but he takes a sip. It's very good. Probably the best latte he's ever had. "The leaf is a little off center," he says, but he's smiling.

"Is it," Park deadpans, leaning forward, still amused. Isaac likes the way his apron bunches around his waist, his arms, the watch on his wrist.

"Yeah. Milk could be frothier."

"Oh, come on," Park complains, grabbing a to-go cup lid and tossing it at Isaac like a frisbee, and Isaac only narrowly avoids it, suppressing his laughter. "Next time I'll give you drip coffee."

"Rude," Isaac muses, taking another sip and licking foam from his upper lip. "It's actually amazing. Thank you." He doesn't want Park to have any doubts.

Park nods, his gaze centered on Isaac's lips, for one second, two seconds, three, until a loud crash sounds from the bathroom, followed by a frustrated *are you fucking kidding me?* that Isaac doesn't think they were supposed to hear. Park glances towards the bathrooms, frowning, and then gestures for the cup lid. "Can you pass me that?" he asks, distracted.

Their hands brush against each other once again, and Isaac wants so desperately for Park to be off his shift so he can take him back to his house for some privacy before Iris comes over. He wants to resume where they had left off the other day, all hands and mouths and blurred vision.

Park's attention has settled once again on Isaac, and he sighs. "Iris scares me a little bit," he admits.

"Yeah," Isaac says, "she's a little intense sometimes. She has the best intentions, though."

Park shrugs. "I'm sure we'll get along in time, I just – she just is intimidating. Intense, like you said." He's picks at his watch strap absently, looking at something just over Isaac's shoulder. "She seems more – distant – than you or the others."

Isaac nods. "She's much more introverted." Quiet. Observant.

"And she's so powerful."

"She won't hurt you."

"No, no, I'm not worried about that. I just feel a little bit out of my element around her, you know?"

The door to one of the bathrooms opens, startling Isaac, and they both turn to watch Riley lug their cleaning supplies into the second bathroom, shoulders hunched in annoyance.

"I get it," Isaac hums, returning to Park's question, amused. "I feel like that sometimes, too." He's almost done with his latte, and he puts it down on the counter so that he doesn't keep the same pace and give himself a stomach-ache.

Park scrunches his nose. "When does it –" He's interrupted by the door opening. He looks back over Isaac's shoulder, offering a customer service hello, which lose its cheeriness halfway through.

Isaac turns to see Cadence coming in, her smile only faltering for a moment when she sees him. "Hey," he says, and she nods. Their moment of peace is gone, and with it, Park's question.

"Must be quiet today?" She asks Park, and he groans.

"You have no idea," he complains, and she sighs. "But, hey, it'll only be quiet for a couple more hours. They'll start pouring in again."

"Will they?" She asks over her shoulder as she disappears into the staff room.

Park checks his watch, and mouths, *ten more minutes* to Isaac just as Riley spills out of the second bathroom, looking annoyed and flustered at the same time.

"The last toilet is plugged again," they grumble, blowing their hair out of their face. "I'm not calling Sky this time."

"Not even if it gives you something to do?" Park asks, his voice as sweet as honey. "I hate calling her."

"I just cleaned the bathrooms!" Riley says, taking their cleaning supplies into the staff room and re-emerging a second later. "And I called her last time."

"I'll do it," Cadence calls out, "I'm by the phone anyways."

Both Park and Riley sigh in relief, and Isaac gives Park an amused look.

"Our manager is a nightmare," he says, "she's always high and she can't take anything seriously to save her life. It took her two months to call a plumber the last time we had this problem."

"Yikes," Isaac breathes, and Park nods.

"Yeah," he says. "But I suppose she's nice enough. I can't complain too much." He checks his watch and it's only been two minutes.

Isaac knows it's only been two minutes because he's been checking the clock on the wall across from him.

"Just go," Riley says, smirking. "Tell Sky you had a family emergency or something, if she asks."

"She won't ask."

Riley raises their eyebrows in a *yeah exactly dumbass* kind of way, and Park looks at Isaac, wordlessly. Isaac swallows, trying not to look too hopeful.

"Jesus fucking Christ you two," Riley says, exasperated. "Just go rip each others' clothes off. Seriously. Please. You're killing me, here."

Park immediately flushes, looking down at his feet, and it's Isaac's turn to smirk. "Can't say no to that, can you?" He asks, and Park opens his mouth, and then closes it again.

"Asshole," he mutters, Isaac isn't certain to whom, and disappears to take off his apron.

Riley and Isaac are left alone in the front, and it's *awkward*. Isaac could cut the tension in the air with a dull butterknife. Even so, he resists the urge to pull out his phone.

"How - ?" he starts, about to ask Riley how they've been doing, but Riley cuts him off.

"He really likes you," they say, "like he *really* likes you."

Isaac blinks at Riley, waiting for a lecture. This must be why Riley's been so weird towards him - they must think that Isaac is only doing what he did in high school. He stuffs his hands in his jacket pockets and nods. "I know," he says, pauses, and then adds, "I really like him too."

"Good."

Isaac looks up, shocked that there isn't more, but Riley is already moving on to scrub out the sink, their tea towel back over their shoulder. He doesn't have time to think about their interaction, though, before Park is rounding the corner, his apron replaced with the hoodie that Isaac lent him that first night at the river.

"Let's go," he singsongs, this time opening the door for Isaac, who follows him out after a quick goodbye aimed at Riley.

Park stays at the door for a second, calling his own goodbyes, and Isaac continues to the car, heart hammering in his chest because he's about to have Park alone again, and he's been dreaming about this for the past few days, for the past few nights.

He unlocks his car, and opens the passenger seat door, waiting for Park. Park bundles himself inside, and Isaac closes the door behind him, hurrying around to the drivers' side.

"I can't wait to kiss you again," says Park, immediately after they're alone, and Isaac's entire body turns to flame. "I can't stop thinking about it."

"Me either," Isaac admits.

"Better drive fast then."

And Isaac does.

✳✳✳

They fall through Isaac's front door, mouths hot on each other, hands grasping and pushing and pulling. Isaac had tried to wait until they were in the house, he really had, but Park was standing next to him, smiling, and he just couldn't. His house key had gotten tangled up in his jacket and he'd dropped it, and the tension was too much.

Park trips over a shoe, and falls closer into Isaac, pushing Isaac into the door and the door into the wall, which is probably not good news for the wall, but Isaac can't bring himself to care. He maneuvers Park further into the house and closes the door with his foot, wincing only a little when it slams. Their mouths don't leave each other as they navigate taking shoes off, and then Isaac's hands are at the bottom of Park's hoodie.

"Okay?" He breaks the kiss to ask, and Park nods, taking it off, taking Isaac's jacket off, and then they're kissing again, all mouths and breathy little noises, and hands exploring bodies. Park slides his hands under Isaac's shirt like he had the first time, and Isaac's breath catches in his throat as Park's fingers dig into his back. He presses forward, moving them so he has Park pinned against the wall, one hand behind his head, the other under his shirt, pressed to his abdomen.

He deepens the kiss, sliding his tongue into Park's mouth, pushing forward even more so their bodies are completely flush against each other.

"Jesus," Park breathes, his voice so soft, "I could do this all day."

Isaac pulls back for a second, drinking in the sight of Park, his pupils so huge there's almost no blue left in his eyes, his mouth red and swollen and parted just a little, kiss-drunk, and so incredibly *hot.*

"Let's do it," Isaac breathes, and Park's lips turn up in a smile.

"Let's do *more,*" he says, and Isaac nods.

"Yeah, okay," he retorts, fingers climbing up Park's abdomen, "you've convinced me."

✳✳✳

Isaac is laying in his bed, on his side, tracing Park's jaw with his fingers, and Park is watching him. He blinks, lazily, and then he leans down to

126

bring the blankets up around them both. The sheen of sweat that was on his skin is drying and it's leaving him cold.

Park gives a small noise of approval and pushes himself closer to Isaac, pressing their legs together and reaching up to rest his hand on Isaac's ribs. He looks like he's going to say something, but then changes his mind, choosing instead to pull himself even closer, so their heads are on the same pillow, so their noses are almost touching.

Isaac adjusts the blanket, giving Park full shoulder coverage, and then lets his hand wrap around him at the waist. "You okay?" He asks softly, closing the distance between their faces and touching their foreheads together.

"Yeah," Park whispers, "I'm more than okay."

"Good," Isaac says, whispering too. Something feels sacred about this moment, as if they speak louder, they'll ruin whatever it is they're sharing. "Me too."

There's silence for a moment, just the two of them, breathing together, and then Park flips and nestles into Isaac's chest, pulling his arm around him and holding his hand at his chest. "You make me feel safe," he says, and Isaac wonders if he was supposed to hear the words, they'd been that quiet.

He doesn't answer, just in case, instead leaning down to press a kiss to Park's shoulder. *You make me feel like I have a purpose*, he wants to say, but he's not sure if that's too much too soon. It's only been a week, and already Park has him so wrapped around his finger it's pathetic. If Park asks him to jump, he will jump. If Park asks him to drive, he will drive. If Park asks him to do that thing with his teeth, he will do that thing with his teeth. He *likes* to do that thing with his teeth.

"I never want to get up," he says, finally, and Park nods.

"Can we cancel tonight?" he asks, turning so he can look at Isaac from over his shoulder, pressing further into him. "Please?"

Isaac sighs. "I want to," he says, and he *does*, but this is maybe the one thing he won't do for Park. They need to regroup. To come up with a plan.

"But you can't." Park relaxes back into the pillows, into the embrace. "I guess I'll just have to come back home with you so we can do it again."

Isaac's heart kickstarts in his chest at the thought of having Park back in his bed later tonight. At the thought of having Park in his bed again, *all night.* "Yes," he says, so fast he almost chokes on the word.

There's a pleased chuckle from Park, and it reverberates through Isaac, warm and hearty, and so so *so* beautiful. Isaac wants to feel it again. "I don't work tomorrow, either."

"I'll make you breakfast," Isaac says, immediately. "What do you like?" He really loves breakfast. It's his best meal for cooking, by far, and he wants nothing more than to share this with Park. "I can do French toast, or pancakes, or – waffles? I think I still have the waffle maker."

Park sits in quiet contemplation for a second, running his thumb along the length of Isaac's, and making Isaac's arm thrum with electricity. Park is good at this, at forming connection and giving Isaac goosebumps, and making his veins sing that he's alive, he's alive, he's alive. "Waffles?" Park asks.

"Fuck yeah, my favourite." And they *are.*

Park lets out a breath at Isaac's excitement, and there's quiet for another moment.

Isaac closes his eyes, and nestles his cheek against Park's spine, trying not to think about the fact that they do still have to get up, trying not to think that they've maybe spent just a little bit too much time in bed, and that Iris's car should be pulling into the driveway any second now. He's trying not to think about how the two of them fit together so well, how the two of them had just done what they did and it was the best of Isaac's life. The way that Park worked to get Isaac's breath catching in his throat, and to get him to release the stupidly embarrassing noise that he knows he makes.

Park had seemed to like the noise, seemed to make it his mission to get it from Isaac as much as possible, and Isaac hadn't been as embarrassed as he normally would have. Something about Park's enthusiasm had made it better – in fact, Isaac hadn't been as embarrassed about anything as he normally would have. The way Park looked at him when he'd taken his shirt off, lips half-parted, eyes three shades darker with want, it hadn't left any room for embarrassment about his body, or about the clumsiness of his hands, out of practice.

Park lets go of Isaac's hand and Isaac almost reaches for it again, but Park flips himself back over, so they're facing each other again.

"When does it start to feel normal?" He asks, and Isaac looks down at him, confusedly.

"When does what start to feel normal?" He tries to clarify, and Park shakes his head, reaching up to trace one of Isaac's worried eyebrows. Isaac's mind immediately went to them, together, but it doesn't seem that close to home, and he lets Park's fingers push the tension out of his face, waiting for an explanation.

"The magic. The pull of it. I can - sometimes I can feel it like it's in my bones." They haven't really talked about Hell Club, mostly talking about themselves, taking turns asking each other to divulge something that they wouldn't know yet. They've talked about Isaac's parents and Park's parents, and Chip, and the stray cat, and Park's co-workers and C, and the restless monster inside Isaac that wants to leave, to get out, about Park's loneliness and Isaac's inability to paint. They've talked about ex-lovers and Isaac's promiscuity and Park's year-long encounter with a man in his mid-twenties when he was only seventeen. Isaac has complained about his struggle with cigarettes, and Park's told him about how C's only concern with him was his addiction.

All this, and they've been skirting around the edge of what brought them together in the first place. The thing that thrums through them like a livewire - the magic of their curse. The lifeblood of the Ghost.

Isaac closes his eyes, sinking into the feeling of Park against him, breathing steadily, waiting for his answer. The truth is that it's always felt normal to Isaac. He's been a gear in the mechanics of the Ghost his whole life, he just wasn't aware of it until he read the Prophecies. It's something to do with the empathy and something to do with Iris - the empathy means he's been absorbing the magic through energy since he could feel emotions, which is why he's such a great conduit for it, and Iris has been by his side since they could walk, adding her own magic, getting under his skin.

"You're thinking so hard," Park muses, and Isaac doesn't open his eyes.

"You asked me a hard question," he retorts, and Park lets out a breath of amused air.

"I didn't think it would be," he apologizes, and Isaac opens just one eye.

"What does it feel like to you?" He asks, and Park stops tracing his eyebrow, his eyes cloudy with thought.

"Like I've joined a cult. Like there's something inside of me breathing with me, like there's a part of me that I'm not in control of."

"Oh." He shuts his eye once again, trying to locate the part of him that feels like that, and coming up short. When he opens them, Park is looking at him with a gaze so intense he wishes he could look away. He doesn't. The back of his neck bristles with fear that isn't his own, and his arms tighten around Park, instinctively. "Does it scare you?" He asks, even though he knows the answer.

"Yes."

"Why?" There are a hundred good reasons Park could give Isaac and Isaac would believe any one of them.

Park swallows loudly, pressing his face into Isaac's chest, to avoid eye contact, to avoid the level of vulnerability that saying it directly to Isaac's face brings. Isaac doesn't blame him. "I can't control it," he whispers, "I don't know how it ends."

Isaac presses his cheek into Park's curls, presses his fingertips into the bare skin of Park's back. He wants to reassure Park that it won't hurt him, that he'll protect him, but the truth is that it's already tried to hurt him and Isaac alone won't be able to protect him from it. Isaac alone is not powerful enough to do anything against the Ghost, none of them are. That's why they're together. That's why they've all been chosen - because together they stand a chance. *Together we stand a chance,* he reminds himself. "To me," he starts, his voice muffled against Park's hair, "it feels like a connectedness. Like learning how to trust."

"Is that what I should do?" Park asks, pushing out from Isaac's embrace, so he can look at him again. "Trust?"

Park doesn't seem like he's talking about magic anymore.

Isaac opens his mouth to tell him that trust is earned, that he desperately wants to earn Park's, when the front door opens downstairs, and Iris announces her presence.

"Fuck," Isaac says, instead, and Park recoils from the harshness of it. "Give us a minute!" he yells, hopefully loud enough for her to hear, and then he returns his full attention back to Park. "That's up to you," he whispers, "but I hope you will - trust - I mean, trust me." He feels warmth in his cheeks, and wants to look away again, but can't.

Park's eyes are burning bright, full of something hidden, and Isaac can't help it, he dips into Park's feelings, letting them wash over him. It isn't trust, it's something more like hope. Something more like a spark into a pile of dry tinder, just waiting to be turned into a blaze. "I think that's up to you, too, isn't it?" Park questions, and Isaac nods.

"Yes." Isaac hopes that Park sees it in him, the need to prove himself. The need to be trustworthy. The need to treat Park right. The desire to curl around him and encourage him to grow, to learn, to change. The desire to know Park like the back of his hand, to smother him in kisses, to learn how to lean on each other when they need to.

"Isaac?" Iris yells up the stairs, "I'm about to break into your cupboards."

Their moment is ruined, Park sitting up and the blankets falling to his waist. Wordlessly, he passes Isaac his shirt, and pulls his own over his head.

"Go for it!" Isaac yells down the stairs, watching Park's muscles stretch and contract as he pushes himself out of the bed, digging on the floor for his underwear and pants, throwing Isaac's at him.

They get dressed without saying another word, and Isaac thinks that maybe Park is angry with him - why he does not know - until they're in the doorway of his room and Park reaches out, touches his arm, stops him in his tracks.

"I think I understand," he says, and Isaac raises his eyebrows at him, asking him to expand. "I mean, I think I understand the connection part of what you said. It's like I'm woven into a bigger picture."

Isaac nods. "Yes," he says, "exactly."

"And you're not scared of it?"

"I'm scared of losing it." Losing it means losing what he's been working towards for so long. It means losing something that brings his friends together. It means change.

Park's gaze softens for a moment, a spot of tenderness, and then he says, "Iris is going to be annoyed if we take any longer," and the two of them are heading down the stairs, ready for Iris and ready for food and ready for the meeting.

17

WHY THE DARK IS FILLED WITH TERROR

C hasn't gone on a run for several days. It's been too cold, or she's been too busy with her homework and her extra-curriculars, which mostly include telling her parents she's in extra-curriculars and finding new places to read where they won't find her. Her favourite place right now is Pippa's while Park is working because neither of their parents want to disturb him.

She would feel guilty about the lie, but sometimes she just needs time to be alone. She just needs time to sink into a book and forget about the world. Besides, she *is* in cross-country running, technically, but she never shows up to practices because she's not as good as the rest of the kids on the team. They're much faster than her, and despite the coach's insistence that the team is for all levels, she can't handle the embarrassment of always being last.

She hasn't been running the last few days so she hasn't been taking note of the new writings at Old John's fence, and she's sure it must have changed at least once by now. John usually changes them weekly, and the last one, *isn't it that we all die? i think that's it, what it is,* had been new nearly a fortnight ago. It's been haunting her, like none of the others have. The ones that came before were simpler, easier to breakdown the meaning. *Look up, the end cometh,* and *guard what you call your own,* and *stay away from the river when she sings.* It's usually doomsday, not existentialism, and C so badly wants to know if he's going to continue down the same road.

She's tuned into his radio channel the last two nights, but all that's playing is static, and she's starting to get the creeping feeling that something bad has happened, though she can't give it a name.

As she approaches the property, the creeping feeling settles heavily in her chest and the hairs on her arms raise. She gets the urge to look over her shoulder, and when she does there is nothing but the empty road behind her, neither comforting nor creepy. She slows down to a walk and rubs her nose on her sleeve, ready for whatever it is that's about to occur. Maybe it's the magic that Old John's been talking about. Maybe it's the magic that Kat has been warning her about.

132

There's a presence in the air and she feels it like she usually does when there's wildlife. It's foreboding thrumming through her saying, *danger, danger, danger, you're in danger, you are not alone.*

She takes out her headphones and there's no sound but the gurgling river, just out of view. There aren't any sounds coming from the highway, just around the corner, and all the birds have stopped their calls to each other. Even the wind has stopped blowing, and the air hangs heavy around her, suffocating. Buzzing. Electric.

Taking her phone out of her pocket, she brings up her brother's contact, about to press call, just in case, when she sees the fence.

It's a new quote, unfinished. *Evil doers beware the time is,* with an ugly streak of white paint arcing upwards, like Old John had been startled halfway through his thought.

C cautiously moves forward, the bad feeling in her gut creeping out to encompass her whole body with every step. Everything in her is screaming to run, to leave, but she keeps going forwards until she sees blackened grass at the bottom of the ditch, like a fire was lit and stomped out. She keeps going until she notices the open paint cans, the paint brush still propped up in one, tacky and matte and full of bits of grass as it dries out. She cranes her neck to better see into the ditch, the dark marks, and she sees the spray paint can, laying forgotten just a foot away from the fence, a small spray of white through the grass.

Something terrible has happened here. Old John has never left a mess at his fence, nor has he left a message incomplete. Something *terrible* has happened here.

The feeling in her gut turns to dread as she looks around, still seeing nothing. No one. The house of Old John is empty, and the road is empty, and the highway is empty and Old John's yard is empty. She is alone. She is completely alone.

She presses call on Park's contact, hoping that maybe he'll have an idea on what to do. Should she call the cops? Would they even care? She doubts it, but she can't leave without doing *something.* How long has Old John's property sat like this without anyone else noticing? How long ago did this terrible thing happen and not a single person has done anything about it.

"Hey," Park says softly on the other side of the line, and a small part of her dread lessens.

"Something's wrong," she says, her hand that isn't holding her phone balling into a fist. She listens as Park tells someone to be quiet in the background, and then there's a chair scraping across the floor.

"Tell me what and where," he says, "we're coming."

She opens her mouth to tell him not to, that she just needs to know what it is she should do, but Kat's words echo in her head from when she'd asked about Isaac – *witches,* Kat had called Isaac and Iris, as if she wasn't also a witch. She had refused to elaborate, but maybe if Park is with Isaac, he'll have some insight into what it is that's happened. "You're with Isaac?" she asks, and Park hums in the affirmative.

There's more background noise from his side of the line, another voice, probably Isaac, asking what's going on, and Park asks her again where she is, what's happening.

"I don't know," she says, truthfully, her eyes finding Old John's house again, the door of it open and gaping like the mouth of a monster. Her fingers dig into her palms, hard, and there's something rising in her throat that tastes like bile. She's sure that the door was closed, only moments ago. "I'm at Old John's house. There's something wrong – I don't know what."

Muffled, Park relays the information back to Isaac, and then to her, he says, "Hold on, C. Iris wants to talk to you."

Before she can answer, Iris is on the phone. "Don't go *anywhere,*" she's saying, her voice dead serious. "Don't *move.* Don't look behind you. We're coming right away."

C swallows and a chill runs through her. "Please hurry," she squeaks, still watching the open door. There is something there now, something black and big and gathering at the entrance, seeping out like a stain over the outside of the house, pulsing and creeping.

"C?" It's Park again, his voice reassuring, steady. "You're going to be fine, okay? We're in the car. We're coming."

"Tell whoever's driving to go faster," she says, and then smaller, *"please."*

The darkness is still moving, and C can't look away. She swallows the bile in her throat again, and Park says something to her, but she can't bring herself to reply. The darkness has completely consumed the house now, and it's still gathering, it's still growing. It's moving towards her, bringing with it a putrid stench, like deadfall and the riverbed at Springtime, like death and rebirth and rotting. She wants to step back, to step away from it, but she's frozen to the ground as it becomes bigger than the house.

Her phone drops from her hands as the smell overwhelms her, and she covers her nose and her mouth, praying for the first time in a long time. *Please, God, don't let this be the end. Please, God, I'm sorry, I'll be better. Please, God, I don't want to die. Please, God, don't let me die.* A constant stream of thought, of terrified begging. She feels her knees give way beneath her fear, and they hit the pavement with muffled pain – she can't feel anything. She can't think anything except *Please, God, please* - and the thing keeps coming and keeps coming and keeps coming. It gets closer and closer and closer, not forming any shape, but somehow getting bigger, consuming everything that it touches, until it, too, is darkness, void of anything at all.

Something settles behind her, and she wants to turn, she wants to look at it, she wants to know what her death will look like, but she heeds Iris's warning. She doesn't look back. She doesn't look back. She wants to look back – she's fighting the urge with everything she has – *Please, God, not now, please* – and then there's the distant rumbling of a car engine, accelerating towards her and her heart leaps in her chest, but only for a moment.

The darkness is at the fence now, ten feet away, and it's all she can see in front of her. Her eyes are open, but it's dark as if she's been blindfolded, and it's cold, the stench all-consuming. Where there hadn't been noise before, is now a humming, dark and deep and so intricate she can feel it in her bones. She can feel it calling to her.

Cecelia, the humming is saying, *Cecelia, I'm hungry, I'm hungry, come with me, come with me, feed me, feed me, feed me, Cecelia, you're the only one, Cecelia Cecelia Cecelia C C C C C feed me.*

"Cecelia!" and this time it's not from the void in front of her, but her brother, and she turns, finally, to see him spilling out of the passenger side door of a red car, a blur of black hair and limbs. Isaac and Iris are also there, on the other side, Iris with her face lifted, a perfect mirror image of Kat, speaking words under her breath. Isaac's hands are open at his sides, and his eyes are fixed on the darkness, angry.

She looks back to the void in front of her, the humming turned into crackling that makes her think of static, electric, and dark, and even closer to her now. If she breathes, she will be breathing in its darkness, so she holds her breath.

Cecelia, it hums, *C, come with me, C. I can give you a place to belong, I can give you peace, I can give you God, come with me C, feed me, and love me, be fed, and be loved. I can mend you, I can –*

A loud screeching starts, like screaming but higher pitched and more terrible. It's coming from in front of her, from behind her, from all around her. She wants to cover her ears, but she can't, and she can't move. She watches as the void starts to crumble into itself, starts to become light again, and then all at once it is gone, and she blinks.

Park is beside her in an instant, his hands on her shoulders, worry written wildly all over his face. "Are you okay?" He's asking, and she wants to say yes, yes she's okay, yes everything is fine, but in some way she thinks she's just seen the end of everything she knows and that is very much not okay.

"No," she croaks out, and then she pulls from his grip and vomits clear bile onto the side of the road, the taste acrid and disgusting in her mouth, mixing with the smell the thing left lingering in the air, making breathing miserable.

"We have to go," another voice is saying, Iris, C thinks, *"now."*

C looks up to see Iris, pointing at Old John's house where there's more of the dark thing gathering at the door, and then C is on her feet, pulling at Park to get up too, grabbing her phone. Her feet are moving before her brain tells them to – fight or flight *or freeze,* and this time she's choosing flight – and she's first to the car, pulling on the back door desperately, wanting it to be unlocked, wanting to get as far from this place as she can, wanting her warm blankets and her warm bed and – *holy fuck, it's even bigger this time.* Her eyes have found the darkness again, and it's pooling out of the house like a cut artery, spilling everywhere, consuming all the light.

"Um," she says, but Iris and Isaac haven't come back to the car.

"Get in," Park says, unlocking the door from the passenger side.

She opens the door, but keeps her eyes on Isaac and Iris, side by side, Iris speaking words clearly, words that don't sound like words, and Isaac open beside her, both glowing like they're caught in the setting sun. The darkness that has amassed in front of them wilting like a dry bouquet, folding once again into itself, and C hears its dying screams just as clear as she had the last.

Shocked, she falls into the car and closes the door behind her, hardly registering the booster-seat, or the sharp smell of man and cigarette smoke. "What," she says, blinking at her brother, who seems more concerned than surprised, "the *fuck* just happened?"

Park sighs, and through the windshield C watches the glow fade from the two witches, watches them turn back to the car, both of their faces drawn tight with exhaustion, with worry. "I'll let them tell you," Park says, and C feels like she might be sick again.

When Kat told her about magic, when she heard about it from Old John, she only ever half-believed it. Despite her curiosity, she didn't really think it could be real, not on this level. Not something like – *that.* Kat seems harmless, with her herbs and her rocks and her wordy spells, so she thought... she thought that was the extent of it. *Witches,* she thinks as Isaac and Iris get into the car. She understands now, why Kat had said it like they were different.

She can only look at them when they introduce themselves, wide-eyed and open-mouthed, feeling like a fool and looking like a fish.

"You have to tell her everything," Park is telling Isaac as he turns the car around on the road, and she meets his eyes in the rear-view mirror.

"We're going to tell you everything," Iris says from beside her, and she turns to her, their shoulders pressed together with the proximity of the car. Iris looks exactly like her sister, so C doesn't feel as bad when she hisses,

"You *better.*"

18

THE DARK AND OTHER ANIMALS THAT BITE

The magic in Iris is still bubbling, and she feels restless, but she's unable to do anything about it. When she's like this, the energy still flowing through her veins and bones and sinew it's hard for her to do anything properly. She volunteered to make tea for everyone, but Isaac shot her a look that read *you'll break my mugs, no thank you,* and so now instead of being helpful she's sitting in his grandfather's chair in the study, listening to Isaac and Park whisper to each other in the kitchen.

She's trying to be nicer to Park, but she can tell that she scares him. Intimidates him. He wears the same expression that so many people – men – wear when they meet a powerful woman. It's not that she thinks he's misogynistic, it's more that she's acutely aware of how being a woman with power shifts others' perceptions of her. It's more that it's easier for her to be cold with new people because that's what they expect. There's a reason *bitch* and *witch* only differ by a single letter.

Really, though, she's going to be warmer. The love she has for Isaac and his growing fondness of Park and the secret he hoards in himself require it. Besides, he seems like he's a good man. A sweet man. A slightly confused and lonely man, but no lonelier or more confused than Isaac is. No lonelier or more confused than Iris is.

She tries to listen to their conversation, but they're talking quiet enough that she can't pick up on anything but the clink of spoons and the whistle of the kettle cutting through the air.

Cecelia, C, has excused herself to the bathroom, but she's been gone for several more minutes than Iris would think is normal, and Iris is starting to become worried. C is friends with her sister, with Kat, and she's sure C's upstairs on the phone asking Kat questions right now. The two have been thick as thieves in the past week, and Kat and Iris aren't close enough for Kat to tell her anything about their friendship. For all Iris knows, Kat could have told C about everything – the magic, the Ghost, the Prophecies – and then C will bear the weight of the Hell Club just like the rest of them, chosen by the Ghost itself.

She should have gotten Isaac to make sure Park told his family to stay away from Old John's house. She should have known that if the

Ghost couldn't get Park it would go for the next best thing, the thing that would make him hurt the most.

She settles further into the chair, letting the plush leather swallow her. She draws her knees into her chest, still hot with magic, still not wanting to risk burning something or breaking something. Isaac's house is as familiar to her as her own home, and she would hate to wreck anything. She would hate for the weird sense of unfamiliarity hanging in the air to keep permeating.

It's different now. Now that Park is involved. Now that there are only a handful of Prophecies left – it's all looming over her like a shadow, ready to descend. *The One who Falls* must be near, which means the rest of the End must be near too.

She's dreading the *One who Falls*. Her and Dahlia have talked about it in length and they've decided that if there's time, if they're able to, they'll jump themselves, to save someone else from the Club, to save *anyone* else. Isaac and Park and her got to C just in time, she thinks, just in time to avoid a last-ditch running attempt to get the Ghost to take her instead.

She's not sure she would have done it, anyways. She's not sure she's as selfless as she likes to think, and her mother's disappearance is always hanging over her, an inch above her head, ready to remind her that no one comes back from the Ghost. Not really. Not for forever.

Isaac and Park enter the study, each of them carrying two mugs of tea, and Iris uncurls herself from the chair, graciously accepting hers from Isaac.

"You okay?" He asks, lingering by her for a moment, his hair tousled and his mouth pinched with worry.

"Yeah," she says, pressing her tea to her chest, relishing its heat. The magic under her skin makes it hotter than it should be, but it doesn't bother her. "I'm fine."

Isaac lingers for another moment, like he's about to say something else, but then thinks better of it and joins Park on the couch, across from her.

"Where's C?" Park asks, suspicion sneaking into his tone, and Iris looks over at him, unsure if the suspicion is directed at her or C.

"Washroom," she says, softly, reminding herself that he is just as scared and worried as she is. That he is probably more scared and worried than she is, and that she has to be nice to him. She's trying to get him to trust her, after all. She's trying to be his friend.

Park nods, and sits back, his leg pressed against Isaac, and a surge of love for her friend washes into her. Isaac is a rock that she can lean on, and Park is learning he can too.

"What do we do now?" Isaac asks, glancing at Park longingly, before looking back to Iris. "I – I think there was more darkness in that house. I don't think – I don't think we got it all."

"We didn't," Iris confirms, and then the shadow is looming in front of her again. According to the records she has, her mom's journals, the Ghost doesn't usually start taking people until it's given Hell Club a solid chance to stop it. The Ghost likes to play with its food before it eats, and what's the point of rushing it? It likes to take pleasure in the chase, in the slow descent into madness. There must be something else happening. Something under the surface that they can't see yet. "We have to figure out why it's trying to take people already."

"Maybe the Sorrow is getting too overloaded too fast," Isaac suggests, taking a sip from his mug. "Maybe the Ghost is running out of time."

Iris frowns. "Maybe it knows something we don't," she says. "Maybe we've finally dug our hole deep enough and it wants to get rid of us before the earth gets past the point of recovery." Maybe there's an extinction event coming that they have no way of predicting. Maybe the Ghost is just getting desperate, ready to rid its master of its parasites like the dutiful guard dog it is.

Iris looks at Isaac and she can tell he's thinking the same thing. What else would be pushing it to act this soon? C can't be the One who Falls, because she's not part of the Club. The Ghost is trying to take her, to get back at Park, to hasten the process. It has to be this.

C finally descends the stairs, her eyes red and puffy, and Park stands, ushering her to sit on the couch with them, offering her the tea they made. She sniffles a weak *thank you*, and Iris's heart aches. Of course, she'd just wanted some time alone to process. Of course, she wasn't in the washroom upstairs conniving with Kat. It must have been terrifying for her, to experience the Ghost for the first time in its full form – the man it wears sometimes is scary in its uncanniness, sure, but the Ghost as a shadow, as a darkness, as the manifestation of dread, is something else entirely.

C doesn't deserve this, she thinks, cursing the Ghost. Cursing herself. *C doesn't deserve to be sucked into this.*

C's eyes lock onto Iris's and there's something in them, an icy resolve that Iris can't help but admire. "You're a witch," she says, and she is not scared.

"Yes," Iris says.

"Old John's radio station was right, then?" she asks, "I kept asking your sister, but she only told me that your magic was different than hers. She said she couldn't talk about what Old John talked about, or what you do because it's too complex and she didn't want me involved."

Iris sends a silent thank you to Kat, glad for her sister's sense. "Old John was speaking truths," she starts, "and yes, Kat and I have different forms of the same magic. I can tap right into the source of the energy and ask it to work with me, for me. Kat must rely on things like blood and herbs and intention for it to do her bidding."

C leans forward, her elbows on her knees. "Why didn't she want me involved?" she asks.

Iris swallows. *Because it's a curse,* she wants to say, but finds herself looking to Park, not knowing how much Isaac has told him, either.

He sighs. "Because once you're involved, you're stuck in Belle until it's over," he says, taking over from Iris. "It's a curse."

C blinks at him, processing. "What do you mean?" she asks, and her voice is an octave higher than it was just seconds ago.

"He means that until that thing that tried to kill you is either dead or it's ended the world, none of us get to leave this town." Iris feels the weight of her words, her own desire to escape Belle a drowned thing in her stomach.

"Is that why you didn't tell me about any of this?" She asks Park, and he nods.

"I know how much you want to leave."

Something passes between them unspoken, and then C groans. "How did you get involved?" She asks.

"What attacked you tonight tried to drown me in the river and Isaac and Iris were in the right place at the right time."

"I thought you met Isaac on a hookup app?"

Park shakes his head, "No. I went to meet the Ghost – the cloud thing – thinking it was someone else."

Isaac gets Iris's attention and mimics the opening of a book. *The Prophecies,* he mouths, *the Sorrow.* She nods at him. *Yes,* she thinks, C is one of them now. She needs to know everything.

Together, the three of them try to explain to C what is happening to the best of their abilities. They tell her about the Ghost and its relationship with the Sorrow, and the Sorrow's relationship with the earth. They tell her about what happens when the Ghost takes someone, where they go, how they never come back. They tell her about the Prophecies and Hell Club and the curse of both. They tell her about Isaac and Park, and the secret that Park supposedly harbours, which she laughs at.

"Park is an open book," she tells them, "he can't keep a secret to save his life."

So, they tell her about Rituals and Artifacts and the power of self-doubt and repression. They tell her that he might not even know what the secret is. They tell her about Old John's contribution to the writing of the Prophecies, and they tell her about Katherine Selene, Kat and Iris's mom.

By the time they tell her about *the One who Falls,* they've drank all their tea and the evening has turned into late night. They've theorized C's importance, her involvement, and they decide it's simply bad luck.

Iris decides that she likes C. She's curious, and she's inquisitive, and now that the initial shock of the Ghost has worn off, she seems determined to learn as much as she can about the world she's been plunged into.

"What happened to Old John?" C asks, concern growing on her face. "Did the Ghost take him?"

Iris shrugs. "Probably. It makes sense that it would have."

"Do you think he's *the One who Falls?*"

Isaac looks at her, and then at C. "She makes a good point," he says.

Iris shakes her head. "That's too easy," she whispers.

"What if that's just what it wants us to think?"

"It doesn't feel right."

Isaac frowns. "No, you're right. It doesn't feel right. Something is still coming."

Park groans and leans to rest his forehead against Isaac's shoulder. "Why can't it just be easy?" he complains, and C gives Iris a pointed look.

It's never easy, she seems to be saying, and Iris agrees.

Isaac stretches and yawns, wrapping an arm around Park's shoulders and bringing him closer. "Anyone staying the night?" He asks, sensing the change in the air. They won't get anything else constructive done tonight.

Iris nods, wanting desperately to stay and wake up in Isaac's house. It's been a while, and she misses their quiet mornings together, his coffee.

"We should get home," Park says, but he looks reluctant.

C picks up on it, too. "You can stay," she says, "I'm probably just going to go to bed to process everything."

"No," he says, "I'll come with you. I want – to make sure you're okay."

C shrugs. "Alright."

"I'll drive you," Isaac says, unpeeling himself from Park and the couch, and the other two follow.

Iris can't help but feel grateful they're leaving. She wants the night with Isaac, to talk to him alone. To plan with him alone. As much as she loves that he and Park are getting along so well, she doesn't want to listen to their flirting or watch the ease with which they operate around each other, and she doesn't want to have to put the effort into being extra nice, so Park doesn't think she's cold.

"Are you staying here?" Isaac asks her, his hand on the arm of her chair as the other two bustle into the mudroom.

"Yes."

"Good," he whispers, and then he, too, leaves the study,

She sinks back into the leather once again and closes her eyes. All of this – their struggle, their desperation – seems pointless, really. The world is already ending. What kind of power do they have to stop it? Why should they care? It's probably a losing battle, anyways, or else the Ghost wouldn't be playing.

Maybe it would be better if they just gave up, let it happen. It would certainly save them a lot of grief.

She doesn't want to tell Dahlia what's happened, but she finds herself pulling out her phone anyways and sending a text to confirm that what they had suspicions about is finally happening. The Ghost is out at Old John's. The Ghost is ready to start taking people.

She sends a text to Kat, too, telling her that C was almost taken but she's okay. That she's part of the Hell Club now and Kat doesn't have to censor what she says to her anymore. She thanks her, too, for keeping the details away from her, for not risking her involvement.

Neither of them answers her, but that's okay, it's late.

It's late, and Iris is starting to think about how easy it would be if they just gave up.

She doesn't know how her mom did it. How her mom worked with the Ghost, how she persevered through it all to keep her promise. She wants more than anything to be able to ask her. To sit down and talk to her, to melt into one of her hugs, to have her tell Iris that she's doing a good job, that it isn't all for nothing.

She wants more than anything to have her mother back, but she can't.

She can't because the Ghost took her, and that rage alone is enough to fuel her to keep going. There's nothing she hates more than the Ghost. There's nothing she can do except keep trying to kill it.

19
INTERLUDE II

Eve hangs up the phone, and looks over to Derek, who is slowly untying his shoes. "They're rescheduling to tomorrow," she says to him, even though she knows that he heard the whole conversation.

"Yeah," he replies, gesturing to his untied shoes, "I got that."

Derek's been pissy lately, and every time she tries to ask him about it, he just gets pissier. He thinks he's going to be the *One who Falls,* but she's talked to Iris about it, and she isn't so sure. Iris and Dahlia are determined to throw themselves into the Ghost, to save the others if they have the chance to, and Eve doesn't doubt that that's exactly what is going to happen.

She runs her hands through her hair and decidedly does not take off her shoes.

When Derek notices, he raises his eyebrows, "Going somewhere?" He asks, and she rolls her eyes.

"Yeah. I'm going to go on a walk, I think," she says, "I need to clear my head a little."

Derek sighs, and mumbles that she should have told him this before he took off his shoes, and while she was planning on going alone, she realizes that it's probably a bad idea, especially if the Ghost is just over at Old Johns. A hop skip and jump away from their basement suite.

Really, what she wants is space, what she wants is silence so she can think. She never has time to think anymore, everything is filled with Derek and Derek and work and Hell Club. She loves Derek so *incredibly much,* but sometimes having a Velcro boyfriend feels like suffocation.

Derek stands back up and offers her a soft smile, an apology for his pissiness she thinks, and she returns it.

"Can we get slushies?" She asks, suddenly, unsure where the craving is coming from, but craving, nonetheless.

"Yeah," Derek hums, patting his pockets to make sure that his wallet is in them, and then opening the door for her, ushering her out. "You know, I'm really worried that they don't actually know what they're doing." He offers her his arm, and she takes it, letting him steady her, ground her.

They've had this conversation before, and they both agree. No one seems to know what they're doing, but she supposes having them is better than having no one. "Me too," she says.

She's been having dreams lately, dreams where the whole town is dark, where she's looking at herself in a mirror and her smile is a little too pointy, a little too red. She's having dreams where Derek is running, and running and running and going nowhere, where her family have sharpened teeth dripping with blood, where her fingers are adorned with garish, dollar store jewellery and her skin is turning green, where something is whispering, always whispering. She can never quite make out what it's saying but it sounds like *justice,* it sounds like *you deserve what's coming to you.*

Bad dreams mean bad sleep, so maybe Derek has been irritable, but she probably has been too. That's how it usually goes – Eve has a bad night, tossing and turning, and so does her boyfriend. She squeezes his arm as they walk, and he looks down at her, that stupid smile that says *I love you so much, you dumbfuck* all over his face.

She feels like something is coming, something bad, something terrible, and she can't lose Derek. She can't lose Derek. If he is the *One who Falls,* then who will kiss her with her morning breath, and who will make her coffee and who will watch stupid reality TV drama with her and who will walk to the gas station with her at seven pm to get slushies?

Velcro boyfriend or not, Derek is her best friend. She doesn't know what she would do with all her love if he left.

At the gas station there's a curly-haired teenager who greets them from the counter, and Derek nods to him, before telling her that he's never been so excited for a slushie.

"I'm going to make it a screamer," he says, even more excited, and she almost wants to cry.

"Me too," she breathes again, unable to match his enthusiasm, but still happy to be here. Still happy even though the floor is sticky, and it smells like sugar, and her head hurts.

She thinks she has to be happy, she owes it to herself. She owes it to Derek. She's not sure how much longer they'll get to be together like this. She's not sure how many more happy moments they have.

***

C is full of anger. Anger and betrayal and something that feels like guilt. It wraps around her chest and fills her lungs, pressing on them as she sinks low into the hot water of her bath.

She takes a deep breath and remembers the terror that coursed through her, the ugly dark things' humming voice in her head, *somewhere she belongs*, and she almost wishes they let it take her. She almost wishes she had stepped forward, let it embrace her, let it bring her to this place.

She knows it's stupid. She knows that's not what would happen, but there's still a small, scared part of her, deep down that thinks maybe it would be better. Then Park wouldn't have to worry about her, he wouldn't have to hover anymore.

She wants to text someone, to call someone, to tell them about what happened, but the only person she can is Kat, and she's already told Kat everything except this, this guilt. She's sure that Kat won't understand. Her panic, her fear that Park is involved in something terrible, the icky feeling under her skin that screams *impure, touched by evil, called out to by the void, impure, impure, impure.* She says she's an atheist, but she's still scared that she'll end up in hell, despite her curiosity. It doesn't matter anyways, she thinks, she's cursed now. She'll never leave this place, and this place is the closest to Hell she can imagine.

She's mad at Park, too. She understands that Park can make his own decisions, and that he kept this from her for her own protection, but she wishes he would have told her *before* the evil thing came for her. She wishes that he was honest with her in how he'd met Isaac. She wishes that he wasn't fucking a witch.

Which is stupid, she *knows,* but now she's carrying around this guilt with her, in her hands, and in her teeth and in her chest, and she's – she doesn't know. She doesn't know how to process this. She doesn't know how to deal with the fact that she would have been okay with the Ghost taking her. She doesn't know why she didn't tell Iris what it told her when she looked at her with her knowing eyes. When she bared her soul about her mother and her struggles with her power.

She slips all the way under the water, wishing she could scream, wishing she could kick and cry and do *something* useful with all the emotions running through her.

There's something sitting heavy in her, something that feels like anger and betrayal and guilt and both a beginning and an end. There's something brewing in the air, in the people around her, and she's caught in the middle of it, a boat at the mercy of the stormy sea. She can't believe that she had wanted this before she was swept up in it. It's all so much more complicated than she thought it would be - all she was looking for was magic and instead she found a monster and a curse and now she'll never leave.

Fuck. This. Place. She thinks, but it doesn't make her feel any better.

***

Mel stinks of Ritual magic, and she hates it. She's taken three showers in the past two days, and it does not want to leave her skin no matter how much she scrubs.

Walt says that he doesn't mind, but she knows he's lying for her sake. There is no one in the world who wouldn't mind this stench.

He's at home with Chip, and she's at the grocery store wearing cheap perfume in the hopes that no one notices she smells like a swamp monster. If they do, they're being nice about it, and Mel is grateful for this, at least. She's pushing her cart down the frozen section when she gets the call from Shannon, and she picks it up with a grunt of annoyance.

"Hello," she says, pushing the cart to the side of the aisle to get out of the way.

"I'm coming home," Shannon says. "I'll be there in a couple of days. Tell Isaac, would you?"

"Su -" she starts, but her sister's already hung up.

She blinks at the rudeness, and puts her phone back in her purse, barely holding down her anger.

She shouldn't be surprised her sister doesn't even have the *decency* to say goodbye; she never has. She's never had decency for anyone but herself.

Mel sighs and decides that she'll wait until tomorrow to tell Isaac that his mother is coming back. She knows that it's been a rough night on him, on the Club, and she doesn't want to pile onto it.

Besides, if she doesn't acknowledge it, she can pretend that it's not happening, right? She desperately does not want this to be happening. She would be okay if she never saw her sister again. She would be *happier* if she never saw her sister again – her sister and the weird man that she married.

Someone asks to get into the freezer beside her, and she startles, moving away and giving the older gentleman a small apology, a small smile. "Rough night?" He asks, and she can only look at him, like a deer in the headlights.

"No?" She says, and he shakes his head as he walks away.

Mel remembers that she smells like the wrong end of a cow, and mutters under her breath. Goddamn Ritual magic. Goddamn old men and their audacity.

20
ACHEY BREAKY BREAKFAST

Park is wide awake at five-thirty in the morning, even though he desperately wants to sleep in. With everything that's happening, with his sister and her anger, and Isaac and his softness, with the world and it's ending, it's a wonder that he slept at all.

He wishes he listened to his sister last night and stayed with Isaac. It wasn't worth it to come back here where C really did ignore him, and he was left to his own devices, left to process everything on his own.

He could have woken up in Isaac's arms instead of tangled in his own blankets, sweaty and disoriented, the remnants of a terrible dream falling away from his consciousness.

He groans, and turns over, finding his phone on his bedside table, finding Isaac's name, and typing out a message.

i can't sleep. c wasn't joking when she said she didn't want me here, she's fine.

Isaac answers immediately, like he always does, and if Park hadn't seen it for himself, he would be sure that Isaac doesn't sleep at all.

breakfast is still an option :)

say no more i'm sold

i'll come get u

that's okay, i'll walk

Park watches the typing bubble start and then stop a few times and imagines that Isaac is having the internal battle of *I don't want to come across as controlling* vs *please let me pick you up so I know you're safe.* If there's anything that he's learned about Isaac so far, it's that Isaac likes to drive. Isaac is like a dog in the fact that he always wants to know where his people are, what they're doing, and if they're safe.

okay. lmk when you leave and if you see anything funky.

okie dokie

Park locks his phone and it drops to his chest, with a thud that almost hurts. It seems so stupid that he's feeling this way when there's so much at stake. It seems so stupid that here, now, with the Ghost nearly taking him and then nearly taking his sister, that he's becoming so attached to Isaac, that he's found someone who's good to him. It seems so absurd that there is a Prophecy in a book that ties them together, and that it did such a *good job* finding two people that seem to complement each other, that it specifically found Isaac and Park.

As Isaac has said before, they would have found each other anyways, but Park still likes to marvel at it.

With another groan he lifts himself out of bed and roots around in his dresser for clothes. He needs to do laundry soon, he needs to clean his room, he needs to buy more toothpaste. It's hard to do normal life things, he thinks, when something more exciting comes around. When *someone* more exciting comes around.

As soon as he pulls non-sleep clothes on and brushes his teeth, he texts Isaac that he's on his way.

okay doors open i'm feeding the cat

i want to meet the act

**cat*

hurry, then

Park pulls on his shoes in a rush and is out the door with his jacket on only one shoulder. It's cold this morning, the autumn finally showing its teeth, and he shivers. Maybe he should have taken Isaac's offer for a ride.

The walk is quick, fueled by Park's chill, and the lingering fear that he'll somehow run into the Ghost, that it will materialize out of thin air and its ugly darkness will slurp him up. He has to remind himself that he'll be safe, that Isaac wouldn't let him walk over if he didn't think that Park would be okay.

Isaac's house looms in front of him too fast for anything to happen, all white and blue and dead plants in the window boxes. The wind chimes hanging at the front sing quietly with the breeze, but the rest of the property seems quiet, still asleep. It's peaceful, inviting, the opposite of the feeling that Park has when he's about to enter his own house – that feels like war.

He opens the door and is met with more peaceful silence. There is no struggle here, no loud anger, and it smells like warmth. It *is* warm. Every time Park comes in here, it feels a little more comfortable, a little more like somewhere he never wants to leave.

He takes off his shoes, and wanders through to the study, where there are blankets on the chair and the couch, left with the impression of people in them. The mugs from last night are still there, too, all empty.

He steps past them, and through the sliding glass door onto the back deck and there he is, Isaac Paige, wrapped in a sweater and pajama pants, leaning against the railing, and shaking a bowl of food at a very, very large tomcat. Beside him is an ashtray, a carton of cigarettes, and Park can smell smoke in the air.

"Morning," he says, softly, not wanting to scare away the cat.

Isaac pushes the bowl as far away from himself as he can and retracts his arm before he turns to look at Park, and Park's heart does a double take in his chest. "Good morning," Isaac says, all sleepy smile and mussed hair; the kind of soft that can only occur before seven am.

Park gestures to the cat, who is eating the food ravenously, like it's the last meal he'll ever have. "Has he let you pet him yet?"

"No. Not yet. I'll win him over soon, though, I think. He's starting to come closer." He glances at the tom, and Park has no doubts that he'll win the cat over. Isaac seems to win everyone over, eventually.

It gets quiet for a moment, while they both watch the cat finish his breakfast and then hop down from the railing to disappear into the woods without so much as a look over his shoulder. Park wishes he could disappear too, if only for a day. Only if he could bring Isaac with him.

"Hey," Isaac says, and Park moves his attention back to him.

"Hey."

"How are you doing?" He asks, and Park shakes his head.

The option to lie is there, but the way that Isaac is looking at him seems to say that he knows that Park isn't doing great, knows that last night was hard. "Not good," he says, and Isaac nods.

"Me either," and Park sees the vulnerability in his eyes, in the small skew to his mouth that says *what can you do about it?* He opens his arms, and Park steps into them quietly, pressing his face into Isaac's shoulder, breathing in his scent, smoky and sharp and warm.

We can do this, he wants to say, to answer Isaac's unasked question. *We can do this whenever you want. We can hold each other.*

Isaac presses a soft kiss to Park's hair and squeezes him tight. "We're gonna figure it out," he says, and Park isn't sure who he's trying to convince.

"I know," he says, just in case and he pulls back so he can look at Isaac. Isaac and his soft hazel eyes, soft jawline, freckles over the bow of his lips. Beautiful. *I hope you will trust me,* his words from the night before.

"Whatcha thinking?" He asks, raising his eyebrows, a smirk making an appearance on his face.

"Nothing," Park starts, and then he realizes there's no point in lying. There's no point in trying to tone down anything that he feels about Isaac. "I mean – I like your face, is all." He can feel his pulse in his throat, and the pit of his stomach, but Isaac's smirk only gets bigger.

"I like yours too," he whispers, and then he presses a kiss to Park's forehead. "This," he says, and then he leans down further to plant one on Park's cheek, "and this."

Park can't help it. He lets out a laugh, and this is clearly what Isaac is aiming for, because he keeps landing kisses all over Park's face until Park is outright giggling, his hands wrapped in Isaac's sweater, right over his chest, clutching on for dear life because his knees are going weak. Isaac places his hands at the small of Park's back, holding him up so the kisses can keep coming, each one soft, each one melting Park even further, until he's a mess of laughter, of warmth, of innocent joy.

"Okay," Park says, and Isaac sneaks another kiss from the corner of his mouth. "Okay, I can't – I can't breathe," Park manages between laughs, and Isaac pulls back, pleased with himself, to look at Park, the goofiest expression Park's ever seen on his face.

He looks like a Labrador retriever, Park thinks, and he says, before he can even think about it, before he's even fully recovered, "Kiss me for real now."

"Yeah," Isaac breathes, and then there they are, kissing on Isaac's back porch, Isaac tasting like cigarettes and toothpaste.

Park melts into the other even further, and the heat in his body moves away from his cheeks, into wherever it is that Isaac places his hands. Weakly, he thinks that Isaac is going to be his undoing, and just as it's about to get good Isaac pull away, gently.

"Iris is still here," he says, "we shouldn't get too carried away."

Park nods and bites his lip. He wants to get carried away, wants to get lost in Isaac, but he understands. Not the time. "Breakfast?" He asks, and Isaac smiles, taking one more second to look at Park, nothing but fondness in his gaze.

"Breakfast," he agrees and Park pulls away.

"I can't wait." And he can't.

✳ ✳ ✳

When Iris comes down the stairs, Park beams at her, any trace of his bad mood completely erased. He and Isaac have shared the duty of making waffles, and they've packed in lots of touching, lots of kissing. There's a flour handprint on Isaac's ass, and Park isn't certain that he knows it's there.

"Good morning?" She asks him, "When did you get here?"

"Very early," he says, mouth half full of waffle. "Had a bad night. Remembered that someone promised me breakfast."

Isaac looks up from where he's spearing waffles onto a plate for Iris. "I did promise breakfast," he replies, "and I made coffee."

"Oh, good," Iris says, and makes her way hastily to the coffeepot, as if she can't take another second without caffeine in her.

Park enjoyed the night before - getting to know Iris a little bit more, getting to see under the cold front she's been giving him. It makes her friendliness seem less like a show.

"I was telling Park what we were talking about last night," Isaac says, pouring more batter onto the waffle machine. They definitely made too much, and now Isaac is going to be making waffles for hours. "About a tarot reading."

"Oh," Iris says around a mouth full of waffle. "Yeah, I mean, I still think it will be beneficial."

Park nods. He's never gotten a tarot reading from a professional, and it scares him a little, especially because it could mean that Iris will uncover the *secret* he's keeping from them and she'll know it before he does. It scares him a little because Iris will be the one doing it and Isaac told him that Iris is very good at what she does, and she's going to read him to filth. She's going to know more about him from this tarot reading than anything he's told her so far.

"Do you trust me?" Iris asks, not looking at him as she replenishes the syrup her waffles have soaked up.

Park opens his mouth and then closes it again, thinking back once again to he and Isaac's conversation the day before. *It feels like learning how to trust.* He should trust Iris, he knows this - she saved him from the river, and she saved C from the dark cloud of the Ghost, and she didn't question her role in either long enough for them to be in more peril. She moved into action as soon as she could, and she's Isaac's best friend. She's Isaac's best friend and Park trusts Isaac.

"You'll have to trust me for this," Iris says, breaking the silence, breaking his thoughts.

"I think I do," he replies, "I'm trying to." He's trying to get over his fear of her, of her power. He's trying to get it out of his head that she's cold, that she's uncaring. She so obviously does care – last night, when she was talking about her mom, when she was worrying about the *One who Falls*.

"Okay," she breathes, "we can work with that."

Park nods, and then Isaac slaps more waffle onto their plates, the slightest hint of a smile tugging up on his lips.

"I hope you guys are still hungry," he says, "because there's still tons of batter left."

***

"Look," Iris says, knocking on her deck three times. "I'll only do one card to start and clarify if we need. That just means pulling more cards."

Park nods, nervously shifting in his chair. Iris's reading room in her parents' metaphysical shop smells like incense, and it's full of macrame and candles, and plants and fairy lights. There's a salt lamp emitting a soft glow in the corner, and crystals *everywhere*.

Park's sure that Iris is just playing up the witch aesthetic for her customers, but it's putting him at ease. There's something that seems clean about this place, peaceful and inquisitive. It feels safe.

"What's your question?" She asks, and her deck snaps as she shuffles.

"My question?" Park isn't sure what he should say. He wants to know what he's supposed to do, how he fits in to this strange world of magic and alternate dimensions, what his job is, but he doesn't know how to put that into words so that the tarot will understand.

"What about: What role do I play in Hell Club?"

He shrugs. That seems about right. "Okay."

Snap. "Think about it," she says, "focus on your question. Let it stay central in your mind."

Park watches her hands as she shuffles again, thinking only *what role do I play in Hell Club?* Thinking only that Iris's hands with their olive painted nails, the gold rings, the eye tattoo on her ring finger, look to be doing exactly what they're meant to do. He thinks about his own hands, *what role do I play in Hell Club? What are my hands meant for?*

Iris cuts the deck into three, and then restacks them. She looks to him now, her eyes serious and all-seeing. It feels like she's seeing him less than she is knowing him, and the air is charged. "Ready?" She asks, and he nods.

It's less scary than he thought it was going to be.

She flips the top card off the deck, and Park is hit with how beautiful it is. "Judgement," she says, and then she laughs. "Of fucking course."

Park blinks at her, confused. "What does it mean?"

Her fingers trace the edge of the card, and she looks at it while she talks, not at him. "Reckoning. A time of reflection, kind of like a reset? Like you're looking back on everything you've ever done and you're deciding if you chose right, if you're ready to move forward or if you've fucked up."

"So, what does that mean for Hell Club? What does that make my role?" Park still doesn't understand. Reckoning?

Iris looks at him, finally, and now Park is certain that she's knowing him. She's looking right through him, to his very core, and somehow it feels okay, it feels nice to be seen, to be known. "You," she says, "you make us rethink everything."

"Oh."

"One more card." She pulls the second from the top, and then she laughs again. "Yeah. Yeah, fuck, that's what I thought."

"That's bad, right?" He asks, and he's pretty sure he's right. Nothing about the card looks good.

"Well, I mean really there isn't good or bad in tarot – but yeah. Yeah, that's bad."

Park nods. Of course it is.

"It's like something coming out of left field and tearing down everything you know about a situation. Something is happening and it's going to rip apart what we think about the Ghost and how we're supposed to stop it."

Park looks down at the card, The Tower, and he swallows. "So, you look back at everything you've done, you start reflecting, and you don't like what you see? So you rip it apart from the bottom up, and you do it all because of something I say or do?"

She shrugs. "More or less. You might not say or do it consciously, but you're going to be the spark that lights the fire."

"Big shoes to fill," he mutters, and Iris chuckles.

She fits the two cards back into her deck, and her deck goes back into its fancy bag. "It's better to be the catalyst," she says, "at least you know you're moving things in the right direction."

Park isn't sure that this is true, but he nods anyways. It makes sense. *When the Ghost calls, one will doom all* - could that be him? Will that be him? Dooming them all?

"Can I tell you something?" She asks, leaning forward.

"Sure."

"Dahlia and I think you might be the next Prophet," she says, "we think that maybe that's your secret - what we have to unlock inside of you."

Prophet? Park isn't a Prophet. Park can hardly string a coherent sentence together, let alone write the future. "I don't know about that," he says, warily.

Iris shrugs. "I want to work with you if that's okay? We can do some meditation, some more tarot readings? Maybe that will unlock something in you. Maybe that will help us get some answers towards what it is you're hiding from us."

Park blinks at her. Could he be a Prophet? Could that be something laying dormant in him, deep down at the base of his spine? Asleep in a corner of his brain, ready to be awoken? He's not sure. "How would being a Prophet be helpful?" he asks.

"If you're a Prophet," she says, standing, grabbing for her coat, "then we know that the world doesn't end with us."

"Oh," he says, dumbly, and then *"oh!"*

She gestures for him to stand, for him to start out of the reading room. "It's just a theory," she says, "but we can work on it, if you want."

He nods. "I want to."

She smiles at him, then, and holds the door open, both stepping out into the brightness of the rest of the shop.

Isaac is sitting in one of the chairs pressed to the wall, seeming shaken.

He looks up to them, and forces a smile, but his face is ashen.

"What's wrong?" Iris asks before Park can, and he sighs, his entire body seeming to deflate.

"My parents are coming back," he says, "they'll be here tomorrow."

21

MILK CHOCOLATE

Isaac is nauseous. Park is in his passenger seat, and they're driving to Park's house so he can get his own things to spend the night, but Isaac has a pit of nerves at the bottom of his stomach, and it's not because of Park.

"Do you want to come in?" Park asks, as they pull up to his house, "No one else is home."

Isaac nods, cutting the engine of his car. He doesn't want to be alone, even for a second. "I want to see your room," he says, and Park groans.

"It's only, like, half unpacked. You'll be disappointed."

"No," Isaac says, because Park's room will be Park's and Park will be sharing it with him.

Park gives him a funny look, but he doesn't ask, and Isaac doesn't explain.

Together, they head towards the house, which looks cheery from the outside. It looks alive in a way that Isaac doesn't think his does, like a family lives within it.

There is no kissing at the doorway, and the two of them step inside without a word. Park is tense, as if someone will enter the mudroom and demand why he's here, why he has a *friend* with him. All the lightness, the bubbliness that was in him at Isaac's, even after the tarot reading with Iris, has been drained.

"I live downstairs," Park says, leading Isaac into the house, "my parents pretty much only come down for laundry."

Park has mentioned that his relationship with his parents is strained, but Isaac isn't sure the exact reason why – although, it's easy to assume, given the cross in the entryway – or to what degree. He's sure that Park doesn't hate his parents as much as Isaac does, but that's not saying anything. Strain is strain. "Is that a good thing?" He asks.

Park flicks on the stair lights and down they go into a carpeted living space, a bathroom tucked into one corner, and a washer and dryer in the other. "I don't really care," he says, "we get along okay, but they –

they think I need to find my way back to God. I came out to them and I though they would be okay with it, but they weren't."

"I'm sorry," Isaac says, wondering what that betrayal must feel like. A dagger placed at the edge of Park's sternum? A trust fall gone wrong? He doesn't have the same problem with his parents - they've never been around enough to care.

"It's okay, really. We just don't talk about it. It'll probably come up again now, though." Isaac senses the lie but doesn't want to call Park out on it. He's sure Park will bring it up, if he wants to elaborate, if he wants to talk it out.

"Oh, why?"

Park opens his bedroom door and looks back over his shoulder, eyebrows raised. "Because of you."

"Right. Gotcha." Isaac could smack himself in the face he feels so stupid. He's out of his element. He's in a house he's never been in, and Park is tense and there's a quietness to this home that he's not used to. Even in his own house, however empty it is, there are still memories. There is still the presence of the past and here he has nothing. Just Park and empty space.

"Well, here it is, in all its glory." Park gestures to his room, which is full of half-empty boxes and various items strewn across surfaces. Clothes litter the floor, and Park starts gathering them, dumping them in his dirty laundry bin. "Sorry about the mess."

"Don't be," Isaac says, taking a seat on the edge of the bed. "Your messy room won't make me think less of you." He gives Park a small smile, and Park returns it, turning to root around in his dresser.

"I'm sorry your parents are coming home," he says, "I know that you're not on good terms with them."

Isaac sighs, and lays back, enveloped in the blankets, in the smell of Park. "I've never been on good terms with them." There's the old burn at the back of his throat, the feeling he would get when they showed up and called him son and knew his name and he couldn't recognize them as his mother and father. The confusion, as they embraced him, and he didn't find any familiarity in them. "They never tried to be on good terms with me."

The thing is it would be easy to like them. It would be easy to let them in if they did try. It's not like Isaac *wants* detached parents - he would love to be close to them, to know what's going on in their lives, to call them a couple of times a week and just talk to them – but they have made it very clear that while they'll keep him financially secure, while they'll invade his space and accept his sexuality, they want no relationship with him. They want nothing to do with their own son.

Park places something at the bottom of the bed, and then lays down so his head is on Isaac's chest, his hands sliding under Isaac's shoulders. The pressure of him makes the tight knot in his stomach loosen a little. "I'm sorry," Park says. "You can come stay here whenever you want, if you need a break."

Isaac places a kiss on the top of Park's head. "Thank you," he says. He wishes that everything in his life could be like this, like what's happening between him and Park. It's not effortless – sometimes it's awkward and Isaac questions whether he's saying the right things, doing the right things – but building something shouldn't be, and connection and vulnerability are the only things worth anything, the only things that hold real beauty. Isaac cares about Park, and Park cares about Isaac and that's all there needs to be.

"You know, I don't work tomorrow either," Park says, "we could sleep in. Maybe do something fun in the afternoon."

Isaac hums an affirmative. "We should. I don't want to be home when they get there. I – I want to be around them as little as possible."

"Do you know how long they'll be here?"

The last time something went wrong with the business his parents were home for almost three months while his mom recovered, but that was a long time ago, when Isaac had just moved out of Mel's house. His mom is older now, more experienced. He doesn't think it'll take her as long this time around. "Hopefully only a couple of weeks," he says, "I – wait, have I told you about our family business?"

Park pushes himself up to look at Isaac, interest dancing across his face. "You haven't told me about your family business," he says, "but I want to hear."

"You're not allowed to tell anyone," Isaac whispers, half joking and half serious. "It's top secret."

"Cross my heart and hope to die."

"We deal in the black market of Ritual magic and Artifacts. I mean – I don't, not yet at least, but the rest of them do. I mean, no – Mel got out of it. She only helps when she has to, but my grandpa and my mom and dad."

Park is looking at him like he's just grown a third ear. "Hold on," he says, "let me get the terms right."

Isaac nods.

"Ritual is magic without being directly connected to the source, right?"

"Yes."

"And Artifacts are objects that have been given magic?"

"Yes!" Isaac feels a small bud of pride in his heart. "My family distributes them to buyers. I guess it's not really a black market, but there isn't a legal option for either Ritual magic or Artifacts, though." Isaac watches Park process. It is strange, but no stranger than Hell Club. The only real difference between the magic Park's already dealing with and the magic his parents deal with is that the business embraces capitalism, takes advantage of it while Hell Club holds it at arms length. Hell Club is old, natural, and the business is what you get when a bunch of old white men want a piece of it.

Park props himself up on his elbows, something working its way over his face. "Isn't that stuff dangerous?" He asks, and Isaac runs his hands up and down Park's back.

He forgets, sometimes, that this can be new to someone. "Yes. Ritual magic is dangerous when it's done improperly, which is why a lot of sellers will pay extra to have someone do it for them. Artifacts are worse – they can usually only be stopped by Ritual magic. The thing my mom is obsessed with has the spirit of a woman who lost her child to illness. When another mother who's lost a child touches it, the spirit enters her body and essentially kills her with sadness until she's removed."

"What the fuck," breathes Park, and he sits all the way up. "Wait, but you're still alive?"

"Yeah, but does she really have me anymore? Did she ever?" Isaac follows his movements, sitting, too.

"Why do people want stuff like that?"

Isaac shrugs. He's asked himself this too many times to count. "I can't tell you, really, but they pay big money for it. I think it's because they like the challenge. They think if they survive it, it's like a badge of honour. They collect things like it."

"Do you – do you collect them?"

"Oh, fuck no. Absolutely not. Usually having one in your home means you're dead."

"And your family just – just sells to these people?"

Isaac nods. Park's growing discomfort is becoming clear, and he doesn't blame him. "They're the best in the game. Listen – don't get me wrong, I hate the business, which is why I'm not in it. Most of them hate the business, but it's easy money when they're down. A lot of the buyers know what they're doing, too. They're experienced." Isaac doesn't mention the ones that aren't. No one likes to mention the ones that aren't.

"That's crazy," Park replies, looking down at his hands. "Do you do Ritual magic?"

Isaac wrinkles his nose. "No. It stinks."

"What do you mean?"

"It leaves a smell on whoever practices it like something three days dead. You'll know if you ever meet anyone who's just participated in one – trust me."

Park lulls into silence, and Isaac watches the gears turning in his mind, hoping that he doesn't seem despicable, hoping that Mel and his grandparents don't seem despicable. He doesn't care so much about what Park thinks of his parents, but he doesn't want to tarnish the impression that Mel's given him.

"Sorry," Park mutters after a few minutes, shifting to look at his hands. "I'm just trying to process."

"No, you don't have anything to apologize for. It's a lot, I know."

"I suppose I should have guessed that Rituals would be sold – that's why Kat is so good at them, right? They must sell them at the shop."

"Yeah, they do. Nothing super serious, though." Isaac reaches out and brushes his fingers against the bare skin of Park's arm, the tips of them disappearing under Park's sleeve.

"Nothing like your parents." Park leans into the touch.

"Nothing like my parents," Isaac confirms, "trust me. You'll meet them, and you'll get it." They look like the kind of people who would sell magic Rituals and Artifacts in the black market. "My mom is like a snake-oil salesman, and my dad is like a mad scientist."

"Ah," Park says, "of course. Exactly who I pictured." He's smiling again, and this is all that matters. Silence for a minute, and Park uses it to press his legs against Isaac's. "You want me to meet them?" He asks, not looking at the other.

"Well," Isaac starts, "I mean, I'm not going to stop inviting you over just because they're there. It's my house, too." Isaac puts his hand over Park's, lifting it from his leg and squeezing. "And don't forget that you invited me to stay here, too."

Park groans, and flops onto his back beside Isaac, pulling him with him and lacing their fingers together. "Yeah," he says. "Yeah, I know. I'm sure you'll run into my parents eventually, but it doesn't matter – they won't admit that you're my boyfriend. They'll only call you my friend."

"Am I? Your boyfriend?" Isaac looks over at him, grinning as he realizes what Park has said. They haven't defined anything about their relationship yet, so Isaac is surprised that Park's said it so casually. He's surprised that Park is rolling his eyes.

"Oh, shut up," he says, "what else would you be?"

"Your very favourite sexy hot fated friends with benefits?" Isaac turns onto his side, so he can see Park better, drink in his knee-jerk embarrassment.

"You want me to introduce you to my parents as that?" He asks, raising his eyebrows.

"On second thought, boyfriend sounds better." Isaac gets closer, hoping that Park gets the hint and kisses him.

He does. He closes the distances between them. "Yeah, I think so too," he says, and then they're kissing, and Isaac can melt into Park and forget about the terrible news he received this morning. He can forget about the end of the world and Hell Club, and he can just be.

✳✳✳

It's windy outside, and it's making the cabin groan around them, as if being out here isn't creepy enough. Isaac thought that he would get over his unease in the clubhouse with time, with continued exposure, but it has never gotten better, even with all his friends in it, even with Iris and Park shoulder to shoulder with him. The hair on the back of his neck still stands up.

"So, it's trying to take people already?" Eve asks, scrunching her nose. "What the fuck are we supposed to do about that?"

Dahlia opens her mouth, and then closes it, her eyes finding Park, searching for something that she must not find, and Isaac puts his hand on Park's leg, hoping to comfort him.

"We're going to have to slow it down so we can figure out our next steps," Dahlia says. "Iris and I want to go back to Old John's and flush it out fully in the hopes that it will take a while to manifest back into our world. Hopefully that'll give Park enough time to figure out what his secret is."

"Have you gotten any further on that?" Derek asks, leaning forward.

"No," Park says.

"We think he might be the next Prophet," Iris chimes in, helpfully. "I'm going to start working with him and see if we can unlock whatever it is."

Isaac feels Park's nerves and is sorry that he dragged Park up to sit with him, where he can so clearly be under scrutiny. *At least he's not alone*, he thinks, *at least he's not the only one trying to explain things.* He squeezes Park's leg, and Park leans in closer to him, just for a second.

"So, our plan is to try and remove the Ghost from Old John's house, banish it, and then wait until Park writes some Prophecies?" Eve asks, as if she thinks it's not enough.

Iris nods. "Yeah. Yeah, that's our plan. Unless anyone has anything better? Anything to add?"

"What about your sister, Park?" Dahlia asks, "Shouldn't she be here, too?"

Park shrugs, his shoulder rubbing against Isaac's. "I invited her," he says, "I told her exactly where we'd be." They'd run into her coming back from school as they were leaving Park's house, and they'd told her about the meeting, told her that she is welcome at any of them from now on, but she'd seemed scared. She'd seemed nervous. She'd seemed angry.

Isaac isn't surprised she didn't show up.

"She'll make her way here, eventually," Iris says, "we all do."

Dahlia nods. She knows the pull of it just as well as anyone else.

"What if the Ghost won't go?" Eve asks, "I keep having dreams where everything is dark, and it keeps getting darker. It feels like dread." She looks tired, Isaac realizes. Her and Derek both – they've been the ones that Isaac and Iris have talked to the least in the last week and they look the roughest.

Isaac wonders if it's because Derek is right, and he's going to be the *One that Falls*. He wonders if Eve's dreams are a sign of what's to come.

"Dahlia and Isaac and I should be enough to make it go. If you want to come, you can. I don't think extra energy would be a bad thing." Iris says.

Eve nods but doesn't look satisfied with the answer. Her hands are held together tightly in her lap, and Isaac has the feeling that there's something else that's worrying her, something bigger. He tunes into her energy for a minute, feeling fear and then guilt. There's something she's not telling them – there's something she's hiding.

Chip, who's been quiet this entire time, reading his book in the corner, finally looks up. "Mom says that evil things like attention," he says, "and it's easy to give them too much." She says the same thing about Shannon, Isaac's heard her talking to Walt.

"More people, more attention," he clarifies when he sees Dahlia raise her eyebrows at Chip.

"Yes!" Chip says. "More attention is bad."

"So just Dahlia, Isaac and I will go, then," Iris confirms solemnly. "Eve and Derek, I think you guys should be with Park, just in case something goes wrong."

Isaac watches Eve nod, and then lean back against Derek. Her guilt has turned into relief.

"I want to go with you," Park says, softly, pulling his attention from Eve. Isaac turns to him, his blue eyes wide.

"It won't be safe," Isaac replies, "if we fail and we go through, there will be nothing we can do to stop it from getting to you, and then it's game over. Especially if we're right and you're the Prophet."

Park blinks at him, searching for something, and Isaac squeezes his leg a second time.

"You'll be safer with Eve and Derek," he says, "please." He hopes that Park sees how desperately he needs him to be safe. He hopes that Park sees how much is starting to be at stake, and not just personally.

"Okay," Park breathes, and Isaac nods.

"Okay," he says, and tunes back into the chatter.

"Tomorrow?" Eve asks, "I mean, tomorrow's Monday. I'm going to be so busy at the salon, and Derek works until five."

"I work, too," Dahlia says, and frustration rises in Iris before Isaac can slam his guards down against it.

It's the end of the world we're talking about, he knows she wants to say, but she refrains herself. "What about the evening? Can we all make tomorrow evening work? After six?"

Voices from around the room confirm, and she nods.

"I'll drive out to check on Old John's place tonight, to make sure nothing's changed, and let you all know if we need to readjust our plans."

"Not alone, you won't," Isaac says, and Dahlia pipes up,

"I'll go with her," and Isaac feels better about it.

"Alright," Isaac says, his energy drained. "I think that's it, is it?"

He makes a mental note to ask Eve what's going on – but not tonight. Tonight they're both too tired, and Iris's frustration has made him irritable, like it always does. He'll text her in the morning to see what's going on.

✳✳✳

Isaac's head is on Park's chest and he's listening to the *thump-thump, thump-thump* of his heart. He never wants to leave; he never wants to move. Park's hands are in his hair, raking through it softly, and he's in the place between wakefulness and sleep, at peace.

"I don't know how to write Prophecies," Park says, in a voice so small. "I don't know how to do any of this."

"That's okay," Isaac replies, squeezing his arm tighter around Park's chest, "we'll figure it out. Together."

Park lets out a long sigh, his fingers stopping their movement on Isaac's scalp. "Promise?"

"Promise."

Park's fingers start moving again, and Isaac presses Park's other hand to his mouth. Together, he thinks, and then he drifts off, into a dreamless sleep.

22
BROKEN LIGHTBULBS

The Ghost is restless. It doesn't like to stay in one place for too long, but here it is, in the Old Man's house, breaking and eating and waiting. There is glass on the floor, on the windowsills, and on the tables. There is twisted metal, and splintered wood and scraps of rotten paper in its wake, but it cannot stop moving. It is hungry - the Old Man did not sate it - but it is also patient. It knows that it will be fed soon, it knows that the twisting, and turning and ceaseless yearning will be put to an end.

It knows a lot of things, and it knows that the Club's plan isn't going to work. It knows what the plan is. It hears them talking in their cabin, about saviours and Prophets and magic, it hears them plotting against it like it's the enemy.

It is not the enemy. It has never been the enemy, it's just that humans can't accept the fate they've created for themselves. It's just that some things can't be saved, it's just that the Wheel keeps turning and the End keeps coming, and it can only be put off for so long.

It can only be put off for so long, and this End has been a long time coming. This End has been hundreds of years in the making, hundreds of years of slumber and rude awakenings and even ruder endings for the Ghost. Hundreds of years of snapping teeth and dripping jowls and hunger like a dagger tucked between its ribs. Hundreds of years of listening to the Sorrow scream, listening to the earth around it scream, listening to the people scream, the trees, the river.

The river used to be passive, used to be docile, used to be only water, but it too is angry now.

Drink me drink me drink me I am crystal clear I am crystal calm drink me drink me drink me, it is singing, singing so sweetly the Ghost is surprised no one's drowned yet. The Ghost is surprised it hasn't taken its blood yet, because underneath it all the song sounds more like:

DRINK ME DRINK ME DRINK ME I AM RAPIDS I AM WHIRLPOOLS I AM ANGRY DRINK ME DRINK ME DRINK ME

and that's a hard song to resist.

It rattles and it shakes, and it pulls upwards, out of the Old Man's house, leaving some of its mass behind, some of its darkness. It is bigger than the witches expect, and it is *so* hungry. It is so hungry they will never be able to understand, these children of men, of those who see themselves as gods.

It wishes that they could see what it does, it does from love. It loves its master, it loves the river, it loves the people who love it back. It is not hungry for destruction because it will bring it power, no. It is hungry for destruction because the Sorrow cries out in pain, and destruction is the only thing which will calm it. Destruction is the only thing that will soothe it, that will stop its sobs, its screams.

It feels them coming, now, the three witches in the gas machine, ready to fight. Ready to call on the tired energy of the earth, the tired energy of the Ghost and the Sorrow themselves. It won't be long before that energy, too, is singing of destruction. It won't be long before the witches see why it's happening the way it is, why fighting it isn't possible anymore.

It knows that they, too, are fighting for what they love. It knows that tonight it will be taking away something the witches love, something the witches treasure. It knows that this is the only way, this is the only way, *this is the only way.*

I am sorry, it wants to tell them, swirling into the night sky, *I am sorry, but I too, cannot control what I love. I too, cannot help but fight. I too, am tired. I too, wish for nothing but the bitter end to this struggle.*

Far away, the Ghost touches a soul, and the soul shrieks and writhes and curses, the soul screams and claws and bites. *Do not fear me,* the Ghost wants to tell it, *I only wish for you to see,* but it does not have the words. It does not have the words, so it soothes the soul with images, with emotions, with visions the soul is familiar with. Despite all the anger, the soul knew her fate. The soul accepted her fate.

The Ghost and this new soul are not strangers, after all. The Ghost and this new soul have been speaking for weeks now, and she's finally starting to understand.

23
INTERLUDE III

C is watching Kat, with her frizzy hair and her glasses. C is watching Kat and she is realizing how much she cares for Kat, how these past few weeks have given her hope for herself, how she's learned so much, how she's found something that interests her. How she's found a friend who can guide her through it and doesn't judge her for her past and doesn't care that she's gay because that's something they share. C is watching Kat and Kat is reciting something from a spell book open in front of her and C can feel the power of her words wash over her.

"Be one," she says, "be one with that who speaks these words, be one with that who braves these currents, be one with that who gives and never takes. Save your hands, save your heart for the one who speaks these words, save your flesh, save your affection."

The words start to blur, turning into static, turning into meaningless sound pulling her, pushing her. All she can focus on is Kat, beautiful, ethereal, her best friend, speaking something that sounds half like a love spell and half like a curse.

Is it for me? She thinks, *Could the spell be for me?*

She doesn't think it is. Kat has made it clear that her feelings towards C are purely platonic, purely nothing more than friends.

Besides, this is a dream. C is dreaming and she knows this because her body doesn't feel real and when she looks down at the ground she's floating. This is a dream because her head feels wispy, like it's made of smoke. This is a dream because if she focuses too hard on anything but Kat, the darkness starts to seep in at the sides. If she turns, there is only a terrifying blackness like night in the middle of the woods, and it is screaming. It is screaming and screaming and screaming and it never stops.

She loses focus. The darkness swallows her, and then she's awake and it's her who's screaming, tangled in her bedsheet, full of sweat and sorrow and tears.

Her mom is there, the door flying open, panic and worry written all over her face, and she's reaching to comfort C, she's turning on the lamp, she's asking *what happened, what's happening, what's wrong?*

I've been touched by evil, mom, C wants to say. *I've seen what's coming for us and I don't know how to choke it down. There isn't a thing we can do about it, mom. Please don't pray for me, mom, it won't do me any good. It has never done me any good.*

It's coming for you, too, mom, she wants to say, *your god can't save you. No one can save you.*

"Just a nightmare," she says, and her mom wraps her arms around her.

"You haven't had one of these in a long time," her mom says. C pushes closer.

"I know." She thinks she knows what they mean now, what they've always meant.

* * *

Eve hasn't slept. She won't let herself sleep. If she sleeps, she sees everything all at once and it's too much. It's too much for her to bear, and she can't wake up to Derek's worried face anymore.

She settles, cross-legged on a pillow, a mug of tea steaming on the floor in front of her. It's been a long time since she meditated, but she's sure it's what she needs to do right now. Maybe she'll get a clearer picture of what's happening, what her dreams are trying to tell her.

She takes a sip of her tea, and then sets it back down, closing her eyes and settling in. She focuses on her breathing for a bit, in and out, until she's relaxed enough to start going deeper. Deeper, and deeper, until there are bright colours, and her thoughts are surface level, distant, background noise.

Here, she can see. Here, she can feel the gross unease that's been settling in her bones since the day she met Park. It pulls at her, like the current, and then suddenly she's standing at the edge of the river, her toes in the water.

In front of her is a tall, burly man, his hair pulled into a low ponytail.

"Who are you?" She asks, and her voice echoes through the woods. Distantly, she thinks she can hear singing.

"You know who I am," the man says, "you know what's coming."

"What's coming?" she asks, and the words in the distance become clearer.

Drink me drink me drink me I am crystal clear I am crystal calm drink me drink me drink me, the words are saying, and she thinks they're from the river. *Drink me drink me drink me I am crystal clear I am crystal calm drink me drink me drink me.*

"Sink deeper," he says, and he snaps, and then she's standing in the dark, her bare feet covered in ash.

She lifts her head, and the wind catches her hair, sending it flying into her face. She reaches up to move it, and once she does, she's hit with how dark it is. How black, how empty. In the distance, there is singing, but this time it's angry.

DRINK ME DRINK ME DRINK ME I AM RAPIDS I AM WHIRLPOOLS I AM ANGRY DRINK ME DRINK ME DRINK ME, it's saying, and its voice sounds like drums.

"Come find this place again," says the man, and she whips around to find him, but she can't see anything. "You'll know when it's time. I'll be right beside you."

***

Dahlia senses that something is wrong as they approach Old John's house. It's in the air like static electricity and it's making her hair stand up, but she doesn't know how to put it into words. She doesn't know how to tell Isaac and Iris that this feels like a distraction, like there's something more important happening somewhere else.

Isaac pulls the Shitbox to the side of the road and cuts the engine. He's full of fluttering, nervous energy today, and Dahlia almost wishes that he hadn't come. Isaac is an emotional person, and sometimes emotions get in the way of things like this. Sometimes it's better to leave them at home, with their lovers.

"Do we want to draw it out?" Iris asks, looking worriedly at Old Johns, which looks like it's been hit by a tornado. "Or do we want to meet it in the house?"

Dahlia is certain that it doesn't matter. She's certain that this whole thing is ass backwards, that they should be the ones with Parker right now. "I think we should leave," she says, finally, and Iris whips her head backwards.

"Why?"

"I get the feeling that we're being led into a trap. I think we should go back."

Iris blinks at her, and Isaac turns his gaze to meet hers in the mirror. "You think Park's in danger," he says, and she nods.

"I think we should have brought him with us."

Isaac is already turning the keys forward in the ignition, even as Iris stutters a complaint.

"I don't think we should be here, either, Iris," he says, maneuvering the car back around. "I have an icky feeling in my chest."

"So do I," Dahlia agrees, and she looks back out to the old house. It may look bad, but it doesn't seem like it's harbouring something evil, not anymore, at least. Maybe not at all. "I don't think we were going to find what we were looking for there."

Iris takes a deep breath, and then she nods. "I – no, I'm glad. I felt it, too, I just –"

Isaac's phone starts ringing, and he hands it to Iris to answer.

"It's Park," she says, and Dahlia watches his hands tighten on the steering wheel.

"Answer it," he replies, and the speedometer increases.

Iris does, and she hits the speaker button. The three of them are met with something that sounds like howling, a deep, deep, primal noise of loss and pain that immediately brings tears to Dahlia's eyes. She can't place the voice; she can't place the pain. It's unlike anything she's ever heard before in her life.

"We were wrong," Park says, his voice tinny, "she's gone."

Suddenly it all makes sense. The animal noise in the background is Derek, and the Ghost isn't at the house. *The One who Falls,* Dahlia thinks, uselessly, and her body slumps down with defeat.

How could we be so stupid? She asks herself, *how could* I *be so stupid?*

24

GLASS FOR DINNER

Park isn't sure what's happening. He's outside of Eve and Derek's house, and Eve and Derek are there, too, both with their gazes to the dark shape in the sky that's blocking the moon.

"Get inside," Eve says, and he's sure that it's directed at him, but she's looking at Derek.

Park takes a step backwards, but Derek doesn't move, his head still craned.

"Derek," her voice is strained. "Take Park and go."

"I can't – I'm not leaving you," he says, "I'm not going to leave you out here alone to fight it."

"You can't do anything, Derek," she replies, tugging at his hand, "I know what must happen. I know that it's me it wants. *Please,* just go. It doesn't want you, but it'll take you, too, if you get too close. I couldn't bear it if it took you. *Please.*"

Derek looks back at Park, but Park is looking in front of them, where a man is materializing out of the darkness.

Every hair on Park's body stands, and he freezes as he realizes this is the man, the *thing* that tried to drown him in the river. *"Watch out!"* He yells, but Eve doesn't react.

"It's time," the man, the thing says, and it holds out a hand to Eve. "You know it's time."

"Eve!" Derek yells, but she's already reaching.

"I'm sorry," she says, and there are tears streaking down her cheeks, "Derek, I'm so sorry. I love you. I love you so –"

And then she's gone.

She's gone, and the man, the thing that looks like a man, is gone, and the darkness that was blotting out the sky is gone.

There's an emptiness in the night, a lack of sound, a lack of everything. A void where Eve had stood.

Derek looks at the spot where Eve just was, and then he looks at Park, and Park sees the tears glistening darkly in his eyes. "She's gone," he says, and then, "she's gone," he wails, and a noise that sounds more animal than human starts coming from his throat.

174

Park doesn't know what to do. Park has no idea what to do. He walks forward, almost in a trance, and he wraps his arms around Derek, who pulls him into himself, sobs wracking his body. He thinks that maybe he should try to say something comforting, but they both just watched Eve disappear into thin air, and no amount of empathy or trauma could train him for this moment. He has no idea what to do as Derek continues to sob, the terrible, terrible noise right against Park's ear.

She was just *gone*, he thinks, and then he's pulling away from Derek. "One second," he says, "I have to - we have to tell the others." And he's messily getting to Isaac's number, pressing call.

"We were wrong," he says, numbly, "she's gone."

"We're coming," Iris says back, her voice taught. "Tell Derek to hold on."

He hangs up. "They're coming," he says, and Derek envelops him back into his arms. "They said hold on," he repeats.

"She's *gone*," Derek wails. "She's *gone!* Park - Park it was - it was supposed to be *me*."

"What do you mean?" He's rubbing concentric circles on Derek's back, but it's useless. He knows it's useless.

"*The One who Falls*, we always thought it was going to be *me*. I - I - I could have dealt with it being me. I was *ready* for it to be *me*, but now *she's. gone.*"

Park doesn't know what to say, so he doesn't say anything, he just keeps rubbing circles. There's an ache deep inside of him that he's not sure he can name, not sure he can categorize. It's too early to have lost Eve, he thinks, he hardly knows her.

It's too early to lose any of them; everything is happening so fast.

There's another feeling, and this one is sitting at the top of his chest. He can name this one, though he feels guilty about it. It's *relief*. Relief that *The One who Falls* isn't Isaac. Relief that the *The One who Falls* isn't him. Relief that the thing that looks like a man but isn't a man didn't reach for him, didn't come close to him at all, didn't even seem to notice that he was there.

Of course, the guilt is gnawing at him. Here is a wailing man that just lost his lover, and he is inconsolable, and Park is standing here, hugging him, being glad it wasn't himself. Being glad that it wasn't his own lover.

Stupid, he thinks. *This isn't about you.*

"We should – we should go inside," he says, finally, thinking that maybe Derek is going to have some concerned neighbours knocking at his door.

"What if she comes back?" Derek replies, pulling away from Park and looking back up into the starless sky. "What if she comes back and we're not here for her?"

Park touches Derek's elbow. "We'll keep an eye out through the window, okay? You're going to get too cold if you wait out here."

Derek sniffles, but Park can see him relent, and he leads him back inside. "It was supposed to be me," he says, again, once their shoes are removed, in the cramped kitchen of the basement suite. "Isaac and I talked about it. We both thought –"

The front door opens, and then other three are there, worry written plainly across their faces, all jostling each other to get inside.

Isaac is the first through, and he touches Park's arm on his way to Derek. "It's okay," he tells Derek, reaching up on his tip toes to plant a chaste kiss on Derek's cheek, and then pulls him in for a hug. "We'll get her back. You know we will." Park's head reels at the gesture – of course Isaac is good at this, of course he knows what to do.

"It was supposed to be me," Derek says, once again, and Isaac's voice is muffled from against his shoulder,

"I know that's what we thought," he says, "but every single one of us was wrong. It's okay. We'll get her back." He says it with such vindication that Park believes him. If Isaac says something is going to happen, it's going to happen.

Iris worms her way into the hug, too, squeezing them both. "I thought it was going to be me or Dahlia," she says. "We – we *wanted* it to be either of us, so we could maybe do something from the inside, but we'll get her out, D." Her voice is strained, like she's going to start crying, too and suddenly it's all too much for Park. There are too many emotions flying around, and he feels out of place.

This is a private apocalypse, and he's intruding. He's the uninvited guest sitting in the corner, grieving when he has no reason to grieve.

"I'll be right back," he says as he pushes past Dahlia, out the front door and onto the steps.

The cool air feels good on his face, as he sits, and he closes his eyes, but all he can see is the thing that isn't a man grabbing him by his arm, wrestling him into the water, the sinking feeling in his chest that he's about to die. He presses his palms to his face and turns his head up, towards the sky.

He never thought he would see that thing again, he never thought that he would come face to face with it. There's a tidal wave of relief and guilt and fear rising in him, and he's sure that it's about to crest and fall, and then here he will be, crying on the front steps of a barely-friends' house, right after he's lost his lover.

This isn't about me, he reminds himself, but it's hard to put aside everything he's feeling.

The door opens in front of him, and Isaac's head pops out. "Park - ?" he asks, and then his eyes adjust to the dark. "Oh, there you are. Are you okay?"

The tidal wave starts falling, and Park shakes his head. "I," he starts, but the words hit a clog in his throat and instead a strangled sob sounds, and Park shudders with embarrassment, with shame and guilt. Between Eve disappearing and that stupid fucking *thing*, he can't seem to regulate his emotions, he can't push them back down.

"Oh," Isaac says, again, more of him appearing in the doorway as he slips through and takes a seat beside Park, his arm wrapping around his shoulders. "Hey, it's okay."

"I'm sorry," Park chokes out, grateful for the comfort, embarrassed by the need. "I'm so sorry."

"What are you sorry for?" Isaac asks, pulling him closer, his voice a comforting whisper.

"I – I could have done something. I could have helped – I – I saw the thing that tried to drown me, and I just froze. I could have pulled her back; I could have done *something.*" The last word cracks, and Park swallows back another sob.

"If the Ghost didn't take her tonight it would have taken her another time," Isaac says, pressing his cheek into Park's hair. "It's not your fault. None of this is your fault. You have nothing to be sorry for."

"But I –"

"No," Isaac says firmly, "we knew it was coming. We knew someone was going to disappear. We tried our best to stop it from happening, but *no matter what* it was going to happen, okay? You're not expected to have to step into these situations and just know what to do,

Park. You're not expected to have to stand up to the thing that tried to murder you."

"I'm glad -" Park starts, and then he hiccups, and keeps going, needing to say something, needing to get it off his chest, "I'm glad it wasn't you."

Isaac sighs, and pulls him in closer, both arms around him now, squeezing tighter and tighter. "I'm glad it wasn't you, too," he says, his voice so small.

They breathe together, for a moment and then two moments, and Park starts to calm down, starts to melt further into Isaac's death grip.

"I'm sorry," Park says again, after a while, not sure what he's sorry about, but feeling the need to say it. To make sure that Isaac isn't holding a grudge against him for being selfish, for being too emotional.

"Mm," Isaac hums, and Park gets the impression that he's deep in thought, not in this realm of the world.

"Hey," he lifts his head so he can look at Isaac's face to see that he was right. Isaac eyes are unfocused, his mouth set in a hard line. "What are you thinking about?"

"I don't know how we're going to get Eve back," Isaac says. "I - God, Park, that *sound* that Derek was making. It broke my heart."

Park closes his eyes. "Mine too."

"Does it make us terrible people that we were both relieved that it wasn't each other?"

"I don't know - I don't think so?"

"I think that we have to believe that it doesn't. We need to get Eve back, and we -" Isaac cuts himself off. "We need to figure out how to end it for real. To get rid of the Ghost, and the Sorrow."

"How are we going to do that? I thought you said that the Sorrow exists because of the sorrow in the world. How do we get rid of that?" Park pulls away and Isaac's death grip on him loosens. Is it even possible? *Could* it be?

"I don't know. I - maybe we're supposed to keep going on despite the sorrow. Maybe we can teach it how to, I don't know, keep existing? I mean, we do it all the time, don't we? Derek will keep existing even though Eve is gone, and you'll keep going even though you were almost drowned, and we - we just learn to keep it with us, you know? Maybe we can do something so that the Sorrow does that, too. So it can let some of its things go."

"You mean like therapy for an ancient energy force?" Park is bewildered. He doesn't know what to think.

"Cosmic therapy," Isaac laughs, and it sounds just a little bit like he's verging on tears himself. A little bit like he's verging on madness. "I - I just don't know what to do from here. That's all."

"We can think about that tomorrow," Park says softly, "we don't have to worry about it right now."

"You're right," Isaac sighs, and he catches one of Park's hands in his own, pressing it to his lips, but his eyes still seem absent, cloudy. Park is sure he's still thinking about their plan moving forward. "Also, you - you don't have to be sorry, especially not about what you're feeling. You're allowed to process your emotions, and you don't have to push them down around me." He finally looks back at Park, and it seems as if he's back. "You're allowed to feel your feelings."

Park blinks. "What about you?" he asks. He's not sure he's ever seen Isaac try to process anything around him. Isaac seems to like to do this behind doors, just as much as Park does.

"I - I'm working on it. I - no, I just didn't want Derek to see how relieved I was that it wasn't you."

"Did you really think that it could have been?"

"I don't know. I don't know anything anymore." He sighs, and seems to crumple to half his size, eyes becoming distant once again, and it's Park's turn to wrap his arms around Isaac.

"It'll all work out," he says, "It has to work out."

"I hope so, Park. I really, really hope so."

25

THE ONLY TREASURE IN THIS CHEST IS WAR

Every time Eve takes a step forward, she kicks up a black dust that makes it impossible to see anything. She reaches with a hand to try to catch some of it as it settles, but it doesn't land on her, instead it seems to move *through* her, and she's intrigued by it.

She kicks more of it up, and then floats her hand through it, watching it move with her, move around her, watching it dance with her hand.

This place isn't as scary as she thought it would be. After reading Iris's mom's journals, after hearing the horror stories of it, after seeing what happened to Old John, she was expecting doom and gloom, fires and demons, screaming and more screaming and an endless river waiting to swallow her whole.

Instead, it's a vast field filled with dust, under a starless sky. Instead, it's a darkness that's tinged amber, a living, breathing thing all on its own.

She is not scared; she has no reason to be.

"It's beautiful here, isn't it?" Asks a voice, and she turns to see the man with the low ponytail coming towards her through the dust.

"Yes," she says, and she reaches up again, to try to touch the dust. "What is this stuff?"

The man shrugs. "Memories? Thoughts? Silt? I can't tell you."

Eve's hand falls back to her side. "You're the one who tried to drown Parker," she accuses, her eyes narrowed. "Why?"

He sighs, and she realizes that he doesn't seem to kick up any of the dust. He moves freely, without it following him. "If he dies, then so does your hope," he says, coming closer, "if he dies you can give up on all of your plans to try to stop the inevitable."

"We didn't even know him then," Eve says, softly, "he would have just been another drowned stranger."

"I realize that *now,*" he says, "besides, there would have just been another one. It probably would have taken longer, but the Prophecy will be fulfilled."

"You know about the Prophecies?" She asks, incredulous. She always operated on the understanding that they were written by humans, for humans, that the Ghost didn't know of their dealings.

"Of course, I know about the Prophecies." He doesn't sound angry, just intrigued. "Why wouldn't I? I know everything."

"Then you know they're about to end," she whispers. "*When the Ghost calls, one will doom them all.*"

"Do you know what it means?" He asks, taking another step closer and Eve realizes with a start that he is barefoot, his jeans cuffed at the ankle.

"Do you?" She retorts, suddenly wanting to be barefoot herself. Suddenly wanting there to be no barrier between her and this ground, this dust.

"It means that your fate is inevitable. It means that one of you is going to realize that," he says, slowly, carefully. This is something that he wants her to remember. "It means that you and your little friends don't get to keep putting it off. It means the End."

"The End?" She asks.

"The End of everything as you know it. The End of the screaming. The Start of something new, something like this." He snaps, and suddenly they're in the woods, trees around them miles high, and the sun is filtering in through their branches.

The ground is covered in moss, and the man gestures for her to follow him.

"Wait," she says, and he does. She leans down to untie her shoes, and then leaves them behind, peeling her socks off, too. "Okay. Where are we?"

"You'll see."

"Do you have a name?"

"I am not in need of a name. I am not a person; merely person shaped. I am of the Ghost."

Eve nods. It makes sense that if the Ghost wants to communicate with her, it needs something with vocal cords. She keeps following the man, the moss cool and soft below her feet, occasionally giving way to a root or a sharp stick, but she doesn't let it slow her down.

Around them, the woods keep going on all sides, and she thinks that she can hear the river flowing, loudly in the distance.

"Are we in Belle?" She asks, thinking that she's been here before, or somewhere around here. *This should be a road,* she thinks.

"Yes," he replies, "this is what Belle would be if there were no Belle."

"How is this the End, then?" She reaches out to press a hand to the trunk of a tree, and closes her eyes, feeling the energy coming from it, enjoying its grandiose presence. "Or is this what our town can look like again?"

"Eventually, it will," he says, "eventually all will come to look like this once again, and the Earth can move forward without the plague of humanity."

Eve closes her eyes and breathes in the scent of damp soil and tree. She can hear birds distantly, higher in the canopy, and the river is getting louder as they walk. It's peaceful here, she thinks, but this isn't the truth. This is the Ghost trying to show her what it thinks she wants to hear. "But if you get your way the world won't look like this," she accuses, withdrawing her hand from the tree, her heart sinking a little with the loss of energy. "This is just a pretty lie."

"You're right," he says, and he doesn't sound surprised. "Do you want to see what the End really looks like?"

She nods.

He shrugs, and then snaps again.

Around them, everything looks exactly how it does outside of the Ghost's realm, except that it's empty. Except that there are car alarms blaring and no one to turn them off, except that there's a fire burning in the distance, a house in flames.

"You take everyone," she says, and takes a step forward, only to find there is glass on the pavement. It doesn't dig into her, doesn't break skin, and she takes another step.

"Yes," says the Ghost, and he reaches out, "I take everyone."

"Do they all die?" Eve asks, and she thinks that maybe she should feel sad, or scared, or something other than apathy, but she doesn't. This is just the way things are, the way they will be, and there is no room for fear. There is no room for fighting it, or arguing, or complaining.

Here, in the Ghost, she understands that the End is coming, and it has been coming for a very long time. She understands that their attempts to prolong the wait aren't going to work for much longer, and she can feel the way that the earth wants it to happen. She can feel the anticipation, the gentle hum of what's to come.

"No," the Ghost says, "they don't die."

"What happens to them?"

The Ghost sighs, and pulls his hair out of his ponytail, only to redo it. He may not be human, but he has habits that help him read as human, and Eve is pierced with a deep feeling of the uncanny. "They come to this place." Another snap. "And they either adapt or they die."

They're back in the place with the dust, except that Eve doesn't move to kick any of it up, and she can see the field that never ends, the real barrenness of it. If she listens, she can hear the anger of the land, the anger of the river just out of sight, singing its ugly song.

DRINK ME DRINK ME DRINK ME I AM RAPIDS I AM WHIRLPOOLS I AM ANGRY DRINK ME DRINK ME DRINK ME. I AM DEADLY, I AM ANGRY. DRINK ME DRINK ME.

"There's nothing here," she says, "there's no way to live. Everyone is going to die anyways."

He shrugs. "That's not my problem."

"Why make them suffer? Why not just kill them while they're still in their homes?"

A smile starts on his face, and Eve notices with a start that his teeth are just a little bit too sharp, his mouth just a little bit too large. "Because they've hurt something that I love. Because they've made the Sorrow suffer, and they've made the earth suffer. Because they deserve it."

Eve blinks. She supposes that this is a fair point; the world has suffered with its plague of humans. Humans who are determined to rule nature and not live with it, but this seems a cruel fate. This place, where they will likely starve or die of thirst. This place where there is only dust and amber light. "Why are you showing me this, then?" She asks, and she kicks up a plume of dust. "Why not just smite me like the rest?"

The Ghost's smile gets impossibly larger, and for the first time Eve remembers that she is completely at its mercy. She remembers that she *should* be scared.

"Because I want you to change my mind."

Eve bites back her shock and tilts her head. "I thought you said it was inevitable."

"I don't have to take everyone." The Ghost snaps a final time, and they're back in the End, they're back in the wasteland of Belle, but around them there are still people.

Around them, the survivors make their way through the mess of cars, turning off alarms, turning off engines. She sees herself and Derek. She sees her parents and Iris and Isaac and his aunt and Chip. She sees Park and his sister, nearly identical, both wearing stony expressions.

"You'd leave just the people that I care about?" She asks, swallowing back bile that rises in her throat.

"No," the Ghost says. "People that can live in the land, not just on it. People who know this is coming. The people you love are just the icing on the cake."

Eve takes a deep breath. She watches her future self, and her friends reconvene, the fear shadowing their every move. She wants to ask *why me*, but she doesn't want to test the Ghost's patience. She wants to ask if she can talk to someone else about the decision that is so clearly laying on her lap, but she doesn't want to risk the Ghost taking away the option entirely.

"What do I need to do?" She asks, instead, stepping up to it and crossing her arms over her chest.

26

CHOCOLATE MILK

C waves her gym membership card at Park "No more running," she promises, "I *already* told you that." Ever since her run in with the Ghost he's been hovering when he's home, worried about how she's doing, how she's feeling, if she's okay.

She doesn't know how to tell him how ashamed she is, how scared that this thing is the start of her undoing. She doesn't know how to tell him that she's been sneaking into Old John's house with Kat, learning as much as she can about magic, so she's been trying to avoid him as much as possible.

It's not like it's been that hard. He's spending almost every night with Isaac, or at their other friends' house – the one who lost his girlfriend to the thing that almost took C.

"Fine, fine," he says, "I'm sorry. I know you can take care of yourself. I'm just worried, is all." He leans on the wall by the door, his arms crossed, his face drawn out in concern. "It's dangerous out there."

"Oh," she says, pulling her second shoe over her heel and standing up, "trust me, Parker, I am *very aware* of that." She's maybe a little bit bitter about the fact that he knew about Belle, about its magic and he didn't bother telling her. And now that she does know she's stuck here.

"Sorry."

She narrows her eyes at him, standing there looking like the picture of innocence. It's hard to not spill everything to him, especially because she knows that he'll listen. Especially because she knows that he'll only be more worried about her. "Don't you have your boyfriend to be worrying about?" She asks, instead of telling him anything.

He sighs, and his arms fall to his sides. "I'm worried about him, too, C. I'm worried about *everyone.*"

"It's not your job," she says, her voice softer, "to worry about everyone. We're going to be okay." She feels the pull of her secrets start at the back of her throat. How easy would it be? To tell him where she's been going to? She swallows it back. "Besides, what you should be worried about is dinner with the Terribles tonight."

He rolls his eyes and turns to head back into the house. "Don't fucking remind me," he says, and then, "have a good run. At the gym."

"Yeah," she replies, watching his shadow fade, "bye."

In a way she's glad that Park has found Isaac. She can appreciate the art of it all, the timing. Here is her brother, alone and lonely, unsure what to do with his life, unsure if he made the right decision to come to Belle, and here is Isaac, unable to leave Belle but wanting to give Park the world.

It isn't hard to see that Isaac is enamoured with Park just as much as Park is with Isaac. She's seen the way they look at each other; like moths drawn to light.

She closes the door behind her and pulls the car keys out of her pocket. She's happy for them, she really is. It's just that Isaac is a witch, and this is a town of magic, and she's been feeling even more out of place than she did before, even if she's been drawn into it. It's just that Kat, her fellow exile, is a part of this magic, too, and despite everything she's trying to teach C, C isn't getting the hang of it. She's out of place, and she can't seem to find her footing and it's *frustrating*. She wants to scream. She wants to cry.

Really, she's being dramatic. It's only been a couple of weeks, and Kat herself said that C is doing well for a complete beginner, but that doesn't stop her mind from telling her she's a failure. That doesn't stop the alienation from wrapping its arms around her organs and pulling tight.

"It's like training a muscle," Kat keeps telling her. "Like riding a bike or memorizing a song. Once you have the hang of it, you'll never forget."

So, C keeps going to Old John's, keeps reading and re-reading the book that Kat has given her, keeps lighting the candles and burning the incense and poking her fingers for drops of blood. She has the words to the first Ritual memorized – the one that's supposed to give her a glimpse of the future, but she hasn't seen anything but darkness, yet.

Darkness like that thing that almost took her, black and all-consuming, but Kat says that it's probably just the shadow of it in the house, that they should be doing this in a more controlled place, like the metaphysical shop. However, C is determined that Old John's is where she's going to learn. She likes to think that Old John's is the place where her interest in all this began, in the words that were written on his fence.

She likes fiddling with his radio equipment and letting the static overwhelm her brain. She likes that she could say anything into the microphone and someone, somewhere, will hear her.

They've been digging into Old John himself, as well. Kat's mom and Old John and the Ghost worked together – on what, they're not sure – but Katherine's journals mention him. Kat has a theory that he's the one whose face the Ghost wears in its marionette form, and that he's the one who wrote the last Prophecy book. She thinks that so much contact with the Ghost drove him mad, and he never truly recovered.

C's been doing some digging on Kat's mom, too, unbeknownst to Kat, and her whole situation seems strange. She disappeared for two days, when Iris was seven and Kat was three, and when she came back, she was *angry*. She motivated the town to protest the old-growth logging that was about to occur in Belle, and she started a movement for the trees to be protected. It seems as if she were a force of nature herself, and people listened to her. They respected her.

She went missing again the next year, and she was never seen again. They didn't find a body, or anything to indicate foul play, so C thinks she was probably taken by the Ghost. It's the only thing that makes sense.

She wants to ask Kat more about it, but she doesn't want to pry. Going through the newspaper articles at the library, she'd found something that Kat has never mentioned before, and it makes her heart ache. Kat's legal name is Poppy, and as far as C knows, her mother was known to most as Kat. Kat must have adopted her mom's nickname at some point, and every time C thinks about it she wants to wrap her arms around her friend and hold her tight. She can't imagine the pain that comes with being so young and losing someone so dear.

She pulls the car into the long driveway in front of Old John's house, and parks alongside Kat's vehicle.

Stepping outside, she calls out, but she isn't met with any greeting from the other girl, so she slips up the stairs and into the house.

The power has been cut off to the old man's house, so they've been trying to meet during the day when there's enough light seeping in through the windows, but there's a flashlight at the door just in case. "Kat?" C calls out and lets out a sigh of relief when the other girl answers from further in the house.

"Yeah?" she asks, "You took your time getting here, didn't you?"

"Sorry," C says, "Park wanted to talk to me for a minute."

She enters what was once the living room, where Kat is sitting on the couch that looks like it's straight from the eighties. The whole house looks like it's straight from the eighties to be honest, and it's covered in this fine black dust that C has never seen the likes of before. She's certain that it must be from the Ghost, but Kat's never paid it any mind.

There's no other sign that the Ghost was ever here, besides the broken lamps and the peeling wallpaper. There's no other sign that the Ghost was ever here, besides the dark stain at the front of the door, where it had sat and waited for C to see it.

She shudders before sitting down next to Kat, their knees touching.

"How is your brother?" Kat asks, pushing up her glasses and pulling the book in her lap closer to her chest. "I heard that he and Isaac are getting along great."

"Great is an understatement," she says, "they're nauseating to be around right now. Honeymoon phase but make it, like, a million times worse than anyone you've ever seen. Isaac is meeting our parents tonight."

"That sounds like fun," Kat deadpans, and C laughs.

"Not even a little bit."

Kat's mouth rearranges into a thin line. "And how are you doing?" She asks, her eyebrows raised, concerned.

C shrugs. She's doing as well as she can, she thinks, considering everything. "I'm ready to learn," she says, and Kat rolls her eyes. *I want to talk to you,* C wants to say, *but I can't even tell myself what's going on.* She can't. She's angry. She's tired. She's sad. She's guilty. She's everything all at once, and half of her free time she spends alone, staring at her ceiling and wishing she had more answers. The other half, she stares at her notes app and rereads Old John's words, trying to make sense of them. They don't, and neither do her emotions.

"Alrighty, here we go, then," Kat says, and she opens the book of Rituals.

27

APPLE CRUMBLE

Isaac is sick and tired of his parents. They're everywhere, and instead of leaving him alone, they're asking him questions. They're asking about his life, like they have an actual interest in his comings and goings when they never have before.

His mom did have the brilliant idea of turning a tote container into a makeshift home for the cat, somewhere he can be warm and out of the oncoming snow and wind, but this is only one of two positive things that have come from their invasion of his space. The second is his dad's insistence on making breakfast and coffee in the morning.

That's all he'll give them. Other than these two things, they've been a pain in his ass.

His mom has started camping out in the study, a perpetual cigarette in hand and a vinyl spinning on the record plater. She starts drinking at noon and she can usually rope his dad into drinking with her. They're in bed by seven pm most days, and up at five am the next morning, ready to do it all over again. Isaac is appalled at the whole ordeal – he was under the impression that she was supposed to be recovering from being possessed by a weeping spirit, not drowning her sorrows. Not that it really matters, he's just tired of hearing their drunken laughter from downstairs, and tired of going out of his way to avoid them.

He's staring at his stash of weed, trying to weigh the pros and cons of a CBD gummy before he goes to Park's house for dinner with Park's parents, who are arguably as bad as his own, in a completely different, sober way. He used to take CBD, for his anxiety, but he hasn't needed to for a while and he's not sure how he'd react. They might just put him to sleep.

Park wraps his arms around Isaac's shoulders, sharing his warmth. "What are you thinking about?" He asks softly, his voice right in Isaac's ear.

Isaac leans back into him and holds Park's wrists, thumb to pulse. "In that bag there," he starts, "I have CBD gummies. I'm just debating whether it's worth it to eat one before dinner."

Park sighs, flopping back on the bed, and stretching his arms above him, examining his hands so he doesn't have to look at Isaac. Isaac knows avoidance when he sees it. "You don't have to come to dinner if you're not up for it."

Isaac closes his eyes and counts back from five. These past couple of weeks he's been an anxious wreck, what with his parents being home and Eve missing, this dinner with Park's parents doesn't seem like it could come at a worse time. It's not that he doesn't want to spend time with Park's parents, it's that he doesn't want to do it while it seems like they're marching into impending doom.

He turns and lays down so that their shoulders press together, both looking up at the ceiling. "I want to meet your parents," he says, reaching up and capturing Park's hand in his own, bringing it down and to his mouth for a kiss and then releasing it. "I'm sorry, I'm just nervous. I don't want to disappoint them – or, I guess, I don't want to disappoint you,"

"I don't think you have to worry about disappointing me, babe. If anything, they're going to be the disappointing ones."

Isaac looks over at him, eyebrows raised. "Babe?"

"Oh," Park grins, his eyes alight with mischief, "you liked that, did you?"

"Maybe a little bit." Isaac bites his lip and reaches out to run his thumb over Park's cheek. "Maybe I just like you."

Park's expression softens, melting into fondness. "I like you too, dork."

"Dork?! What happened to babe?" Isaac feigns shock, but his whole body feels light and airy, like it's full of cotton candy. He loves it when Park is like this, when he's open and flirty, and there's a smile on his face instead of that small, scared expression that he was wearing the night Eve disappeared, right before he started crying. The one he's been wearing whenever they start talking about the future, and what they're supposed to do about it. Isaac *hates* that face.

"I mean, you can be both, can't you?" Park has fully turned so he's facing Isaac, and he's smiling.

"I guess I can. Only for you, though."

"Yeah," Park nods, smug. "Only for me."

✳✳✳

Isaac's nose turns up with disgust as soon as he steps through Park's front door, and he looks over to see if Park is doing the same. He is.

"Hey, C!" He calls into the house. "Maybe don't leave your stinky gym shit right at the entrance!"

"Sorry!" Comes the reply, and then C is there, grabbing her gym bag from where it sits by the shoes, her hair damp around her shoulders, freshly clean. With her, she brings even more of the terrible smell. "I meant to get it before y'all came over. Hi, Isaac."

Isaac raises his hand in hello, biting back his suspicions.

C disappears back into the house, and Park turns to him, eyebrows raised.

"That's what you meant when you said Ritual magic smells like something three days dead, right?" He asks, his thumb pointing over his shoulder to where C was just standing.

"Yeah," Isaac confirms, "yeah, that's exactly it."

Park sighs and takes off his shoes, his shoulders slumped. "I don't even want to know," he mutters.

Isaac chews on his bottom lip and pulls his phone from his pocket. If there's anyone who could have given C Rituals, it's Kat, and that would mean she's probably in the same situation. "I'm texting Iris to see if she can talk to Kat. Or really, just smell Kat. They're probably doing it together."

"Is it dangerous?" Park asks, his eyes drawn with worry.

"I mean, alone, yes, but if she's working with Kat, Kat's been doing Ritual magic for nearly as long as Iris has been doing tarot. I don't think there would be anyone safer to learn from."

Park nods. "Alright, I guess. I'm pretty sure she won't be at dinner, though. Mom will kick her out as soon as she gets a whiff."

Isaac grins, "Yeah. Honestly, good for her, though. I mean, it's kind of cool what you can do with them, if you don't get too carried away."

"Would be nice if she told me." Park gestures for Isaac to follow him to the basement, and Isaac does so, looking around warily. As much time as he's spent here, there's still something about the house that puts him on edge, something that makes him feel like he's being watched, like someone is about to jump out from behind a door and yell *gotcha!*

Caught in the act. We know what you two do behind closed doors and it's not okay, you're going to hell you're going to hell you're going to burn. It leaves him feeling slick with shame, even if he knows they're doing nothing wrong.

"Are you and C okay?" He asks, earnestly, as they descend the stairs, and Park sighs.

"I think so. She's not really talking to me, but I haven't been around as much, obviously."

"Sorry," Isaac feels obligated to say, even though he isn't really that sorry. Spending time with Park has been good. It's been the one thing that he's able to navigate. It's been the one thing that hasn't thrown any surprises at him.

"Don't be. You and work are like, the only things that are going okay right now."

They enter Park's room, and it's in the same state of disarray that it was the first time Isaac saw it, the same as the countless times that Isaac's seen it since. "I know what you mean," he sighs, taking a seat on Park's bed, and watching as he scoops the discarded clothes on the floor into his ever-growing dirty laundry bin.

Park finishes his task, and flops down onto his back, just next to Isaac, his eyes closed. "I just want tonight to go well," he says, "I - I mean, I hope it will."

"It's not like it was even your idea," Isaac remarks, reaching over to run his hands through Park's hair, messing up his perfect assortment of curls, "so if it goes bad it's one hundred percent on them."

Last week, right after Eve disappeared, Isaac spent the night here, accidentally running into Park's mom, Georgia, in the kitchen while she left for work. The conversation was awkward, but Isaac introduced himself as Park's boyfriend, and she had merely blinked in surprise.

"You'll have to come for a proper dinner," she told him, on her way out the door, and when Isaac recounted the experience to Park, Park's lips had formed a thin line of worry, which made Isaac think that maybe he should have not introduced himself as *the boyfriend.* Something which he's still worried wasn't okay.

"I don't think mom is expecting you to show," Park says, now, "I still don't know what either of their angles are. They keep calling you my *friend* and saying how nice it is that I've found *friends.*"

Isaac pokes Park's shoulder. "I mean you did find friends."

"Ouch!" He exclaims, batting Isaac's hand away, and flicking his knee in retaliation, sitting up on his elbows. "You know that's not what I mean."

Isaac does know that's not what he meant, but he's only trying to make Park feel better, trying to alleviate some of the stress. He had introduced Park to his own parents, but they hadn't requested a formal dinner with him. It had been a handshake, and a *nice to meet you, Park,* and that was it. He could imagine that if the roles were reversed, he would be just as stressed as Park is. Their laughter from this morning seems worlds away. "I know," he whispers. "I still think that it's going to be okay."

"Okay and good are two different things."

"Park."

"What?"

"I know you're nervous, but if you're convinced it's going to be bad it probably will be! What if they love me? I'm incredibly lovable, you know."

Park rolls his eyes. "I know they're going to love you. I just – I just want them to acknowledge that you're more than just my friend, and that me being gay isn't going to change just because we haven't talked about it."

Isaac nods. "Yeah," he says, "I don't know. Maybe they'll surprise you." Maybe they won't. Maybe it will go exactly as disastrously as Park thinks it will.

Park groans, and flips over so he's laying on his abdomen, hands reaching out to tug on Isaac's hoodie, asking him to join and Isaac obliges, wrapping his arms around Park's shoulders as he settles in beside him. "I don't want to think about it anymore," he says, "just wake me up when they're here."

"Alrighty," Isaac says, digging in his pocket to produce his phone with one hand, and securing his second in the fabric of Park's t-shirt. "Have a good nap, babe."

"Mmmfthanks," says Park, and Isaac's heart swells, just a little bit.

***

Isaac is seated awkwardly between Park and C, and he's trying not to let the Ritual smell bother him too much, but it's strong, and it's making his nose hairs bristle. Park was wrong, and Georgia doesn't seem to be concerned about the stench – the only thing she's concerned about is asking Isaac every question she can think of.

Park's father, Alex, is doing the complete opposite. He introduced himself at the beginning of the dinner and he's hardly spoken a word to anyone since. Instead, he mechanically lifts his food from his plate to his mouth and nods along with the conversation when appropriate. Isaac can almost feel the distaste coming from him, the judgment, and he's trying to avoid all eye-contact, but it seems futile. Alex's gaze has hardly strayed from Isaac all night, and it's making Isaac sweat. His guards have been up all evening, but it's not hard to imagine what he'd be feeling from Alex if they were down. It's written so clearly across his face: *you are an unnatural thing. You are an unnatural thing, and you are at my dinner table, and I do not like it. I do not like you. I do not like that you're a reminder my son is like you.*

Under the table, Park presses his knee into Isaac's sharply, and Isaac blinks up at Georgia, who's just asked him another question which he's missed. "Sorry," he says, "I didn't quite catch that." His voice feels static, limp, lifeless and full of insecurity.

"Oh, I was just wondering what it is that your parents do," she says, taking a sip of her wine, the dark liquid swirling in its glass as she sets it back on the table, "and why they're always out of town."

Park's knee presses into his own again, this time not sharply, and Isaac presses back, grateful for the point of contact, the anchor. "My mom is a lawyer," he says, "more specifically, a divorce lawyer. She's a senior partner at a firm in the city."

Georgia nods, "And what does your dad do?"

Isaac almost snorts. *Follows my mom everywhere,* is what he wants to say, but instead he manages, "Paralegal. They work at the same firm."

Georgia's eyebrows raise, and she cuts into her baked chicken. "That must be a lot. Working and living with your spouse." Isaac notices how she doesn't look at Alex, how Alex still is keeping most of his attention on Isaac.

"Yeah, I mean, they get along great, though." He focuses on his own chicken, and there's a lull in the conversation, an awkwardness that feels more tangible in the silence. "What is it that you do?" He asks, finally, just a few moments too late for it to feel authentic.

C sighs beside him, and he looks over at her, but she's pointedly avoiding eye contact.

"I'm a kindergarten teacher," Georgia says, proudly. "And Alex is a conservation officer."

Isaac nods, amiably, and presses into Park's leg. "Wow," he says, thinking that he's about to say something stupid like *very cool jobs,* when Park interjects.

"One of Isaac's friends is working on that remediation project at the old forestry site," he says, looking at his dad, "maybe you've met her? Dahlia?"

Alex thinks for a second, and then shakes his head. "I don't think I've met her. I haven't really been out there for a while, now, not since Joe stopped trying to convince us they were on his land."

"Ah," Park shrugs, and his knee is against Isaac's again, implying, *sorry, I tried. I'm trying.*

It goes on like this for an incredibly long time. Georgia and Isaac making up most of the conversation, C and Park interjecting whenever they can, and Alex mostly ignoring them all, only speaking when directly spoken to. There's nothing terrible about it, and there's nothing remarkable about it, either, except that the food is good, and the awkwardness lingers over every moment.

Finally, Georgia leans forward, a small smile over her face, the sticky remains of an apple crumble on the plate in front of her. "So, how long have you two been together?" She asks, her tone matter of fact.

Park, in all his grace, chokes on his mouthful of apples, drawing the attention of the table to himself. Coughing, he wheezes out, "What?"

"Are you alright, dear?" Georgia asks, and when Park swallows several gulps of water and nods, she says, "Isaac introduced himself as your boyfriend?"

"Yeah," Park says, blinking at her, "I mean, yeah, he is." His knee finds Isaac's again, pressing hard.

"So?"

"About a month and a half?" Isaac blurts, feeling a blush race across his cheeks. "Maybe less or a little bit more." He's not sure about this. Time has felt both like molasses and a racing river in the past few weeks.

"About that," Park confirms, seemingly fully recovered from his crumble incident. "I –" he starts, but Alex interrupts him by pushing back his chair and leaving the table abruptly.

He doesn't say a word as he heads into the kitchen, and there's the sound of running water, and the opening and closing of the dishwasher. Somewhere in the house, a TV turns on, and Georgia mutters under her breath.

"Sorry, Isaac," she says, "he's been rude all evening. We're just – we're acclimating, is all. You seem like a nice kid, and you seem to make Park happy. That's all we care about, really, he's just having a hard time coming to terms with – with –"

"Me being gay," Park finishes, "us dating."

Georgia's face pinches as if she's in pain for a brief second, before she recovers. "Yes," she says, "I – I've been doing some research, Park. I know we haven't talked about it for so long, but I think that as long as you're happy – I'm – I mean, we're okay."

"Um," Park says, "that's good?" He looks over at Isaac, and there's confusion in his eyes, his eyebrows furrowed.

Georgia's nods, and she pushes out from the table. "It was good meeting you, Isaac," she says, sweetly, "we'll have to do this again. Now, if you'll excuse me." And then she's gone.

"What the fuck," C says, her fork clutched tightly in her hand, the same bewilderment clear on her face. "Park, what was that?"

"I have no fucking clue," Park says, and it comes out as half a high-pitched laugh. "Is this real?" He looks to Isaac for confirmation and Isaac nods.

"It's real," he says, and hope floods into Park's expression, overflowing into his smile. Into his everything.

"I guess this is good," he says.

"Or it's really, really bad." C puts her fork down.

"It sounds good to me," Isaac says, softly, unable to think about what it means if it's bad. Unable to picture the hope in Park being crushed, unable to handle it. "It sounds like she's trying to start to make amends."

Park smiles, then, and Isaac would do anything to keep that smile on his face. "Yeah," he says, "I hope she is."

MORNING BREATH

"Are you sure that he doesn't want us to stop by?" Park asks, peering over Isaac's arm to read the text message that Derek has just sent.

i think i just want to spend today by myself. thanks, though :), it reads.

"Yeah," Isaac replies, "I mean, I don't want to push him to see us."

"No," Park says, biting his lip. "How was he the last time you were over?"

Isaac shrugs, his thumbs moving over the screen, *okay,* he types, *no problem.* "As good as he can be, I think? I mean, he's still functioning. He said that he's been spending a lot more time with his family."

"That's good, I guess," Park says, letting his head fall back onto his pillows. "I mean, I can't imagine what he's going through right now."

"Yeah," Isaac sighs, throwing his phone to the side of the bed, out of sight. *What Derek's been through* has felt like a taboo subject. With the Ghost around it could happen to anyone, and the less they talk about it, the less likely it is to happen. "What are we supposed to do today, then?" It's Park's day off and this was their only plan. Everyone else is working and there's nothing happening with Hell Club, not really.

It seems like they've hit a dead end. The Ghost hasn't reared its ugly head back in Belle since it took Eve and everyone has gone back to life as usual, besides Derek. Besides the gaping hole that Eve's left behind in her absence. Even Park's noticed it, and he hardly knew her.

He's trying to remain positive that they'll get her back somehow, but no one except Derek and Isaac seem to believe it's possible. No one except Derek and Isaac are even looking into options – not that they're finding anything – and their frustrations are rubbing off on Park. He doesn't understand why the others, the ones with more power, aren't trying to understand why she left, what it means that she went willingly, how the Ghost weaseled its way into her mind and made her trust it. It could happen to anyone, Park thinks, and he wants to prevent it. He doesn't want to watch someone else take a step towards the awful man that is the Ghost and let themselves be taken.

He wants to do *something.* He wants to be *useful.*

Iris has been talking about teaching him meditation and small divining techniques, so that they can figure out his secret and he can tell them the thing that's supposed to change it all for them, but their work schedules conflict. Park is never free when Iris is and if he is, he's exhausted and all he wants to do is crawl into Isaac's arms. C is calling them codependent, but she says it less like it's a joke and more like it's jealousy. Every time she says the word, *codependent,* it's a reminder that they might not have much longer together. She knows it and Park knows it and Isaac knows it.

Neither of his coworkers know it, though, and they poke fun at him relentlessly. Isaac will show up, sometimes, when he's bored, and he'll sit quietly in the corner table if it's busy or he'll stand by the register if it's slow. Usually, he has a book with him, but sometimes he just sits, and Park is sure that he's only trying to get some peace from his parents.

He told Riley this, and Riley nodded understandingly. "Shannon is not a nice woman," they told Park. "I wouldn't want to be under the same roof as her, either." They were a little warmer to the idea of Isaac in the corner after this, and even Cadence's jealousy seemed to tone down a notch or two.

Park doesn't like Shannon, either. There's something slippery about her – Isaac was right with his snake-oil salesman description – and whenever she's around his hair stands up on end, and his skin itches with discomfort. It's not that she hasn't been pleasant to him, because she has, but he knows what she's done to Isaac, and he can't forgive her for it. He's glad that no one else seems to like her, either. It seems fitting.

At least the dinner with his own parents went well. Park had his doubts, a churning feeling at the bottom of his stomach, turning to acid reflux while his mother grilled Isaac, but it had gone well. Mostly. Except for his dad. His dad's reaction to Isaac had scared Park a little, and the whole time he was staring, Park half expected him to lunge across the table and strangle him, even if his father has never shown violence before. Whatever made his mother warm up to the idea of Park being gay hadn't made it into Alex, and Park isn't sure if he'll be able to make eye contact with him for a while – not after his anger had been so apparent.

It's not that Park is ashamed – he isn't, especially when being gay has given him the chance to be with Isaac, someone who is kind and gentle and *good* – but his father's blatant disapproval doesn't sit well on his chest. It's a weighted blanket that's several pounds too heavy, and he struggles to breathe. He wants to avoid it if he can.

Georgia surprised him. Her attentiveness to Isaac, her interest, had been genuine, as had her apology for Alex's behaviour. Park remembers C saying something about her trying to turn over a new leaf a while back, but he'd ignored it, scared that she was wrong, scared to start hoping that maybe one day she'd be okay with him bringing home a man, but she was right. He should've known – C is usually right.

His mother even seemed to like Isaac, which is not surprising because Isaac is genuinely likeable, but the idea that she could enjoy the presence of his lover is not something he's ever allowed himself to think about. It feels strange that his mother could grow a relationship with his boyfriend, that they might one day become family.

It's exciting. It's a butterfly flapping its wings in the dark part of his mind where he locked these hopes and desires up when he came out. He wants to sit down with his mom and talk to her about it. He wants to tell her more about Isaac. He wants to bring Isaac home again and let them talk more.

"Babe?" Isaac asks, turning his head, his eyebrows raised. "What are we going to do?"

Park groans, and rubs his eyes with his fists, still tired. Not much sleeping had been done after the dinner, and Isaac accidentally woke him up at the ass-crack of dawn, like he usually does. "Nothing?" He asks. A day of doing nothing with Isaac seems like heaven, but much to his dismay, Isaac's expression fissures with doubt. "Please?" He asks, and Isaac relents easily.

"Nothing as in stay at home in bed and sleep all day or nothing as in we camp out on the couch and watch movies?"

"Uh," Park starts, thinking. "I mean, I'm going to fall asleep if we watch movies, anyways."

"Right," Isaac hums, "bed, then?" He opens his arms to Park, and Park graciously wriggles himself closer.

"Bed," he whispers, his face pressed into Isaac's pajama shirt, Isaac's heart thumping steadily underneath his ear. *Thump-thump, thump-thump, thump-thump.* Park could get lost in it. "I never want to get out of bed."

"That can be arranged," Isaac whispers back, rearranging the blankets so they cover Park's shoulders, and pressing a soft kiss to the top of his head. "We'll never leave again."

Park's eyes shut, lulled back into his sleepiness by the *thump-thump* and Isaac's arms wrapped around him. Here, he can convince himself that there isn't anything he needs to be worrying about. Here, he can sleep knowing that at the very least, Isaac will be there when he wakes.

✳✳✳

Much to Park's dismay, they are out of bed. They are out of bed, but that's okay because Isaac is making food, and the steam from the boiling pot of water that he's standing over has made his hair damp and frizzy, his cheeks red from the heat.

Park is sure that Isaac has caught onto the fact that he's being stared at, from the slight upturn of the corner of his mouth, but he hasn't made a comment on it – something very un-Isaac-like.

"I had a weird dream," he says, instead, scooping out one poached egg, and then another, not looking up from his work. "You were in it."

Park leans forward from his seat on the counter, almost over-balancing and falling off, but righting himself at the last moment. "Oh?" He asks, hoping that Isaac didn't notice. "Tell me about it." Isaac's dreams, when he has them and feels like sharing, are usually strange, and they amuse Park to no end.

"I saw that," Isaac grins, confirming Park's fear. "It was so weird. You were you but you were also different, somehow? Like, there was you and then there was a second you, and the second you was only slightly different. It was something about the way you moved, maybe? Or the way you held yourself?" He dumps the egg water down the drain and starts to arrange the plates, full of breakfast food.

"That's creepy," Park remarks, although it doesn't seem creepier than some of the other dreams Isaac's told him about. They're usually dark, with something chasing Isaac or something luring him somewhere. He accepts his food, and then slides off the counter to grab them both forks. "Was the other Park evil?"

"Mm," Isaac follows Park into the dining room, where they sit in perpendicular seats, feet knocking together. "Not really? Like, your other was just colder. Like he didn't want to talk to me, ever, and he mostly brushed me off."

Park's eyebrows furrow, and he watches Isaac take a bite of his food, avoiding eye contact. "What about me, me?" he asks, cautiously, thinking that maybe this dream of Isaac's could be more than a dream.

"Oh, you were you. We talked about everything – which I think is why the dream was so disorienting." He doesn't elaborate.

"Because there was such a difference?" Park prompts, wanting to hear more.

"Because I know that the real you would never blow me off like the fake you did, so I knew he was fake the whole time? Like, it was almost as if my dream was trying to play a trick on me to make me miserable, but it did a piss-poor job. It was more comical than anything."

Park blinks at him, not sure what to think. Not sure what to say. "I mean, I'm glad you know I wouldn't brush you off like that," he starts, "but is that something that you're worried about?" There's still the underlying concern that maybe, despite Isaac's claim that it was comical, this is something that Isaac is afraid of. Those that he holds dear no longer finding the time for him.

Isaac sighs. "I mean, in a broad sense, yes? Isn't that something that we're all scared of? But I don't think that you would do that, I think you're just the one that I'm spending the most time with right now."

Park nods, accepting the answer. "Okay," he says, poking Isaac's foot with his big toe. "As long as you know I love talking to you."

"Oh, of course," Isaac replies, a stupidly adorable smile taking up his entire face, his eyes alight with affection. "I love talking to you, too, you know."

It's impossible not to smile back at him, so Park does, and Isaac is lucky that there's a table in between them, because Park has never wanted to jump him as bad as he does in this moment. Park has never wanted to shower him in kisses and affection as much as he does right now, and Park thinks that if anyone else was sitting in the chair across from him, it would be a dangerous feeling.

But Isaac is Isaac and Park is Park and there's no danger between the two of them. Isaac feels more like home to Park than anything else, and he's sure that Isaac feels the same. Together, they can build something where there is no anger, where there are no loud voices, where it's okay to share what they're feeling, even if it isn't positive.

Together, they have something that Park desperately wants to be able to live in for a very, very long time.

He's not sure he'll have the chance, though. He's not sure that they can stop the End.

29
CARING IS THE NEW PLAGUE

Eve is sitting on the ground, drinking from a juice box that the Ghost snagged from her world. The black dust is floating around her, glinting in the amber light, and she can't help but wonder what fragments of thoughts or dreams are resting against her skin.

The Ghost is sitting a few feet away from her, looking off into the distance as if it is not truly here, and Eve supposes that it isn't. The bodily form of the Ghost only seems to be alive when it's interacting directly with her, and when it's not, it's more like a marionette than a human. It was kind of creepy, in the beginning, but Eve's been here for what feels like a decade now, and she likes to think that she's used to it.

Or, as used to it as she can be. It's still fucking weird.

This place, this dimension, this other realm or space or time, isn't what they thought it was. The Ghost isn't what they thought it was, and Eve is itching to tell the others what she's learned. She's bursting at the seams to explain everything, the whole plan, the whole process, why it's going to be impossible to stop the Ghost this time.

Unfortunately, according to the Ghost, her fate and its fate are still walking together, intertwined, and she hasn't yet convinced it that there are people worth saving. Though, at this point, she's not sure that any of them *are* worth saving, whether she loves them or not. The things the Ghost has shown her, the things she's heard come from the mouths of despicable people – the love she holds for those closest to her might not be enough for her to want to stop the Ghost.

It's hard because she knows that the people she loves are good people, incredible people, even. It's hard because she knows that most people are good people. Lots of them have some sense of how the world works, how human beings are interwoven into what's around them, the necessary steps that come with healing their relationship with the world. It's just that there are things in the way. There are money problems. There are time constraints.

Sure, everyone would love to be making their own clothes, growing their own produce, and recycling all their waste, but these things take time and time is a resource that many people don't have.

It's hard to walk barefoot in the grass, free of responsibility other than the one between humans and other creatures when there's no money to buy food. No time to make the food. It's hard to prioritize a relationship with the natural world when someone is drowning in the human one.

It's hard to listen to the screaming of the Sorrow when the screaming of the poor is louder. It's hard to focus on the dying world when most people are dying under the feet of those above them on the economic hierarchy.

Eve knows this now. She's seen it.

She's also heard the Sorrow, how beautiful and melancholic the sound of the End seems, how it gets under skin and into the marrow of bones and it aches and aches and *aches*. She immediately started weeping. Her hands felt so useless, her body something that couldn't possibly understand something so incredibly, intricately raw and painful. All she could think of was a cheese grater repeatedly grating the same spot on her skin, never ceasing, cutting through blood and bone and muscle. Cutting through nerves and sinew.

"How do you live with it?" She'd asked the Ghost, and when she looked over at it, it was crying too.

"How do you live knowing that the thing you love the most is hurting?" It asked her, and she's been thinking about that question ever since.

Everyone everywhere is hurting. Trauma and guilt and shame and imperfections and should-haves and could-haves. Invisible hurts, scars, burns, missing fingers, missing limbs. Fucking *arthritis*.

Derek, the person she loves most in the entire world hurts. He stops dead in his tracks when he sees sunflowers, and he cries every time his grandmother's favourite song plays on the radio. He's scared of Alzheimer's and cancer and there are scars across his legs, long faded now, a memory of a time when he hurt so much he couldn't handle it. She's held him and she's comforted him. She's made him tea when he didn't want to talk about it, and she's yelled at him when he couldn't put his hurt into words she understands.

She would do anything to exact revenge on those who caused him unjust hurt. She would do anything to protect him from needless pain, to never see him suffer over someone else's poor decisions.

It's going to happen, though. People are going to hurt him, and she'll bear witness to it. She can't swath him in bubble wrap and keep him in a cage. She can't protect him from everything, even if she so desperately wants to.

This must be what the Ghost feels, when it hears the Sorrow, when it sees the swirling mess of colour and earth and energy writhing in pain. The Ghost just wants to end the needless suffering of what it loves most, and Eve understands this.

She drains the last drops of juice from her juice box, and sighs, her eyes falling back on the Ghost. "Hey," she says loudly, and watches as it jerks back to life, its face reanimating and its limbs jerkily pushing itself off the ground.

"Yes?" It asks, only the whites of its eyes showing until it blinks and the irises roll forward again.

Eve shivers with something like disgust, and then holds out the juice box. "I want to see more," she says, "and I want to let Derek know that I'm still okay."

The Ghost lets out what could be a growl, if it were an animal, and then it snaps its fingers and they're standing in the kitchen of Derek and Eve's suite. It drops the juice box onto the table, and gestures for her to do something.

Hurriedly, knowing the Ghost won't allow her much time she grabs a pen from the junk drawer and scrawls *I'm okay. I'll be back soon. Love you xxxx - E* on the back of a take-out receipt and slides it under the juice box.

The Ghost snaps once again, and the world is exploding around her.

30

HOLD THE FUCK UP

"What were you up to, today?" Asks Isaac's mom, behind him, and Isaac wants to slam his head against the deck railing until he doesn't have to answer. Time is slipping around him like a freshly caught fish; wriggling and impossible to catch. His parents have been home for too long, and they're breaking his rules, they're entering his sacred, safe places.

He doesn't turn around, but he says, "Not a whole lot," his words a sharp edge in the evening air. In truth he spent most of the day with Park, and they really did *not a whole lot,* but even doing nothing with Park feels like something.

After the dinner with Park's parents, Isaac was worried that Park would be upset with him, that he said or did something wrong. He was worried that Park would be upset with his mother's insistence that she's trying to change her views and her ways with very little evidence to back up the claim, but Park seems hopeful. When they talked about it this morning, there was a light in his eyes that could only be the dogged hope that maybe his mom is turning over a new leaf, looking for reparations. They didn't talk about his father much, but the positives with Georgia seem to weigh out the negatives with Alex, and Park still seems excited to move forward with his mother's new outlook.

Isaac wishes that he could feel the same hope with his own parents, that there was still a part of him that thought they would make the effort to patch their relationship with him, but that hopefulness was stamped out of him years ago.

He used to think that they would come and show interest in him; that those people that called themselves his mother and father would call him in the evenings or make the trip out on the weekends to visit with him and take him to his favourite park so they could push him on the swings. This fantasy turned into one where he wished they would come to his track meets and see how good he was at running, at jumping, and then when he quit the team and quit sports altogether, the fantasy changed into him feeling okay with them seeing his art, them paying for the painting lessons that he wanted so badly.

It was never them, though. It was always Mel or his grandparents that were there, cheering him on. It was always them who uplifted him, who comforted him. He didn't have to think twice about sharing his art with Mel, or his grandma, and it was his grandpa who paid for the lessons. His parents were never around, and the hope that they would try to fix it now, two decades later, is laughable.

"Did you spend any time with that boy? Park? He seems nice." His mom leans against the railing beside him, and wordlessly asks for his lighter, which he gives to her with an annoyed sigh.

"He is nice," he says, hoping that she hears how much he doesn't want to be having this conversation and she'll leave him alone.

His mom nods and takes a drag of her cigarette, handing him back his lighter. The two of them have the same hair, his mom's starting to go grey around her ears, and they have the same eyes, his mom's tired but smart. "How long have you two been together?"

Isaac shrugs. It feels like it's been forever, but it's only been just over six weeks since they dredged him out of the river. He doesn't want to be specific, so he says, "Only a little while."

"Oh," she sounds surprised, "I thought – I thought it'd been longer, I guess. You two seem so close."

The end of the world kind of does that to you, he wants to say, but replaces the words with another shrug.

"That's what it was like with your father and I," she starts, and Isaac refuses to look over at her, instead focusing on the treeline at the edge of their property, the clouds in the dark sky that cover the stars and promise that snow is coming. "We just went together. It didn't matter that we only knew each other for a few months before we got married – we both knew it was right. He felt like home."

Isaac swallows. He doesn't want to be hearing this – he doesn't want to *know this* about his parents. He doesn't want there to be more that link him to them, he is *nothing like them.*

"I know you're mad at us, Isaac," she keeps going, "I know you've always been mad at us. I don't blame you – I would be mad at us, too. For what it's worth, I wish that it could have been different. I wish that we could have been there for you. I wish that I could have really been your mom."

There's anger that's rising from the pit of Isaac's stomach, and it burns brightly. He opens his mouth to tell her off, but nothing comes out except the small noise of the words getting caught in his throat. *How dare you,* he wants to say, *how dare you come back here and say this? How dare you think that you have the right?* But his anger won't let it out. His anger sets his jaw, and grips the railing harder, making his knuckles strain white.

"I'm sorry," she says, and her voice is too soft, too kind. "That was too much. I know it's not fair. I came out here to tell you that we're leaving tomorrow."

Isaac's head whips around to look at her, his eyebrows raised. "It's only been two weeks," he says, bewildered. Certainly, she can't be recovered yet.

A small smile starts at the corners of her mouth, and she stubs her cigarette out in his ash tray. "I know."

"Are you going back to work?"

She shakes her head, "No. Not yet. We've booked a week stay in a resort in Jasper, and from there we'll see where we go."

"Oh," Isaac says, not sure there's anything else he *can* say.

"We probably won't see you tomorrow morning," she continues, "so I'm going to say goodbye now. It's been nice seeing you again, Isaac, and I hope that everything works out in your favour."

He blinks at her, as she pushes herself from the railing. "Bye," he says, and she nods, and then heads back into the house.

Without thinking, he pulls a cigarette from the carton in his pocket and lights it. Something inside of him feels like this is another ending, but he's not sure what kind. He's not sure if it's a beginning, too, and despite his best efforts, the anger in him is subsiding, leaving him empty and shivering and exhausted on the deck.

Whatever that was, whatever he's hoping that it could morph into, isn't healthy for him to obsess over. His mom has said kind things to him, before. He's sure his mom is full of kind things to say to him, but this doesn't mean that anything has changed. This doesn't mean that he's any more inclined to be hopeful that she's changed, or that there's something there they can fix.

He looks back up to the sky, to the clouds, and he lets out a deep breath. *They're leaving tomorrow,* he thinks, and for the first time in a week, he can relax his shoulders.

* * *

The door to Derek's basement suite opens to reveal Derek, grinning. "Hi?" Isaac says, both glad and surprised to see Derek in such a good mood.

"Hi!" He exclaims, ushering Isaac in, "You're never going to guess what I found last night!"

Isaac raises his eyebrows in suspicion and removes his shoes. As he's unzipping his coat, he asks, "What did you find last night?" Whatever it is it must be good, because Derek has the giddiness of a child on Christmas morning.

Derek flips a couple of papers off the dining room table, and then produces a take-out receipt. "Here," he says.

Isaac looks at it in disbelief. "Dinner for two from the diner?" He asks, and Derek lets out a sigh.

"Flip it over."

Isaac does so and scrawled messily across the back is a note, which sends a chill up his spine. The hairs on his arms raise, and he blinks up at Derek.

I'm okay. I'll be back soon. Love you xxxxx -E

"Do you think this was actually her?" He asks, flattening the receipt and reading it again.

"It's her writing," Derek starts, excitement still buzzing around him like electricity, "and – wait, this might sound weird, but there was an empty juice box on it. It was mango flavoured, and that's her favourite."

Isaac hands Derek back the note, his mind racing. If Eve can come back to leave Derek something tangible, then that means that she's able to move around in the Ghost, in the other dimension, the place where the Ghost exists. It means that at the very least, she's eating and drinking.

"You don't have those juice boxes in the house, do you?" Isaac asks, and Derek shakes his head.

"We buy jugs."

There's silence for a minute, and Derek's excitement seems to die down a little, his expression fading into something a little more like worry. "This is a good thing, right?" He asks. "This means that she's okay?"

"I mean, I guess so? She says she's okay, so I think we should believe her. At least we know she's hydrated."

Derek looks down at the receipt in his hands, and then cups it to his chest like it's something sacred, something to be cherished. "I don't think she would lie about being okay. I don't think she would lie about any of it. She has to know how worried I am about her, and I don't think that – I don't think that she would lie, is all." He nods to himself, and Isaac sees the darkness under his eyes, the desperate, unfailing hope that this is real, that this was Eve, that this is her telling them that she really is alright.

"I don't think she would lie, either," Isaac says, looking down at his hands. In fact, he's one-hundred percent sure that she wouldn't. "I just hope that whatever she's doing, she's okay, and she can come back soon."

"Do you think she's working with it?" Derek asks, plopping himself onto the couch, receipt still against his chest. "The Ghost, I mean."

Isaac falls to sit beside him. "She must be," he says, "it doesn't make sense for her to be able to leave notes and stuff for you if she's not. I don't think anyone has been able to do that before."

Isaac is sure that no one's been able to do that before. If they had, then maybe the Ghost would seem less terrifying, less of a death sentence.

"She *is* special, you know," Derek muses, "she's been having – I mean, she was having these dreams before it took her. She said it felt like something was trying to talk to her. She said that it always felt like everything around her was cracking at the foundation."

"It sounds like the Ghost was reaching out to her." Isaac sits up straighter on the couch. "Maybe it chose her, maybe the One who Falls isn't random?"

"Do you think that means that maybe the Ghost is trying to work with us? Instead of just smiting us all? Could it be, like, wanting to make a truce?"

"I don't know," Isaac says, his mind racing. He's never thought of it like this before – it's always just been an End that they're fighting against, an End that the Ghost is supposed to bring to them. He hasn't considered that the Ghost would try to reach out to them, would allow a white flag to fly, which *must be* what the note is.

Derek shrugs. His hands are still around the note, but now they sit in his lap. Isaac can only imagine how relieved he must be, knowing that Eve is okay, knowing that she'll be coming back.

Another possibility occurs to him – this could be a lie. This could all be a lie. The Ghost could be playing with them like pawns on a chessboard, and the note could be a set up to lure them into thinking it isn't as dangerous as they think it is.

He doesn't dare say it out loud. He doesn't dare mention it. He knows that it would wipe the hope from Derek's face, and he couldn't do that. Not in a million years. Derek deserves to hold on to his hope, and Isaac needs to believe that this is real. He needs to believe that Eve wouldn't lie to them, that she wouldn't leave something so hopeful even if there was a gun to the back of her head.

***

The meditation music playing on the shop speakers tells Isaac everything he needs to know as he steps inside. The gentle jingling of the bells on the door makes Kat look up from where she's perched on the counter, and she presses a finger to her lips. "They're in the back," she whispers, and Isaac barely hears her.

He nods, and stuffs his hands in his pockets, working his way through the maze of the metaphysical store until he's at Iris's reading room. He opens the door cautiously and sticks his head through to see candles lit on every surface.

Iris and Park are both sitting on the floor, facing each other, Iris with her eyes open and Park with his closed. Iris looks over at him, and waves her hand, ushering him in. She, too, presses a finger to her lips and he rolls his eyes at her.

He takes off his coat, and places it as quietly as he can on the small table by the entrance, and then joins them on the floor, his knee pressed to Iris's.

Park's face is set in a soft kind of concentration, relaxed but present, and Isaac knows he shouldn't stare, but it's hard not to. Park is *beautiful*, maybe even more so now than the first time that Isaac met him. Isaac loves the way his eyelashes cast shadows onto his cheeks in the candlelight, and the spattering of freckles across his lips that are so faint you have to be as close as he is to Park to see them. Or closer. Isaac would love to be closer.

Iris pokes his arm with a sharp fingernail, and he turns his head to her. *No staring,* she mouths, and he rolls his eyes yet again, but averts his gaze to his hands. He wants so badly to tell her what he found out at Derek's, but he knows he's going to have to wait.

Whatever it is that's going on in Park's head right now is just as important.

Park shifts, and when Isaac looks back up, he's stretching out his fingers, his eyes wide open. "Hey," he says.

"Hey," Isaac repeats.

"That was only three minutes," Iris says, sounding annoyed. "Did you see anything?"

Park's jaw clenches, and he shakes his head. "I don't know if I can try again," he says, "all I can think about are my parents. And my ass hurts."

Iris sighs and pushes herself off the ground. "Fine," she says, "we're going to do this again tomorrow."

"I have to *sleep* -"

"Park."

"Fine."

Isaac watches the exchange wordlessly. As good as it is that Park and Iris are getting along better than they were in the beginning, they're still a little bit awkward, and he isn't sure that there's anything he can do. Park needs sleep, and they need answers. They need him to be their Prophet. The *world* needs him to be their Prophet.

He slaps his hands onto his knees, and says, loudly, "Eve left a note for Derek."

There's a clatter from where Iris has started blowing out candles, and a white pillar rolls slowly across the floor. "She *what?*"

31
INTERLUDE IV

"I can't tell you anything about the Ghost," Mel sighs. "The only person who can tell you anything about the Ghost is your son." Of course she knows about the Ghost, but she would rather walk into traffic than tell Shannon anything.

Her sister glowers at her, the morning sun illuminating her hair, making the grey stand out more than usual. "What about *your* son?" She asks, and Mel can't stop the laughter that bubbles out of her throat.

"If you think you're getting anywhere near Chip, *think again.*" She pulls the door closer to her body, so that Shannon can't even see into her house.

"Think about it, though, Mel," Shannon tries a new tactic. "Think about how much money we could make if we found a way to bottle it, to sell it. Everyone wants a little bit of the end of the world."

Mel's nose twitches, and her hand tightens around the door. Of course, it's all about the *money.* Not about her son, who's risking everything to stop it, and not about the people who will be taken if he fails. No, of course, it's about a *profit.* "You disgust me," she says, but it doesn't hit Shannon hard enough, so she continues. "I'm disgusted by you. You think you can waltz in here and just know everything? You couldn't touch the Ghost even if you tried."

Shannon's eyes have turned cold. "Oh, believe me," she says, "I'm going to try."

Mel can't stop herself. She slams the door shut in her sister's face and slides the lock into its home. She tries to say something witty, but her tongue won't move. She's full of anger, and it's closed her throat too tight for words to slip through.

"Oh, *fuck you!"* Her sister yells from outside. "You think you're *any better* than me? You ran the business too, or did you *forget* about that? You were better at it than I *ever* was! Fuck you, Mel. Get off your *goddamn* high horse."

Angry footsteps stomp off Mel's front porch, and she leans her forehead against the coolness of the door. Shannon's right, of course – she likes to pretend that she's better than her sister, but she's sold things she shouldn't have before. She's inadvertently caused deaths. She's profited from the pain of others, and she might have done it to *take care of her family*, but that doesn't change that she's done it. That doesn't change that she's a terrible person, too.

"What's happening?" Walt asks from behind her, and she turns to see him standing at the bottom of the staircase, still half-asleep, his robe draped across his shoulders, undone in the front and flapping open to reveal his chest.

"Just the wicked witch of the West coming for a visit," she mutters, "it's all good, babe. She's leaving."

Walt blinks, looking several degrees more awake. "What did she want?"

"Just came to give me shit about the business. Made a point to say that I'm no better than her for it."

Walt shrugs. He's never been bothered by the ethics of Mel's work, and she's not sure if it's because he truly doesn't care or if it's because he doesn't know the extent of what she's done. Part of her always hangs on the precipice of telling him, but she never does. She doesn't want him to see her like she sees herself. "You did it for your family," he says, "She's only doing it because she has a debt to pay."

Mel hums in agreement and opens her arms for a hug. He obliges, enveloping her in his warmth. She presses her cheek against his beard, and says softly, "I love you. I'm sorry this woke you up."

He rocks them back and forth gently and presses a kiss into her hair. "I love you too," he says, "and don't worry about it. I'm just sorry I didn't get down here soon enough to chase her off for you."

Mel chuckles at the thought of her sweet, non-confrontational husband trying to do anything to dissuade Shannon from approaching their house. She doubts it would have gone well for him, but she appreciates the sentiment, anyways.

"Why are you laughing?" He asks, pulling away from her, grinning. "You don't think I would have done anything, do you?" He raises his eyebrows, and she only laughs in response. "You *don't*, do you?"

"No," she says, smiling. "I don't think you would have."

"Well, next time she comes around, just you watch."

"I hope there isn't a next time."

Walt nods, his eyes serious. "Me the fuck, too."

***

Iris taps her fingers absently over her favourite tarot deck, enjoying the sound of her new acrylics. It's something that she's only recently started treating herself to, but she thinks that it helps her aesthetic - the new ones are dark black, almonds, a single swirl of purple down her ring fingers. She's already gotten three compliments today.

There's a knock on her door, and panicking she looks down at her schedule before she remembers that she asked Park to meet her here after her readings were finished. *Right,* she thinks, *right right right.*

"Yeah, come in," she calls out, and the door opens and there Park is, the man that has her best friend wrapped so *completely* around his little finger.

"Hi," he says, unzipping his coat and hanging it cautiously on the coatrack beside the door.

"Hey," she replies. "Are you ready?"

He sighs, deeply, and Iris notices how tired he looks. "Ready as I'll ever be, I guess."

***

In Derek's dream, Eve is sitting at the dining room table, drinking a juice box, and humming annoyingly loud. "Would you stop that?" He asks, and she puts the juice box down.

"This is the last time you'll see me," she says, "and you're going to be rude about it?"

He opens his mouth to say *no, no, of course not, I'm sorry, I'm so sorry, please don't leave,* but then she disappears just as she did that night with the Ghost, and all that's left in her wake is a take-out receipt. He reaches out to grab it, and when he does, he sees that there's a note at the bottom of it. He tries to pull the receipt towards him, to read the note but every time he does, he's met with empty paper.

"No," he says, softly, "no, please." He keeps pulling on the receipt, but all it does is pile around him until he's knee deep in it, and he gives up. "Please just come back," he begs, throwing his hands up. *"Please!"*

Around him, there's the hiss of a whisper, a single word, reverberating around the basement suite until he's standing alone in a field, one bathed in a low, amber light. "Eve?" He asks, his voice verging on tears.

"Soon," says the world around him. "Soon."

"How soon?"

"Soon. Soon. Soon. Soon. Soon."

The word repeats until the earth opens in front of him, creating a gaping black maw, a mouth that doesn't seem to end. "Soon," it says, "soon," it promises, its earth lips pushing the word out with Eve's voice.

Derek wakes with a start, sweaty and wrapped in his sheet, his left arm asleep beneath him. "What the fuck?" He croaks to himself and reaches for the bedside lamp. His dreams, while weird, are not usually this weird.

His hand brushes against a sticky note that's been left on the lampshade, and he grabs it, hurriedly, waiting for his eyes to focus.

Soon,

Xoxoxoxoxo – E

32
WHAT WAS THAT BULLSHIT ABOUT STARS

Park's alarm rings loudly in the morning, and he groans, reaching blindly to turn it off. Much to his surprise, Isaac is still beside him, and one of his hands lands solidly on his shoulder. He grumbles a soft sorry.

"Mmmf," Isaac says as Park navigates over him to the bedside table, turning off the alarm.

"Morning, sunshine," Park whispers, collapsing back down in his spot, pulling the blankets up to his chin.

Isaac opens one eye, the other still pressed against his pillow. "Morning," he says, his voice groggy and deep. "Do we have to get up?"

Park smiles and reaches to run a hand through Isaac's hair. Last night Isaac convinced him to come back to his house, so they could enjoy the newfound silence of his parents' absence. Park was reluctant, because he needed to sleep, but much to his surprise Isaac had crashed before he did. It all must be catching up to him because Isaac is usually downstairs by the time Park's alarm goes off.

"I do," he says, his thumb tracing over Isaac's eyebrow. There is so much fondness churning in his stomach that he can hardly handle it. He almost closes his eyes so he doesn't have to look at Isaac's face – his heavily-lidded eyes, his pout half-smushed against the pillow, the stubble on his cheeks – but instead he adjusts the blanket over Isaac's shoulder. "But you can stay in bed, sleepy."

Isaac's eye shuts once again. "Gotta bring ta work," he slurs, "five more minutes?"

"Okay," Park whispers against his better judgement. He's awake, but he's not sure if he's awake enough to get up in five minutes. He's awake, but he's not awake enough to be able to resist when Isaac opens his arms and invites Park into an embrace.

He presses into Isaac's warmth, breathing in the smell of him, settling against him like a puzzle piece finally in the right place. Isaac's started sleeping with his shirt off, and Park is a big fan of this new development. He likes the skin-on-skin contact, the softness of Isaac's abdomen against his own, the tickle of armpit hair on his chest.

He closes his eyes, his ear pressed against Isaac's chest, the slow and steady thump-thump of his heart mirroring his own pulse. He's sure that Isaac has already fallen back asleep, and he tries to resist the pull to do the same.

Five minutes, he thinks, *just five more minutes.*

***

When Park wakes again there's bright light streaming through the window, and instant panic hits his heart, jolting him out of Isaac's grip. "Shit," he says, throwing the covers back, leaving them both exposed to the cold morning air. "Shit, shit shit."

Isaac blinks, and then sits up, looking around, rubbing his shoulders with his hands.

Park stands on unsteady legs and grabs his phone. Three missed calls from Sky, and one from Riley show up in his notifications. The time reads 9:49AM, nearly four hours late for his shift. *"Fuck!"* he says, dropping his phone and listening to it clatter on the ground.

He knew that it was a bad idea to stay in bed. He knew it, and yet he still did it. He still let Isaac talk him into it. No – it's not Isaac's fault. Park didn't want to go to work, anyways. He knew what was going to happen and still, the anger at himself twists his stomach violently anyways.

"Hey," Isaac says, softly, wrapping his arms around Park's shoulder and pulling him into him. Park wants so badly to melt into him, to let him comfort him, but the anger presses its fingers into the base of his spine and starts to climb upwards. "It's okay. You needed the sleep more than you needed to work. Give them a call, let them know what happened. It'll be okay."

"I –" Park starts, about to snap at Isaac, and then closes his mouth. It's not Isaac's fault. Isaac is trying to make him feel better. He pulls out of Isaac's grip and grabs his phone from the ground, opening his voicemail.

"You have three new messages," the mechanical voice on the other side of the line says, and then it's Sky. "Hey, Park, it's six-ten. I'm just wondering what's going on - are you okay? Please let me know." He deletes the message, and then she's in his ear again. "Hey, Park. It's six-thirty. Just wanting to check in. Hope you're okay. Please get back to me as soon as possible. Don't worry about coming in today, we've got it covered." Delete. Sky again. "Hey, Park. It's seven-thirty, sorry for calling so many times, I just want to know that you're alright. Please call me back. I'm worried."

Isaac falls back, sitting on the edge of his bed, looking at Park with a soft expression, guilt creeping in at the corners of his eyes. Park sighs. "I'm sorry," Isaac says, and Park shakes his head.

"Not your fault," he says. "It's okay. Sky doesn't seem mad. Let me just - hold on."

He dials Sky's number and she answers on the second ring. "Park!" She says, "Oh, thank God. Are you okay?"

"Yeah," he says, "I'm fine. I'm really sorry, I just - I just -"

"Don't worry about it," she cuts him off, "honestly. It's okay. I'll just put down that this is one of your sick days. Will you be in tomorrow?"

Park's eyebrows furrow, and he looks over at Isaac. "Yeah," he says, "yeah, I'll be back tomorrow. Thank you, Sky."

"No problem. See ya." She ends the call.

Park puts his phone back on the nightstand, and Isaac reaches out a hand for his, pulling him easily so that he's standing right in front of him, looking down.

"Are you okay?" Isaac asks, and his voice is velvet soft, cotton soft.

Park doesn't want to talk about it. Not yet. He's still trying to douse the anger inside of him, and Isaac's hands around his are helping. "I could ask you the same thing," he retorts, changing the subject, avoiding. "I've never seen you sleep that much."

Isaac shrugs. "I think my parents being here was stressing me out more than I thought it was. I'm glad they're gone."

Park nods. He's seen how stressed Isaac's parents being in his space made him - he gave him a shoulder massage a few nights ago and the tension in them had been incredible. It's no wonder Isaac hardly sleeps. "I'm glad they're gone, too," he says, and then there's quiet for a moment. He looks up to the ceiling, so he doesn't have to look at Isaac with his silent, probing gaze. Finally, he says to the ceiling, "I don't know what happened this morning."

Isaac squeezes his fingers. "Okay," he says, "but I'm here to listen, if you want to talk it out."

Park sighs and finds Isaac's gaze again, weighing his options. There's a reason he was so easy to sway back into bed this morning, and he knows exactly what it is, he's just not sure how to approach it, how to make it make sense to anyone else. Finally, he says, "I just don't know what the point is, anymore."

Isaac nods, persuading him to continue.

"I mean, the End is near, isn't it? So why the fuck am I wasting time at work? Even if we're able to stop it – I don't – I don't know. Maybe if we stop it I'll go back to school." Working is pointless. Working at a café in Belle is even more pointless than working anywhere else in the entire world. The world isn't going to last for much longer, so why should he be making overpriced coffee for the people actually working jobs that matter when he could be here, at home, at Isaac's house, spending what little time they have left with Isaac?

"I get it," Isaac says, immediately, and his eyes have darkened. The rest of his face is open, honest. "I keep thinking about that, too. Like, if we can't stop it, then why are we still trying? Why aren't we just enjoying the time we have left together, you know?"

Park slumps back onto the bed, their legs pressed together. They're both quiet for a moment, and Park realizes that it was a good idea to talk to Isaac about this. It's usually a good idea to talk to Isaac about most things – he brings a rationalization, a levelheadedness that Park can rarely find on his own.

"I have some money saved up," he blurts out, "I mean – I have a lot of money saved up. I could – I could quit my job, for now. We could just –"

Isaac puts his hand on Park's thigh and turns towards him. "Is that what you want?" He asks, and Park feels giddy with excitement, with the prospect of not having to return to work, of getting to spend more time, here, with Isaac. Of getting to sleep in, of getting to sit in the last bit of sunshine they have before winter really hits.

"I think it might be what I want," he says, and the last bit of anger that was keeping its hold on him slides away. "I want to spend more time with the people that matter to me. I'll figure out what I want to do after we stop it." *Or after we don't.*

Isaac nods. "Okay." It's all he says. It's all he needs to say.

Park sighs. It feels good to have voiced the doubt that's been building in him. It feels good to have admitted to someone, Isaac, of all people, that he doesn't think normal life as it's going is worth putting energy into anymore. "Okay."

Isaac smiles, and he presses his face into Park's shoulder. "Okay."

****

Park is sitting in front of Iris again, both cross-legged. Iris had the foresight to set pillows on the floor this time, and Park is eternally grateful. The floor is hard, even through the yoga mat.

Isaac is sitting in the corner, a blanket draped around his shoulders, and he's been switching between scrolling on his phone and reading chapters of the thick book he brought with him. He also has a pillow, but his has migrated to separate his lower back from the wall. He hasn't said a word since they started, almost two hours ago, but Park is getting the feeling that he's antsy to leave and is just too polite to voice his discomfort.

It doesn't matter, though. Iris is relentless, and they won't be leaving until Park can stay in his own mind long enough to see something that's relevant, to come up with something viable as their next move.

The shop outside of Iris' reading room is quiet, and Park can only assume that the sky has gone dark.

Isaac stands, abruptly, and both Iris and Park look over to him as he sheds his blanket cape. "I'm going to go get food if we're staying here late. I'm *starving.*"

Iris looks over her shoulder at him, her eyes narrowed. Isaac's mouth flattens, and his eyebrows raise, as if to say, *are you going to deny me food?* and then she nods.

"Fine," she says, "I guess we should take a break, too."

"Oh, thank god," Park says, almost involuntarily, and Iris rolls her eyes at him.

"Has it been *that bad?*" She asks, and he shakes his head.

"No," he says, and he's telling the truth. Sitting in silence with Iris, sitting in silence with himself, isn't that bad. He's enjoying it, really, he's just tired, and his muscles are going stiff, and he's also hungry now that he's thinking about it. "I'm just ready for food."

She nods. "Me too, honestly. A milkshake sounds great right now."

"Alrighty," Isaac says, and slides his coat on over his sweater. "Milkshakes it is."

The three of them bumble out of Iris' reading room, and Isaac offers his arm to Park in the dark store to keep him from bumping into anything, and Park graciously accepts. What little light that's able to filter in through the windows seems to be enough for Isaac to guide them out, even though Park's eyes are only starting to adjust by the time they get to the door.

Iris tells them to wait while she sets the alarm, and while she's pressing buttons, Isaac reaches out to press a finger to Park's nose, grinning when Park makes a face in protest.

"Asshole," Park mumbles, feeling his cheeks go red, but Isaac's grin only gets bigger.

You love it, seems to be what he's saying, and he's right. Park does love it.

"Okay, everyone out," Iris says, shooing them with her hands, and Isaac turns to open the door, pulling Park with him.

They stop to wait for Iris to lock the deadbolt, and then all three of them start for Isaac's car without hesitation.

"Shotgun," Park says, cheerily, and Iris groans.

"Fine," she says, "but I call shotgun on the way back."

"That's cheating!"

"Says who?"

"Says me."

"How is it cheating?"

"You're calling it too far in advance!"

"I say it's fine," Isaac says, opening the driver door and looking across the top of the car at Park, the small beginnings of a smile on his face.

"Rude! This is betrayal!" Park says, and he smiles back.

"Hah!" From Iris, as she closes her door behind her.

There's silence in the car until Isaac's music starts playing, and it's not uncomfortable. Park thinks that at this point he mostly trusts Iris, and she's done everything she can to gain it. She's funny, and she's determined and she's smart. She's good at what she does, and she knows it. She's been teaching Park in the kind of way that he's understanding, and she's building up his confidence in himself, something that he's incredibly impressed by.

She's a better person than she puts off, and Park is only a little bit surprised by this. What he's more surprised with is how well the two of them get along. Even without Isaac around, Park likes hanging out with Iris.

Even if she is determined that his mind holds an answer when all he can see is the End, and fire. Even though he keeps telling her that he's probably not a Prophet.

Isaac pulls the car into the 24-hour diner, and the three of them get out of the car, and hurry to get out of the cold. Inside Iris asks for a table for three, and the waiter tells them to sit anywhere. The entire place is empty, and a creeping feeling starts at the base of Park's neck, but it's stopped when he sits beside Isaac in a booth, their legs and shoulders pressed together.

There's nothing creepy about the diner, Park, he tells himself, *it's just a diner.*

Iris squints at the paper menu on the table, and traces down the milkshakes absentmindedly. "I think I'm feeling like chocolate," she says, and hands the menu over to Isaac, "and a burger. Obviously."

Isaac nods, and immediately hands the menu to Park. "I'm getting the same," he says, and under the table his foot hooks around Park's ankle.

Park tries hard not to react and reads through the menu to take his mind off what Isaac's doing. He gets the creeping feeling that there's something wrong again, and the light above their table flickers. He looks up, and watches as a fly crawls across the lightbulb, its red eyes staring right at him.

Under the table, Isaac's foot has disappeared and he moves his to find it again, but he's met with empty space.

He looks over and Isaac is gone. Iris is gone. It's just him alone in the diner and when he sets the menu back on the table, it reads: *SINK INTO ME, I AM SOFT, I AM FORGIVING, I AM COMFORTING. SINK INTO ME, I AM HOME, I AM HOME, COME HOME. I AM SOFT, I AM FORGIVING, I AM COMFORTING.*

Park feels anything but comforted, and he stands, nearly tripping on the table leg. "Hello?" He calls out, and his voice echoes through the diner. No one answers. "Hello?" He tries again, and the light above him sparks and goes dark.

Shit, he thinks, and the light in the booth ahead of him does the same. *Shit shit shit.*

He wills his legs to work, to get him out of the diner before it goes completely dark, and he barely makes it out of the door, the bell chiming and announcing his exit before the last light sparks, and then he's standing in the glow of the streetlamp, looking up and wondering if it, too, will go out.

It doesn't.

He breathes a sigh of relief, and then from behind him he hears the soft whisper, "Sink into me, I am soft, I am forgiving," and the ground beneath him starts to melt. "I am comforting. Sink into me, I am home, I am home, come home."

He tries to pick up his feet, but he can't. They're stuck in the pavement like quicksand, and the voice is still speaking. His heart is a jack hammer in his chest, and he tries to even his breaths, to keep control.

"I am soft, I am forgiving. I am comforting. Sink into me, sink into me, sink into me."

"Stop!" He yells, demands, and he stands very still. It stops. He ignores the shaking in his hands.

"You know nothing," the voice hisses, sounding like it's right beside his ear, but when he turns his head there isn't anything there. "You think you can stop it." The other side.

"Can we stop it?" He asks, his voice wavering. The streetlight flickers, along with it.

"Can you stop a tornado?" It hisses, in front of him now, "Can you stop a volcano? Can you stop a tsunami? Can you stop a heart from falling in love?"

Park closes his eyes, just as the streetlight sparks and goes black. *That's what I thought.*

When he opens his eyes again, he's looking at Iris, who's sitting on a pillow on the floor in front of him, and Isaac is tucked into the corner, his phone screen light illuminating his face.

"Fuck," Park whispers, and Iris leans forward.

"What did you see?" she asks, her face inches away from his own. "You must have seen something?"

He nods, and swallows. His hands are still shaking, his heart is still racing. "I saw something, alright," he says, "and I think it means we're fucked."

33
WISHING IN BOLD

C presses the old, leather-bound book she found in Park's room closer to her chest and glances over her shoulder at Kat, who's standing just out of view of the door in front of them. "Are you sure this is where we should be?" She asks, and Kat nods, once.

"Mel knows a lot more about Rituals than I do," she says, "she'll know if there's anything we can do."

C sighs and reaches out a hand, hesitant to press the doorbell, thinking better of it after a second. "What if she's upset that we took the Prophecy book?" C *feels* the eyeroll from Kat.

"She probably doesn't even know it exists," Kat says, moving forwards and pressing a slender finger to the doorbell. "It'll be fine, don't worry. Mel is super sweet."

C's jaw clenches, and there's yelling from inside the house.

A woman's voice, "Walt! I'm not answering the door this time!"

The door opens, only a little, and through it half of a man's face appears. He's ruggedly handsome, and he looks at C with suspicion. "Hello?" He asks.

C opens her mouth, about to say something along the lines of *Can we talk to Mel?* But his gaze slides over to Kat.

"Ah," he says, "hi, Kat." The door opens fully, revealing that he's still wearing his bathrobe even though it's noon. He calls over his shoulder that it's Kat and cuts himself short. "Who are you?" He asks C, not unkindly, his eyes a striking blue.

"Cecel – C. Just C."

A short woman with her hair pulled up into a messy bun appears behind the man, Walt, and nods at Kat. "Hi," she says.

"This is C," Walt says, gesturing, and Mel smiles, holding out her hand.

"Nice to meet you," she says, "I'm Mel, this is my husband, Walt."

C shakes Mel's hand, and is surprised at how warm she is, how firm her grasp is. She's reminded immediately of Isaac, and how he felt familiar to her, the first time they met. It's no surprise that the person

225

who raised him has the same easiness to her. "Nice to meet you, too," she mutters under her breath.

"What brings you two over?" Mel asks, pleasantly. "Did you want to come in?"

C opens her mouth, about to launch into her story of Park's betrayal, of her near-death experience with the Ghost, with the others' inaction. They seem to think they're looking for ways to undermine the Ghost, but what are they really doing? It doesn't seem like a whole lot. "Um," she says, not sure where to start.

"It's about Hell Club," Kat says, from behind her, and gestures for C to give the Prophecy book to Mel. "We thought maybe you could help us with something."

Mel's eyebrows furrow, and she takes the book, flipping through it absently. She gives a hum of disapproval, and then snaps it shut. "You two better come in, then," she says, and shares a look with Walt.

"I'm going to go check on Chip," he says, softly, and then disappears as soon as C and Kat have stepped inside, the door shut gently behind them.

As Mel leads them further into the house, which is tastefully decorated in greys and plastered with photos of Mel and Walt and Isaac and the small boy that must be Chip, C realizes with a start that Mel is pregnant. She realizes that Mel has a life, a family, and here they are just barging in on it, asking for help.

She looks over her shoulder at Kat, wanting to ask her to leave, but Kat only shoos her forward and she has no choice but to follow Mel into the dining room, where she gestures for them to take a seat.

"Do you want anything to drink?" She asks, and both Kat and C shake their heads. "Alright."

Their chairs screech in synchronization with each other as they all sit, and Mel opens the book again, reading through the first page more thoroughly.

"What is it you want to know?" Mel asks, after a second, and C looks to Kat, because she's not entirely sure herself.

"The book predicts the End of our world," Kat says, reaching out and flipping the pages to the end of the book, where the last Prophecy is written.

Mel reads aloud. "*When the Ghost calls, one will doom all.* Yes, Chip and Isaac have told me about it. They're the ones who know what's going on - I don't know what it is that I can do for you."

Kat *hm's* softly. They're coming to Mel because C found the Prophecy book at the back of Park's closet three days ago and no one's noticed it's missing. They're coming to Mel because it doesn't seem like anyone has a solid plan to stop the Ghost and the End is creeping closer and closer.

Sure, Iris and Isaac have a plan to rely on Park, but what is plan B? What happens if that doesn't work? What happens *when* that doesn't work? C doesn't think that Park can write Prophecies. C is almost *entirely certain* that Park can't write Prophecies.

It was Kat's idea to investigate the Rituals they could perform to stop the Ghost, to stop the End and every day since finding the book, Kat has spent the afternoon at her house, or the evening if she's working. One time, she even invited C to come sit with her in the shop, and C took her up on the offer. Together, the two of them poured over the Ritual books that Kat's family keep in the storeroom of the shop and they hadn't found anything. It was then, that Kat had the idea to come to Mel, and now here they are on a sunny Saturday morning, in her dining room.

"We're hoping you can help us find a Ritual to stop the Ghost."

C sits up straighter in her seat, trying to look older. Trying to look like she knows what she's doing. There's something in the back of her mind, scratching, waiting to be let out, waiting to be realized, but she isn't sure what yet. There's a missing piece of the puzzle and she knows it's missing, she's just not sure where it's missing from.

That's why they're here. That's why they're asking for help.

Mel looks down at the book, tracing over the last Prophecy with her fingertips. "I have some old Ritual books I can lend you, but that's about all I can do. I don't know enough about what the Ghost is or how it works - Isaac and Iris are probably your best bets for that."

C doesn't have to look over at Kat to know that she's rolling her eyes. "Their big plan is to write more Prophecies," she says, "but that will only prolong the problem. We want - we want to know if we can get rid of it for good."

Mel looks taken aback for a second, but she recovers quickly. "You mean you want to -"

"Kill the Ghost," C finishes. "We want to kill the Ghost."

Mel pushes the book across the table back to her. "I see," she says, and then she stands. "I'll go get those books for you." She disappears through the kitchen without another word.

"She doesn't seem like she wants to do more than give us the books," Kat whispers, and C nods.

"I mean, I wouldn't want to get involved if I was her, either. She probably doesn't want to be stuck in fucking Belle forever."

"But her son already is. Wouldn't you think that she'd want to know what's going on with him and help?"

C shrugs. She can't even wrap her own mind around her own thoughts, let alone someone else's. Let alone someone else who's been involved in the world of magic for her whole life – there must be a reason that Mel is keeping her nose clean of Hell Club. "I feel like she must have her reasons."

"Maybe she just doesn't have the time – I mean, I can't imagine being in the business she's in and trying to raise a kid and take care of Isaac too. I mean –"

"Here we are," Mel says, appearing again, a stack of books high in her arms. "This is everything I keep in the house, but I may be able to get something from my father if there's nothing in here."

Kat moves before C can, taking the books from Mel. "Thank you," she says.

"Yes, of course," Mel says, pressing her palms into the small of her back. "Just be careful with what you find. Please."

"We will!" Kat says, moving towards the door and leaving C to hurry after her.

"Thank you," C also says to Mel, "it was really nice meeting you."

Mel nods, but there's something sad behind her eyes. "Just be careful," she warns, and C follows Kat quickly. She feels like she's still missing an important part of the puzzle, something that Mel knows and doesn't want to tell her – something that Isaac and Iris and Park know and don't want to tell her, but she can't put a finger on it.

Back in the car, Kat immediately starts flipping through the books. "Even if we don't find what we're looking for, these are gold," she says. "There's shit in here that shouldn't be touched with a nine-foot pole."

C starts the engine. "Isn't it weird that she just gave us the books? No questions asked?"

"Yeah," Kat says, "it is. But I'm trying not to question it too much. She has a family, so she can't want the End to happen, you know? Maybe she knows that Isaac and Iris and them aren't doing shit to stop it."

"Or maybe there's something else that we don't know about."

Kat looks up at her, eyebrows furrowed. "What do you mean?"

C shrugs. "Maybe it's useless. Maybe there isn't a way to kill the Ghost."

Kat frowns. "Everything has to die, C," she says, "and besides, Mel said herself she doesn't know that much about it."

"Yeah," C mutters, but she's sure that isn't it. There's still something *missing*. There's no Prophet yet. There's no life-changing decision. There's only an endless amount of time in-between Prophecies and the promise of an unstoppable End. What's Park's role in it? Martyr? What's her own role? Why would the Ghost go after her if it didn't have a reason?

It doesn't seem to work senselessly. Everything it's done has had a reason. Why did it choose her? Why does it show itself in her dreams?

Maybe she's the missing puzzle piece. Maybe she's the one who's going to find a way out of the mess they're in.

She can only hope – she's always wanted to be the hero.

34
FEAR

Isaac is shivering in the cold morning air and there are emotions welling up inside of him that he can't begin to comprehend. It's enough to make the back of his throat ache like he's about to cry, and he's trying desperately not to think about it.

Instead, he's chain-smoking, and staring across the yard into the trees like they'll give him the answers that he needs. Instead, he's trying to distract himself by picturing Park last night, in a blur of soft colours and fondness, hands everywhere and soft noises pressed into Isaac's neck, the inside of his wrists.

Instead, he's putting off getting a jacket because the cold on his bare skin is grounding him, and the goosebumps are a painful reminder that despite it all he's alive. Despite the End coming at them so rapidly, despite the changing of the seasons, despite the pit of dread that's gotten large enough to encompass his entire body and not just his stomach, he's alive.

Everything feels so hopeless.

"Isaac?" Park calls from the door, sounding worried. "Baby, it's freezing outside. You left the door open."

Isaac doesn't remember leaving the door open. He's certain he closed it. He – no. No, maybe he didn't close it. Everything is foggy from his lack of sleep, from the thoughts and the nicotine buzz in his head. He's so cold he can hardly feel his fingers or his toes. He doesn't want Park to see him like this. He doesn't want Park to know that his coping mechanisms mostly involve numbing himself, hurting himself however he can.

Park's footsteps crunch across the icy deck towards him, and he doesn't turn. "Hey," Park says, softly, reaching to take the burnt-out cigarette from Isaac's hand and placing it in the ashtray. "How long have you been out here?"

Isaac shrugs. He looks down to the railing in front of him, suddenly feeling very vulnerable. He's been outside long enough that the chill is bone-deep, long enough that he's smoked the entire pack, long enough that the sky has bled from dark to dawn.

"It's freezing," Park's hands find Isaac's elbows and they pull him so he's facing his boyfriend whose expression is very worried and very serious, "you're freezing."

"Yes," Isaac replies, moving his gaze from Park's. He swallows, waiting for Park to chastise him, waiting for Park to say something along the lines of *why are you doing this to yourself?* but the words never come.

Instead, Park sighs, and grabs the empty carton of cigarettes and the lighter from the railing, stuffing them into his sweater pockets. "You're not even wearing socks," he says, softly, and takes Isaac's hand in his own. "Your toes are going blue."

The feeling that's been at the back of Isaac's throat all morning threatens to show itself, and he opens his mouth and closes it again, finally letting his eyes meet Park's for more than a second. *Please understand,* he thinks, hoping that Park will. *Please don't make me explain myself.*

Park's eyes darken, still very worried, and his fingers tighten around Isaac's, tugging him forwards towards the door. "In," he says, and Isaac starts stepping cautiously back to the warmth, his toes tingling painfully. Park starts behind him, his hand at the small of Isaac's back.

Isaac steps into the house, still shivering, and waits as Park closes the door behind them. He wants to be ashamed that Park is pulling him out of his own self-punishment, but he has no idea how he's supposed to be feeling. He has no idea how to take what's in his head and explain himself, no idea how to put anything into words. He's always taken his misguided thoughts and feelings and turned them against himself as punishment – he's always taken the things he doesn't know how to work through and pressed the sharp edges against his own skin. He's better at it than he used to be, better at finding healthier outlets, but sometimes old habits fight to the surface.

"I'm getting you into the shower," Park says, once again putting his hand on the small of Isaac's back. "That'll get you warm again. Come on, love."

Love. Isaac wants to cry.

He lets Park steer him upstairs, and into the bathroom, lets him take off his shirt and sweatpants and boxers as the water warms. Naked, in the bathroom light, he fights the urge to cover himself, to hide himself from Park, whose fingers are gentle as they lead him into the hot water.

He flinches – too hot – as prickling spirals of pain shoot down his arms and shoulders, his nerves suddenly awake.

It only takes a few seconds before Park is also naked and stepping into the shower after Isaac, rubbing more feeling into Isaac's back and arms, into his thighs and his chest. He doesn't say a word when Isaac stops him.

"I'm sorry," Isaac says, softly, "I'm so, so sorry."

Park's hands are on Isaac's upper arms, but they move to cup his face, and he's looking at Isaac with eyes so incredibly warm and full of love, full of worry. "Don't be stupid," he replies, "nobody is expecting you to save the world."

"No," Isaac says, because that's not what he means. That's always been hopeless. They've never stood a chance. "I'm sorry that I didn't go looking for you sooner – I – I just wish we had more time."

The corners of Park's lips curl upwards, just a little bit. "Me too," he says, solemnly, "but we still have *some.* We'll figure out what to do with it."

Isaac nods, and then Park is pulling him into a hug and the dam behind Isaac's eyes finally releases, the itch at the back of his throat finally scratched. Relief and release settle around him like the steam from the water, and he buries his face in Park's shoulder.

35
WINE BLUES

"God, I don't know what we're supposed to do anymore," Iris says, exasperated. She leans back dramatically in her chair, wineglass in hand. She let Dahlia convince her to go for drinks, and she's being a little bit too loud about the situation they've found themselves in but it doesn't matter anymore. The world is going to end and there's nothing they can do about it.

So, she's going to get drunk with one of her favourite people, and she's going to complain – two of her favourite things to do when the future is bleak and there's no hope left in the gas tank.

"I just don't understand how Park had that strong of a vision? Like, do we trust that that's really what he saw?" Dahlia, more composed than Iris, leans forwards over the table, digging her elbows into the scarred wood. She's wearing purple lipstick.

Iris remembers the look on Park's face when he opened his eyes, and she doesn't think there's any way that he could have been lying. He was terrified. "Yes," she says, taking a big gulp of her wine. "Yes, we trust that it's what he really saw." He doesn't have any reason to lie.

Dahlia nods, and then lets out a long, slow sigh. She's three mojitos in and Iris can see the mischievous glint in her eyes. The one that suggests she's thinking about something that Iris isn't going to like.

"What?" Iris asks, wanting to be let in on the secret.

Dahlia leans further forward, her fingers wrapping around her fourth sweating mojito glass. "Do you think there's a portal into the Ghost's world?" she asks, "Like, instead of –"

"That's a terrible idea," Iris says immediately, not even wanting to entertain it. "We don't have any power in the other place. What would we do?"

"We don't know for sure that we don't have any power there," Dahlia points out, but Iris has her mother's journal that says otherwise. "Besides, do you have any other ideas?"

Iris shrugs. She's all out. She has been for a while. "It still seems like the worst possible thing we could do." Not to mention the fact that they don't even know if it's possible. Not to mention that they've already lost a friend to the Ghost, and going there willingly, purposefully, seems like a death sentence.

"You're right," Dahlia concedes, and the mischievous glint in her eye is replaced with something more like disappointment, or hopelessness, and then she starts laughing, something empty and mocking. "Why did we think we could change things?" she asks. "Why did we think we could fight against the Ghost and *win?* Maybe we deserve what's coming."

Iris laughs, too. It's hard not to. Maybe Dahlia is right – thinking that they could do anything is exactly what got them into this mess in the first place. They're not special. They're no different from anyone else who sees themselves above nature.

The laughter starts to feel dangerously close to tears and she brings her wine glass back to her lips, draining the rest of it. "I don't know," she says, "how do we tell Chip and Derek that our plan has turned into *we're just letting it happen?*" How can they tell Chip that he won't get a chance to do anything, to grow up and make something of himself, for himself? How do they tell such a hopeful child that his hope is for naught?

"We don't," says a voice that's not Dahlia's, and Iris looks up to see Eve sitting across from her, too, her hair disheveled and half-pulled back into a ponytail. There's dirt on her face and under her fingernails and the dark bags under her eyes make her look like she hasn't slept since she disappeared.

"Eve!" Dahlia exclaims, drunkenly enthused and less shocked than Iris. She reaches over to press a hug awkwardly into Eve's shoulders and Eve hugs her back, smiling. "I missed you."

"I missed you, too," Eve replies, and Iris sees the glassy sheen of tears over her eyes. Dahlia pulls back and Eve holds out a hand to Iris, which Iris takes. "I missed you as well."

Iris squeezes her hand, not trusting her voice to be steady if she were to say anything.

"I have so much to tell you," Eve starts, "but we have to get everyone together."

"Tonight?" Dahlia asks, surprised.

Eve nods. "Tonight," she says. "The Ghost starts taking people tomorrow."

36

THERE'S NO SUCH THING AS LOVE

C smells like Ritual magic once again, and Park narrows his eyes at her as she enters the kitchen. "You're not doing something stupid, are you?" He asks, pressing start on the microwave.

She sighs and adjusts the gym bag that's slung over her shoulder which looks suspiciously heavy. "Define stupid," she says.

He shrugs. "Something that could get you killed." He doesn't understand why she's being so secretive – he doesn't know why she isn't talking to him or showing up to the meetings that she's been invited to. All he wants is to know what it is she's planning, and if he can help. All he wants to know is that she's safe in her new-found hobby.

"I don't think it'll kill me," she says, her expression turning strangely sober in the kitchen light. "The only thing we're trying to kill is the Ghost."

The microwave beeps behind Park, loud in the silence between them. He doesn't know how to respond to C, doesn't know what to say to his little sister who's gotten so involved in something she never should have. It seems like she has a better plan than the one that Hell Club has, which is relying on Park. Which is to do nothing. "Have you found anything?" He asks, not sure what else there is he can say.

C shakes her head, her long hair shuddering with the movement. She cut her bangs last week and Park can't believe how much they've changed her face – she looks so much older now. So much wiser than he's ever thought she could be. "Not yet," she whispers, "but we might have something after tonight."

Park nods, and then looks away. He pulls his leftovers out of the microwave, so he has something to do with his hands. "Okay," he says, softly, shifting the contents of the bowl. "Please be careful."

"Yeah," she says, pushing past him on her way to the door, "you too."

She leaves, and he's left in the kitchen by himself, dishing out stir-fry into two bowls, one for himself and one for Isaac. His mind is spinning, and he isn't sure what about. He wants desperately to protect C from the dangers, but he's also glad she's not as lonely as she was. He's

235

glad that she's found a friend and a purpose in this place. He's glad that she's not using him as a crutch as much as she was before, but he *misses* her. He wants to broach the gap between them, but he isn't sure how.

He's about to turn to put everything back in the fridge when he hears Isaac coming into the kitchen, his footsteps hurried.

"We have to go," he says, and Park turns to him in confusion, the container of food held against his chest like a shield.

"I just heated the leftovers," he says, blinking at Isaac, whose face seems strained. Whose entire being seems strained. "I - what's going on?"

"I know, but we - we have to go."

Park brushes past him, opening the fridge. "What's going on?" He asks, again.

Isaac only blinks at him. "It's an emergency."

Park stands and looks at Isaac, silently willing him to explain further, but Isaac is already moving away from him, into the mudroom, and there's an obnoxious jangling of keys that lets Park know he's waiting impatiently. "What about the food?" He asks, conflicted. Why isn't Isaac telling him what's going on? Why can't he just talk to C?

He's so tired.

"I'll eat later."

Park takes another second to worry, and then packs Isaac's food into a lidded container, and piles his own bowl on top, finally meeting Isaac in the mudroom. He passes the food to Isaac to hold while he puts his shoes and coat on, and when he gestures for them back Isaac looks half shellshocked with worry and half like a lovesick puppy. "For later," Park shrugs, and Isaac presses his fingers into the small of Park's back as he ushers him out the door.

"Thanks," he whispers, and they pile into the car.

"What's the emergency?" Park asks, once again, his seatbelt clicking into place.

"Eve is back."

Excitement sparks in his chest, but when he looks over at Isaac, Isaac's eyebrows are furrowed. "That's good, isn't it?" He asks, unsure. Shouldn't this be a good thing? He's so far away from his body. He's *so tired.* "Tell me it's a good thing," he whispers, "I want to be happy for someone."

"It's a good thing," Isaac confirms, reaching over and squeezing Park's knee. He gives Park a small smile, before he backs out of the driveway. "Iris says she has a plan, too."

A *plan!* "Something better than the one we have now?" He takes a bite of his stir fry, his mood vastly improved. "Something that doesn't involve relying on me?"

"I don't know," Isaac's hands tighten on the steering wheel. "Iris was cryptic on the phone. Didn't really say much other than we have to call a meeting *right now.* I think she's drunk."

Park almost chokes on his mouthful of food. Iris drunk seems foreign to him – she's usually so serious, so in control of herself that to imagine her drunk is nearly impossible. "How is she getting to the meeting?"

"We're picking her up."

Park nods. "Is she alone?"

"No, Dahlia and Eve are with her."

"What about Chip?"

Isaac shrugs. "He's just going to have to get caught up tomorrow."

"He's going to hate that."

Isaac's nose scrunches, and he pulls up to the curb of the local pub. "Yeah," he says, softly, "I know."

Park looks over at him, at the stress pushing his mouth into a thin line, at the tension in his jaw. "It'll be okay," he says, wishing that he could ease some of Isaac's worry.

Isaac's lips curl up into the smallest of smiles as he turns to Park, and he reaches for Park's hand, pressing a quick kiss into his palm. "I know," he says, and Park presses his hand into Isaac's cheek, running his thumb across the bow of Isaac's lips, and then along his cheekbone.

Something shudders in his chest, and a small voice deep inside his head says, *drink this in while you can,* and another voice says, *you get to have this forever.* He's not sure which one he trusts more, but certainly they don't have to cancel each other out. He can cherish his moments with Isaac *and* he can have Isaac until the end. The end of the world, or the end of one of them, or the end of their relationship; just the end.

There's a pounding on the back door of the Shitbox, and it snaps the two of them out of their moment, Park's hand snaking back to his bowl of food.

"Shit," Isaac says, flustered. He hurriedly presses the unlock button, and then Iris and Dahlia and Eve shuffle into the backseat ungracefully.

Park turns to watch them over his shoulder, and his gaze falls on Eve, who looks exactly like she's just returned from an enlightening trip into the forest, her eyes wide with something akin to the wild. When she notices him looking, she gives him a quick smile and a nod, and reaches out to tap his shoulder and then Isaac's.

"It's good to see you two again," she says, and Isaac nods.

"We missed you," he replies, and a private flash of love shows in her eyes.

Park looks away and takes another bite of his stir fry, not wanting to intrude, but wanting to be a part of it all the same. He's glad she's back - so, *so* glad, but it's hard for him to process his own emotions in the wake of everyone else's. He's glad she's back, not because he knew her and missed her presence in his life, but because he missed her presence in Isaac and Iris and Derek's lives.

"Did you not miss us?" Iris asks, her tone mocking and sarcastic, louder than usual. Her jacket rustles as she assumedly points to herself and Dahlia. *She* apparently has no qualms about intruding.

"Of course," Isaac says, pulling the car back onto the road. "I missed you both dearly." He says it with only a minimal amount of sarcasm.

"Park?"

Park swallows hurriedly. "Oh, yeah," he says, "me too." Park's must seem less believable as it earns him a scowl from Iris, and a muttered insult.

Isaac grins at him privately, and Park would do anything for it.

They pull into the cabin's long driveway and Eve lets out a strangled noise when she sees Derek's truck already there. Derek himself is leaning against it, looking out towards the road, a hopeful tilt to the way he's holding his head.

The car isn't even stopped by the time Eve is pushing the door open and stumbling out, crashing into Derek, who buries his face into the side of her neck and shoulder. Park can't hear anything they're saying, but he can imagine it's a string of assurances, of *I love you* and *thank god you're okay.*

"Should we give them a minute?" Iris asks, shutting the door that Eve jumped out of.

"Yeah," Dahlia whispers back, her gaze stuck to the other two. "I think they need a second."

Park looks over to find Isaac watching him, and he raises his eyebrows.

"How are you doing?" Isaac asks, quietly, and Park nods.

"I'm good," he says, depositing the food on the passenger seat floor. He looks past Isaac, at Eve and Derek, and his heart clenches. "I'm glad she's back."

Isaac follows his gaze. "Me too."

They give them a couple more seconds, and then Iris asks, "Ready?"

There's a chorus of yeses, and then car doors opening and the crunch of frost under feet.

As soon as the cold air hits Park's face, he shivers, and the reality of their situation hits him. *This is it*, he thinks, *this is when we find out how it all ends.* His hand find's Isaac's as they file towards the cabin, and Isaac gives him a reassuring squeeze, which Park returns.

37

SOCKS WITH HOLES IN THE TOES

Eve's leg is pressed against Derek's and she can feel the eager eyes of all her friends on her, but she isn't sure how to tell them what happened. She can't take her gaze off her hands, the redness of them, the way that they betrayed her.

She doesn't know how to tell them that she faced the judgement of the Ghost and that she was found wanting. She doesn't know how to tell them that she's failed them, that she's failed everyone. Somehow, she thought that this would be easier; somehow, she thought that admitting what happened in the Ghost wouldn't feel like reaching into her chest and ripping her heart out for everyone to see, for everyone to judge.

She opens her mouth, about to start her story, but she makes the mistake of lifting her head and making eye contact with Isaac, whose face holds nothing but careful curiosity. He's holding Park's hand close to him, as if it's the most precious thing in the world, and suddenly Eve wants to cry.

"It's okay," Derek says from beside her, his voice warm, "take all the time you need, babe."

She looks over at him, and the love in his expression, in the softness of his eyes, in his encouraging smile, sets her stomach roiling. *I've failed you especially,* she thinks, and it's all because she can't imagine a life without him.

"The Ghost showed me terrible things," she starts, swallowing down her shame. "It showed me how awful people are to other people, and it showed me how awful they can be to other living things, but that was only the start. It showed me good things, too. It showed me how kind people can be, how selfless."

She watches Park glance at Isaac, almost automatically, and a small smile sneaks onto her face. *Of course,* she thinks, *of course Isaac is a good thing.* All her friends are good things. How could they not be?

"It took care of me as best it could, I think, but its domain – its dimension or timeline or whatever it is isn't good for people. I wasn't sleeping properly, and it was starting to affect me, so it finally told me that I have to choose."

"Choose?" Iris asks, leaning forward, her elbows on her knees. Eve isn't sure if it's from curiosity or from the need to steady herself.

"Yes," she says, "it told me that I have to choose between everyone or everyone it deems as good."

"What did you choose?" Dahlia now.

"It was a trick," Eve sighs. "I told it it should leave the people that it thinks are good here, especially if there's a chance that they can do better, that they could do good in the world, and it told me that I was right. It told me that there were people I love who weren't – who wouldn't make it. I – In the beginning, it showed all of us. It said that all the people I love would stay here, if I made the choice, I mean – if I saw everything it wanted to show me and still made the choice." Her voice is shaking. She doesn't know how to make it stop shaking.

"Wait," Park says, "I just – it made you make the decision of who it's killing?"

Eve nods.

"Everyone in the world or everyone except those it thinks can right the wrongs done?"

Another nod. "I don't know how exactly it deems someone worthy," she whispers, "there are a lot of factors, I think, but –"

"But I'm not worthy," Derek states, "it would have kidnapped me and left you here."

She closes her eyes, and the tears start to silently fall down her cheeks, warm and wet and shameful. "Yes," she says, "and Park."

Derek's arm wraps around her shoulders, and he pulls her towards him, kissing the top of her head. There's silence from the rest of the room.

Her eyes are still closed, but she can imagine everyone's expressions as the implications of her decision sink in. She hopes they can see that there was no other choice, that she can't imagine a world where her and Derek aren't together. She hopes that they can see that she couldn't be the deciding force that tears Isaac and Park away from each other. They have to understand that after the things she's seen – the death, the betrayal, the cruelty – it wasn't worth it. They have to understand that it was an impossible decision, and any of them would have made the call she did.

"I don't understand – why Derek and Park?" Iris is still leaning over her knees, and she's looking between Derek and Park like she's trying to piece together a puzzle. "Have you done something bad that we don't know about?"

Park snorts and shakes his head. Eve can imagine that he's trying to piece together why, that he's going back through his life to try to understand.

"I'd like to know, too," Derek whispers, in her ear. Private.

Eve nods. "You work at a bank, Derek," she says, "a bank full of greed and materialism. A home of capitalism."

Derek hums a flat noise of annoyance, and Isaac, who's been uncharacteristically quiet, echoes it.

"Is that all it takes for the Ghost to decide?" He asks. "Wouldn't anyone who has ever had a job be counted as not good, then? Is that why Park's on the shit list?"

"No," Eve leans heavier into Derek. "It's only those with jobs in the government, or banks; jobs that perpetuate greed and power. It told me that Park is included because he was always supposed to die."

"I mean, that's not really true, is it?" Dahlia asks. "The Prophecies say otherwise."

Eve shrugs. She can't justify anything that the Ghost told her – all she can do is repeat it.

"So, is there a way for us to stop it?" This is from Park, who just looks tired now that he has an answer for why he's on the cosmic naughty list. "C told me that her and Kat were trying to find –"

"A Ritual," Eve confirms. "Yeah. There is one. I saw a group like us perform it – I don't know if it'll work when the Ghost is this powerful, or once it's started abducting people, but it's worth trying, I think." Now that she's doomed the world.

"Where do we find it?" Iris asks.

Eve grins. "C and Kat already have," she says, "they just don't have the manpower to do it alone."

"Jesus Christ," Park mutters, "C smelled like Ritual magic when she came home today."

"I think that they're smarter than we give them credit for," Eve says, "they put it together faster than we would have."

"How?"

"I don't know. I just know that they have it." Eve looks down at her watch, and her heart sinks deep down into her stomach. "Fuck," she whispers, and then, "we're out of time."

Derek squeezes her tighter to him. "We never would have made it anyways," he says, "at least now we have a plan."

Eve closes her eyes. She knows that he's right, that they wouldn't have had time to finish the Ritual before the Ghost started its taking, but it still hurts. It hurts that she knows exactly what those people will find when they open their eyes, that she knows exactly the fate that they face.

It doesn't seem fair that she got out and they won't.

It doesn't seem fair that she's the reason they're there.

38

WHO KNOWS WHAT ABOUT TRAGEDIES

The Ghost, in its human form, is walking down Main Street in Belle, under the star-filled sky. Below its feet, it can feel the energy building, amassing, swirling and ready to spill over into the physical world, ready to do the Ghosts' bidding. Ready for revenge, ready to reclaim what has always rightfully belonged to it.

It knows that Eve, the one that it thought was worthy, is telling her friends of her little plan, of the little Ritual that it let slip the cracks into her visions. It is all happening as it should.

The Ghost had a feeling from the start that Eve was going to crack, just like everyone does. Just like humans do. It thought that this might happen, this choice. It would have been stupid to go through with its plan without fail-safes. It would have been stupid to count on Eve to make the decision to damn her loved ones.

It would have been stupid to show her something that it didn't plan for, and if there's one thing that the Ghost isn't, it's stupid.

It keeps putting one foot down in front of the other, and it feels the people around it, asleep in their beds, unbothered by what's happening right outside their houses, right underneath their dreaming bodies.

The Ghost does not choose who it takes. It does not discriminate. It feels their dreams, and it seeps into them at the edges, turning everything black, corrupting them.

It does not reach everyone, not tonight, it is not greedy, but it takes its full share.

It feels a grin working its way across its face, and it stops, drinking in the fear that its already causing, drinking in the nightmares, the pain.

It snaps its fingers, and then it is gone and so are those whose dreams have been touched by its darkness. It snaps its fingers, and it slides back into its home, taking its victims with it, as pleased as it can be.

Somewhere, in the distance, the Sorrow pauses mid-scream, and finally, finally, the Ghost gets a moment of peace. If it had lungs, it would breathe a sigh of relief, but it does not have lungs. It does not have lungs and the Sorrow is already screaming again.

39
INTERLUDE V

Don't panic, don't panic, don't panic, Mel is chanting to herself as she gathers her bathrobe around herself and hurries to the guest bedroom, the bedroom that used to be Isaac's. Walt has been sleeping here, lately, when she's too uncomfortable and keeping them both awake.

"Walt?" She asks, softly, as she sticks her head into the room, expecting to see him sprawled out over the bed. He isn't.

She stands for a moment, thinking, trying her hardest not to panic. If he isn't in their bed, and he isn't in this bed, maybe he's downstairs on the couch – maybe he couldn't sleep last night, and his compromise was the couch. It isn't unthinkable, he's done it before.

She hurries down the stairs as fast as she can. *Don't panic, don't panic, don't panic.*

She hits the living room lights as she enters, and on the couch is a conspicuous lump of blankets. A breath of relief escapes her lips. "Walt?" She calls out again, but there is no answer. Stepping forward, her heart in her throat, she pulls the blankets off the couch to reveal several of Chip's stuffed animals, and a couch pillow.

Tears burn at the back of her throat, and she swallows them back. It's too early to cry, to early to come to conclusions. She has no idea what's going on – Walt could have just gone for a morning run, like he used to do. He could have gone out to get them coffee, he could be over at his shop, getting some work done before he becomes too busy with Chip and with her.

Chip, she thinks, and then she's rushing back up the stairs, opening her son's door, the sound of blood deafening in her ears. *Please, God.*

Chip is there, sleeping silently, his blankets pulled all the way up to his nose.

Mel's knees buckle, and she has to shut the door quickly, so that Chip doesn't hear the sob of relief, of terror, that she lets out. For a moment, she leans her forehead against the cool wood of the bedroom door, and she regroups.

Maybe Walt is just out. That's it. She slept through him getting up, and now he's out doing business, or out getting coffee. He's on a run.

Everything is okay, she's just being ridiculous. She's overreacting. Nothing is wrong.

Downstairs, the front door opens, and something falls to the ground.

"Fucking hell," a familiar voice grunts, and then Mel is moving,

"Walt!" She yells, rounding the corner to see her husband, standing there with a bag of take-out breakfast food in one hand and an iced coffee in the other.

"Hey, you," he says, surprised at her loudness, at her haste. "Is there something wrong?" He asks, as she embraces him,

"Yes," she whispers into his chest as he maneuvers them towards the bench in the entryway, so he can put his goods down.

As soon as his hands are free, they're wrapped around her, pulling her tight. "What is it?"

"The End," she says, "Isaac texted me that the End is here. I thought you were *gone.*"

He lets out a small noise and squeezes her. "No," he says, "I'm sorry. I'm right here. I just got us breakfast."

"Yeah."

"Wait – Chip?"

"He's still asleep."

"Thank God."

Mel nods. She realizes how lucky she's gotten. None of the people that she loves are gone – none of them have been taken. She can only imagine what it's like to be on the opposite side of the coin, to have lost someone.

***

Shannon is standing in the wreck of Old John's house. All the lightbulbs are broken, and glass covers the floor, crunching under her feet with every step. There's a fine layer of black dust over everything, and Shannon thinks that this must be remnants of the Ghost.

She can feel the echo of it here, the energy pulsing through the walls, the ebb and flow, the sound of static only audible when she's not trying to listen to it. There's a sense of dread that's creeping in, making the hair on the back of her neck stand up, and she's glad she asked Carter to stay outside. He doesn't do well in situations like this, and she's starting to think that maybe she shouldn't have involved him with this at all. He's been telling her that she's crazy, tracking the Ghost, trying to collect fragments of it.

She blinks, and suddenly there is a man standing in front of her. She would be startled if this wasn't exactly what she expected. Of course, the Ghost needs to have something that looks human, something with vocal cords, something to talk to interested parties with ears that can hear.

The man has a low, blond ponytail, and a smile that's just a little bit too big for his face. "I've been expecting you," he says, and his voice is low and full of gravel.

"Have you now?" She responds, trying not to let her fear show through.

"Yes," he says, and his smile gets impossibly bigger, "I want to make you a deal."

Her heart stutters in her chest. She didn't expect it to be this easy. She *did not* expect the Ghost itself to offer this. "Okay," she says, triumphant, "I'm listening."

***

C is sitting at the dining table, staring at the wall across from her. In the kitchen, she can hear her mother talking to a 911 operative.

"What do you mean, people have just *disappeared overnight?*"

Exactly that, mom, she wants to say. *They're gone.*

She had been woken up by her mother this morning, her eyes brimming with tears. She explained quietly that C's father was gone. His clothes were still in the closet, his phone was still plugged in, and his shoes were still at the front door, but he was nowhere to be seen. *Gone. Vanished.*

Immediately, C had been hit with a wave of nausea and it still hasn't passed. Her text to Parker is still unread, and she has no idea how to console their mother.

Somehow, knowing that this was coming isn't helping her cope. Knowing that this was coming is only making her feel worse – it's filling her with guilt.

She *knew* this was coming. She *knew* this was coming, and here she is, sitting at the dining table, listening to her mom plead with the 911 operator.

"Please! You have to *do something!"*

But there is nothing to *do.* This is the world now, until everyone is gone. They're too late, and their Ritual didn't work. They're too late and there's nothing left to try.

With a sigh, she opens the notes app on her phone, and scrolls to the list of fence quotes from Old John that she's been adding to, rereading the last one.

The world starts its descent on a Thursday night, or a Friday morning. Whichever counts as midnight.

She starts typing underneath it, and then something clicks in her brain. She slides down her notifications and sees the date: *Friday December 17.*

Heat starts to rise in her chest, and she goes back to her notes app. The nonsense sentence before it says: *Ritual be found, Ritual be useless, two cannot fuel the flame,* and the one before, *Darkness touches those who are found worthy,* and the one before that, *the sister is sacred.*

"Ah, shit," she says, dialing Parker, her feet already taking her out of the house.

"Where are you going?" Her mom asks, her voice drawn tight with worry.

"To go find Park," she says, and her mom nods.

"Good idea," she says, and then Park is talking to her on the other side of her phone.

"We have to get everyone together," she says, "I have something to tell you and Dad's gone."

"Gone?"

"Gone. Mom is really upset about it. She's losing it at the 911 operators. I don't know how to feel – I don't think it's sunk in yet."

"Yeah," he says, and his voice is lower, softer. There's a pause and then he changes the subject. "Bring the Ritual that you and Kat found."

She's not even annoyed that he knows she found a Ritual. She doesn't even care. She's glad he didn't say anything else about their dad. "Yeah," she says, stepping out into the cold. "Okay."

The back of her mind whispers, *Prophet, Prophet, Prophet,* and she can't believe that she didn't put it together before now. It was never Parker.

Parker wouldn't even be a part of this if it hadn't been for Isaac – but C? C would have been. C was following the magic happening in Belle before she even knew that's what it was.

Parker might have been prophesized to fall in love, but C? C is the fucking Prophet.

40
FREEZER BURN

Isaac's heart is pounding in his chest. The news is playing on the TV in front of him, and he regrets putting it on. Guilt and terror are multiplying inside of him uncontrollably. *We're complicit in this,* he can't help but think. *We didn't stop it, so we're complicit.*

"Citizens of Belle are reporting that their loved ones have disappeared without a trace overnight – initial estimates on the number of missing stands at about one quarter of the population," says the monotonous voice of the newsperson, sitting at a desk, their panic veiled only slightly.

"One quarter of the population," Isaac whispers, the words feeling like lead in his mouth. "That's like five-hundred people, just poof, overnight." Five hundred people who have families, whose children and partners and parents don't have an explanation for where they've went. Five hundred people who have been doomed.

Beside him, Park is pressing his fingers into the couch as he hovers right at the edge. "Imagine when they're *all* gone," he whispers, "when it spreads outside of Belle."

"No," Isaac replies, pressing the power button and shutting the TV off. "No, I'm not going to think about that. We're going to do this Ritual, and we're going to get rid of it."

He remembers their conversation about just letting the End happen, about how greedy and selfish and terrible humans are, about how it's been coming for so long. Now that it's here, now he can see the pain that it's bringing, now that he can taste the oncoming mass panic, and now that he has his own guilt, he's not sure that they were right.

"Isaac," Park says, his voice soft, and Isaac hates it. He feels like he's about to be talked down to, condescended to like a hopeful toddler. He can't even look at Park. "You know that all we can do is try, right?"

"I know," he says, and his voice is strained. "But I want to – I want to believe that it's going to work. If I don't believe that – I don't – I don't know. I don't want to feel like that yet." He hates that Park is right, and he hates that Park isn't as condescending as he thought he would be.

He's a being full of hate and guilt and dogged hope that he cannot let become bitter.

He's also a being full of love, and as much as Park is getting on his nerves today, he knows that Park is just as lost. He knows that Park is just as scared.

He reaches out and grabs Park's hand in his own. He's grateful that Park is here, and he's grateful that Park tolerated - more than tolerated - his mood swings, his hopelessness, and his lack of knowledge. His terror as things started spiralling into something that he cannot fix.

Park traces his thumb over Isaac's, and the corner of his mouth lifts, just a little bit. "I want to believe it's going to work, too," he whispers, his voice quiet, as if he's scared that saying it out loud will ruin its chances at coming true. Like a wish on a birthday cake, or a dandelion, or a star.

Isaac pulls him in close and rests his chin on Park's shoulder. He wishes, desperately, that they could tell the future. "We'll all be together," he says, "for as long as we can be. I think that's what matters."

Park nods against him but doesn't say anything. He doesn't have to.

They stay pressed together for another moment, and then Isaac pulls back. "The cat," he says, remembering that this morning there was a feeling he was forgetting something. He gives Park a quick kiss on the cheek, and stands, readying himself to step into the cold weather.

The cat has been staying in the container that his mom made for him, and Isaac has only needed to top up his food every couple of days. He still isn't letting Isaac pet him, but if he's in his shelter, he'll give Isaac the pleasure of a small *mrrow*. Isaac likes to think that it's his way of saying *thank you.*

He hears Park behind him as he opens the glass doors out to the deck, a scoop full of cat food in his hand. "Isaac?" Park says, his voice now loud and sharp, full of concern. "Isaac, look."

Isaac looks up, following Park's pointed finger with his gaze.

Sitting outside, just within the line of the yard, is a fox and it is looking directly at the spot which Isaac disappeared into.

"Do you think that it's eating your cats' food?" Park whispers, as if the fox can hear him.

Isaac watches it for another minute, as it seemingly nods to him, and then slinks back into the woods. He remembers at the beginning of this all, when Park was newly drowned and there was hope in the air like a virus – when the fox first appeared. He never *had* looked into what it could mean, but it appearing here and now, seems like the closing of a loop. The end credits.

He swallows and dumps the cat food into the bowl in the tote, which is disappointingly empty. "No." He steps back inside and closes the door behind him, joining Park to look out at the spot the fox had been standing. "I think it's a sign that we're getting close to the End."

Park opens his mouth to say something, but the shrill ringing of his phone interrupts, and he gives Isaac a dark look before he answers. "Hi," he says, not breaking eye contact with Isaac as the voice on the other line says something. "Gone?" He asks, and Isaac watches as he closes his eyes, turns his face, his jaw tightening. "Yeah. Bring the Ritual that you and Kat found." he breathes, and then he hangs up, stuffing his phone back in his pocket and swallowing, not looking up.

"Who was that?" Isaac asks, thinking that he already has an inkling.

"C."

"Who's gone?"

Park looks at him, then, and takes a deep breath. "Dad," he says, "and she says she has other news."

"Other news?"

Park shrugs, looking away again. "She wants to meet at the Clubhouse. Says to bring everyone."

"Do you want to talk about your dad?" Isaac asks, wanting to step forward, to put his hand on Park's shoulder, but unsure if it's what Park would like him to do.

"Let's just get this over with," Park says, leaving to head towards the front door, seeming smaller than usual, silhouetted by the outside light filtering in through the windows.

"Are you sure –" Isaac starts, following him.

"Please, let's just get it over with."

"I –"

"Please," Park's voice breaks.

Isaac grabs his keys, an excuse to go to another room, to give Park a second of privacy. "Yeah," he says, through the wall, "yeah okay." He takes out his phone, sends the meeting notification to the group chat, to Mel.

In the car, Park reaches over and gives his hand a squeeze, and when Isaac takes it off the steering wheel and offers it to him, Park takes it, interlacing their fingers. Isaac steals a glance at him, but Park is looking stubbornly forward, into the oncoming road.

I love you, Isaac wants to admit, has on the tip of his tongue. *I love you,* he wants to say more than anything. It's implied, he knows that, but there's something about saying it out loud that will make it concrete. He opens his mouth to say it, but then his voice dies in his throat. *I love you,* he wants to say. *I love you I love you I love you.* He should say it now, before they get to the Clubhouse. He should say it now, while they still have time. He should say it now, because he doesn't know if he'll get the chance to say it again.

Instead, he squeezes Park's hand, and Park squeezes back.

***

Mel opens the door when Isaac knocks, and she ushers him inside, complaining about the cold. "I think this is a bad idea," she says, as he stands on her welcome mat, uncomfortably adjusting his jacket.

"I don't know what else to do," he says, and he knows that he's told this to Park and Iris and the others but saying it to Mel makes him feel smaller and more useless than ever. *Nobody is expecting you to save the world,* Park's voice is in his head.

Mel swallows, and reaches out her arms to him, a small pitying smile on her face. Isaac tries not to think about it as he buries his face in her shoulder. "I love you," she says, pulling away to look at him. The pity is gone.

"I love you, too."

"Can we go?" A smaller voice, from further in the house. Chip is sitting at the bottom of the stairs, watching them with distaste.

"Yeah, dude," Isaac smiles at him, and then nods at Mel.

Chip is out the door before Isaac can even blink, and then Mel is telling him, "You better bring him back here to me."

And he's promising her that he will, but he's not sure if there will even be a here to bring him back to by the end of the night. With whatever news C has for them, and whatever her and Kat's Ritual ensues, he's not sure about anything.

The door closes behind him, and he watches as Park turns around in the passenger seat of his car, saying something to Chip as Chip buckles himself into his car seat. He takes a deep breath, and then steps off Mel's porch, less ready for what's coming than he was when he got here.

41

THE LOVE GIVEN WHEN THERE WAS
NO LOVE LEFT TO GIVE

"Isaac?" Park calls out, waiting for Isaac to turn to look back at him. They're the first ones to the Clubhouse, and Chip is already inside. He had raced to get out of the cold, despite Isaac's warning that it wouldn't be any warmer in the cabin until they started a fire.

"Yeah?" Isaac's eyebrows are raised, and he holds out a bare hand, which Park takes immediately.

Fuck, he thinks, now that Isaac is looking at him, now that Isaac is touching him. The words were right on the tip of his tongue, but now he's thinking about them, and *yeah sure,* they're true but saying them feels sacred, like maybe he should wait until this is over, maybe he shouldn't force it. But he has no idea if they're even going to be here afterwards, he has no idea –

"What's going on?" Isaac has stepped directly in front of Park, and both of his hands are on Park's forearms and Park can't help but think about how lost he would be right now if his father had disappeared and he didn't know what was happening. If he wasn't here, if there wasn't Isaac to lean on, if he had never decided to trust the people that saved him from the river.

Is it too early? Park is sure that it's been implied for so long. "Nothing I just – I – I love you, is all. I just wanted to say it before whatever happens happens." He feels his cheeks get warm, and he looks away from Isaac for a second, only to look back and see him beaming.

Before he can protest, he's being pulled into a tight hug, and Isaac is chuckling right into his ear. "I love you, too," he says, "you had me worried for a second, you know."

"Did I?"

"Thought maybe you were going to run away on me."

Park pulls him in closer. "Never," he whispers.

"Me either."

Park lets his eyes shut for a fraction of a second, and then he steps back. "Ready?" he asks, and Isaac shakes his head.

"I'm scared."

"Me too."

"It's all going to work out."

"Do you think that the people the Ghost took are gone forever?"

"I don't know."

Park swallows. "I hope not."

"I do too."

Behind him, Park hears the engine of a car getting closer, and Isaac sighs.

"Let's do this?" He asks, and Park nods.

In the cabin, Chip is huddled in his jacket, looking annoyed that Park was right and it isn't any warmer in here than it is outside. "Fire?" He asks, and Isaac nods, starting the work of setting a fire in the fireplace.

Park perches beside Chip, and the vehicle that he heard outside pulls into the drive, gravel crunching under its tires. The engine cuts off, and a lick of flame starts from Isaac's kindling.

"Aha," Isaac says softly, and three car doors slam in succession.

"What's going to happen?" Chip asks Park, leaning closer so Park can hear his whisper.

"I have no idea," Park admits, and the cabin door creaks, revealing C and Kat and Iris and Dahlia, all with solemn expressions on their faces.

At the fireplace, Isaac stands, and turns to face the newcomers. "Hey," he nods, and Iris moves forward to wrap him in a hug, whispering something in his ear that Park doesn't quite catch.

She moves towards him and before he can protest, she's hugging him too, and as soon as her arms are around him, he feels something settle deep down in his chest. Something like belonging. "I'm glad you're here," she whispers before she pulls away.

"Me too," he tells her, and she gives him a small smile. He can't believe that this is the same person who intimidated him so much, that this is the same person he was so reluctant to trust. It feels like the first time he met Isaac- the first time he met Iris- was a lifetime ago.

Isaac sits beside him, pressing their legs together, and Iris leans against the table next to him.

Park leans forward to catch C's attention, but she seems keen on avoiding eye contact with him, instead wringing her hands out in her lap and whispering something to Kat. *Dad's gone,* he hears in his head,

Mom's losing it at the 911 operators. He wants to tell her that he's sorry he wasn't there, that he thought about it, that after Eve's revelation last night he should have told her, he should have gone home but he couldn't. He couldn't leave Isaac alone in his massive house, and he couldn't invite Isaac home to witness the private apocalypse he had a feeling would happen this morning.

The guilt is eating at him, though – his first thought was *at least it wasn't mom,* and he knows that's terrible of him. He *knows* it is, but he can't change it. He's pretty sure C is thinking the same thing, and he wants to ask her, wants to lessen his shame.

Another car pulls into the cabin driveway, and Isaac leans over into his space.

"Is it just me or is C avoiding looking over here?" He asks, and Park nods.

"Maybe it has to do with whatever she's going to tell us?"

"What do you think it is?"

"Oh, she's probably found some kind of loophole that's going to save us if the Ritual doesn't work."

"I hope so."

"Yeah," Park says, resting his head on Isaac's shoulder. He wants there to be a back up plan to their back up plan. He wants C to have found something that no one else has yet. He doesn't want to keep imagining losing her, losing Isaac. He doesn't want to have to think about his last moments with them, in whatever terrible hellscape the Ghost is.

The door opens for a final time and then Eve and Derek are there, giving hugs to everyone and settling in for C's news. Eve says that her grandmother is gone, as well as her aunt, and Derek sets his jaw as he tells of a missing older brother and cousin. Everyone gets quiet, unsure what to say.

"I," C starts, biting her lip. "Can I tell you guys my news now?"

She finally looks at Park, and he nods, holding Isaac's hand just a little bit tighter.

"I'm the Prophet," she says, and her hands are shaking.

42
INTERLUDE VI

The Ghost has been taking people all day. Its reaches have expanded past Belle into the neighbouring towns, leaving pulsing dark energy lines in its wake.

It does not take as many as when it started. It's harder when they're awake. It must choose those that are thinking of it, fearing it. They must already hold some of the Ghost in their mind.

It starts slow, at their feet and creeps upwards like a sense of dread. It winds slowly around muscle and bone and cartilage. It passes through their organs, filling stomachs with bile, making its way to the spine, where it climbs the vertebrae like a ladder, infusing spinal fluid with inky darkness.

Finally, it reaches the brain and with a sharp noise like a snap, the person with all their fear, all their thoughts and darkness, is gone from this world and onto the next.

The Ghost, never sated, is already on the hunt for another. It will not stop until there is nobody left.

***

Shannon is staring at the thirteen jars of writhing black in front of her. She's just finished dripping wax around their edges, and she can't get over how ugly her new Artifacts look.

Of course, aesthetics aren't everything and she's sold uglier, but it seems to her like the bite-sized portions of the end of the world should *look* pretty.

She reaches out and swirls one of the jars, watching as the dust angrily follows the motion.

"I don't think it likes being in there," says Carter from behind her.

She knows he doesn't agree with what she's done, but he won't say anything. He won't admit it. Besides, he's aware that these thirteen jars will give them a fortune. A monopoly over the Artifact market – new Artifacts are rare and now they have thirteen of them. *Thirteen.* Not to mention the fact that everybody wants their own little piece of the apocalypse.

"It doesn't have to like being in there," she says, putting the jar back. "It just has to stay where it's safe."

"Safe from what?" Carter is standing at her shoulder, keeping her between him and the jars. There's something like fear in his voice, in his energy. This is something Shannon has seen from him so rarely, despite everything.

"Safe from our son," she says. It doesn't quite make sense to her, but it doesn't have to. She has what she wants. She has what she needs. She's about to be *rich.*

***

Mel did not wake up this morning thinking that today would be the day for the birth of her second child. Not when her first is currently trying to save the world.

It doesn't matter now, though. Here she is.

"Walt," she says shortly, gritting her teeth, "did Sharon answer?" Sharon, of course, is her midwife. In the beginning, Mel was appalled that her name was so alike her sister's, but there is a world of difference between them. Mel likes Sharon much more.

Walt, who is trying his best to remain calm, shakes his head. "Straight to voicemail," he says. "What if she was one of the ones taken?"

Of fucking course, Mel thinks, *of fucking course that's how things are going to go.*

All she wanted was a *quiet. home. birth.* and God forbid she actually get one.

Walt, bless his heart, blinks at her, awaiting some kind of reassurance, some kind of instruction on what she wants next. He's already packed a to-go bag – he packed it weeks ago and it's been sitting by the door. It had warmed her heart in the moment, but now she's in too much pain. She wants to strangle him for doing this to her, she wants to scream.

She does neither of these things.

The contractions are getting closer together and she's guessing that they don't have much more time until the baby is here. Chips' delivery was quick, so this one should be even quicker. Supposedly. Things haven't been going the way they're supposed to.

"Okay," she says, grabbing onto the stairway railing and hauling herself up. Walt reaches to help her, but he steps back as soon as he sees the murderous expression on her face.

"Mel –" He starts, but she shakes her head.

"Plan B. Take me to the hospital."

43
PEACH LIPSTICK

Isaac is staring at C like the rest of Hell Club is staring at C, but she's staring back at him. *Try and argue with me,* her expression is saying, *try and tell me I'm wrong,* but Isaac isn't going to try anything of the sort. He's relieved.

Does this mean when this is over Park and I can leave? His heart is beating faster in his chest, and he swallows. No, he's not allowed to think like this. He's not allowed to have that glimmer of hope – besides, he's not even sure what he would do outside of Belle. He's not certain who he will be without the familiar roads, the familiar trees, the familiar people. He's not certain that they'll even survive this, so really, there's no point in thinking like this. *But still –*

"How do you know?" This comes from Dahlia, who's looking at her, incredulously. All of the ideas and plans that Dahlia had come up with and none of them involved C.

None of the ideas that *any* of them had come up with involved C. Isaac and Park had both been worried about her getting involved, about her getting hurt, about her going missing in the Ghost. They all thought that the Ghost's attack on her was random but it's true that they could be wrong. It's true that the One was never explicitly stated to be the *secret to the Secrets skimmed from the river's edge,* but it didn't make sense that they would be anything else. It's true that Park could still be the One and C is the missing puzzle piece that he brings to Hell club.

C pulls out her phone, and wordlessly hands it to Dahlia, who scrolls, reading with her eyebrows drawn together. "'The sister is sacred,'" she starts, and then, "'Darkness touches those who are found worthy,' 'Ritual be found, Ritual be useless, two cannot fuel the flame,' 'The world starts its descent on a Thursday night, or a Friday morning. Whichever counts as midnight.'"

"I am the sister and the Ghost attacked me," C says quietly, pushing her hair behind her ears, suddenly seeming shy. "Kat and I found a Ritual that supposedly will end the Ghost, but we can't perform it alone – we tried. Neither of us are powerful enough. And – well, today's Friday. The Ghost –"

261

"The Ghost started taking people at midnight!" Eve exclaims, "Oh, C! You're brilliant!"

C smiles awkwardly and averts her gaze to the floor, clasping her hands in front of her. "Thanks - I - uh - I hope you don't think I wrote those after the fact. They were all before, um, and the last one -"

Dahlia is talking over her now, "'Follow the Prophet, burn what needs to be burned, sacrifice whom-so-ever must be sacrificed.'"

" - the last one is from this morning."

"Oh, great," Derek says, and he's placed a protective hand on Eve's leg, his arm crossing over her body like a seatbelt. "We're going to lose someone." Eve pushes out from under his arm and holds his hand in her lap, stroking his thumb with hers. *Not me,* she seems to be reassuring him, *not you.*

Dahlia scrolls upwards on C's phone. "What are the rest of these? Were they all you?"

C shakes her head, "No, they're just what Old John was writing on his fence. I - uh - I thought that maybe I would be able to make sense of it."

"Well, you're certainly making sense of s*omething,*" Dahlia mutters, handing her phone back.

Park, who's been eerily quiet this whole time, leans against Isaac more heavily, sighing. He still doesn't say anything, but Isaac is sure he's just as relieved as Isaac is.

"What about Park's meditation vision?" Iris asks.

"We don't know if that was Prophetic," Dahlia counters, "what if it was just the Ghost planting a seed to misdirect us?"

Park tenses against Isaac. "So you're telling me that not only did it try to drown me, but it's been messing with my head?"

"Clairvoyant," says a small voice on the other side of Isaac, and when no one acknowledges him except his cousin, he says louder, "Park is clairvoyant."

"Oh, *god,*" Park groans. "I don't want to be that."

"Or he could just be tied to it," Dahlia says, sitting forward, her elbows on her knees. "It did try to kill you, and not the normal way it would."

"I don't want to be *that,* either."

Isaac leans back as Chip reaches across, tugging on Park's sleeve until Park offers him his hand, and Chip takes it, holds it, says nothing.

Isaac looks at their hands, and then over Park's head to Iris, who's biting her bottom lip. He knows what they're both thinking, *Chip is just like him when he was younger,* and he looks away quickly.

Chip pulls his hand back, and Park blinks, bewildered. Isaac wants to cry.

He realizes that Dahlia and Kat and C are talking, still, and no one else seems to have noticed the interaction. Quickly, he leans down and plants a kiss on Chips head, and then he wraps his arm back around Park's shoulders.

It seems absurd to him, that they're all here, that they're all dancing around the reason that they're here. That the room he's in is filled with people that he loves and that outside this room there are people disappearing, people dying and they're still talking about the logistics of it. They're still debating whether they can trust something that Park saw, as if this whole situation isn't already so abnormal. Who cares anymore? C is the Prophet and Park had a terrifying vision. The world is ending, and they have a chance to save it and they don't have time to be questioning it. *Nothing* that's happened so far has made sense, and none of the plans they've come up with have worked. They've been wrong about so many things, so what's the point of putting off the Ritual they're here for by trying to logic their way through it?

"What about the Ritual?" He asks, and when Dahlia turns her gaze to him, he realizes why no one's mentioned it yet, why they're all skirting around it.

They're all scared, just as scared as he is. Everyone has put on their brave face until now, but the cracks are starting to show. This situation is just as terrifying to them as it is to him, and now, C's Prophecy - *follow the Prophet, burn what needs to be burned, sacrifice whom-so-ever must be sacrificed* - has made it even more so. None of them want to be the whom-so-ever and none of them want the others to be them, either.

C sighs, and from her coat, produces a piece of crumpled paper and the book of Prophecies that Isaac had given to Park, so long ago now.

"Where did you get that?" Park asks, and C rolls her eyes.

"You hid it at the back of your closet, Park," she says, "come on."

He huffs, and Isaac fights the urge to smile. *Serious,* he reminds himself, *this is serious.*

C uncrumples the paper, and passes it to Dahlia, who reads it silently, and then passes it to Eve, who holds it out in front of her so both her and Derek can read it.

"It seems pretty straightforward," she says, and then hands it to Iris, and the four of them press further together to read it.

As Isaac skims through it, he realizes that Eve is right. It *is* straightforward. First, they must cleanse the space and protect themselves as much as they can, but this is standard. This is something that happens before any Ritual, regardless of its consequence or difficulty.

Second, they must all provide something small of themselves, a trinket or a hair or a segment of their handwriting, something to tie themselves to those around them. This will be put in a small bag at the center of a circle they will make with their bodies. This will make it easier for Dahlia and Iris to draw their power from them when they need it.

Third, they must burn a book that contains powerful words, and hopefully they will conjure the Ghost. (He knows when Park reads this part, because Park shudders and Isaac remembers, once again, the night he dredged Park out of the river, sopping wet, and the man with the ponytail and the empty eyes. He doesn't want to see the Ghost again, either.) Once the Ghost is here, Dahlia and Iris will speak their intentions into the air and turn their magic towards the Ghost. The combined energy of the group will act like a magnifying glass – essentially, Dahlia and Iris will suck out the Ghosts' energy and return it back to itself several times stronger. Too strong for it to handle. It will die, and then they will thank each other, and burn the bag of things they have accumulated, so none of them become Artifacts.

"We have to burn a *book*?" Chip asks.

"Yeah," C gestures for the paper. "We think that for it to really work, it should be the Prophecy book. We tried burning one of the copies we made, but it didn't give us enough *umph*."

Kat, who hasn't said anything this whole time, nods in agreement.

Isaac knows that he and Iris don't talk about how much Chip resembles him, when he was younger, but he thinks that maybe he should mention to Iris how much Kat reminds him of her, especially right now. She looks determined, she looks calm, her jaw is stubbornly set in the way that Isaac sees from Iris only when she's about to start something and see it to conclusion. He admires her – he remembers how much she didn't want to be involved with Hell Club, how annoyed she was with Iris when it first started, how angry she was at Iris when C was attacked – her dedication, even if this is the opposite of what she wants.

Eve clears her throat, "If we call the Ghost here it will try to kill us."

"Not with Dahlia and Iris."

"But as it gets weaker, so will we," Iris protests.

"That's what the rest of us are for," Isaac says, softly, "so you can have our energy and you don't have to rely on the Ghost."

"Which is why C and I couldn't do it," Kat finally chimes in. "We can't harvest our power directly from other sources, but you guys –"

"We know how to."

"If we kill the Ghost, does that mean that no one will be able to do Rituals anymore?" C muses, and Dahlia shrugs.

"Does it really matter?"

"It will for a lot of people."

"Do we not kill the Ghost just for them?"

C shrinks, "It was just a question," she mutters, and Dahlia softens.

"I know," she says, "I'm sorry. I think that Rituals will still be available – there are other energy sources that aren't the Ghost, and really, the Ghost is just an amalgamation of those."

"Okay," C says, "that's good."

Good for who? Isaac wants to ask but doesn't. He knows who it's good for: his parents, Mel, his grandpa, even himself. The people who profit from these things.

"Can we get this over with?" Asks Park, who has huddled into himself. "Please?"

There's a collective silence for a moment, in which they all seem to be afraid to move, afraid to speak, afraid to breathe, and then, finally, Iris unzips the backpack she's brought and digs around until she's produced a bag of dried herbs, a bowl, salt and some matches.

"Dahlia, can you do the salt?" She asks, not waiting for an answer before she hands off the bag,

"What do you have to burn?" Dahlia replies, and Iris scrunches her nose. "Dad made it," she says, "I think it's got mint, and rosemary and –"

"Lavender and rose petals," Kat cuts in, "it was all we had at home."

Park nudges Isaac, and whispers very quietly, "What are the herbs for?"

Isaac leans in closer to him, and whispers back, "Cleansing and protection. Iris will burn it and it'll get rid of any negative energy. The salt will prevent anything evil from coming in."

"Oh," Park replies, and rests his head against Isaac's shoulder. "Is there anything I can do?"

"Focus on keeping a guard up against things that are meaning you harm. It doesn't have to be super special or anything, just the intention."

Beside him, Chip slides off the table they've been sitting on and finds a new spot beside Eve, who starts talking with him animatedly. Iris cranks the single window open, and Dahlia props the door open with a piece of firewood.

The resulting chill makes Isaac shiver, and he closes his eyes as if that could keep the cold from his bones. There's so much he could be saying right now, he thinks. There's so much he could be thanking his friends for, there's so much that he could be listening to, but he doesn't have the energy. It feels like he's been fighting this fight for eternity and he's so tired. He's more tired than he's ever been before.

Park takes Isaac's hand in his own, both freezing, and tries to rub some warmth into Isaac. *I love you,* Isaac thinks, but he doesn't say it.

Iris lights the herbs and the cabin smells briefly of mint and rosemary before the breeze wafts it away, and Kat passes around a small drawstring bag which is meant for their personal things.

"What do you have?" He asks Park, and Park lets go of his hand to dig through his pockets, revealing a diner receipt from the last time they went for midnight pancakes, two quarters and a tube of mandarin orange-flavoured chapstick, which is undeniably Isaac's favourite.

"The chapstick?" Park questions, and Isaac nods.

Park slides it into the bag, and it's Isaac's turn to empty his pockets. "Lint," he says, after the first pocket, and then he finds a loonie, a lighter and a pack of rolling papers. He chooses the rolling papers – the lighter probably would be better, but he's not sure he wants to set it on fire after the Ritual.

The bag continues its route through the group, and Iris shuts the window and the door as her herbs finish burning. Dahlia starts a salt line on the inside of the door and on the windowsill, and then they both join the circle of bodies.

"Ready?" Iris asks, and the rest of them nod.

No, Isaac wants to say, but he knows they can't put it off any longer. This must end now.

44
WISHBONE

Park is trying not to think about the words that Iris and Dahlia are speaking and he's trying not to think about the thing that they're summoning. He's trying not to think about the disappearing people and he's trying not to look over at C because there's something in her expression that makes him nauseous, and he's trying not to think that they might die out here, they might both disappear, and their mother will be worried.

Instead, he's thinking about Isaac's hand in his and he's thinking about brick walls between him and the Ghost. He's thinking about laughing at Iris's dry humour and Eve's doctor hands probing carefully at the back of his head the first time he met her, her reassuring smile. He's thinking of Derek and his devotion, he's thinking of C's jaw set in determination after she saw the Ghost for the first time. He's thinking of Dahlia and her omnipresence in everything they did, everything they do, her dedication to finding a solution, to plan building.

He's thinking of Riley poking fun at him on their shared morning shift and Cadence rolling her eyes at them. He's thinking that he didn't even remember to text Riley or Cadence, to ask them if they lost anyone, to check if they're lost themselves. He's thinking of Sky and the three missed calls when he didn't show up on that day, so long ago now. He's thinking of his mom and the dinner where she invited Isaac, how much she's tried since then.

He's thinking about how he's going to miss this if the Ritual goes south. How cruel it is that he's just found people he doesn't have to be afraid around and he's just found someone who is the kind of gentle he's dreamed about in a lover, and it could all be ripped away from him in seconds. How cruel is it that he's just started to feel like himself again and it might end, here, tonight?

Isaac squeezes his hand and it brings Park back into the moment.

Everyone except Iris and Dahlia are standing on the outside of a large salt circle, and they're holding hands. To his right is Isaac and to his left is Eve, whose hand is sweaty and damp in his. Out of all of them, she seems to be the most worried, the most stressed.

Inside the circle is another circle, which contains only the Prophecy book and Iris is squatting beside it, a barbeque lighter in her hands. She looks at him for a second, her mouth set in a straight, grim, line, and then she flicks the lighter on.

The pages of the book light instantly, and Iris stands and takes a step back.

"Here we go," she says, and her voice is soft.

The book burns for a surprising amount of time, it burns until there is nothing left but ash. There are a painful number of seconds between it finishing and something happening. Park looks across the circle to his sister and then to Kat, and Eve is starting to say something when the laughing starts.

It echoes through the cabin, high-pitched and mocking, and it makes every hair on Park's body stand upright. He knows this laugh. Between the time it takes for him to blink, the thing that tried to drown him in the river appears in the smaller salt circle, in the ashes of the Prophecy.

It sees him, and it grins at him, its eyes full of hate, full of anger. "Hello, Dead Man," it says, bowing mockingly, before its grin gets wider. "Hello, Fallen," it says to Eve, and she stands up straighter beside him.

"Fuck you," she says, and it starts laughing again, cruel and loud.

Finally, it brings its attention to Iris, and it tilts its head. "And you, Witch," it says, "do you really think you can kill me?"

Park watches as Iris lifts her chin, looking at the Ghost directly in its eyes. "Yes," she says.

"Even if killing me means killing the world?"

"We still have time to save it."

"Funny," it trills, "that's not what your friend thought. She was all for me ending it, until I told her that her survival came at a price."

"The world is better with Park and Derek in it."

The Ghost looks away from her now, to Dahlia. "And you agree with this? You believe I should die? You believe that the earth deserves to suffer for your own sakes?"

Dahlia makes eye contact with Park, and he sees the glisten of tears. "I believe that we shouldn't have to sacrifice the people we love for the greater good."

"Do you?" He asks again, mocking. "Do you really?"

"Yes."

"Then tell me why I don't believe you."

"I can't."

"I'll make you a deal, Dahlia Martin," it continues, and she swallows, looking away from Park. "I'll spare you all, I'll spare the people that could make this world a home again, if you give me one of your friends."

The air becomes tense, all eyes on Dahlia as she sets her jaw. At her sides, her hands are trembling, and Park understands that she's considering it.

"I'll even let you choose which one," it continues and her eyes flick back to him.

The floor seems to drop out from underneath him, and he opens his mouth to say *no, no please don't send me away,* but no sound comes out. Isaac's hand gets even tighter around his.

"No," Dahlia says, and her voice is firm. There's no room to reason.

"How predictable," the Ghost sneers.

"Killing you will save so many people," Dahlia says, and her glance sways back toward Park. She nods at him, just the slightest inclination of her head and a wave of embarrassment flows over him for even thinking that she might sacrifice one of them.

For thinking that she might sacrifice *him.*

"If you kill me here, tonight," the Ghost says, a grin on its face, "I will not die. I have sold pieces of myself, and they will grow in time to become something just as big and just as powerful as I am now. If you kill me here, tonight, you will only be putting off the inevitable."

Beside him, Isaac tenses, and he almost turns to see the frustration that he knows Isaac is feeling, but Iris lets out a noise so angry, he can't tear his eyes away. "You *bastard,*" she howls, and then louder, "I banish you. I curse you. I want you to suffer the fate you made others face."

The air in the cabin shifts, becomes colder, sharper. Park tastes the fire in the corner, feels the burn of the salt on his skin, the rise of the blood in his body to the call that Iris has made. In between one moment and the next, Park has become a vessel for the energy she needs, and he imagines it flowing through him, flowing through Isaac, too, enveloping them in light.

"Killing me isn't going to win you the war," the Ghost chides, its edges blurring into the darkness.

"It's going to make me feel a whole hell of a lot better," Iris says, and she raises her hands, in sync with Dahlia. Their palms are glowing, just as Iris's were the night Isaac pulled him out of the river, and the energy flowing from them is strong enough, bright enough, that Park closes his eyes.

The pull of his energy is something that almost hurts, something like a day-old sliver or the sudden re-opening of a scabbed wound. It's as if something that has been asleep inside of him is being awoken, rudely, loudly. He likes it, and then it gets stronger, and he hates it, over and over and over again he flips between the two until all he can think about is how much he wants this to end, how much he wants the Ghost to die.

The Ghost lets out a strangled cry, and Park forces his eyes open to see that its edges have blurred further into the darkness, but the smug expression on its face hasn't changed. Its eyes are black holes in its face, and its teeth are pointy, so sharp that when it closes its mouth they dig into its lips and draw blood. Any semblance of humanity it was clinging onto has disappeared. "I'll be back," it trills, and it sounds as if it's laughing, "I'll be back and I'll be stronger than ever."

"Jesus fucking Christ," Dahlia says, her voice strained, "just *die* already!"

And then it does, fading into the darkness with a final fizzle like a firework.

The whole group stands for a moment, stunned that it had been so easy, stunned from the sudden return of their energy, stunned from the thought that maybe they did make a mistake, and Park is the first to stir, shaking his head. "We didn't even ask what it meant by selling pieces of itself," he says.

"We didn't have to," Isaac replies, his voice full of guilt. "It's my mom."

"You really think she'd do something like that?" Iris asks, the glow from her hands fading.

"You don't?"

She shrugs in agreement, and Dahlia, behind her, picks up the bag of trinkets they gathered.

"I guess we're going to have to find Shannon, then," she says, pushing through Eve and Derek to dump the bag into the fire. "Do you think we have a chance at getting those pieces?" This is directed at Isaac.

"Probably not."

"She has to know –"

"She knows exactly what she's doing," Isaac says, "and exactly what kind of money it'll get her."

Park squeezes his hand and he squeezes back. "We'll figure it out," Park whispers, but Isaac doesn't say anything.

"Well," Eve starts, swinging her hands back and forth, "they say no rest for the wicked, but I'm drained."

"I can't believe that killing it was that easy," Chip remarks, saying what everyone else is thinking.

Isaac wraps his arm around Park's shoulders and pulls him in close. "Can I come home with you?" He asks privately, and Park nods.

Isaac's lips find his temple, then, and Park lets his exhaustion take over. He leans on Isaac, vaguely hearing the plans that he and Iris and Dahlia are making – find Shannon, take the Ghost pieces, destroy them.

C, across from him, is still avoiding eye contact. *When will we talk about it?* He wants to ask her. *I want to talk about it.*

He pushes himself up, watching out of the corner of his eye as Dahlia lights their trinket bag on fire, and stops in front of C. "Hey," he says, and she sighs.

"Hi," she says. "Are you coming home tonight?"

"Do you want me to?"

Kat, who C had been talking to, turns away to give them a moment of privacy.

"I don't care what you do."

"I'll come home, then."

"Okay."

"Do you want to talk about it?"

She sighs again and crosses her arms in front of her chest. "Not yet," she whispers, "I don't want to think about it yet."

He nods. "Isaac is coming over, too. We'll be there after we drop Chip off."

"Okay. I – I guess I'll see you then."

He opens his arms for a hug, and she allows it, returning it at just the same level. "I'm so happy it's over," she whispers, "and you're still here."

"I'm happy you're still here, too." And he is. The worry he's been harbouring for her can be let go of, just a little. She's still here, and he's still here, and they can talk about it. He stays with C until Isaac finishes talking to Iris and then he says goodbye and bundles himself into Isaac's car with Chip.

They sit, watching the other vehicles pull out onto the road, their headlights cutting neatly through the dark as they ferry their friends towards their homes.

"Aunt Shannon's made a lot of trouble, hasn't she?" Chip asks, and Isaac sighs, leaning forward so his forehead hits the steering wheel.

"Yes," he says, "she sure has."

Park puts a hand on his back, hoping to provide some sort of comfort.

"Are we going to fix it?"

"I don't know if we can, Chip."

<h1 style="text-align:center">45</h1>

THOSE WHO CRY WHEN THINGS GET TOUGH

Iris is staring blankly at her hands. Her hands helped banish the Ghost, destroy it. Her hands hold the power to do such things, and yet there's an emptiness inside her, still. The Ghost was as old as time, as old as everything and it had just *died* because of her hands, and it doesn't feel right. Nothing about what's happening feels right.

The Ghost can't be dead.

Even if it hadn't fragmented itself, Iris can't imagine that it's truly gone. The energy from the earth, from the trees and the river and the mountains is still flowing which means that somewhere the Sorrow is still crying, which means that the Ghost must be keeping guard like the dog that it is.

"What are you thinking?" Kat asks, leaning against her doorway, her hands shoved deep into her pockets.

"It's never going to be over," Iris replies, and she swallows.

They may be ending a cycle with the Ghost, but it's not *the* end. It wasn't the end for the people who ended it the last time, and it won't be the end for the next people, either. The struggle with the Ghost is a spiral and it curves around and around and around forever.

They were fools to think otherwise.

"It's almost over for you, though," Kat whispers, "that has to be exciting, doesn't it?"

Iris sighs, and falls back on her bed, joined a second later by Kat. Hell Club has been exhausting for her, right from the get-go. It's taken so much of her future, so much of her current time, so much of her energy. She's going to be sad to see it go, but more so because it's a bridge between her and her friends. More so because weekly meetings have been grounding. Less so because she enjoys the magic, less so because she enjoys trying to piece together hundred-year-old Prophecies.

At least whoever takes over is going to have C, someone who doesn't seem keen on writing in riddles. Someone who's still around and willing to interpret her own goddamn Prophecies.

"I guess so," she says, and turns her head to look over at Kat. "Less exciting for you."

Kat shrugs. "I kind of expected that I'd get involved at some point."

"That doesn't mean you have to be happy about it."

She looks away, to the roof. "It means that I get to spend more time with C," she says, "it means I get to feel closer to Mom."

Iris lets out a breath. Working in Hell Club made her feel farther away from her mother – her mother who had always known what to do, who had marched directly into the fire without a second thought, who *really made* a difference, and didn't just prolong what's coming – but she doesn't want to tell Kat this. Kat deserves to be able to make her own decisions about what she feels, what she doesn't feel, what she wants.

Except that she doesn't get to decide if this is what she wants. Just like Iris didn't.

"I hope that it works out better for you," Iris whispers instead. She wants to reach out, to brush her sisters' hair out of her face, to bring her closer, to comfort her. It's been so long since she's done this, she's not sure she knows how – she's not sure if it would be welcome. They haven't been this close together in years, both harbouring their own hurt, their own anger.

"I'm sorry I pushed you away," Kat says.

"I'm sorry I didn't try harder to keep you closer."

Kat gives her a weak smile.

It might not be perfect, but it's the start of something.

***

Eve is sitting in the passenger seat of Derek's truck. The engine has been shut off, and neither of them have made a move to get out, instead sitting in the cold. She's shivering.

Neither of them has said anything to the other, but it's not uncomfortable. Eve thinks they would be hard-pressed to find something that's truly uncomfortable while they're together. Instead, it's contemplative, frustrated. All this time they've been racing towards an end and now the end has been ripped out of their grasps.

The Ghost could rise back to its original power at any point. All that needs to happen is for someone to open one of its containers, and everything is back where they started. Their work will have been for nothing.

"I can't believe that Isaac's mom fucked us over," Derek says, finally, breaking their silence. After all this, Eve thought that he would be mad – but he doesn't sound it. He just sounds exhausted.

"Have you met Isaac's mom?" She asks, incredulous. Eve thinks that out of everyone in the world, the most likely to pull a stunt like this would be Shannon.

"No."

"She used to come to town on some weekends," Eve starts, "I did her eyelashes for years. I don't even think that Isaac knew she was here."

Derek stares at her, incredulous. "What the fuck," he says, flatly, and Eve nods.

"Despicable," she whispers. Shannon *is* despicable and not just because she abandoned her only son – because she abandoned the entire world.

Eve remembers her own decision, standing there, in front of the Ghost, unable to choose whether to give up Derek or to give up everything else she knows. It was a decision not completely unlike the one that Shannon made, and she can't help but think that maybe this also makes her despicable. She clenches her hands, and Derek raises his eyebrows at her.

"What's up?" He asks, and she sighs.

"Do you think that I made the wrong decision when I –"

"No."

"But –"

"Eve," he says, and his voice is so soft, like velvet against her skin, "everyone would have made the decision you did. You didn't make it to gain something. You didn't make it without a heavy heart. You're not despicable."

She blinks at him, feeling the burn of tears as he reaches out, and takes her hands in his, which are so warm. "Thank you," she whispers, squeezing his fingers. She loves him so much. She loves him *so* much. She wouldn't want to be doing this with anyone else.

"It'll all work out, you know," he says, and she smiles at him through her tears.

"I really hope so," she sniffles, and then he's wrapping his arm around her shoulder the best he can over the truck console, and he's kissing the top of her head and she so desperately needs for him to be right.

She doesn't know what she's going to do if he isn't right.

46

TEN THOUSAND SHADES OF PURPLE

The key to his aunts' house is shaking in his hand as he tries to guide it into the lock, and he drops them once, then twice. He almost swears, and then remembers that Chip is standing right behind him, watching, so instead he sets his jaw and takes a deep breath. If only Mel hadn't texted him that she was in the city, that her baby has incredibly poor timing. If only Isaac could drop Chip off and go to Park's house where he wouldn't have to face the overarching shadow of his mother. If only Shannon hadn't *ruined everything.*

"Hey," Park says, and Isaac closes his eyes. He doesn't want Park to see him like this, so incredibly frustrated and angry and confused and *worried.* Park reaches out, touches Isaac's shoulder, and then tugs the keys from his death-grip.

The squeaky hinge of the door sounds, and Chip rushes past them both, excited by the prospect of sleeping over at Isaac's, excited by the news of a new baby sister. Isaac wants to be excited, too, but he just – *can't.* Too much has happened today, too much is swirling around in his head, and it's all so *loud.*

Park's hands find him again, tugging him over the threshold, and then wrapping around him tight, burying his face in Isaac's shoulder. "I'm so tired," he whispers, and Isaac sighs, pressing a kiss into his hair, and then another one.

"Me too," he says.

"How does Chip do it?"

Isaac laughs, sharp and loud in the empty foyer. Upstairs, there's a crash followed by a "I'm okay!" as if Chip is trying to illustrate Park's point.

There's silence for another second, and then Park pulls away, keeping his hands on Isaac's hips, looking up at him, contemplating something.

"What?" Isaac asks.

"Do you know what they're going to name the baby?"

Isaac blinks, trying to think back to a time where Mel mentioned a baby name. He's been so preoccupied lately that his visits haven't been

278

as frequent, haven't been as long. "I can't remember," he admits, and Park shrugs.

"Do you think they'll make it go with Chip?"

"Oh, God," Isaac groans, "nothing goes with Chip."

"Is that actually his real name?"

"No, his real name is Matthew." Isaac grins. He hasn't thought about Chip being Matthew aside from paperwork at the school in so long. "Walt used to call him a chip off the old block and it just kind of stuck."

"Oh, Matthew is easy to get something to go with," Park says, and then he's smiling, and Isaac understands that this is a ploy to get him to smile, too, to get their minds off what happened today. "Moira?"

Isaac wrinkles his nose. "Madison?"

"Maddy and Matty?"

"No, you're right – too similar."

"Maeve?"

Isaac's blood pressure drops. Maeve was his grandmother's name. "It's going to be Maeve," he says, and his voice is soft. It's lost its playfulness. "My grandma."

"Oh, Isaac," Park whispers, opening his arms, beckoning Isaac into them. "I'm so sorry," he says, and Isaac knows he's not just talking about his grandma.

"I wish that could have been the end," he whispers into Park's neck, closing his eyes, soaking in the moment.

"Me too," Park whispers back, tightening his grip around Isaac. "Me too."

***

Chip requested another movie night, and just like the first, Isaac is sandwiched between a sleeping Park and a sleeping Chip. The movie, *Rise of the Guardians,* is rolling into the end credits, and Isaac doesn't want to wake either of them.

He leans his head against the back of the couch and closes his eyes. It's been a long time since he's felt this betrayed by his mom, by *Shannon.* So much for taking a break in the mountains, so much for *seeing where we'll go.*

So much for her saying, *for what it's worth, I wish that it could have been different. I wish that we could have been there for you. I wish that I could have really been your mom.*

So much for her shitty apology.

The stupid tote idea didn't even work - his cat is *gone*, anyways, and Isaac never did get the chance to pet him.

Nothing that his mother has said or done has ever been enough and yet he still let himself fall into believing that maybe this time would be different. His anger had faded into acceptance, and he had even *hoped*, God forbid, that his mother was turning over a new leaf, and was going to start *trying*.

All she's done is fuck up even more, and now she's probably disappeared with her stupid pieces of the Ghost. Maybe she's even sold them by now - who knows? If she has, they'll be impossible to track down and get back, they'll be impossible to destroy. If she's sold them, they will have all lost, and the stupid part about it is that he doesn't even think his mom understands the implication of her actions. Or if she does and she went through with them anyways, she's so much worse than he could even imagine.

To doom the world for money is despicable. To betray your son to doom the world for money is unforgivable. It's worse than despicable.

He never, never, never, never wants to see her again.

On his right side, Chip stirs, and lets out a deep breath. The credits are coming to an end on the TV, and the digital clock on the DVD player reads 11:34PM in dim red light. He's uncomfortably warm, having managed to kick off most of the blanket that he and Park are sharing, but he's sweating where he wasn't able to move it, for fear of waking someone.

He blinks, and then decides it's time, whispering first into Park's ear, and then shaking Chip. As expected, Chip hardly responds, and Park opens his eyes slowly, confusedly.

"Movie's over," he whispers, pushing Park's hair out of his face. "Bedtime."

"Mmm" Park groans, and Isaac's entire heart lurches in his chest. He's glad that Park was able to stay with him, even if it's selfish.

"I'm gonna bring Chip to his room," Isaac says, softly, waiting for Park's gaze to focus. "Meet you upstairs?"

Park nods, and then closes his eyes again, and Isaac isn't entirely sure he will be upstairs when Isaac is done tucking Chip in, but that's okay.

He pushes himself out from under both of them, and turns off the TV, using the light of his phone to maneuver his hands under Chip, lifting him from the couch. Chip stirs long enough to wrap his arms around Isaac's neck, and Isaac feels dangerously close to tears.

Upstairs he turns on Chip's bedroom light with the back of his hand, and then, struggling, deposits Chip on his bed. He's not sure how much longer he can carry Chip, but he's absolutely going to try for as long as he can. Falling asleep on the couch and waking in his bed was always something Isaac loved as a child, and Chip is growing up so fast. He deserves to have this piece of childhood for as long as he can.

Isaac pulls back the covers, and tucks them around Chip's shoulders. Chip murmurs something under his breath, and Isaac says, "Pardon?"

"Thank you," Chip murmurs again, and then he curls up on his side, out cold once again.

"You're welcome," Isaac replies, lingering, brushing a strand of Chips' curls back from his face, reflecting. "You're surrounded by so much love, kid," he whispers, and then he leaves, his heart in his throat.

As expected, Park has not made it upstairs, so Isaac takes a moment to brush his teeth, not looking at his reflection, and then goes back down to the living room. "Babe?" He asks, from the doorway, and there's a sharp intake of breath.

"Sorry," Park says, "I wanted to be - ouch, Jesus! That was my hand."

"Oh shit, sorry," Isaac accidentally sat on his hand, and he moves off quick. "Sorry, sorry. You okay?"

"I've been mortally wounded," Park complains, and Isaac's eyes are adjusting quick to the dark. He can see the grin on Park's face. "I don't know if you'll ever redeem yourself."

"You don't, do you?" Isaac asks, his tone verging on playful. "I'm sure there's something I could do."

Park sits up, looking at him from under his eyelashes. "Oh," he says, "there sure is."

***

Finally, they stumble upstairs, shirtless and love-drunk, hands still not sick of touching each other. Isaac presses against Park on the stairs, and Park has one hand on Isaac's leg as he brushes his teeth and Isaac watches him, sitting on the counter.

There's toothpaste on the side of Park's mouth after he finishes, and Isaac reaches out to wipe it with his thumb. He catches Park's jaw with his other fingers and presses his lips open. Park responds immediately, letting Isaac's thumb enter his mouth, licking the toothpaste off, not breaking eye contact. His hand slides ever-so-slightly up Isaac's thigh, and every hair on Isaac's body stands up. Park's mouth is hot and warm around his thumb, and his jaw is trembling.

"You're so fucking beautiful," Isaac whispers, and pulls his thumb out between Park's teeth, down his lip, down his chin. "Did you know that?"

Park swallows, his cheeks reddening. "I do now?" He questions, "You make me feel beautiful."

Isaac's hand drops, his fingers along the side of Park's neck, his thumb tracing a line across his Adam's apple, making Park's breath shaky, sharp, and then shallow. "Good," he says, his pinky hitting Park's shoulder, his thumb in the hollow between Park's collarbones. He breaks eye contact for a second, to watch Park's chest rise and fall, and then he's back, staring into Park's eyes, their pupils wide with desire, with hunger. "You're so beautiful." He doesn't want to sound like a broken record, but he's feeling vulnerable. He's so tired, and so frustrated and betrayed and he loves Park so much. He needs Park to know he's beautiful, he needs to let Park know that he's wanted, and he's loved, and he's so scared that one day something will happen, and they'll grow apart. He's so scared that Park will leave him, just like his parents did. It's not fair on Park. It's not fair on Park that this fear lives inside him, but it's there. It's there and it terrifies him – the magnitude of his feelings for Park, and they could all come crashing down in an instant.

He pushes them down. Park isn't leaving him. Park would tell him if he was unhappy. Park would talk to him. Park is *here,* and his cheeks are red, and his mouth is open, and his breath smells like toothpaste.

Isaac's hand drops from Park's shoulder, and he stands, then leans down to whisper into Park's ear. "Fuck me, you beautiful, beautiful, man." He extends his hand to Park, who takes it and presses the palm to his mouth, kissing it, and then brushing his tongue against Isaac's wrist, right at the pulse. Isaac shivers, and Park moves up his arm, making his veins sing.

He lets out a soft moan when Park hits his elbow crease, and he can feel Park's smirk against his skin, but neither of them say anything. Park makes his way to Isaac's shoulder, across his collarbone, stopping at the same place Isaac did on him, nipping Isaac's skin with his teeth, making Isaac shudder with *want.*

"Fuck me," Isaac says again, his body alive with goosebumps.

Park drags his bottom teeth up Isaac's neck, landing behind Isaac's ear, and his voice is low, sultry, when he says, "You want me to fuck you?"

"Yes." Isaac's breath is gone. His mind is blank, all that's running through it is *Park Park Park. Want want want.*

"Yes?" Park asks, and his hand traces Isaac's spine, down to the waistband of his sweatpants, making Isaac whine.

"Fuck me," Isaac says, knowing what Park wants him to say, wanting to draw it out longer, wanting to see how long Park will wait.

Park's hand follows Isaac's waistband to the front, and then he sticks his fingers under it, eliciting another whine before snapping them back, moving his hand up Isaac's chest, finding his left nipple. "You want me to what?" His mouth moves along Isaac's jaw. *Rude.*

Isaac doesn't know how much longer he can hold out. He's hot, flustered, so turned on it aches in him. "Fuck me*,*" he says again, aware of how whiny he sounds, aware of Park's fingers pressing down on the soft skin around his nipple, his teeth on Isaac's throat.

"Okay," Park whispers, coy, and then his hand and his teeth are gone abruptly, and he's tugging Isaac forward, out of the bathroom and into the bedroom, where they both lose their pants, and then their underwear, and Isaac lets himself make more noises, soft, so they don't wake Chip up, and Park pushes and pulls all the right buttons and all the right levers until both of them are breathless. Isaac finishes first, and then pins Park to the bed, with one hand, reaching down with the other until Park's belly becomes slick.

They both clean up, and then fall back into bed, tired and sated, and full to the brim with love. Isaac's head is on Park's chest and he's listening to the rise and fall of his chest, his lungs, while Park runs his fingers through Isaac's hair.

"I love you," Isaac whispers, tightening his grip on Park's forearm. It's the first time he's said it after the looming end of the world and it almost seems scarier to mention it now, when they know they have more time together.

"I love you," Park says back, without hesitation, quelling Isaac's fear. A moment later he adds. "So much. I'm spilling over with love for you."

Isaac laughs and pushes himself up so he can see Park's expression. There's nothing but genuine happiness in it, genuine feelings. He raises an eyebrow and Isaac shrugs, settling back down against him. "Just wanted to see your face," he whispers, explaining himself, "the overflow."

47
SHOTGUN

Park is brewing coffee and making breakfast while Chip ecstatically reads aloud from the book he took out from the library. Park didn't feel like talking this morning, so when Chip asked if he could practice his reading out loud, it was perfect. Apparently Chip is competitive in everything at school – reading aloud, math questions, capture the flag, and science. He seems very proud to be the smartest in science.

Park flips over the toad-in-a-hole he's making Chip and glances at the clock. "Sorry to interrupt," he says, "but what time does your school start?"

Chip blinks at him, "Eight-thirty."

The clock changes from 8:13 to 8:14 and panic starts to rise in Park. "Shit," he says, and then "sorry. We have to leave soon – I'm – oh, screw it, this can wait a minute. I'm going to wake Isaac up."

Chip looks annoyed that his reading has been interrupted, but he closes his book and slides it into his bag. "Come back soon," he says, and Park wonders if he's hurt the boy's feelings. He really hopes not.

He runs up the stairs and opens the door to Isaac's room quietly. He left Isaac to sleep this morning because of all the tension that was on his face the night before. There's only so much fucking can resolve, and if anyone deserves a morning to sleep in, it's Isaac, but that sentiment came crashing down when Chip reminded him that he needed to be at school.

"Isaac?" Park asks from the door, and when he doesn't get a response, he goes to the bed, and sits on the edge, peeling the blanket that Isaac has up to his nose down to his shoulders. "Isaac," he says again. Still nothing.

He sighs and shakes Isaac.

"Babe?"

Isaac starts awake and Park feels even worse. Isaac looks up at him, confused, and Park reaches out to brush his thumb along Isaac's cheek.

"Sorry to wake you," he whispers, "but I forgot that Chip has school and –"

"Oh, fuck," Isaac says, and then he's up and out of bed, "what time is it?"

"Um," Park watches Isaac pick up the sweater he was wearing the day before, and a pair of sweatpants from the basket of folded laundry on his desk chair. "It's like 8:15."

Isaac makes a noise that's unintelligible, and Park cringes.

"Sorry," he starts, "I thought maybe it'd be nice for you to sleep in, but -"

Isaac turns back towards him, shaking his head, and places a chaste kiss on his lips, his morning breath so strong Park almost recoils. "It's okay. Thank you for trying - really. Thank you." He smooths Park's hair back, and gives a little smile, and the knot at the base of Park's throat releases.

"Has he had breakfast yet?"

"Ah, shit," Park stands up, and runs back downstairs to check on the breakfast he's cooking, which, thankfully, doesn't seem to be burnt. He flips it onto a plate and hands it to Chip, who has taken his book back out of his bag and is mouthing the words to himself.

"Thanks," he says, taking the food. "Is Isaac up?"

"Sure is!" Park turns the burner off.

"Is my lunch packed?"

"Lunch?" Park opens and closes his hands, "Um - what do you want for lunch?" He looks around the kitchen aimlessly, trying to come up with something that's easy, something that's yummy.

"Sandwich," Chip says between bites of egg, and Park nods. He can make a sandwich.

He's halfway through sandwich-making when Isaac appears in the kitchen, hair pushed back from his face, seeming just as tense as he was the night before. Park's stomach sinks. He hoped that after last night, after a good sleep, Isaac would feel better, wouldn't seem so *upset* about it all. He knows it's not realistic - not everyone can shove down their feelings as well as he can - but still. He was hoping Isaac would have at least looked a little bit less like a truck had run him over.

"I'll get the snacks," Isaac says as Park tucks the sandwich into a container.

"Perfect."

Chip finishes his breakfast, and Park takes his plate. Isaac grabs the sandwich container and an apple and a granola bar and two bags of fruit snacks and stuffs them into a lunch bag, and then zips them into Chips backpack.

The three of them file towards the door, and Isaac makes sure Chips coat is done all the way up.

"When will it snow?" Chip asks as they head to the car, and Isaac looks up towards the sky, which is just fading into morning light.

Park drinks in the way he smiles, just a little bit, and says, "I don't know, but I have a feeling it won't be today."

"Why?" Chip hops into his car seat and Park does up the buckles.

"I don't know," Isaac says, and he slides into the car, turning the keys in the ignition.

"What about tomorrow?"

"I hope not."

"Don't you like the snow?"

"Not really."

"Why?"

"Too cold."

They pull out of the driveway, and Chip and Isaac continue their banter all the way to the school. They pull in at 8:35, and Isaac sighs.

"I have to drop him off at the office," he says, and Park nods.

He says goodbye to Chip, and that he hopes Chip is the best at everything today. Chip thanks him earnestly, and then he and Isaac are gone inside, and Park is left to stare at the reflection of himself in the window. Isaac leaves the car running, so the heat won't go out, and Park wonders if he ever gets tired of doing so much for everyone, all the time.

He knows Isaac gets tired of doing so much for everyone, all the time.

Park lets his head fall back against the headrest and closes his eye, replaying the last twenty-four hours in his mind. His dad is gone, and the Ghost is dead except it's not really dead, and his sister is the Prophet that he was supposed to be and Isaac's mom is more terrible than Isaac thought, and Mel is having her baby and Isaac is so torn up and Park isn't - shouldn't he be torn up? About his dad? Shouldn't he feel worse than he does?

It almost seems like relief, the thing welling up out of his chest. He and his dad never got along, and of course it didn't get better when Park told him he's gay. He remembers the day after, when his dad brought home that stupid cross that he said *reminded him of Park,* and how that burned more than any of the tears his mother had cried. All the snide comments throughout the years, the investment in Park's life only to a certain point. How he avoided the topic of love, how he avoided Park's eyes when Park showed up at home with love bites that he'd asked the boy he was sleeping with not to give him. How ashamed he'd made Park feel without even opening his mouth, and how he never tried to redeem himself. Since the dinner with Isaac, he hadn't even seemed to want to interact with Park at all, despite all the urging from Georgia to make nice. Isaac, of course, won over Georgia without even trying, and Park and her have been talking more. Getting to know each other like they hadn't had the chance to before.

He knows how heartbroken she's going to be that his dad is gone. He's not sure he wants to go home and witness her pain, especially when his is so much smaller.

The driver side door opens and snaps Park back into reality, and he looks over to see Isaac, grinning at him. "Chip really likes you, you know," he says, and Park's eyes widen.

"I was under the impression that he didn't, actually."

"Oh, no," Isaac says, "he's just giving you a run for your money. He thinks you're cool. He likes that you just let him talk."

"Do most people not?"

Isaac shakes his head. "Not a lot of people are good at listening."

"You're good at listening."

"You're even better."

Park sighs, and Isaac puts the car into gear, pulls out of the parking lot. "Can I take advantage of your listening?" He asks, quietly, and Isaac nods.

"Only if I can take advantage of yours after."

Park shrugs. They have a lot to talk through. "Yeah," he says, and watches as Isaac drives past the turnoff to his own house, and then Park's, pulling onto the highway. "Of course."

48
INTERLUDE VII

C is staring at the cat in her windowsill. She's surprised that the flower box on the side of her house is sturdy enough to be holding it up as it's massive. It has cheeks the size of cherry tomatoes, and it's staring right back at her, two glowing eyes in the growing dark.

"Hi," she says to it, moving forward, wanting to open the window and the bugscreen, wanting to see if it'll come inside, if she can touch it, but there's a knock at her bedroom door and it startles, dropping to the ground. Disappointed, she watches it run back into the woods.

"C?" Park asks from the other side of the door.

"Yeah, come in," she replies, sinking into her desk chair.

Park pushes through the door, his hair disheveled and his eyes red and puffy like he's been crying. She isn't surprised – their mom is in such a state of despair it's hard to not cry around her. "How are you doing?" He asks, and she shakes her head.

She's been trying to write more Prophecies, but every time she opens her notes app, she ends up staring at the last one that came out of her - *follow the Prophet, burn what needs to be burned, sacrifice whom-so-ever must be sacrificed* – and remembers that they haven't sacrificed anyone.

"I just – I can't figure out what we're supposed to do now. The Prophecy says sacrifice someone, but who? And why? Shouldn't we just have to find Shannon?"

Park shrugs, flopping down on her bed and disappearing into her pile of fluffy blankets. "Isaac tried texting her a few times this morning, but she obviously didn't answer."

C sighs. "She could be anywhere, couldn't she?"

"Isaac thinks that she's still somewhere around here. He said that a lot of her buyers are Canada-based, and she probably wouldn't risk selling to someone she doesn't know with something so powerful."

"But that's not for certain."

"None of this is for certain, C." He seems frustrated, and she gets it. The thing they're not talking about hovers in the air above them, just

289

out of reach. The thing that Park ran away from last night, and the thing that she had to come home and face alone.

"What if we do have to sacrifice someone?"

"I guess then we have to sacrifice someone."

"But *who?*"

"I don't know, C," he wraps a blanket around his shoulders and sits up, "you're the one writing the stupid things."

She *is* the one writing the stupid things. She sighs, and looks back down at her phone, at the stupid notes, at the stupid Prophecy, and her vision starts blurring. She's been trying not to think about their dad, about how tense their relationship was, about how she sometimes heard him talking to their grandma about how he felt like a failure. How he wished his family was normal. If only he had known about the magic!

There's another knock at the door, and her head snaps up to meet Park's gaze. *Mom?* He mouths, and she shrugs.

"Yeah?" She asks.

"Is Park with you?"

"Yeah, Mom," he says, still looking bewildered. It isn't often that their mom disturbs them like this when they're together.

"Can I come in?"

Shit, C mouths, locking her phone. "Of course," she says, instead, and then there is their mom, full of sadness and looking wretched, standing in the doorway of her bedroom.

She takes a deep breath, and then joins Park on the bed. Silently, he gives her part of the blanket around him, and she takes it, wrapping it around her, their shoulders touching. "Do you remember," she starts, looking at them both in turn, "that Halloween where you went as a witch and a wizard?"

"Yeah," C says, and she does remember. They were very young – maybe three and six – and it had been so cold that they'd had to wear full snow suits over their costumes. C had refused to wear a toque because she had a witch hat, and Park's wizard beard had frosted solid from his breath's condensation, so both were freezing. It hadn't mattered, though.

"Dad pulled us around on that sled," Park says, looking at his hands, "we never wanted the night to end."

C nods. "And we got so much candy."

"You were both so happy," Georgia says, sniffling, "we were all so happy. I – I think about it a lot."

Park looks at C, something unintelligible in his eyes. He wraps his arm around their mom, and she leans into him, crying. When he looks back at C, he tilts his chin towards Georgia in a *get over here* motion, and C sighs.

She gets up, and wriggles her way under her mom's other arm, letting herself be embraced.

What if this is the sacrifice, she wonders, *the ones who were taken.*

***

Mel is exhausted. She's exhausted and sore and she just wants to go home. They're holding her at the hospital for an extra night and she wishes they wouldn't. She's *fine* and the baby is *fine* so why do they insist?

Walt is sitting in the chair beside her bed, crafting a text to Isaac, and Maeve, their new baby, is bundled against her, asleep.

"I want to go home," she complains to Walt, and he slides his phone back into his pocket.

"I know," he says, gesturing for her hand, "but it's only one more night. We'll make it."

"Will you get us food?" She asks, sweetly, unable to fathom eating the hospital food for dinner. "Something greasy?"

Walt nods.

"What did Isaac say?"

"He's okay with Chip for another night – he said to take as long as we need."

"Sounds like Isaac."

"I don't think last night went as well as they were hoping."

She sighs and lets go of Walt's hand to brush a careful finger across Maeve's cheek. "As long as we're still here," she whispers, "that's all that matters, isn't it, baby Maeve?"

49
FUCK YOU, ANYWAYS

Isaac is sprawled on the floor of Iris's reading room, his thumb hovering above the button to call his mom. "I don't know if I can do it," he says, his intestines brewing with nerves.

Iris sighs and pushes back out of her chair to join him on the ground, arm to arm. "I can call her from my phone, if you want," she offers, but they both know that Isaac isn't going to let her do that. At least not yet.

"I think I have to do this," he says, and then his finger dips down, pressing the button.

As it rings, the door to the reading room opens, and Park slips inside, nodding at them as he takes off his scarf and then his jacket, and then his boots. Isaac doesn't watch him, but he follows the movements with his ears, unable to focus on the ringing coming from his phone.

"Hi! You've reached the voicemail of Shannon Paige; leave a message and I'll get back to you as soon as I can!"

Isaac hangs up before the beep, and Park joins them on the floor, his arm pressed against Isaac's other side.

"I didn't think she was going to pick up," he says, the nerves he was feeling earlier giving way to something more like defeat. "I don't think she'll ever talk to me again."

"Is that really a bad thing?" Iris asks, gesturing for his phone. "Are you sure that you don't want me to try? She might pick up an unknown number."

Isaac sighs, and lets his whole body deflate. After his talk with Park yesterday, he feels better, but he's still angry. He's still defeated. He desperately wants his mom to pick up the phone and he desperately wants to never speak to her again. "Try it," he says, and Park's hand wraps around his wrist, his two middle fingers pressed against Isaac's palm, half comfort, and half electric.

Iris enters his mom's number into her phone, and the ringing starts again.

For a moment it seems like she's picking up and Isaac's breath catches in his throat before his mom's voice says, *"Hi! You've reached the voicemail of Shannon Paige; leave a message and I'll get back to you as soon as I can!"*

Iris hangs up.

"What the fuck are we supposed to do?" Isaac asks, and Iris wordlessly returns his phone.

"Maybe we don't have to do anything," Park says softly, "we've done our part, haven't we? The only way anything more can go wrong is if the Ghost gets let out of one of those jars, and who knows when or where or if that's going to happen."

"He has a point," Isaac says, nudging Iris' shoulder. "We could just be done with it."

Iris threads her fingers through Isaac's and squeezes, once, twice, three times. "I want to," she whispers.

"Then it's settled, isn't it?" Park whispers, "We move on."

"We move on," Isaac confirms, and beside him he feels the moment that Iris agrees.

"Fine," she says, "we move on."

EPILOGUE

BUBBLE TEA WITH EXTRA BUBBLES

Isaac sucks air through his straw at an extraordinarily obnoxious level of loud, and then he puts down his cup and grins at Park, waiting for Park to say something like *stop that,* or *Jesus Christ, Isaac, we're in public,* or *please stop being a gremlin,* but he doesn't say any of those things. He only raises his eyebrows.

"Done?" He asks, and Isaac nods.

Park rolls his eyes, then, and takes the empty cup, stacking it in his own, and leading the way out of the shop, throwing the cups in the trash as he walks by. "I can't believe you haven't had bubble tea before," he says, once they're out the door.

The wind kicks up around them, and Isaac sinks deep into his scarf, reaching for Park's hand. "There's no place you can get it in Belle."

The two of them have moved into the city for university, and while Isaac has had almost a year to adjust, there are still some things he isn't sure about yet. It was hard for him, in the beginning, and the loud noises and crowds of people were something that he didn't want to face. The transit system scared him, and so did the idea of driving. He didn't like the apartment they shared with Iris, and he was terrified that he could only see the mountains he grew up surrounded by if he squinted into the distance.

He used to imagine walking into a store and seeing his mother standing there, or running into her on the street, but of course he hasn't. No one's heard from her since she made her deal with the Ghost, and Isaac isn't sure if it's a good thing or not. Maybe she's dead. Maybe she's fled the country. He's trying his hardest not to care.

He's better at being in the city now, of course - especially since Park has taken it upon himself to introduce Isaac to all of the simple pleasures that he's never been able to have – but there's still a part of him that yearns for his home, his real home. Sometimes, late at night, he asks Park if Park is still okay with them moving back when they've finished school, and Park will smooth his hair back from his face and smile at him.

"Yes," he says, "of course I am." But Isaac can see how much Park loves this place. He can tell how hard it will be for him to leave it for a second time, especially after everything that's happened in Belle.

"Hey," he says to Park now, swallowing the sugary taste of the bubble tea down, and Park turns to him, his eyes so full of love.

"Yeah?"

"Thank you," and his voice catches in his throat.

Park's eyebrows raise again, but he nods, swinging their hands between them as they walk. "Thank *you*," he replies, and neither of them have to elaborate.

It's enough to be here, together. It's enough to know that the people they love are okay. It's enough to be able to hold onto the image of a future where they can be happy. They are happy.

Isaac is happy, and nothing is ever going to be able to take it from him again.

THE END

Acknowledgements

Overflow has been in the works for the better part of the last decade, and I am so happy to have a finalized version Out There and available for people to read. So, thank you to everyone who has interacted with the different versions over the years! Especially thank you to Alicia for beta reading, to Chelsea who never did get to reading it but was still supportive, and to my parents who remained excited to read it despite my warning they would probably not like it. Thank you to the team at AOS for taking a chance on me. Most of all, thank you to Fiona who helped me plan, listened to hours of ranting and suffered through the first and worst draft chapter by chapter as I wrote it. It means the world to me.

Thanks for reading <3